Now that she thought on it, Ash had *never* seen Ignitus worried. Angry, yes; offended, of course. But not worried. All gods seemed to go directly from prideful to furious.

I have heard no similar rumors, Hydra had told Ash back in Igna. *Stop worrying.*

At first, Ash had thought Hydra's message was in response to some slight Ignitus had committed. But she had wanted *him* to stop worrying about something.

Dizziness set Ash's head spinning. No, it wasn't dizziness—it was . . . hope.

Someone or something existed that could worry a god.

Also by Sara Raasch and Kristen Simmons

RISE UP FROM THE EMBERS

SET FIRE TO THE GODS

SARA RAASCH
& KRISTEN SIMMONS

BALZER + BRAY
An Imprint of HarperCollins*Publishers*

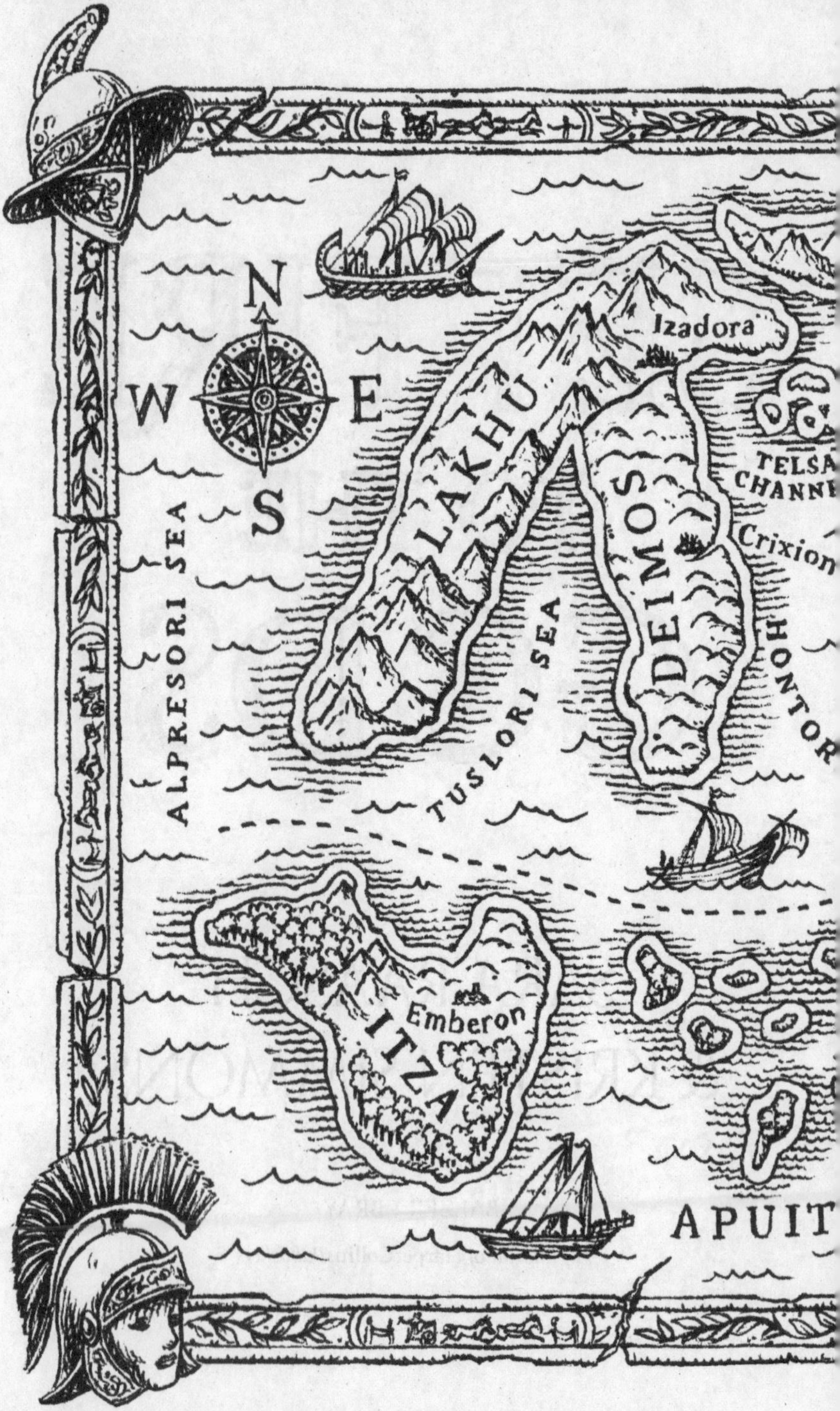

N
W
E
S
ALPRESORI SEA
LAKHU
Izadora
DEIMOS
TELSA
CHANN
Crixion
HONTOR
TUSLORI SEA
ITZA
Emberon
APUIT

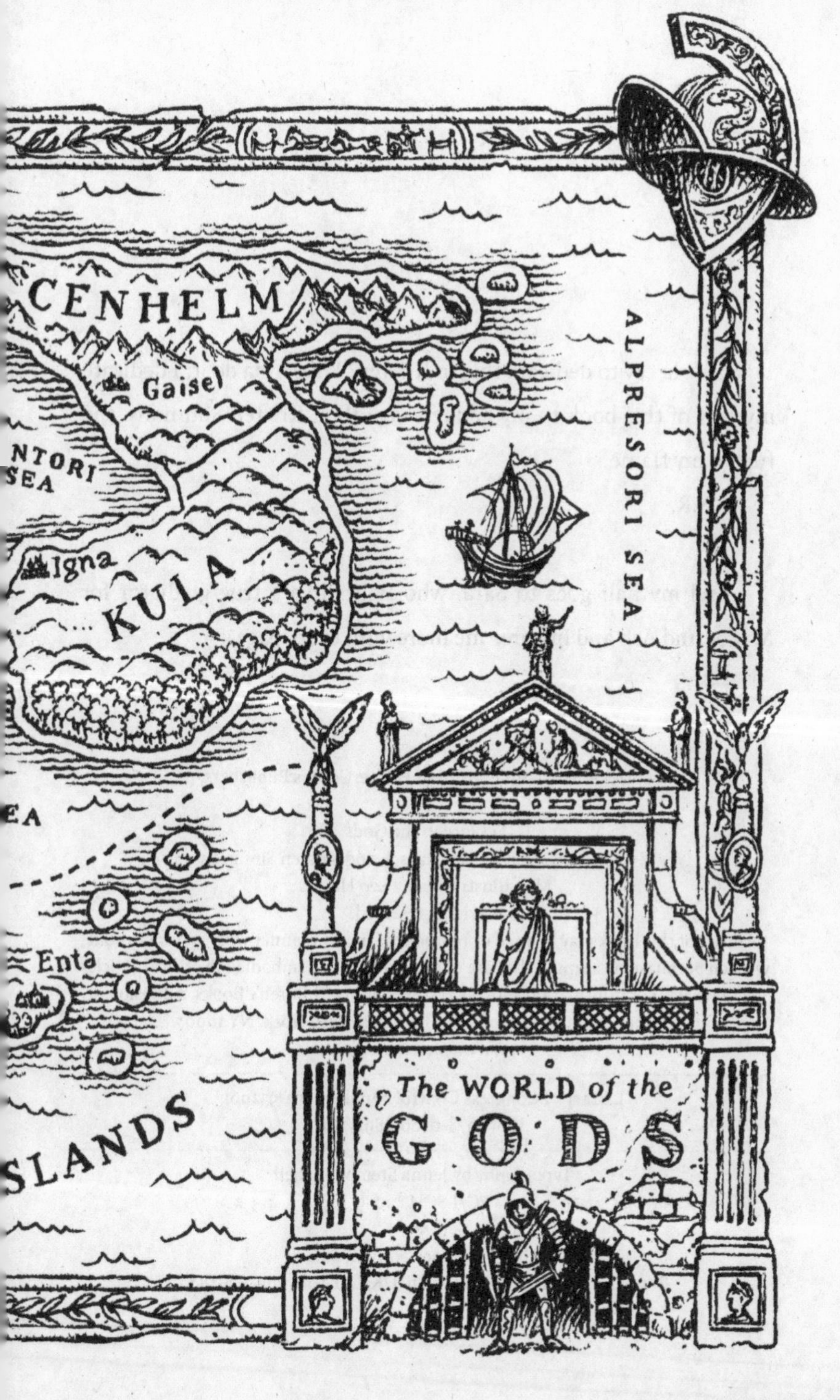

CENHELM
Gaisel
NTORI
SEA
Igna
KULA
ALPRESORI SEA
EA
Enta
SLANDS
The WORLD of the
GODS

Is it cheesy to dedicate this to Kristen? I'm gonna do it: I dedicate my half of this book to my goddess coauthor, Kristen Simmons, the fuel to my flame.

—S.R.

And my half goes to Sara, who fights like a true gladiator for Madoc and Ash and inspires me more with every page.

—K.S.

Balzer + Bray is an imprint of HarperCollins Publishers.

Set Fire to the Gods

Map Illustration by Leo Hartas

www.epicreads.com

Library of Congress Control Number: 2021932061
ISBN 978-0-06-289157-0

Typography by Jenna Stempel-Lobell
21 22 23 24 25 PC/LSCH 10 9 8 7 6 5 4 3 2
❖
First paperback edition, 2021
Printed and bound by CPI Group (UK) Ltd, Croydon, CR0 4YY

THE CREATION OF THE WORLD

Before time, there was energeia, and that energy was a goddess.

But she was lonely in the ether, so she harnessed and shaped her energy until she formed the world. Jagged mountains sprang into the sky; flames sparked in the dusty air; water frothed; animals prowled through towering plants. But the goddess was still lonely, so she pushed her soul into the rocks and the fire, into the air and the water, into the animals and plants. From this came her six children, keepers of each energeia, and she was their Mother Goddess.

These six godly offspring populated the earth with mortals. But when her offspring began to love the mortals more than they loved her, the Mother Goddess grew jealous, and she sought to destroy them all. Blood soaked the earth; war all but decimated the population. To protect the mortals they had each made, her children united their energeias, and that power led to the Mother Goddess's destruction. They vowed from that moment on to settle their disagreements with honor, glory, and minimal loss of life.

To this day, all wars are resolved in the arena by gladiators.

ONE

MADOC

SWEAT DRIPPED INTO Madoc's eyes, soaking the frayed neck of his grime-streaked tunic and burning an open wound on his jaw. Blinking back the sting, he swiped an impatient hand across his forehead and lowered his stance. The thick, corded muscles of his thighs flexed as he rocked forward, preparing for his opponent's next strike. Though his arms trembled with fatigue, his hands lifted, loose and ready.

The night air reeked of wet earth, dead fish, and blood—the perfume of South Gate, the seediest fishing port in Crixion, Deimos's capital city. Madoc had broken a sandal early in the fight, and the toes of his right foot dug into the cool soil of the old boatyard, the location of tonight's match.

Above the rush in his ears, Madoc could hear the taunts of the crowd that had gathered, hungry for his opponent's victory. Fentus had been training to be a gladiator in Xiphos, on the eastern seaboard of Deimos, when he'd been kicked out of his sponsor's facility. Word was he lacked the discipline to control his Earth Divine gifts and had killed his sparring partner in practice. On the streets they called that murder, but for one of the Father God's blessed fighters, it had been ruled an unfortunate accident.

Fentus had knocked down three challengers already tonight. Elias had said the odds were now ten to one in Fentus's favor, and anyone who dared go up against him was a fool. But if that fool could win, he'd carry home a purse so heavy he'd be a king.

Which was precisely why Madoc had taken the fight.

A large part of him regretted that now. The match had gone on too long—Fentus's strikes had been unrelenting. He had battered Madoc with waves of dirt that now coated his olive skin and dark hair. He'd knocked Madoc down with hunks of rope and sharp, rusty fish hooks, debris he'd picked up from the swirling earth. Over and over Madoc had fallen, only to rise again to take another blast of gravel from his attacker's spindly fingers.

If Madoc could get close enough, he could beat him. But to do that he had to stay upright.

"Take the fall, pigstock!" A male voice rose above the others, eliciting an eruption of laughter.

Madoc brushed off the insult, a common reminder that even though the Undivine made up half the world's population, those without power were no more useful than cows, sheep, or pigs.

"Give me strength," he muttered to the Father God, his stare alternating between his attacker's broad forehead and his hands, which were now resting at his sides.

A familiar rush filled Madoc's veins, cool against the oppressive heat of the night.

Almost, a voice whispered in his mind. *Almost.*

Fentus smiled, half his teeth black holes in his mouth, but even from twenty paces away, Madoc could see the sheen of sweat on the other man's brow and the sag in his shoulders. Still, it was something else, something deeper, that stirred Madoc's unusual sixth sense. He could feel the fatigue as if it came from his own muscles—a dip in energy, like some might feel the coming rain—a subtle change no one else could perceive.

The ore was growing heavy in Fentus's blood.

Those with geoeia could pull only so much strength from the earth. Too far past the threshold, and the power turned to poison, making the mightiest fighters as slow and clumsy as any Undivine. Most knew their limit and did not push past it. Others, like Fentus, were too proud or stupid to quit.

This was precisely what Madoc had been waiting for.

A quick glance to his left revealed a skinny stonemason on the edge of the crowd, his tunic stained with telltale splashes of gray mortar.

"Pigstock!" the stonemason called again, his grin, familiar to only Madoc, as wide as a sickle moon. He raised his fist, encouraging those closest to join the chant of *Fen-tus! Fen-tus! Fen-tus!*

The people called for the bookmaker, the gold coins in their outstretched hands glinting off the tall torches surrounding the boatyard.

Madoc tapped his left fist on his thigh twice. To the crowd, it would look like a nervous tic. But the stonemason's dark hair fell over one eye as he dipped his head.

"Submit, boy," called Fentus, though at eighteen Madoc couldn't have been more than five years younger than him. "Or I'll bury you in a grave so deep not even your mother will know where to start digging."

The crowd roared.

"That's not very nice," Madoc answered, tapping his thigh faster.

Fentus grinned and, with a snarl, swung his thin arm toward the ground. Before he could touch the earth, Madoc dropped to one knee, digging his right hand into the tossed soil.

The quake began instantly, cutting Fentus's battle cry short. Madoc gritted his teeth as the ground dipped beneath his palm and rose up like a wave before him. The flying gravel was thin, not nearly as dense as Fentus's efforts had been. Still, it surprised Madoc's opponent. When the blast hit Fentus in the chest, it knocked him back three full steps.

Madoc lunged up, sprinting through the cloud of dust toward the other man. He might not have been trained in Xiphos, or have mastered the skills of arena fighting, but he'd been lifting rocks at the quarry since he was a child, and his back and shoulders could carry a weight twice his own.

Three more steps and Madoc had closed the space between them.

Fentus's eyes, red from the dust, went wide just before Madoc arched back his elbow and punched him in the jaw.

Fentus fell like a rock, flat on his back, and did not rise.

Frenzied excitement squeezed Madoc's chest. The crowd was quiet—no more calls of *pigstock* sounding out in the night. They'd finally seen his true intent, his strategy played out: wait until the other man tired, then attack.

If only they'd known that sensing Fentus's weakness was all Madoc's powers entailed.

Ten-to-one odds. They should be higher now; no one would doubt Fentus's victory after all the falls Madoc had taken.

A shout built inside him. Petros's hired thugs were falling, one by one. The senate's corrupt master of taxation set up these matches knowing he'd win—the entry and attendance fees, the heavy bets, all of them went into a pot that he kept unless a challenger could take down his fighter. It was just another way Petros sucked the poor dry.

But Geoxus had smiled on Madoc, and tonight Petros would leave empty-handed.

"Cheat!" shouted a man to Madoc's left. The bookmaker. One of Petros's many employees. "No one beats Fentus! He must be a cheat!"

Madoc's eyes narrowed on a blue toga surrounded by centurions in silver and black armor. Centurions policed the city, enforcing the senate's rules with an iron fist. Of course Petros would have them standing by.

A few others around the bookmaker took up the call.

"Great." Madoc held up his hands in surrender. He tried a smile, which drew even louder cheers from the crowd. He wasn't the only one who wanted to see Petros's fighter defeated.

"Arrest him!" shouted the bookmaker.

Madoc bit back a curse. It was a shame Cassia, Elias's sister, couldn't be here. Her life's goal was to be a centurion, and she'd make a good one. She'd been telling on him since he was seven.

As three centurions moved into the ring, drawing rocks from the ground with their geoeia to hover above their ready hands, Madoc gave a weak laugh. He took a step back, then another. A quick glance over his shoulder revealed two more centurions coming up from behind.

"It was a fair fight," he tried. "You all saw it."

The centurions continued their steady approach, wariness curling their spines. They had Geoxus's blessing to use lethal force, but Madoc made them nervous. Any fighter who could take down Fentus was to be approached with caution.

"Leave him alone!" shouted a woman from the edge. A rock slapped against the nearest solder's breastplate with a ping. "You want to arrest someone, arrest that crook Petros!"

The soldier spun toward the edge of the crowd, but the woman was nowhere to be seen.

From the opposite side came another rock, then another. Soon shouts were rising into the night. Some came to Madoc's defense, others to Fentus's. Guilt panged through Madoc. Half these people were counting on tonight's winnings to feed their families or cover their debts. The bookmaker's shrill call for order was brushed aside as a fight broke out to Madoc's left.

That was his cue to run.

He sprinted into the crowd, gravel flying behind him. More fights broke out, shouts ringing into the night, as Madoc bounced off bodies blocking his way.

"There he is!"

"Get him!"

"Run!" called a man nearby as a flash of silver and black whipped behind them. Soon, people were shoving in all different directions, and the shouts turned to screams as the crowd stampeded back to the safety of the buildings.

Madoc charged on, keeping his head low and his shoulders slumped to hide the fact that he was taller than most full-grown men. The urge to turn back pulled at every step. He'd weathered half a night's beating for that purse. He didn't want to leave without it.

"Bull!"

Madoc flinched at the sound of the name he used in fights. He ignored it, pressing on, but a fist grabbed the back of his tunic and dragged him beneath a stairway. Madoc spun, braced to fight, but as soon as they were hidden by shadows the other man immediately released his hold. Madoc assessed him in a single breath.

He'd seen that scarred jaw and silver-streaked hair somewhere before.

"Lucius wants to talk to you."

Realization struck Madoc like a fist to the gut. This man was a trainer for Lucius Pompino, one of the premier gladiator sponsors in Deimos. Lucius was an esteemed member of the senate—and a grandson of Geoxus himself. Elias and Madoc had watched people like him in the parades before a war. Sponsors would ride in elaborate chariots, wearing the finest clothing, tossing gems—worthless to the Divine, who could pull them from the earth with a flick of the wrist. Even more worthless to the Undivine, who couldn't even sell the stones for a loaf of bread. There was little value to a rock that even a Divine child could make.

"Stop gaping like a fish," Lucius's trainer said. "You know the man I speak of?"

Madoc closed his mouth. "Yes. Dominus." He added the title of respect, though it pained him to do so. The Divine in this city cared little for anyone who didn't have the Father God's gifts. Not even Petros bothered to attend the fights he ran in South Gate. The upper class normally didn't dirty their hands in the Undivine districts.

The trainer pulled his hood over his head. "Good. Then you know where to go."

The villa on Headless Hill, a plateau in Crixion's wealthy Glykeria District, so named by those who looked up at it. Everyone knew where Lucius lived and trained his fighters. You could see the stone walls and the glimmer of his turquoise-studded insignia all the way from the quarries.

Though Madoc wanted no part of the risks involved in fighting real gladiators, he couldn't help the smirk pulling at his lips. Lucius's top trainer had been at this fight. The man thought he was good enough to see the biggest sponsor in the city, to fight on his god's behalf in official arena matches against their enemies during wars. At Headless Hill, he'd be given all the food he could eat, and go to parties that went late into the night, with wine and games and girls.

While others like him—*pigstock*—continued to suffer.

His grin faded.

"Thanks for the offer, but Lucius will have to find someone else." The words were as dry as dust in Madoc's throat. The trainer's mouth twisted with impatience, but before he could berate Madoc for declining this rare opportunity, a shrill whistle filled the night.

Madoc blinked, and the trainer was gone.

Panic raced through his blood. Outside the stairway, more silver and black glinted from the edge of the crowd—centurions flooding the streets to stop the riot. If Madoc waited around much longer, he was going to find himself locked up in a legion cell.

His feet hit the stone, one sandal clapping against the street while the other bare, callused foot absorbed every bump and rock.

From the front of the alley came a shout of surprise, and Madoc lifted his eyes to find a centurion on horseback blocking the path. The crowd before him shifted, turning back the way they'd come. Spinning, Madoc tried to go with them, but soldiers pressed from the other side. The hard, metallic clang of their gladius knives against their shields streaked a warning through him moments before the ground quaked, then lifted to block the nearest escape.

Fear raced down Madoc's spine. The centurions were using geoeia to corral the crowd.

Cutting sideways, Madoc dived beneath the damaged wheel of a broken cart shoved against the side of a stone building to the right. Tucking his broad frame against the splintering wood of the axle, he watched the other runners disperse, escaping or caught by the legion. Soon, Madoc could hear the clap of hooves against the street. A centurion on horseback was coming closer. Even in the low light, it was impossible that Madoc would remain undetected. His right shoulder stuck out from the back of the cart and his legs were too long to tuck beneath him.

The darkness was his only ally.

Keep going, he willed the soldier. *Keep going.* He knew of people the legion had taken. They never returned. If he was caught, and the centurions learned he had been one of the fighters, what would they do? He knew, better than most, that prisoners were often shoved into training arenas as fodder for real gladiators.

Instead of being sponsored by Lucius, he'd be ground to dust by the fighters Lucius chose.

Keep going. Madoc willed it so hard his vision wavered.

The soldier passed, his black and silver regalia muted by the star-lit sky.

A hard exhale raked Madoc's throat. He waited until the horse and rider were out of earshot and the centurions no longer beat a warning against their shields. Until the street went quiet.

An alley across the road caught his eye, and he slipped out from beneath the cart and sprinted toward it. As he ran, his feet sloshed through puddles of stagnant water and the waste of emptied chamber pots from the apartments above. Keeping to the twisting alleys, he carved a path through South Gate toward the Temple of Geoxus, where he was supposed to meet Elias.

As in the other four Undivine districts, the houses and shops here weren't soaring visions of marble, gleaming with gold leafing and wrapped in gems. Simple brown brick apartments lined the streets. Beggars slept on corners. Even this late at night, children dug through rotting garbage for bits of food to calm their twisting bellies.

They had Petros and his impossible taxes to blame. It didn't matter that being born with the gods' power was a chance of fate—that geoeia was often, but not necessarily, inherited from one or both parents. When the Divine held the power, the Undivine paid the price.

A chill crawling down his spine, Madoc took the final turn out of South Gate and into Market Square, an area where Divine and Undivine mingled. An open-air temple protecting the giant bronze statue of their Father God towered high above the empty street. In a few hours, vendors would fill the square, selling clay gladiator dolls and silver and black banners alongside food and textiles, but for now it was still, lit only by the beaten copper streetlamps.

Madoc's remaining sandal caught a raised stone on the street and tore the leather strap. With a curse, he took it off and tucked it into the back of his belt. Now he didn't even have the coin to replace it.

Maybe he could sweet-talk Cassia into fixing it tomorrow. She would, after she smacked him upside the head with it. She had informed Madoc and Elias on more than one occasion that she did not have the time or patience to coddle giant babies.

With a resigned sigh, he headed for the corner where an olive seller sold his wares during the day. Elias always chose this place to meet because he liked the look of the merchant's daughter.

"Took you long enough."

Madoc turned to find the scrawniest stonemason ever to live jogging across the street. As he approached, a grin dimpled his right cheek, half hidden by his shaggy black hair.

Relief broadened the smile on Madoc's lips, masking the fear that prickled beneath his breastbone. Now that he was with Elias, Madoc realized just how close they'd been to getting pulled apart.

"I had a few stops on the way back," Madoc said. "Had to get a drink. Picked up some pickled bull testicles from the South Gate market for Seneca."

At the mention of their eccentric old neighbor, Elias snickered. "Courting gifts won't help. She's not interested, you sorry pigstock."

Madoc chuckled, used to the good-humored insult from his friend's smart mouth. Elias knew that Madoc's strange intuitions were far from ordinary, but he enjoyed reminding Madoc who had the real power.

"Did you enjoy yourself tonight? I gave the signal ten times before you decided to step in."

Elias frowned. "What was it again?"

Madoc gave an exaggerated tap of his left hand against his thigh.

"Oh, right." Elias laughed, and Madoc shoved him to the side. "It's okay. The Great Quarry Bull can take a hit or two."

Madoc groaned at the name Elias had chosen so that no one would be able to trace Madoc back to their home. It was true that he tended to heal quickly, but that didn't mean he hadn't felt each grain of sand flung in Fentus's assault. Only a true Earth Divine could use geoeia to harden their skin like a rock.

They turned toward the river and the stonemasons' quarter. Madoc had lived there with Elias Metaxa and his family since Elias's sister Cassia had found him begging on the temple steps eleven years ago. Though Elias and Cassia were Divine, their mother, Ilena, and her other children were not, and when her Divine husband had died, leaving them with unsurmountable debt, they'd been forced to move into the slums with the Undivine.

"It was quite a show, wasn't it?" Elias's voice had quieted but was still pitched with delight. "Did you see how far I sent that dust wave? I'll bet I'm the only one in the city aside from Geoxus himself who can throw geoeia like that." He grinned, but his sandals scuffed the ground with each heavy step. It appeared their opponent wasn't the only one who'd pushed his limits at the fight.

Madoc gave a snort. Elias might have put on a show tonight, but it was Madoc who had sensed Fentus's weakness. Most of the time Madoc tried to ignore the constant battery of emotions people generally thought they were hiding beneath the surface, but at times like this it came in handy. He was learning to use empathy to his advantage. Where Elias was getting stronger, Madoc was getting smarter.

For months they'd practiced their routine, failing in the first three fights before finally finding their rhythm and securing a sloppy win. Madoc, looking the part of a fighter and trueborn Earth Divine, faced the opponents while Elias, who'd sworn to his mother never to enter a fight, stood on the sidelines, throwing his geoeia from a distance.

Making it seem like Madoc was the one doing it weakened the strength of Elias's blows, but what the attack lacked in power, Madoc himself made up for in brute force. No one had any idea that he didn't have geoeia, and due to the severe punishments imposed on cheaters, no one suspected their lie.

Not even Lucius's trainer had seen the truth.

Madoc's mouth opened, his conversation with the trainer ready to spill out, but he stopped himself. He was bound by the same promise as Elias—they'd both sworn they wouldn't fight in the high-stakes matches Petros hosted around the city each week—and telling him about Lucius would only lead to trouble. Elias was distracted by shiny things, and a chance to earn real coin, like the payouts the gladiators made when they fought for Geoxus, would have them facing foreign competitors twice as formidable as Fentus, or leave them in a cell pondering their fates.

Anger sliced through Madoc's disappointment as his mind returned to the boatyard. They'd beaten Fentus and walked away with nothing.

"We had him," Madoc muttered. "That much coin could have gotten us through the rest of the month." The half they would've given to the temple could have kept a kid off the street, or paid for new cots in the sanctuary, or kept someone out of Petros's greedy grip.

"Oh." Elias removed the swollen leather purse tucked inside his belt and slapped it against Madoc's chest. "Did I forget to mention I snatched this from the bookmaker while he was carrying on about you being a cheat?"

Madoc grabbed the satchel, the thrill of his victory slamming back through him as he pulled open the strings and looked inside. Gold glinted back at him, dimly lit by the moon above. Geoxus had blessed them after all.

"You could have started with this," Madoc said, clutching the purse.

"I could have," Elias agreed. "But it wouldn't have been nearly as dramatic."

They veered to the opposite side of the street, up the broad stone steps of the temple where a dozen homeless Undivine slept, moaning softly in hunger or pain. As Madoc drew closer to the gates of the sanctuary, he felt as if a hand were closing around his throat. It didn't matter how many years had passed since he'd first come here, he would never forget that thin, desperate hope that had pushed him to reach his skinny arm into the offering box, praying for a coin to steal so that he could buy something to eat.

Thirteen years later that same slot remained in the weathered wood of the door, beneath the line of gemstones people touched for luck or prayer. His large hand wouldn't fit through now, but the coins did. They fell to the bottom of the box with a quiet jingle.

He would never be that boy again. As long as he could fight, he would fill these coffers, returning what he could of the money that Petros stole from the people.

The Divine might turn away pigstock like him, but the temple never would.

"There goes my new chariot," Elias whined. "I hope you're happy."

Madoc grinned. "I'm sure your mother wouldn't be at all suspicious if we came home in a chariot." They couldn't even afford a carriage ride across town. After their first win, Elias had brought a fat duck home for dinner, and Ilena had accused him of gambling and made him give the bird to Seneca to teach him a lesson.

Elias scowled.

Ilena wasn't their only concern. Half the take usually went to the family to pay the bills and keep Petros and his dogs at bay, but if word got out that they'd bought new clothes, or spent more than they could pull at the quarry, Petros would hear of it and have them arrested for hiding taxable income.

"Does killing my dreams make you happy?" Elias asked, his glare scalding.

Madoc laughed all the way down the steps, but the truth needled deep beneath his skin. Tonight's winnings were a bandage over a gaping wound. The Undivine would suffer as long as they were powerless, and they were powerless because they would never be afforded the same jobs, homes, and schools that those with geoeia had. In Deimos, if you were born pigstock, you died pigstock, and one man made sure you remembered your place.

Madoc would not be truly happy until Petros had lost everything.

TWO

ASH

THE GREAT DEFEAT dance was Ash's favorite, but the story it told was a lie.

The dancers waiting with her on the sun-warmed arena sands wore costumes representing the six gods, with another dancer in white to symbolize the long-dead Mother Goddess. Around them, the largest arena in Kula hung as quiet as the windless noonday sky; the crowd's enthusiasm had simmered down from boisterous to a tense, eager silence.

"They recognize what dance we're going to do," whispered the boy who was playing Biotus, the god of animal bioseia. He shifted in his costume of heavy furs, sweat beading along his brow, but he nodded at the watchful crowd. "Look at them—oh, this is going to be *good*."

Ash could taste his—and the crowd's—anticipation on the air. It tasted of salty sweat covered by one of the other dancers' too-sweet tangerine perfume.

The god of fire always staged performances before arena matches—just not *this* dance, the extravagant costumes, the undeniable insult. This dance was typically reserved for the holiday marking the Mother Goddess's defeat.

Ash rolled her eyes. "It's a waste. Geoxus isn't even here."

Not that she wanted the earth god here. But his absence made this dance feel unnecessary.

The gods rarely traveled for anything less than gladiator wars, two-week affairs of pomp and arena matches that settled blatant offenses and gave the winning god huge prizes: ports, land, trade routes. The cause of this fight had only been Geoxus accusing the fire god of letting his people fish in Deiman territory—the fight after this dance would resolve that, and give a small reward to the winning god, a chest of gold or a season of harvest.

On Ash's other side, the dancer representing Hydra, the water goddess, sighed, rippling her sheer blue veil. "I *know*," she moaned. "Geoxus is nice to look at."

Ash snapped a sharp look at her. "That is not what I meant."

Music cut off their whispers. The dancer playing Hydra gave Ash a grin from behind her veil, clearly not believing her denial. The gods were all painfully beautiful.

Ash shot air out her nose and dropped her eyes to her bare feet. This was why she tried not to talk with the other fire dancers—most people saw the gods exactly as they wanted to be seen. Gorgeous and immortal, powerful and fair. Poverty wasn't their fault; they always wanted the best for their children. Even when they were cruel, they were still merciful and avenging.

But those were all lies, too. Lies as potent as the Great Defeat dance. Lies that made Ash feel alone, though she was standing in the center of hundreds of people.

This self-pity was not helping. Ash bit down on her lower lip. She knew that all the lies were worthwhile. She would dance in a moment and get a reprieve in the music and movement; her mother would fight in the match that followed, and she would win. Then they'd get to walk out of this arena, together and alive.

She'd tell a thousand lies if it meant another day with her mother.

Her eyes lifted to the stands. The arena was an imposing structure of black granite, obsidian, and jagged spikes of lava rock built in the usual tradition, where audience seating ran tiered laps around the center fighting pit. People filled every bench, some clasping orange and red streamers while others held signs painted with *CHAR NIKAU*—the fire god's best gladiator.

Ash noted a new addition with a startled flinch. A few people wore garish masks in Char's likeness. One showed her sticking out her tongue, her eyes wide and cut with squirming red veins.

Ash wrinkled her nose. People saw the gods as beautiful, but they saw her mother as *snarling*?

The music swelled. Cymbals crashed, reverberating into silence.

"Here we go," the dancer playing Biotus cooed.

Ash twitched to right herself, narrowing her mind to the performance.

A harp rippled, and the dance began.

Ash swayed her arms in practiced movements alongside the other dancers. For a moment, she felt a thrum of connection. She had nothing in common with these dancers, couldn't even choke out a conversation with them for the lies she would have to tell, but in this dance, they were unified.

And Ash wasn't alone.

The girl representing the goddess of air waved a flurry of streamers to symbolize air energy, or aereia. The Mother Goddess struck her down with a single elegant twirl.

Next went Biotus. He stomped, vicious and growling. The Mother Goddess hurtled into his arms and dispatched him with her limbs twining around his broad body.

Then came Hydra, with flapping cerulean silk to show the hydreia of water, and Florus, with vines for floreia.

When most of the dancers lay sprawled around the Mother Goddess in defeat—not death, but rather their energies merely spent, or so the story went—the second to last stepped forward: Geoxus, the earth god, played by a tall boy covered in dust and sand. He lifted one foot before the Mother Goddess spun on him, blowing him a lethal kiss, and he fell. The crowd roared with laughter.

The only performers left standing were the Mother Goddess and Ash—who played the lead role. She wore a tight bodice with silk pants that hung low on her hips, both in a wine red that made her brown skin gleam. Sheer orange fabric spooled down her shoulders, ending at the tips in bursts of vibrant blue, and her hair hung in thick black ringlets to midback. Kohl rimmed her eyes and blue paint coated her lips, giving a frosty edge to her smile.

She loved this dance for the outfit she wore, for the connection she felt, for the swell of rapture that bubbled up from the core of the earth itself and filled her with power. This dance was a love letter to igneia, fire energy in its most beautiful, enchanting form.

But she hated this dance for the role she played: Ignitus, the god of fire.

Ash had a few more beats before her cue. Her eyes leaped to the arena's grandest viewing box. On the right were a half dozen centurions from the western country of Deimos; they wore silver breastplates and short pleated skirts, bags at their waists holding stones they could control with geoeia. On the left, Kulan guards wore armor made of dried reeds that, when treated, proved as strong as leather and, better, fireproof.

Divine soldiers like centurions and guards enforced laws among mortals; the immortal, unkillable gods technically didn't need them for protection, but having them was a display of power.

The Deiman centurions stood behind a plump man who had been chosen as Geoxus's proxy for this fight, one of his many senators. The Kulan guards stood behind Ignitus.

Ash's earliest memory of her god was at a feast following Char's first win. Ignitus gave Ash a candy in the shape of a sunburst, doting on the daughter of his next prodigy.

The candy had been bitter, and Ignitus's smile had been sickly sweet.

It always struck Ash how normal her god looked in his ageless physical form. At will, Ignitus could become an inferno, or dissolve into a blue-white flare, or appear as a candle flame on a table. Now, he was dressed in baggy silks dyed orange and scarlet, his brown chest bare, his black hair adorned with gold baubles and scarlet garnets that caught the sunlight.

Each of the six gods was the manifestation of their respective energies, the result of the Mother Goddess pushing her own soul energeia into fire, earth, air, water, animals, and plants. All the gods Ash had seen looked like their mortal descendants—save for that expression. The one Ignitus wore as he gripped the edge of the viewing box and ran his tongue over his lips: bloodlust.

He didn't care that with each match he fought against his god-siblings, he wagered gold, crops, or stakes in Kula's exports, such as their glass. He didn't care that he risked his gladiators' lives, or that even if they won, they stockpiled memories of murder. He didn't care that out beyond this packed arena, the capital city of Kula was a mess of poverty and starvation because so many harvests were lost to other countries, and resources were stripped to pay Ignitus's debts.

He just stared down at Ash portraying him and demanded glory.

The music crashed, cymbals banging hard and fast. Ash's heart lurched and her limbs took her into the movements from memory, the thrill of dancing driving all else from her mind.

Three braziers spaced around the fighting sands thrashed with orange flames. Fire would give constantly if igneia was taken in steady, unselfish sips, one of the first tricks Ash had learned. But for this dance, she needed a great deal of power quickly—she called on the igneia, and all three braziers snuffed out, the fire energy darting into her heart. There, she could channel it into her body, make herself move faster or heal quicker—or she could shoot it back out in powerful flames.

Ash kicked a leg high, and as she twisted under it, she shot fire at the Mother Goddess. This dancer was Fire Divine, so the flames wouldn't hurt her. Even if an esteemed position could be given to someone Undivine, the simple fact that they were descended from the fire god made all Kulans resistant to flame, no matter if they couldn't control it.

The Mother Goddess dipped backward to mimic being struck.

Ash fed igneia out slowly, growing a whip until it coiled around the entire fighting pit. She whirled, twisting it in a high funnel that rose above the crowd. Arcs of orange cut through the powdered turquoise sky, each loop alive with dozens of sharp, stabbing tongues.

This was the pinnacle of igneia: life and vibrancy and passion. This was proof that Ash's power could do more than kill.

The crowd gasped at the tornado of fire. Voices cheered, "Ignitus! Ignitus!"

Ash yanked the funnel of scarlet fire down around the Mother Goddess. The dancer toppled with a piercing wail, her body limp alongside the prone bodies of the other gods, her children.

Only Ash still stood, the god of fire, now the savior of humanity.

This was the boldest lie. That, centuries ago, Ignitus had been solely responsible for defeating Anathrasa, the Mother Goddess who had created her six god-children at the beginning of time—then tried to kill them and their mortal descendants when she realized she couldn't control them. She had nearly succeeded in wiping out all mortals, drenching the world in blood and war, before the gods stopped her. Ash had heard variations of that story in every country she had been to—each god claimed that *they* were responsible for that final assault. The truth of how Anathrasa had been defeated had been lost to the ages, buried under each god's need to declare themselves a hero.

The stands thundered with whistles and applause. Only Geoxus's representatives scowled.

The dancers peeled themselves off the sands and bowed, grinning at the fanfare. They had done well; Ignitus would heap gold on them, enough to forget that once it ran out, their bellies would be empty until he called them to dance again. Even so, it was a preferable life to being born Undivine. They were the rabble, the workers, the people who suffered first—and most—when resources were scarce. For every ten children born to a Divine, one was likely to be Undivine; but children born to only Undivine parents were always powerless—and ignored.

Ash didn't stay to bow for the audience or risk getting pulled into another conversation with the dancers. Performing as Ignitus was one thing; she could use igneia beautifully, show its other sides. But she'd rather live out the rest of her days slowly freezing to death in the icy northern mountains than wave to the crowd and pretend she was proud of playing her god.

Besides, an announcer had begun to speak. The main event was starting.

"Most Merciful Ignitus, god of all igneia, stands accused of encroaching on the fishing grounds of Deimos by Powerful Geoxus, god of all geoeia."

Ash turned toward one of the arena's tunnels. Sand trickled over her bare feet as her pace quickened, faster and faster until she slid into the hall.

Her vision blackened in the shadows, but lit sconces brought shapes into view. Tor, his towering form making his head brush the ceiling, stood with his shoulders bent protectively around Char, who sat on a bench against the wall. She had her head tipped back, eyes closed, black hair in a sleek braid. Her armor, made to be as a second skin, rose and fell with her steady breaths.

"Mama." Ash darted forward.

Tor looked up at her approach. "She's fine. Just preparing."

He wasn't much older than Char, but gray peppered his black hair and a few wrinkles cut through a crescent-moon scar around his eye. Those wrinkles deepened when he gave Ash a look that said *Don't push her. Not now.*

"As decreed by the gods, this conflict warrants a single match," the announcer was saying. "The winner shall be declared based on the surviving gladiator, and the losing god will forfeit the fishing grounds and pay twenty gold bricks."

Char gaped up at Tor. "This fight is for gold *and* fishing rights?"

Tor shrugged, but what could he say? The gods determined the prizes, and mortals suffered their losses.

Ash lowered herself to her knees on the rocky floor. "You brought home ten gold bricks from your win against the air goddess last week. That will help."

Char dug her knuckles into her temples. "It doesn't make up for the thirty gold bricks he lost to Biotus while I was gone. More than most Undivine see in a lifetime of work. *And* three full years of wheat harvest when he's barely able to keep his Divine fed as is. He keeps gambling away resources in multiple arena matches at once instead of just waiting for me to be ready—"

Char blinked down at Ash, startled, seeming to realize who she was talking to. "Ash. Sweetheart. I—I get carried away." She batted her hand, but it trembled. "Don't let my ramblings worry you. Your dance was lovely. The new lip paint was a striking addition."

Ash gave a weak smile. They had bought the blue paint yesterday in the market. She and Char had tried yellow first, and cried laughing at how it made them look ill.

She warred with making light of it by mentioning those awful masks in the stands and how Char should paint her mouth too so people would make the masks even more ridiculous with wild lip colors. But Ash's voice came out soft. "Kula's suffering isn't your fault, Mama."

She wanted to add, *Let me help. I can fight some of these battles for you. You can't trust other gladiators to always win, but you can trust me—you've taught me how to fight.*

Char walked into every arena and dispatched Ignitus's enemies precisely so Ash could stay *out* of those arenas. It was one of Ignitus's few mercies—as long as Char had his favor, Ash was unwanted. Char had only taken over for her own mother once she had been killed.

For now, Ash was a dancer. She used igneia as an accessory and prop. Not as a weapon.

"Ash," Char sighed. She put her fingers around Ash's wrist and squeezed.

"Fighting on behalf of Deimos is a great-great-great-grandnephew of Geoxus—Stavos of Xiphos!" the announcer bellowed.

The mostly Kulan crowd met the introduction with boos and hisses.

Behind Ash, Tor huffed. "Remember what we talked about, Char. Stavos is a brute, but he's overconfident and slow. Use that."

Char started to stand when Ash tightened her grip on her mother's hand. Her heart stuck in her throat as the flames in the sconces behind them pulsed, yellow and hot.

No flame was ever just *a flame*. Each god could spy through their energeia—fire was an eye, an extension of the god Ignitus himself.

Ash had asked Char and Tor once why no one stopped Ignitus. He could choose not to declare fights against his siblings. He could dole out food and money equally if he wanted. Kula's sufferings were *his* fault.

Char had smacked her hand over Ash's mouth and cast a horrified look at the fire in their cottage's hearth. "Ignitus could be listening," she had said as Tor snuffed out the fire. "You must never speak of harming him."

"But *why*?" Ash had pressed.

Char's eyes had teared, so Tor had answered, his own eyes shadowed in the absence of flames. "He is a god. Mortals cannot defeat him. But we have moments like these"—he motioned at Char, Ash, himself—"alive and together. Obeying him is a small price to pay for that."

So Ash held her tongue when Char's leg snapped in a match. She silently scrubbed blood out of Char's clothes and braided her mother's hair over her bruises. She choked down the food she was given freely as a gladiator's daughter while people begged along the streets.

But Ash knew, through every soft moment, she was waiting for her mother to die.

"Mama," Ash whispered now. Agony cut into her, visceral and searing. She tried not to ask this often. "Let me take your place. Ignitus may let you retire. You could have a *life*, you and Tor. I'm younger; I can buy us time until Ignitus finds a new line to favor—"

Color drew across Char's brown skin, chasing away the paleness that had become too normal. "Stop." Her tone was rigid, but she touched Ash's cheek. "I'm fine. I won't lose. How could I, when I have the strongest fuel and the brightest flame cheering for me?"

Ash bit her lip. Char sacrificed everything to bring resources to Kula. The least Ash could do was not make things harder on her.

But silence was killing Ash. Silence with Char. Silence with the other fire dancers. Silence with *Ignitus*. She wanted to race into the arena and scream her hatred at him.

She wanted to stop having to hide *everything*.

"Fighting on behalf of Kula," the announcer began, "is Char Nikau, granddaughter of Ignitus, beloved of the fire god."

Ash braced at her mother's title. Though every mortal, Divine or Undivine, was descended from the gods, the Divine with the closest connection to their god were thought to be the most powerful. It was absurd, of course—Tor was just as skilled with igneia as Char, and he was so far removed from Ignitus's direct descendants that he couldn't trace the relatives.

Char covered Ash's fingers with her own and squeezed. "After the fight, we'll practice making fire orbs. You could do wondrous things with them in the Great Defeat dance, I bet."

Ash managed a brittle smile. If she had been more selfish, she would have begged Char to run. But there was nowhere to go—Ignitus and his immortal god-siblings ruled each of the six countries and wouldn't risk offering asylum to Kula's best gladiator.

This was their fate. This choking monotony of blood.

Ash let Char stand, her hand falling limply to her lap as her mother walked toward the wide, waiting glitter of sand.

The moment Char passed into the sunlight, the crowd howled with excitement.

Tor was already at the edge of the pit, just within the hall's shadow. Ash joined him there, her body vibrating.

"She'll be fine," Tor assured her. He gave a firm nod, but his eyes were tense.

"She'd listen to you," Ash whispered, "if you told her to let me fight."

Tor frowned. "What makes you think I want to see you in an arena any more than I want to see her out there?"

"What you want; what she wants. I don't get a choice at all?" The question cut Ash's tongue. She knew the helpless answer.

"No," Tor told her, bittersweet affection in his eyes. "Not when it means risking your life."

Ash turned away, knowing it was childish to sulk, but what else could she do?

Her own father had been an arena worker from Lakhu—not an uncommon thing, for people from two different gods to be together. If they were both Undivine, where they lived was of little consequence—but if they were Divine, that caused more difficulty, as both gods had claim to their powers. The only reason Ignitus had allowed Char to keep Ash was that her father had been Undivine, so there was little chance of her being Air Divine or even Undivine, with Char as her mother. But her father had died long ago, before she had even gotten to know him, and she couldn't remember a time when Tor hadn't been in her life.

"To the glory of the gods," the announcer shouted. "To the death. Fight!"

At the proclamation, Stavos stepped in front of the rock pile that had been provided for him. He was tall and bare chested—a bold choice to sacrifice protection just to show off his muscles—and his shaved head made his large eyes appear feral. He stretched out a hand over the rocks and they shriveled into a great puff of dust. All of them, gone.

Ash hissed through her teeth. Some gladiators chose to harness their energeias externally—Animal Divine could control creatures; Earth Divine could move stones and rocks. Others chose to absorb energeia into their bodies, letting it add speed, strength, and endurance to their physiology. Though the arena boasted other sources of stone, the gods' firm rules limited each gladiator to what energeia sources had been provided. Stavos had taken all his geoeia at once.

A wash of nausea pinched Ash's stomach. She had seen gladiators infused with smaller amounts of geoeia cleave through stacks of logs with a single blow. She imagined that fighting one powered on so much of it would be like fighting a landslide.

A firepit sat opposite the former rock pile, near a weapons rack. Char stood before it, eyes closed. *It sharpens my other senses*, Char had said, but seeing her mother defenseless froze Ash's lungs.

The crowd roared encouragement. Stavos drew a broadsword from the weapons rack that sat near his tunnel and took a step forward. Char still didn't move.

"Come on," Ash whispered.

Tor was rigid beside her. "Patience," he said tersely.

Stavos took off at a sprint. The arena was large enough for him to be winded by the time he reached Char, which had to be her intention. His broadsword was aloft, glinting in the sunlight.

Ash's attention went to Ignitus. He gripped the box's railing, his lips quirked. He knew Char would turn the fight. He knew she wouldn't fail him.

The broadsword came down over Char, and finally, *finally*, she moved.

The firepit sputtered as she pulled on igneia. She cartwheeled to avoid the broadsword and got in a solid kick to Stavos's jaw before her feet planted back on the ground. Stavos reeled, his sword thundering against the earth and giving Char another opening: she chopped her leg against his hands, dislodging his grip. She kept going, pulling more igneia—but this time the fire came in a hypnotic arc of gilded scarlet, swooping through the air on Char's command. She twisted, and the ribbon washed into Stavos, slamming him onto his back as he gave a bark of pain. The fire knotted into a ball to sit heavy and hot on his chest, keeping him down, pinned, as the bare skin on his sternum began to crackle and burn.

Stavos shrieked.

Ignitus pulled back, arms crossed, grinning. Geoxus's senator shouted something at his gladiator that Ash couldn't hear. Her eyes, her focus, her soul, were fixed on her mother.

Char bowed forward and the flame dropped torturously slowly, sweat beading down her face with effort as the crowd hooted. She would drive the fire into Stavos's chest. How long had this fight lasted? Not even five minutes? A new record, surely.

Stavos squirmed in the dirt at Char's feet. The fingers of his left hand slipped to his thigh—finding a holster hidden under his pleated skirt.

"Wait!" Ash screamed. "Mama—"

A knife flashed in Stavos's palm. He swatted his hand up, looking as though he was batting at Char's legs. But the blade sliced Char's ankle, and she buckled enough that her igneia wavered.

Stavos wriggled free, launching himself to his feet and scrambling for his broadsword. His chest was a red-black mess of fresh burns.

Ash's lungs screamed from lack of breath as Char stumbled away from Stavos.

"Char!" Tor bellowed. "Get to the weapons rack! Go for long range—the spear!"

A single thin line of blood welled on Char's leg where Stavos had cut her. It wasn't deep, but Char teetered as though dizzy. She lost hold of her igneia, the fire sizzling out into nothingness, and there was no fire left in the braziers. She would have to fight without igneia now.

"Something's not right," Ash managed, unease prickling down her arms. "She looks—ill."

One of Tor's hands balled against the stone wall. "Not ill. Drugged."

Ash flicked a look at Tor. Drugged?

It connected. Stavos's knife had been tipped with poison. An illegal move.

"We have to tell Ignitus." Ash whirled on the flickering sconces. "We have to—"

But Stavos swung his sword, and Ash realized that Tor had been right before. She didn't have a choice when it came to her fate—but not in the way he'd meant.

Even if she'd wanted to stay in this hall with Tor, she wouldn't have been able to.

She refused to let her mother die like this.

Ash moved as though music was forcing her into a dance.

She grabbed for the igneia in the sconces and sprinted into the fighting pit. The sand was unsteady under her feet. Tor screamed for her from behind, but she pressed on, pooling igneia into her palms, forming it into a whip like the one she had made in the dance.

Ahead, Char shook her head, her fingers pushing into her temples. She blinked, registered Stavos's coming sword, and shot to the side to dodge the blow. The momentum caught her wrong and she faltered, sprawling on the dust.

The sand was red. Had it been red before?

Ash gasped, sweat pouring down her back. The tone of the crowd's cheering shifted, but their incessant noise dulled to a hum as she ran, her fire whip lengthening, lengthening—

Char heaved herself backward, then back again, leaving a trail of maroon in her wake.

Stavos dragged the tip of his sword through the sand. He noted Ash coming with a wicked sneer.

Char followed his gaze, her lips moving. Maybe, *Ash, no!* Maybe, *My fuel and flame.*

Stavos lifted his sword and hurled it through the air.

Ash reared, her fire whip snapping to fill the circumference of the fighting pit as it had during the dance. She tightened it until the flames knotted around Stavos and hefted him above the sand. He shouted, thrashing, and she tossed him across the pit, as far away as she could.

She swung around, eyes scrambling for Char.

Mama, don't do this, please. She had been eight, begging Char to stop. She had been eleven. She had been eighteen, this morning, *Mama, please stop, he'll kill you—*

Stavos's broadsword pinned Char to the sand. Her body lay sprawled and delicate like the dancers depicting the vanquished gods, only she didn't rise for a finishing bow.

The world blurred. The blue sky, the heaving crowd—and movement in the viewing box.

Ashi's own grating breath deafened her as she looked up, numb.

Each god could spy through their energeia. Try as Ignitus did to limit his siblings' access, he couldn't get rid of all other energeias—which meant the earth god had been able to watch this fight.

And he was here, now, standing in the viewing box next to Ignitus.

Geoxus's body was half dust and dirt, a product of traveling through stone, as all the gods could do with their elements. He formed as he rose over Ignitus, rock yielding to flesh and blood. He was his brother's opposite in all but their black hair and brown skin; where Ignitus was long and slender, Geoxus was all chiseled solidity and muscle.

He spoke, breaking into Ash's shock with a searing crack as his voice came from every pebble and rock and particle of sand in the arena: "Your mortal interfered, brother. You cheated. I declare war on Kula."

THREE

MADOC

"CAN YOU BELIEVE it?" Elias huffed, a wild light in his eyes as they raced down the narrow street. Madoc had seen the same excitement in half the faces they'd passed since the foreman at the quarry had dismissed them early from work, and felt the rush of anticipation buzzing from the crowds that had gathered on the street corners.

War was coming to Deimos. The fire god, Ignitus, was bringing his best Kulan gladiators to battle the fiercest of Geoxus's champions in the arena. For two weeks and four strenuous rounds, the competitors would battle their fellow fighters for a chance to advance and represent their country in the final match to the death. People would swarm to see their favorites attack with earth and fire. Parades would jam the streets and parties would last until dawn.

There was nothing the people of Deimos liked better than blood soaking its golden sand.

"That we're at war with Kula? Or that we got a half day off work?" Madoc asked. They'd been creating the foundation for a new bathhouse near the market for the last two weeks. When news of war had hit the streets, the foreman had been in such a hurry to join the thousands signing up for gladiator tryouts that he'd tripped over a bale of straw.

Madoc didn't blame him. Those lucky enough to become trainees made one hundred gold coins a week. Those good enough to make Geoxus's prized Honored Eight—the finalists who would compete for the chance to fight in the final match—made a thousand coins for each level they advanced. It was rumored that several spots had opened, too, on account of some illness running through the gladiator barracks. Three of the champions from the last war ten months ago against Cenhelm had died of it, and their positions could be anyone's.

Madoc's thoughts returned to Lucius's trainer, and his offer in South Gate. That much coin would have been nice, but he had no intention of dying for it.

"Both," Elias said as they turned the corner into the stonemasons' quarter. Signs were already posted outside the apothecary declaring death to the Kulan gladiators, and showing images of their fire god snuffed out by sand. "We'll be off for all the trial matches, as well. That's two weeks' vacation thanks to Ignitus."

"Unpaid," Madoc added, and received a jab to his ribs from Elias.

"In case you forgot, we raked in a winning purse last night. No digging for our dinner in Divine trash heaps this week!" Madoc winced, remembering a rough spot last month when he and Elias had searched for scraps of food in the Glykeria District—a wealthy, Divine area of the city—but Elias's joy was unrelenting. He spread his arms. "Welcome to Deimos, Kulans!"

From across the street came a stream of *boos*.

Madoc grabbed Elias's sleeve, dragging him around a mule-drawn cart on the bricked path. Still, he grinned. His back ached from double shifts churning the vats of sand, water, and cement into mortar. His hands were blistered and sore from slopping the gray sludge into the spaces between stones shaped by the geoeia of the Earth Divine masons. Elias's geoeia abilities were fit for the more refined jobs of masonry—shaping towers or carving intricate doorways—but his father's debts had tarnished the Metaxa name, so he was forced to work with Madoc and other Undivine, doing whatever cheap labor they could get.

Neither of them was complaining about some time off.

They cut through a narrow alley toward the small courtyard the Metaxa family shared with four other families. The air here smelled faintly like dust and simmering stock, and the top of each door was lined with broken gemstones—Geoxus's eyes, people called them, though the truth was the Father God could see, hear, *move*, through any kind of earth. He was always close, and even in a place thick with thieves and hunger, reminders like this warmed Madoc.

It meant he was never alone, however much he felt that way.

But as they drew closer, wind gusted down the narrow alley, carrying a spray of dust from the ground and an uneasy quiet. There was no laughter, no arguments carried from the courtyards or from inside the open windows. Even the street beyond, normally filled with horses, carts, and beggars, was still. Just as the wrongness of it registered in Madoc's brain, Elias stopped, his head tilting slightly.

In wordless vigilance, they crept forward, past a splintering blue door and a small bronze prayer statue tucked into an alcove near their courtyard. The dried flowers and incense Madoc had placed beneath them before their last fight were crushed, as if someone had stomped through them.

His heart raced faster.

They reached the gate to their home but found it open, swinging on its hinge with a quiet squeal. The white and green stones of a children's game had been abandoned beneath the potted orange trees, and the community meal table was empty. Including the six of them in the Metaxa home, eighteen souls shared this tight space, and yet no one seemed to be here.

Dread curled in Madoc's gut as he registered the glowing embers in the central hearth and the tunic left halfway out of the washing basin beside it.

It was as if everyone had disappeared, or hidden.

Madoc scanned for intruders. Thieves were not unusual in the quarter, but they would have taken the clothes on the line, or broken into one of the homes. His gaze jerked up the stairs, to the balconies that led to the tenants on the top floor. The windows were shuttered. The doors, closed.

"What is . . ." Elias stumbled over a broken bowl but caught himself before falling. "Mother? Cassia! *Danon!*" He called for his younger brother, racing toward the first-floor apartment. "Ava!" Elias shouted, making fresh fear swell within Madoc's lungs. He didn't know what he'd do if five-year-old Ava was hurt—if any of them had been harmed. They might not be his family by blood, but they were all he had.

The door swung inward at Elias's push, and Madoc blinked to adjust his eyes to the group of people crowded in the small kitchen.

Danon stood closest, gripping his bony elbows as if he might fall apart if he let go. Cassia and Ilena were gathered on one side of the table with Seneca, the old woman from upstairs. Their strained stares flicked from Madoc and Elias to the two men in clean, white togas standing beside the door. One of them, a guard, was nearly as tall as Madoc, and built like the bricks he could undoubtedly crush with a flex of his fist.

The other was Madoc's father.

The senate's master of taxation and organizer of off-book street fights. The man who had kicked Madoc out at five years old for being Undivine.

"Ah, good. Just the young men I wanted to see." Petros Aurelius dabbed at a line of sweat that carried the black powder he wore in his hair down his jaw. His paunch stretched over his belt, a sign that he could afford to live in excess, and his cheeks were flushed. "Leave the door open. It's as hot as a sauna in here."

Panic needled through Madoc's skin. What was Petros doing here? Taxes weren't due until the end of the month. And what did he mean, *Just the young men I wanted to see*? He didn't even know who Madoc was. He'd been to this house many times over the years on his collection circuit and hadn't once spared Madoc a second glance. Madoc had figured he'd either forgotten his own son or didn't care that Madoc had survived.

At first, that indifference had been worse than Petros's hate, but over time it had cured Madoc's shame. If he meant nothing to his father, his father would mean nothing to him.

With a nod from Petros, the guard edged past his master and began sweeping through the main room, looking in jars, then tossing them to the ground, tearing aside the woven mats on the chairs. The space was so tight, he nearly knocked over the table on his way past.

"What's going on?" Elias asked as a flash of white darted around them and latched onto Madoc's legs. Madoc lifted Ava into his arms, blowing out a shaky breath as her small hands wound tightly behind his neck.

"There's been a misunderstanding," Ilena said. "Petros heard a rumor that you boys had been stealing, but I assured him that wasn't the case." Elias's mother was slender and could fit under Madoc's arm, but she was the fiercest woman he'd ever known, and when her pointed gaze landed on him, he knew he'd better play along.

"Hardly a rumor," Petros said. "You know I run the amateur matches at the South Gate fishing port, don't you? A little hobby of mine to keep people entertained." He nodded to the guard. "Search the bedrooms."

Madoc's stomach dropped as the guard shoved past Cassia, entering the room she shared with Ilena and Ava. Petros didn't run just the fights. The poor districts were filled with his other business ventures: bathhouses, seedy taverns, and cheap brothels. Half the South Gate district belonged to him, and the other half paid their dues for the right to live there.

His amateur matches collected enough coin to replace the

dilapidated homes in the stonemasons' quarter. Instead, it went into Petros's pocket and paid off fighters like Fentus, who were sure to win.

It was a shame when they didn't.

"I've heard of it," Madoc said, out of the corner of his eye catching Elias twitching. From the bedroom came a crash, as if the pallet they slept on had been tossed against the wall.

Petros smiled tightly. "Then perhaps you know of the Quarry Bull. He's been raking in quite a purse these past months. Four matches he's beaten my best fighters."

"We don't know anyone named the Bull, we told you," said Cassia. Her dark hair was pulled back in a knot, showing the angry crimson of her cheeks.

"Easy, my dear," said Seneca. "There's no need for disrespect."

Petros smiled.

"There's little use denying it, girl. I have eyes everywhere." Petros sighed, stepping closer to Madoc. "The Bull, as he's called, ran off with last night's take. I'd very much like to discuss that with him."

Ava gave a quiet wince, telling Madoc that he was squeezing her too tightly. He loosened his grip, trying to look casual.

"How can we help?" Elias asked.

Petros chuckled, glancing at Elias's dirty tunic. "You can tell me where to find the young man who fights with mortar stains on his clothes, who's built like he's spent long days hauling rocks with the strength of his back, not his geoeia."

It didn't matter how tall Madoc had become, or how many years had passed. When Petros narrowed his beady gaze on him, he wanted to disappear.

He hadn't been careful enough. Few Divine did manual jobs, not when they could use their power to make more money.

Petros knew they'd been fighting. That they'd been winning. As much as Madoc had longed to confront his father, to own that he had been the one to take the winnings, he had not seen it playing out like this, with his family and Seneca standing watch.

"There's no money here, dominus," said the guard, resuming his place at Petros's side.

Madoc's pulse beat between his temples. He wanted these men out of this house, far away from the Metaxas. He wanted to forget the anger, and the pain, and the memories he'd locked so deep inside that he could almost pretend they weren't a part of him. But they *were* a part of him, and now with each breath the past dug its claws deeper into his lungs.

You don't belong here. You're a disappointment to any god.

Elias laughed weakly. "I don't know anything about that. We're stonemasons, not fighters."

"There you have it," said Ilena. "Now, if you—"

"You used to live in one of the Divine districts, did you not? Glykeria? No, Kyphus."

Ilena dipped her head, hiding the clench in her jaw. "Yes, dominus."

Petros knew they had lived in Kyphus because six years ago, he'd taken Elias's father for his unpaid gambling debts. Ilena had been left alone, pregnant and with three young children, as well as Madoc. And when they'd been unable to pay off what he owed, the tax collector had sold him to the arena, to be used as practice in the matches against real gladiators.

No amount of stonecutting skill could help him. Elias's father had lasted only a week.

Behind Ilena, Cassia was gripping the edge of the table with white knuckles. She'd once told Madoc that the reason she wanted to become a centurion was to stop men like Petros. She'd applied every year for the legion since she was twelve, even though they didn't take anyone under eighteen. Barely a day went by that she didn't practice their training exercises in the alley behind the apartment.

He prayed she didn't lose her temper now.

"I'm sure you think there isn't much farther to fall than this heap of rubble and filth, but believe me, there is." Tension thinned the air as Petros stepped closer to Madoc, forcing Elias to cram against the wall to stay out of his way. "It would be a poor decision to lie to me."

"Please," Cassia said. "We know—"

"Quiet," Seneca cautioned her. Her eyes were water blue, nearly translucent as they landed accusingly on Madoc.

"Tell me, Madoc," said Petros. "When did your geoeia reveal itself?"

Madoc froze. Petros remembered his name.

It shouldn't have been a shock, but it was. Madoc hadn't heard his father say his name in thirteen years. He'd assumed Petros had forgotten it, just as he'd forgotten him.

"Dominus, please." Ilena stepped closer to his side, edging in front of Madoc and Ava. "My son is Undivine. He has no geoeia."

"*Your* son," said Petros, bringing a wash of shame through Madoc's chest. Birth mother or not, Ilena was the closest thing to a parent he had. Madoc could hardly believe Petros was challenging the claim. "Did I not tell you it was unwise to lie to me?"

Petros raised his hand. With a twitch of his finger he summoned a stone from the wall and sent it hurtling toward Ilena.

"No!" Cassia shouted, launching herself forward. She was fast, but not fast enough. As she pushed her mother aside, the stone glanced off Ilena's head, drawing a gash the size of a fist across her forehead.

Chaos erupted inside Madoc. With Ava still in one arm, he dropped to catch Ilena, terror punching through his ribs. As his adoptive mother blinked up at him, dazed, Madoc caught sight of a ceramic bowl flying off a shelf, crumbling to pieces in midair.

"Cassia, stop!" Elias cried, trying to block the fragments of clay before they hit Petros or his guard. It was illegal to use Earth Divine gifts against a government official. Citizens were imprisoned for even suggesting they could.

The guard swung in front of Petros, turning the shards to dust before they reached their mark. With a roar, he cut his arms in a wide arc, clapping his hands before him with a deafening boom. The walls around them shuddered as gravel and loose bits of stone came flying toward Cassia. Danon dived under the table, and Madoc thrust a screaming Ava toward him, dragging Ilena to safety as Elias tried to contain his sister.

"Please!" From somewhere across the room, Madoc heard Seneca's voice. He looked frantically for her through the dust—the old woman could hardly stand without support. She couldn't make it down the stairs without assistance. A blast like this could topple her. "You'll bring the house down!"

The rumbling halted, but dust floated in the air, gleaming in the light from the door.

"Enough," said Petros. Madoc coughed as he rose from beneath the table. He glanced to Elias, the gasp withering in his throat as he found Cassia's arms pinned to the wall by molded clay. She struggled against her bindings, back bowing. Strips of hair clung to her dirty face.

"She's sorry," Elias was saying. "She didn't mean anything by it. She was just trying to protect our mother."

Tears of frustration streamed down Cassia's cheeks.

"Are we done lying?" Petros asked.

Madoc wanted to kill him. Wanted to tear him limb from limb. He could barely feel the buzz of all the warring emotions in the room over his own hate.

"Let's see your geoeia, Great Quarry Bull," said Petros. "A little demonstration. I doubt anyone will notice if you make a mess." He motioned to the chairs, tipped over or broken. The fragments of dishes burrowed into the red mat at Madoc's feet. The candles were snuffed out and broken against the ground; the only light came through the open door.

"I have no geoeia."

Petros lifted his hand again, and the bindings tightened around Cassia's wrists. Her scream of agony cut him to the marrow. Frantically, Elias pulled at the clay with his geoeia, but each effort only doubled the bonds. Petros would not loosen his hold.

"It doesn't take much pressure to crack the bones of the wrist," Petros mused.

"Stop!" Madoc shouted. He caught sight of Seneca leaning heavily against the far wall behind Petros's guard, her long white hair coated with gray dust. He couldn't tell if she was injured.

"How about we sweeten the pot?" Petros taunted. "Show me how you fight, and I'll let the girl go."

Rage hardened Madoc's veins. He glanced at Elias, his stare hard. If Petros wanted a show, he would get one. Sweat and dust burned Madoc's eyes. He stepped away from the table, bits of dishes crackling beneath his feet. His hand dropped to his thigh, ready to give the signal.

This was a test, just like the tests in his youth, only now he wasn't five years old and afraid. Now he had Elias. Now he had a family.

He tapped his thigh, but nothing happened.

Petros's gaze pinched.

"Come on," Madoc muttered. Elias could lift a broken cup off the floor, flick a stone across the room, anything. But when he tapped his thigh again, the earth stayed quiet.

Panic laced through his ribs.

"My mistake," said Petros bitterly. "It looks like you are just pigstock after all." He snapped his fingers and his guard stepped forward. "Bring the girl."

Cassia's sobs gave way to a soft moan as her bindings loosened.

"No." Madoc lunged toward Petros. "Please. I'll do whatever you like. You want to see geoeia? Let's go outside in the courtyard. I'll show you."

Petros's disappointment turned to disgust. "The girl attacked me.

I could ask Geoxus for permission to execute her. Taking her to my house is a mercy."

"Your house?" Elias balked. The guard had crossed the room and removed a set of cuffs from his belt. They were wooden and spiked along the inside. "Wait. You're shackling her?"

Madoc could feel his own control slipping. He'd seen the centurions shackle Divine lawbreakers so they could be taken to the jail. The wooden spikes in the cuffs that encircled the wrists and ankles could not be manipulated by geoeia. If the prisoner moved too fast, or tried to summon the earth to their bidding, the spikes impaled their skin and destroyed their focus. It was supposedly excruciating. A Divine man who mixed mortar with them had worn the shackles once after drunkenly attacking a centurion and now could barely bend his wrists.

Cassia wanted to be a centurion. She was supposed to be the one keeping order, not breaking it.

"Cause me more trouble, and you'll be next," Petros told Elias as the spikes were fastened around her thin wrists. "We'll set her indenture at fifteen hundred gold coins. That's only fair for her actions today."

"That's more than we make in three years at the quarry!" Elias cried.

"We'll pay it," Madoc promised. "Let her stay, and I promise we'll make good on it."

"I don't think so," Petros said. "The Metaxas have defaulted on the payment of their debts in the past, if I recall."

Rage hardened Madoc's muscles. This wasn't happening. He had to stop Petros. He'd been foolish thinking a few gold coins earned in a fight would hurt his father. The man was a monster. He needed to be destroyed.

"Stop." Cassia glanced up to Madoc, a fierceness filling her gaze even as the guard jerked her upright. "Don't be stupid." She lowered her chin toward the table, where the rest of the family hid.

He couldn't fight for one of them without risking all of them.

He couldn't let her go.

It didn't matter if they lived in the quarter, or if they had to eat other people's scraps or nothing at all. They had each other—that was what Ilena always said. They could get through anything as long as they stayed together.

"These alleys are so small," Petros complained. "We had to leave the carriage on the corner. Such a walk in this heat."

"Don't be stupid," Cassia said again as the guard pulled her from the room. "I'll be fine."

With a smirk, the guard closed the door behind him. A moment later, the wood was sealed to the frame by a wall of clay from the outside.

"No!" Elias rammed his shoulder against the exit, but it gave only a small crack. He lifted his hands, trying to peel away the earth with geoeia, but it was solid, like Cassia's wall bindings. Elias could chisel through it with his power, but it would take time and concentration.

Madoc wheeled on him as he shoved back the table. "What was that? Why didn't you use your geoeia when I gave the sign?"

"And have him take you too?" Elias shot back as Madoc dropped to his knees at Ilena's side. "You use geoeia and it proves you're the one he's looking for. He could have killed you on the spot!"

"Would you two shut up already?" Danon shouted.

On the ground, Ilena moaned and jerked beneath Madoc's grip. He didn't realize he'd touched her arm, or even how hard he was holding on to her, until he drew back, revealing the pink imprint of his fingertips.

"Are you all right?" Elias dropped to his knees at her side, worry drawing his tone tight.

Ilena blinked and prodded her forehead. "Yes . . . I . . ." She grabbed Elias's arm and pulled herself up. "Where is Cassia?" Her unfocused gaze slid around the room. "What happened?"

Madoc's head fell forward.

"Petros happened," said Danon.

"What does that mean?" Ilena's voice pitched. "Get me up!"

"She should stay down." Seneca had hobbled over, leaning against the corner of the table as she extended a dusty towel in their direction. "That's a nasty cut."

Madoc took the cloth, holding it to Ilena's head. His nerves were frayed, his blood pumping too fast. He needed to get out of this house. He needed to bring Cassia home.

Ilena paled further as Danon explained what had happened.

"When is Cassia coming back?" Ava asked, latching onto her mother's side.

Ilena didn't answer. Her gaze had turned to Madoc and Elias.

"Fighting?" she whispered. Then, like a shot, she snagged the front of Elias's tunic in her unrelenting grip. "*Fighting?* We don't use *energeia*—or our *fists*, Madoc—to hurt anyone!"

Shame sliced through the jagged edges of his emotions. She didn't want them fighting because of her husband, and they had done it anyway. He pressed his fingertips to his closed eyes. He couldn't explain why he'd done it. He couldn't make this okay. He'd wanted to hurt Petros, and instead, Petros had hurt him, just like always.

Elias peeled her fingers away with a muttered apology.

"I'll talk to Petros. Tell him this was a misunderstanding." Bracing herself against Madoc, Ilena stood, but one step had her stumbling into the side of the table.

"You need to lie down," said Madoc.

"Don't you tell me what to do," she snapped, but when she wavered again, she gave a reluctant nod. "Just for a bit then."

They helped Ilena to her room, righting the cot that had been overturned in the guard's search. While Danon and Seneca attended to her, Madoc and Elias returned to work on the door.

"We'll go to his house," Elias muttered as he chipped through the clay along the jamb with his geoeia.

"And what? Ask nicely to get her back? You know what Petros will say." With his foot Madoc cleared away the gravel that fell. "His house is a fortress, anyway. We'll never get past the front gates."

"Then we'll wait until everyone's gone to sleep. I'll make stairs with the stones against the outer wall. We'll climb over and find her."

The throbbing at the base of Madoc's skull increased, spurred now by Elias's anxiety. Madoc wished he could shut it off—at least dull the sensitivity. Not for the first time, he wondered if something was wrong with him. As far as he knew, no one else could sense others the way he did. It had started when he was young—a flicker of anger or excitement that matched that of someone close by, a hunger in his belly when he saw Ilena hiding her tears. But each year it was getting a little stronger. Now their small house was too loud with everyone home, and big crowds like the market gave him headaches.

He blew out a stiff breath, trying to focus. "If we break in, Petros will come to the quarter, arrest Ilena and Danon, send Ava to the poorhouse, and ask for Geoxus's blessing to run us all through with wooden spikes."

"Well, what are we supposed to do then?" Elias threw back. "Let your father keep her?"

Madoc turned away. In all his years with the Metaxas, Elias had not once referred to Petros as Madoc's father.

"Look, I'm sorry." Elias groaned. "I can't stand it, all right? I can't sit here and do nothing." He sent another burst of geoeia against the door, and finally the blockade shuddered, chunks of stone falling free. Madoc dropped his shoulder and rammed through, the wood splintering as it exploded into the courtyard.

The sun was setting, painting the horizon bloodred.

Your father. Your responsibility.

They needed to get Cassia back—Petros had her in *shackles.* But how?

There had to be a way. There was always a way.

He crouched, one hand pressed to the earth. *What do I do?* The Father God would guide him. He'd always come through for Madoc.

"We can't hurt Petros." Madoc rose as Elias joined him in the empty courtyard. "He's Divine. He's surrounded by guards."

"Oh, and he's a senator, appointed by Geoxus," Elias added, patting the dust off his arms.

"The only option is to pay off her indenture." Which meant they needed money. *Fast.* And more than they could get at the quarry.

They needed to fight. They needed to win.

Madoc's arms dropped to his sides as an idea flickered inside him.

Elias raked a hand through his hair. "Are we thinking the same thing?"

"I doubt it," said Madoc.

"We rob the temple offering box," Elias exclaimed, just as Madoc said, "We become gladiators."

"What?" Elias frowned. "That wasn't what I was thinking at all."

Madoc lowered his voice. "Lucius Pompino's trainer saw me fight at South Gate last night. He wants me to train. We could sign up, earn the money we need, and free Cassia."

"Hold on—you got invited to train at Headless Hill?" Elias checked the volume of his voice, stepping closer. No one was outside, but that didn't mean they weren't watching and listening. "Sorry. I forgot to mention that Geoxus himself stopped me in the market the other day. He told me I could have all the olives I wanted. And that he likes me much better than you. I didn't want to say anything because I thought it would hurt your feelings."

"Great. Then you can ask the Father God to release Cassia."

Getting physically close to Geoxus was impossible. He was a god, surrounded by advisers and guards and half the legion wherever he went. But if Lucius really wanted to make Madoc a gladiator, he might be able to earn the money they needed to set Cassia free.

Of course, there was a good chance Lucius's trainer would laugh him away for declining his initial offer, but Madoc couldn't think of that now.

"I would," Elias said. "But I wouldn't want to steal your glory." He frowned, then turned his eyes west, toward the Glykeria District, where Lucius Pompino's training facility sat atop Headless Hill. "You really think this could work?"

Madoc blew out a tense breath. "We've beaten Petros's best. Even just training, we'd make a hundred gold coins a week." *And stay alive.* He'd seen fighters who'd trained with the sponsor around the city. Some of them had been wounded badly enough that they couldn't continue at Headless Hill.

He'd worry about that later.

"You're sure Lucius would let me stay with you?" Elias asked. "I don't mean to piss on your delusions of grandeur, but you're not exactly moving mountains on your own."

He was right. Madoc wouldn't have won a match without Elias using his power from afar.

"Lucius's gladiators each have a servant to help them prepare before a fight," Madoc said. "If anyone asks, you're the only one I trust."

Elias must have been nervous, because he didn't object to being called a servant.

"Mother's going to kill us," he said instead.

"If the other gladiators don't first."

Elias nodded. He glanced back at the house. "Danon!" he shouted.

When his brother's head appeared in the hollowed door, he said, "Tell Mother we're going to get Cassia back."

Danon's eyes widened.

They didn't wait for a response. As quickly as they'd come, Madoc and Elias departed, racing out into the alley, to the streets that would lead to Headless Hill.

FOUR

ASH

WHEN ASH WAS younger, Char would steal her away from her tutors early. Leaving behind lessons on mathematics and letters, they would race down to the dock market in Igna, Kula's capital. Food shortages had not yet become dire, and there were still vendors who sold luxuries like flaky pastries and cloud-soft cakes and—Ash and Char's favorite—cacao.

One time, Char bought a paper sack filled with mango slices dipped in dark, creamy chocolate, and they played their favorite game while they ate.

"You could be a glassblower," Char said, pointing at another vendor. "That's what you can use your igneia for. You can create beads that will make Kula beautiful."

"Or a baker!" Ash pointed syrup-sticky fingers at a booth, her belly full of richness. "I'll use fire to turn dough into bread and cake."

Char smiled. "It's so easy to forget that there are wondrous things about fire energy." Her smile faded. "It's important to look for the beauty in igneia, Ash."

These special moments always came after Char had had difficult training sessions or brutal arena matches. She wanted Ash to see beyond Ignitus's future. She wanted Ash to want *more.*

And Ash did want more. She wanted her mother to smile. She wanted Tor to laugh. She wanted to not feel so alone.

When she danced, sometimes she got those things. But they never lasted, and she feared the moment when Kula would cease being beautiful forever.

That moment came as Ash stood on the blood-soaked arena sands, staring down at Char's body. The broadsword protruded from her chest.

Ash couldn't move. She heard the crowd shouting, someone distantly calling her name.

No, it wasn't her name—it was a word. *War.*

Tor set upon her, his hands like vises on her arms. "Ash, Geoxus has declared war. Get behind me—I need to get you out of this arena."

Awareness trickled into Ash's mind. Tor's eyes were bloodshot, his face rigid. Behind him, Kulan guards were charging into the fighting pit.

"Halt, Nikau!" they ordered. "Surrender!"

She wasn't resisting them. She wasn't moving at all. There was nothing she could do that would fix anything, nothing that would bring Char back.

She let the guards rip her from Tor's hands and drag her out of the arena.

Ignitus's dormant volcano palace was a dark maze of magma tunnels that connected rooms of polished obsidian, granite, and peridot—stones that were made from fire, and therefore impervious to Geoxus's control. The air was thick with ashy smoke, which made it more difficult for the goddess of air to manipulate; there were no animals, no guard dogs or pets, to prevent Biotus from spying. Ash had heard visitors from other countries describe Ignitus's palace as dank and eerie, but she found it lovely in the same way she loved igneia. It was something her god had made; she should hate it. But it was still hers too, part of her blood and her history she couldn't ignore.

Ignitus's guards hauled Ash to one of the palace's highest floors. When they pulled her into a foyer, the opulence stunned her silent. The ceiling was several stories tall, with closed ivory doors leading to other rooms, and garnets, Ignitus's signature gem, embedded in the molding along the floor. The walls were hardened panes of gold that reflected the light of the chandelier.

Stationed next to each door, Kulan guards stood armed with live flames in their palms. Secretaries moved in and out of a few rooms, their arms laden with scrolls and books. They eyed Ash as though she was an investment Ignitus was considering. Had they heard what had happened?

That question broke through Ash's shock, and the bottom of her stomach dropped out.

She had interfered in an arena match. She had broken one of the rules of gladiator fights, the only things the gods held sacred. Geoxus had watched through the stones and declared war.

Ignitus was going to kill her. If she was lucky.

A vile tartness filled Ash's mouth and she steeled herself against the urge to throw up. She should have run, Tor was right—but she couldn't *think*, she could barely feel her own aching feet under her, and every blink brought back the image of her mother's body speared through the chest.

One of the guards opened a door. Ash eyed the sliver of light that crept out.

"Touch nothing," the guard said. "He will be here once he's done with Geoxus."

Ash stiffly walked into the room. It was a sitting chamber with a wall of glittering Kulan glass windows that showed the late-afternoon sky and the startling, multistory drop. Scarlet and butter-yellow tapestries covered the walls, draping in lazy sweeps between golden statues of Ignitus and furniture in dark polished wood. A red padded lounge filled the middle of the room, surrounded by stacks of paper, scrolls, and books.

The door shut with a thud behind her. She was alone.

Ash's nerves caught up to her. Her fingers started to shake, her arms, her chest. She dropped onto the lounge and braced her hands on the edge, her curled black hair falling in straggly chunks around her face as she strained in one full breath of the smoky air.

A sob bubbled past her lips, horror and rage lashing to break free.

Ignitus had gotten Char killed. In trying to stop it, Ash had brought more death to Kula.

What had she done?

A golden bowl full of water sat on the floor next to the lounge, a damp cloth over its edge. Something was odd about the water. It rippled, but Ash hadn't touched it—

The water bubbled, frothed like seafoam, and formed a face.

Ash jerked back on the lounge. The watery eyes shifted around the room. They landed on her, and an expression like annoyance crossed the face. "I thought my brother was in Kula."

Hatred and fear usually overpowered any sense of wonder that Ash could feel about the gods—but being so close to this water face, watching the features ripple and glisten, she was rendered speechless. She knew Ignitus communicated and traveled in fire, and only moments ago she had seen Geoxus come to Kula through stone.

Recognition brought feeling into Ash's limbs. *Brother.* A face appearing in water.

Hydra, the goddess of water energy who ruled the Apuit Islands.

Ash nodded. "He's here."

The goddess of water glanced around the otherwise empty room. An eyebrow lifted.

"In Kula," Ash said, dumbstruck. "Not *here*. Yet."

Hydra heaved a sigh, the water undulating around her face. "Who are you—a servant? Actually, I don't care. I'm not waiting for him. Pass along my response: I received his message. I have heard no similar rumors. He should stop worrying and leave me out of his squabbles with Biotus, Aera, and Geoxus."

Hydra sank back into the water with a parting splash.

Ash started. Ignitus had sent Hydra a message? Why? Only four of the six gods treated their people like disposable objects; two hadn't used their arenas in so long that they were falling into disrepair. That was only a rumor—the two peaceful gods, Hydra, of water hydreia, and Florus, of plant floreia, had long ago formed a coalition against their warmongering siblings. No one other than their own people had been to their countries in decades, as any mortal who tried to cross into either Hydra's or Florus's lands was immediately stopped and sent away.

Ash hadn't heard of the other gods speaking to Hydra or Florus—though that didn't mean it never happened. What did Ignitus want with Hydra?

A flash of orange and blue filled the room.

Ash hurtled to her feet. Her foot caught on the golden bowl and sent the water spilling across the carpet, soaking books and scrolls. She lost her balance and crashed to her knees.

Ignitus appeared, grim faced and fuming. His silken robe fluttered around him, showing strands of glass beads draped across his chest. A few torches were already lit throughout the room; five more flared to life at his presence. He eyed them, then looked at Ash, merely because she was in front of him, and he would have had to make a great show of ignoring her to look elsewhere.

Ash almost told Ignitus about Hydra. But her fingers dug into the soaked carpet, and her mouth tasted like sand.

She was bowing before the creature who had murdered her mother.

The last remnants of Ash's shock shattered beneath the heavy drop of rage.

Ignitus may have been the god of fire, but he didn't know what it was like to feel *this* kind of fire, an anger so pure and absolute that even the sun shied from it.

She wouldn't tell him. The reason Hydra and Florus had had to form a blockade around their countries was to prevent their warmongering siblings from drawing them into fights. Whatever dispute Ignitus wanted to start with Hydra, a *peaceful* goddess, Ash would let him fail at it. She wouldn't assist him in anything that would lead to more bloodshed.

"You," he started, "broke our holy laws. Your mother lost. The Nikaus today have nearly undone their lineage's good deeds."

Sweat pasted Ash's orange-and-scarlet dancing costume to her skin, and her breaths came in stunted gasps. She bit back a whimper, calling on her fury to keep her strong.

But one of his words hooked her. *Nearly*?

Ignitus took slow steps around her, his bare feet squishing in the water-soaked carpet. He didn't mention it, merely nudged the empty bowl out of the way as he left her direct line of sight. "My brother's gladiator, though," he continued, "was the most foolish of all today."

Slowly, Ash stood. Her legs tingled at being unbent, but she felt better not being on her knees. "Great Ignitus," she said, turning to follow him, "I didn't—"

"Stavos thought that his poisoned knife would not be seen." Ignitus's eyes locked on hers. "He thought that my Kulans would not meet his cheating with violent force."

Was that a spark in his eyes, a smile on his lips?

"Aren't you angry with me?" Her voice was no higher than a whisper.

Ignitus grinned. "I have every right to be, don't I? Geoxus denied any wrongdoing on the part of his gladiator—but I owned *your* wrongdoing, Ash. Though it may be difficult to believe, I am proud of you. Some of my guards and a few gladiators have mentioned seeing Stavos of Xiphos's hidden blade. But who took action against him?"

He waited, the wonder in his voice unmistakable.

Ash gawked at him. "I did, Great Ignitus."

Ignitus tipped his head. A lock of hair fell across his shoulder. "You used igneia dancing techniques to subdue Stavos. It was elegant."

He was taller than her, his eyes dark and endless, and Ash couldn't remember ever looking at him directly for so long. She felt drugged, fuzzy, her mouth filled with cotton.

To break the spell, she swept her eyes to the side. The hair that had fallen across Ignitus's shoulder glinted in the flame light. A few strands underneath were gray-white. Ash frowned. Was that coloring a sign of age, like in mortals? Doubtful. Likely they were strands of silver Ignitus had had servants weave into his hair.

"Geoxus's war declaration holds," Ignitus said. "We sail to Deimos tomorrow. Kula stands to lose much. But"—he leaned closer—"I am not angry, because I have found my next victor. You."

Ash gaped at her god, seeing the smile of hunger he gave before he urged his gladiators to face death. The smile he had given before a sword pinned Char to the fighting sand.

"I'm a dancer," Ash tried.

"You're a Nikau. I know Char taught you how to fight. This is what you were born to do."

No, Ash wanted to say. This wasn't her destiny.

This wasn't what her mother had wanted for her.

But Ash wasn't only herself, standing there before Ignitus. The Nikau legacy was strong—a line of fierce igneia gladiators who had brought Ignitus hundreds of wins. She was her mother, her grandmother, her aunt, a cousin, a living corpse of all the Nikau gladiators who had died over centuries of fighting. Char had tried to resist by making the best of this role and bringing as many wins as she could to Kula's coffers. But she had still died, and Ash would still take her place.

A sob gripped Ash's throat and she choked on it, coughing, wanting to break. Char was dead and nothing would change. Nothing would—

A question struck Ash like lightning, cutting into her spiral of panic and dread.

What *would* change this dangerous, bloody cycle?

Ash remembered the Great Defeat dance. The Mother Goddess, who had decimated the world, dead at the end—probably not by Ignitus's hand alone. But she had been killed by *something*. That was the truth in the story: the Mother Goddess was dead.

So there had to be a way to kill Ignitus too.

The revelation blossomed in Ash's heart, swelling like a surge of drums and a crash of cymbals. She wanted that, she realized. She had wanted that her whole life: wanted Ignitus to die.

As one of Ignitus's gladiators, Ash would have access to him. He would dine with her, discuss fighting strategies and the best uses of igneia. She could use that. Unlock his secrets.

And kill him.

That would change their world. That would free Kula from this bloodshed.

Ignitus's ivory teeth glowed against his dark-brown skin. "Geoxus thinks to shame me for your interference. But you are angry that his gladiator defeated Char. Let it fuel you. Be one of my champions and avenge your mother."

This close, he smelled like cinders and coal and sunlight.

Everything else fell away. "Yes, Great Ignitus," Ash said. "I will avenge my mother."

Ash had gone with Char to Deimos for a lesser arena fight three years ago. They had stood at the bow of Ignitus's ship with Tor's Undivine twin sister, Taro, who had chuckled and said that Crixion's lighthouse looked like a part of a man that should not be on display.

Taro had elbowed Char. "Do you think Geoxus modeled this after his own *lighthouse*?"

Char had laughed, bright and clear and real. It had made Ash laugh too, though she didn't entirely understand the joke.

Char had misinterpreted her reaction and seized Ash's arms. "Have you been with a man?" she had asked, a quiet whisper. "Are you careful?"

"Mama—no," Ash had managed. She had been fifteen at the time, and when would she have had time to? On Ignitus's crowded ships or in rooms she shared with Char in foreign arenas?

The few private moments Ash got, when she had a room to herself or a lock on the washroom door, her fingers had trailed over velvet-soft skin that made her flush with a heat not unlike igneia. But she had never met anyone she cared to *be* with. Any conversations she had with people her own age ended in Ash abruptly leaving, distraught by how devoted they were to their god or goddess. The only time she felt anything like connection was in dancing, but even in Ash's limited experience, she knew a relationship built on physical movement wasn't worthwhile.

Char had looked unconvinced. She pulled her into a hug, shoulder digging into Ash's throat. "You *must* be careful. You're the last of the Nikau line. Our blood is a burden."

Had Char been any other mother, Ash might have heard that as *You are a burden*. But she had never once doubted Char's love for her.

Now the captain of this Kulan ship hammered a bell above deck. Everyone onboard had waited three long days to hear that signal—they were entering Crixion's main port. The lighthouse would be just beyond the wall Ash was staring at, the one hung with a round mirror.

"This is madness," Tor said for what had to be the hundredth time. He was sitting on a chair, letting Taro style his hair for the welcoming ceremony. "You can't fight in a war."

Tor's distant lineage from Ignitus hadn't stopped the fire god from naming Tor one of his other war champions, hoping that his grief at losing Char would fuel him like it fueled Ash.

"It's the least I can do, isn't it?" Ash used her pinky to clear a smudge of golden paint under her eye. She was shaking; the gold smeared. "I caused it."

"You did not." Tor's tone was cutting. "We all saw Stavos cheat. You reacted, but you did *not* cause this, Ash. Don't let me hear you say that again."

Ash dropped her eyes. Guilt rubbed her soul, but she tried to believe what Tor said. This was Stavos's fault. It was Geoxus's fault, Ignitus's. This war, the impending bloodshed, wasn't her burden to bear.

The structure of gladiator wars was meant to be distractingly opulent. Prizes like land and resources deserved fanfare, and the glory drove most people into a frenzy of love for their god.

At the start, each god selected eight champions. Those champions fought among themselves in nonlethal elimination trials, with the winners of each round earning gold and prestige. Between rounds, the hosting god threw lavish dinners, theatrical performances, fireworks displays—whatever best showed off their wealth and power. The war ended when each god's remaining champion fought in a to-the-death match. The victorious god received riches and resources from the losing god—as well as incomparable bragging rights.

Though the elimination rounds were nonlethal, that did not always mean they were harmless. The two weeks of a war flowed with opulence and blood in equal measure.

One of Ignitus's other champions was also in this ship's lower-deck room: Rook, a distant great-grandson of Ignitus. Rook had once been a loyal fighter, but the birth of his Undivine son, Lynx, had altered how he viewed Kula, and Undivine, and Ignitus himself. Rook now hated being a gladiator more than Char ever had.

"I think she's got a good plan to press Ignitus for weakness," Rook told Tor. He held his arms lifted while Spark, Taro's wife and a healer, an Undivine woman with nimble hands and endless patience, painted golden sunbursts on his bare chest. "About time someone took a stand."

"She's a child," Tor snapped.

"She's eighteen. Ignitus doesn't let any of our children get to be children. You need any help"—he nodded at Ash, his black curls shifting—"you let me know."

Rook's fighting schedule often left Lynx alone. He was seven now, cared for mostly by the servants in Rook's Igna villa. But Lynx had fallen gravely ill while Rook was traveling two weeks ago. Lynx's mother had run off years back and Rook had no other family—and Ignitus had denied Rook's requests to stay with his Undivine son.

Ash bowed her head at Rook and inadvertently eyed the lantern Taro had put out earlier, as though the flame might still spring to life and Ignitus would overhear them all.

"Don't encourage her," Tor snapped. "Trying to kill a god is folly. Remember Wolfsbane."

It wasn't a question. It was a battle cry, a warning, an omen. *Remember Wolfsbane.*

More than thirty years ago, a gladiator named Wolfsbane had come undone. Too many fights, too much death, too much loss. At a postfight celebration, Wolfsbane had taken a knife from the dining set, walked up to Ignitus, and stabbed him in the heart.

A mortal would have died. But a god retaliated.

Ignitus put Wolfsbane on display so everyone would know what happened to Kulans who turned on their god. Only Ignitus's fire could burn a live Kulan. He seared Wolfsbane's mouth shut, and he had Wolfsbane's limbs removed in increments. He cauterized the wounds himself.

Wolfsbane had stayed alive for eight days.

Ash swallowed a kick of revulsion. "I won't end up like Wolfsbane.

Ignitus thinks my mother's loss rallied me to his side, and he is proud enough that he believes I am fighting *for* him, seeking justice from Deimos. I'll get close to him and figure out what it was that killed the Mother Goddess so I can kill him the same way. I can't stand aside anymore. I shouldn't have hidden while Mama—"

Ash stopped, her voice wavering. She braced her hands on either side of the mirror, her sparkling reflection staring back at her in the light of the porthole window.

"Char loved watching you dance, using igneia to create beauty," Tor tried. "She didn't want this life for you."

"Well, I didn't want to watch my mother die. Rook doesn't want to be away from his son. You don't want to have to worry about me dying, too, and Taro and Spark want more out of life than playing our nursemaids. Show me even one person in this room who got what they wanted."

Tor went silent. Taro, putting oil in his curls, watched Ash in the mirror with a pained gaze, the same she knew Rook and Spark were giving her.

But Ash straightened, fighting to ignore them, and adjusted a curl here, a bead there. She had prepared her mother this way dozens of times. As a child, she had begged Char to let her wear the makeup and clothes too, just to play. But these weren't toys.

This Kulan armor, made from reeds dipped in gold—it was ceremonial and dense.

These wrapping sandals fit with garnets at the intersections—they weighted Ash's feet, made her feel unable to walk or run.

The weave of even more reeds that stretched across her thighs—her legs ached at the bulk.

The iron curlers that had styled her thick black hair. The sparkling garnets and golden picks that held it off her face. The sweeps of makeup: kohl to highlight her dark eyes, shimmering gold on her lids and across her cheekbones, sticky scarlet on her lips. This all made her a gladiator now. She had to be strong.

She had to be emotionless.

Ash glared into her own eyes.

"You and Rook. I heard Ignitus mention Brand and Raya." Ash shifted her gaze to Tor in the mirror. "I don't know the other fighters Ignitus named as champions."

A few of Ignitus's lesser-known gladiators had been selected to fill the other champion positions, leaving slots for gladiators like Brand and Raya who were currently in other countries, fighting battles over minor offenses. They were on their way to Crixion now.

For a moment, Ash thought Tor might not respond. But after a long pause, he sighed.

"The lesser-known gladiators are strong but unpracticed in wars. Ignitus is hoping their loyalty will compensate." He didn't look at Ash, as if refusing to admit that he was giving her this advice. "He will select the first fight pairings after the opening ceremony. Rook and I will help if you're paired against us, but if Brand gets here in time, you'll likely be pitted against him. He's the only one who outranks you by blood, so Ignitus will be curious to see which of you fares best."

Tor looked up at her reflection. "Brand loves making Ignitus proud, and he will only consider it a victory if he kills or maims you. When you fight him, you must intend the same."

Ash felt the world shift with Tor's bluntness. She wasn't a child, deserving of softened half-truths. She set her hands into fists, hoping the action hid her fear. What had she said to comfort Char?

Let me fight for you, Mama. Let me take your place.

Ash chuckled bitterly. She had gotten what she wanted after all. She would wind through Crixion in a grand parade and begin the painstaking work of murdering people for Ignitus.

To earn Ignitus's favor, Ash reminded herself, *and destroy him.*

"Let's get this over with," Rook said as Spark put away her paints. His chest was covered in dozens of golden sunbursts. "The sooner we start this, the sooner we get back to Kula."

"The war will last two weeks no matter what we do," Tor said. If he meant to sound comforting, it came out short. He stood and added, "It will pass quickly. It always does."

"And they make those clay marbles here," Ash added. "For that game Lynx loves?"

A smile puckered Rook's cheeks. It didn't reach his dark eyes, rimmed with kohl and gold. "When I dropped him off at the infirmary, the nurses said he was so ill he'd have to be confined to his bed."

Tor put his hand on Rook's shoulder. Spark cast a sullen glance at Taro, the room sobering.

"For Lynx," Ash whispered, dipping her gaze to the floor.

Out of the corner of her eyes, she saw Rook's hand rise, dabbing at his face.

For Char, Ash added to herself. *For Thorn.* Tor and Taro's Undivine cousin, and his two children, also Undivine. *For Wisteria.* A woman who ran one of the orphanages in Kula, and had been helping Taro and Spark work to find a child. *For all the other fire dancers.*

A bell tolled above deck. Silently, Taro left, followed by Rook and Spark. Tor lingered.

"You look just like her," he offered. "Her fuel and flame."

Heat welled in Ash's chest and tears rose, threatening to streak kohl down her cheeks.

Tor offered her his arm and led her through the ship, up into the high, burning light of day.

Crixion's main port, Iov, was a bay with a narrow opening to the Hontori Sea. At one side of the entrance, the lighthouse rose in a jut of ivory; a military fort stood at the other.

Hilly and steep, Crixion unfurled around Iov as if for inspection. Igna's buildings were all black, volcanic materials, but these structures were shining and white. Old trees had made themselves comfortable among the buildings instead of being burned to the roots. The air was rank with city grime and body odor and the salt of the sea, but not with charcoal or sulfur.

Geoxus was a warmongering god, but he wasn't petty. He rationed his resources and engaged in fights without draining his country. This was what Kula could look like if Ignitus made decisions for the good of his people instead of his own pride.

Ignitus had chosen to complete the final stretch of the journey to Crixion on his ships instead of by materializing there in his fiery form. A physical arrival was more impactful to the Deimans, to make them arrange the necessary welcome throughout the city.

The ships docked in the shadows of the Port of Iov temple, a marble building with an exact likeness of the earth god in rose quartz on its steps. Couuntless Deimans stood in front of it, stretching in long lines into the city, highlighting the parade route that the waiting carriages would follow to the grandest arena in the city center.

Holding back the crowd—though no one fought to press closer—were two unbroken lines of Deiman centurions in pleated leather skirts and polished breastplates, gray-silver capes pinned to their shoulders and helmets glinting in the afternoon sun. Each one had their left hand extended, palm up, spinning a small funnel of stones with geoeia. Not throwing them, not shouting threats; just reminding the crowd and the Kulans that they were trained in using earth energy.

The sheer number of geoeia-wielding centurions made Ash's mouth go dry as the ship's gangplank lowered. Geoxus wanted to intimidate Ignitus and his champions.

It was working.

Ignitus was already descending the long wooden gangplank of his lead ship. He wore scarlet robes and orange glass beads that glinted even from this distance. Blue flames twisted around his lifted arm—a greeting, a threat, a reminder that he was the god of fire.

The Deiman citizens packing the parade route started a cheer when Ignitus came into view. Bits of silver-painted confetti and fragrant flower petals peppered the air.

"Geoxus!" they cried. "The mightiest god!"

Ash gripped the ship's railing. Of course they weren't cheering for Ignitus. But if he heard the taunts of the Deimans, he overlooked them with a sharp, soulless smile.

His last war with Geoxus had ended in failure for him—not Char's fault, thankfully—and now Ignitus had just lost his best gladiator in a rigged fight. But he seemed high on good fortune.

Tor and Rook started down the gangplank, but Ash stayed on the deck, her heartbeat bruising her ribs as a realization bruised her mind.

Ignitus was unworried. Relaxed, almost, tossing his shining black curls down his back and flinging random bursts of fire into the air.

Now that she thought on it, Ash had *never* seen Ignitus worried. Angry, yes; offended, of course. But not worried. All gods seemed to go directly from prideful to furious.

I have heard no similar rumors, Hydra had told Ash back in Igna. *Stop worrying.*

At first, Ash had thought Hydra's message was in response to some slight Ignitus had committed. But she had wanted *him* to stop worrying about something.

Dizziness set Ash's head spinning. No, it wasn't dizziness—it was . . . hope.

Someone or something existed that could worry a god.

FIVE

MADOC

MADOC HAD BEEN to Geoxus's great arena as a spectator many times. Every year Ilena brought them to the Festival of Sand and Stone, where the Divine competed to lift the heaviest boulder with their geoeia. During Conquest, a weeklong festival in the summer commemorating Geoxus's greatest arena victories, there were exhibition battles in which all the city's top gladiators fought costumed soldiers from foreign lands. And, of course, Madoc and Elias flocked to the stands like the rest of Deimos when Geoxus waged arena fights with his god-siblings.

But never had Madoc set foot on the sands within the arena, or in the tunnels below, where they now waited in lines with Lucius's other trainees for Geoxus to make the formal announcement of which gladiators would fight in the war with Kula.

"Sounds like a lot of people out there," said Elias, bouncing on the balls of his feet.

Madoc pulled at his golden breastplate. It weighed him down, along with the belt lined with squares of rose quartz and his silver-plated sandals. When he'd seen gladiators take the arena in full armor, they'd always moved with ease and certainty. He didn't understand how. The metal was cumbersome and hot. His tunic beneath was already soaked through with sweat.

He forced his shoulders back. It had taken extensive groveling to convince Lucius's trainer—Arkos, Madoc had learned—to give them this opportunity after Madoc had turned him down after the South Gate fight. He wouldn't let Arkos question his second chance. For one hundred gold coins a week, he'd be the best trainee Lucius and Arkos had ever seen.

He just needed to stay alive long enough to get Cassia away from his father, who by now probably had her laundering his clothes or scrubbing his floors, berating and belittling her every chance he got.

He prayed she could keep her head down until he had the money.

The last days had been a frenzy of activity. After arriving at Lucius's villa, they'd found the house staff in chaos, preparing for the war. It was dark by the time Arkos led them to the library, a dusty room filled floor to ceiling with leather books and scrolls, and presented them to Lucius. The great sponsor was poring over records of gladiator statistics and was so preoccupied that he only gave Madoc a passing inspection before shoving a contract at him—a pledge that Madoc would fight for Lucius alone, for the glory of Deimos, until his severance or death.

With a knot in his throat, Madoc signed his name and became a gladiator.

He had not been the only new trainee. There'd been a flood of recruits for the war, especially following the plague that had killed the three most respected gladiators, and twenty other fighters, male and female, had spent the night in the dormitories crammed onto bunks stacked three high. The best, he learned, sparred with real gladiators. Some of them had fought in exhibitions, or in lesser matches around the city. All of them were equally desperate for glory in the great arena, and the payout that came with it.

Madoc peered around the broad shoulders of a boy named Narris, who'd told Madoc that the last trainee to fill Madoc's bunk had lost the front of his skull in a hailstorm of gravel. When Elias had responded that they'd once defeated Fentus, an expelled fighter from the facility in Xiphos, Narris had laughed like this was a joke, slapped them on the backs, and told them they were all right.

They were in with the trainees. Now they just needed to make sure no one caught on that they were cheating.

The golden circle of light at the end of the hall was blinding. The crowds in the stands shouted, their stomping feet quaking the arena and shaking sand through the gaps in the stone ceiling.

The arena needed new mortar. Under other circumstances, Madoc and Elias would have been called in to fix it.

"Stand ready!"

The order came from the front of the line and caused a ripple of excitement down the ranks. Whispers bounced off the narrow walls and low ceiling. Leather armor creaked, flicking at Madoc's raw nerves. He was the last of the dozen trainees in his line, which ran parallel to the trainees from Xiphos. Another sponsor's gladiators would come from the opposite side of the arena and meet them in the center. They were to stand behind Lucius's real gladiators as Geoxus chose the Honored Eight who would fight in the war against Kula. The trainees were to look menacing and ready to attack. That's what Narris had said, anyway.

The rumbling outside quieted, then gave way to silence. Madoc's stomach pitched, but he tightened his jaw and glared ahead. He'd lived as pigstock long enough to know that the only way to fit in with the Divine was to pretend to be one of them, or to be tough enough that it didn't matter.

Now he had to be both.

"What are we doing?" Elias muttered. "There has to be an easier way to get Cassia."

"Like robbing a temple?" Madoc hissed. "You want to steal bread from starving children, be my guest."

In truth, he wasn't above it at the moment.

Narris's attendant, a boy called Remi with silver-painted lips and streaks of gold in his hair, glared at them. "Quiet! The officials have begun the ceremony!"

"Was I talking to you?" Elias motioned with his hand for Remi to turn around, which he did only after giving them another dirty look.

"It's fine," Madoc told Elias. "This is just for show. The money is what matters."

"Don't let Geoxus hear you say that," Elias muttered.

A tremor ran through Madoc as he recalled this morning's inspection at Headless Hill. The trainees had been talking about the lavish parties the Father God threw in wartime, how the light from his palace burned straight through until dawn, when Arkos had called them into formation. For long minutes, they'd stood in silence, gladiators side by side with trainees. Madoc had waited for Lucius to address them but found him at the front of the group, staring forward, as still as the rest of them.

That's when the sand beneath their feet began to churn, like ripples in a pond, and the stones around the training arena had begun to groan and shift.

A chill had crawled over Madoc's skin as he realized the inspection had already begun. They were being watched through the earth, by Geoxus.

Maybe it was his sixth sense, or maybe they'd all felt scrutinized, but Madoc swore he could feel the Father God's eyes on him alone. He'd expected to be called out on the spot, shamed for his lie and his lack of divinity, maybe even killed. But the earth had settled, and they'd been ordered to load into the carriages that would bring them to the great arena.

"Listen up, dust mites," came Arkos's growl from the front of the line. "You will march out there with your heads high and your backs straight. If you fall out of formation, I'll sand your skin raw. If you so much as flinch when Geoxus chooses his gladiators, I'll give you to the real fighters to play with. Are we understood?"

The response from the other trainees was instant and bone-shaking. "Yes, dominus!"

"He seems friendly," Elias muttered.

Outside, the crowds roared.

Madoc pulled again at the golden breastplate. A cool rush trickled through his veins, coming faster and more powerful with each passing second. He felt like he did before a fight. Ready. *Eager.*

"In stone!" shouted Arkos.

"And blood!" responded the recruits.

"In stone!"

This time Madoc was ready.

"And blood!"

The line moved forward.

Remi pounded a fist against his trainee's breastplate. Narris's mouth tightened into a sneer.

Elias's eyes grew wide. "Don't trip. I don't want to see what you look like without skin."

The attendants moved to the side. A brief moment of panic cut through Madoc when he realized Elias wouldn't be going with him. What would he do if they were forced to demonstrate their skills? It would be immediately obvious that Madoc was not who he claimed to be. He'd be given to the real gladiators to *play with*, cut down faster than Elias's father.

Elias must have been thinking the same thing, because all color had drained from his face.

"Move along!" A centurion shoved Madoc from behind. "Come on, keep in line!"

Madoc followed Narris's lead, shoulders back, chin high. He'd faked his way through fights; he could fake his way through this. Still, his doubt grew with every step he took toward the mouth of the tunnel.

Geoxus would know.

The Father God could have seen Madoc in his youth through the stone of Petros's villa or the brick of the Metaxa home. Rumor was he could sense divinity in his mortals, and though Madoc had been sure he'd never get close enough to the Father God for that to matter, he'd counted on Elias's presence beside him just in case. Now he wouldn't even have that.

He was a dead man, and Elias along with him. Cassia would be broken down by Petros's will, and the rest of the family, dependent on their income, would be thrown to the streets.

The scaffolding of his plan was buckling. What was he doing? This was a war, not some street fight. The fate of Deimos was resting on the shoulders of the men and women around him.

Four more steps and he would be outside.

He had to turn back. There was still time. They could still think of a new plan.

Three. *Two.*

He crossed the threshold into the light, blinded by the brightness of the sun and its reflection off the hundred pounded gold mirrors encircling the arena's upper deck. The roar of the crowd shook through his bones and stole the breath from his lungs. He trained his eyes on the back of Narris's shaved head but could still see the stadium behind it, rising four magnificent stories skyward, every seat filled with cheering Deiman citizens.

It was as if he'd missed a step going down the stairs. For a moment, he wasn't thinking about Geoxus, or Cassia, or even his own skin. The crowd was cheering for them. He was wearing the armor of a gladiator and marching with Lucius Pompino's fighters as half of Crixion screamed his praises.

It was a rush unlike any he'd ever known.

Mounted centurions were posted around the arena floor, each carrying the silver and black flag bearing Crixion's city seal. The Father God's artists must have been hard at work all night, because a stage Madoc had never seen before had been erected in the center of the arena, massive onyx spires twisting skyward at each of its four corners. Mosaics of white, black, and silver braided across the front like a river of metal, while the supporting stones were carved in the shapes of ferocious Deiman gladiators.

Lucius Pompino, wearing a fine white toga and a crown of turquoise, stood atop the stage beside two other senators in white and red robes. A few lesser sponsors joined him, but none stood as tall, or as proud, as Geoxus's favored great-grandson. People said he was the most beloved descendant of the Father God since the gladiator Galitus, son of Geoxus, had lived seven hundred years ago.

On the opposite side of the stage stood Petros, wearing thick opal bracelets and black powder in his hair. His presence made Madoc's stomach twist—Petros knew exactly what he was and wasn't capable of, and if he spotted Madoc, he would surely inform Geoxus.

Across the yellow sand, the other line of trainees snaked toward them. Both groups slowed as they neared the center of the arena. Madoc sighed in relief as his line crossed in front of the other to create two layers of trainees who faced Geoxus's private box in the center of the stands, blocking him from Petros's view.

As the crowd thundered on, the trainees stopped, and Madoc

became as acutely aware of Petros at his back as he was of the Father God himself, just before them. Geoxus was standing at the edge of his box, his thick chest and arms bare and glistening in the sun, his black, fringed toga hanging neatly off one shoulder. The crown of opal and onyx encircling his head caught the light and shone in Madoc's eyes, forcing him to look away.

Not just because his being here was a lie, but because he was here at all. This wasn't like the inspection at Headless Hill. The Father God was present now, and there was no denying that he could see Madoc.

A movement beside Geoxus lifted Madoc's gaze again, and a surge of anger ripped through him at the sight of Ignitus, whose cheating gladiator had caused this war. Madoc had seen him before, from much farther away, during the last war with Kula. Geoxus's brother hadn't changed a bit. His face bore no lines of age or hardship. Only a single stripe of grayish hair graced his otherwise black locks. But where Geoxus was sturdy and muscled, Ignitus was thin and lithe. He moved like the flames he so loved, like he had too many joints and not enough weight. He slouched against the railing, keeping to the opposite side of the box.

Maybe Madoc wouldn't be the champion to send him home defeated, but Ignitus *would* be defeated, as he had been at their last war.

Madoc's gaze flicked to the tunnel entrance, searching for Elias, but there were only shadows.

"Eyes ahead," muttered Narris. "You want to get us in trouble?"

Madoc's head snapped forward.

The crowds screamed louder, their excitement pressing against Madoc's temples as the gladiators of the top Deiman sponsors emerged. Each was taut with muscle, from the cuts on their forearms to the bulging knots of their thighs. Their chosen weapons hung from their belts or were carried in their fists—knives, hammers, even long, gilded swords. Sneers pulled at their mouths. There were fifteen of them, and Madoc was relieved that they were on his side.

The cheers in the arena suddenly plummeted into boos as a small group emerged into the box behind Ignitus and gathered near the railing beside him. They did not march in formation, or brandish any weapons. They wore gold and red Kulan armor and glared down at the Deiman gladiators they would soon face off against.

Chills whispered down Madoc's spine.

"Children of Deimos!" Geoxus's voice echoed like thunder in a cave, though he did not appear to strain at all. He raised his hands, and again Madoc felt the urge to look down and drop to his knees.

Instead, he turned his gaze toward the small band of Kulan gladiators. One was as muscled as Geoxus himself, with long ringlets of black hair and hands big enough to crush a man's skull. Another was older, and didn't look like much of a threat.

Then again, neither did Elias, and he could knock down walls with a flick of his fingers.

Madoc felt the itch of someone watching, and when his eyes landed on a girl in the center of the group, he startled.

She was younger than the rest, close to his eighteen years, with long, graceful arms, and wild raven hair cascading over her shoulders. Her waist was narrow, her legs lean and strong. She had high cheekbones and a sharp chin, and when she caught him looking, she quickly turned away.

A morbid curiosity rose inside him. Plenty of trainees were young, but he'd never before seen a champion his own age. Could she throw ribbons of fire like the other Kulan fighters he'd seen? Could she summon a flame to dance in her bare hand? He knew it was wrong to want to see it—she was the enemy, and any skills she possessed would be used against good Deiman gladiators—but he was intrigued all the same.

"Today we enter into war with Kula!" Geoxus called. When the crowd grew quiet, the Father God stabbed a hand in his brother's direction. "Last week, in a match with Kula over their barbaric attack of a Deiman fishing boat in the Telsa Channel, one of Ignitus's mortals interfered." The arena erupted with boos and angry threats, but Madoc's eyes were drawn to the god of fire and the sour pinch of his expression. Ignitus hated Deimos and had attacked many times in Madoc's lifetime, but this war felt desperate—he'd never heard of a god sending another gladiator in to win a match.

"The great Stavos would not be beaten, and though he defeated Ignitus's champion, this violation of our sacred rules will not be ignored," Geoxus thundered. "The stakes of this war have been set. Deimos and Kula wager fishing rights in the Telsa Channel. Kula wagers a twenty percent stock in their glass trade. And in addition, two seaports of the winning god's choice, including all taxation and docking rights, will be surrendered indefinitely."

Gasps gave way to more cheers, but Madoc could only gape in surprise. In the past, stakes of war had included a single port, or trade for wheat or some other crop with another country. But the entirety of the Telsa Channel, which ran between Deimos and Kula, or *twenty percent* of Kula's glass trade, plus two seaports—such a prize was unheard of. And a testament to Geoxus's anger.

Only a god who valued the lost lives of his citizens would put so much at risk. Still, Madoc couldn't help thinking what would happen if the Deiman champion did not succeed.

Geoxus raised his hands to quiet the crowd. "We will delay no longer. Ignitus has chosen his champions. How will they fare against the pride of Deimos?"

Jeers and laughter erupted around the arena. Madoc's gaze turned again to the Kulan girl, who was now half hidden behind the giant warrior in her group. Her jaw flexed in hatred as she stared across the box toward Geoxus, standing beside her god. It reminded him a little of the way Cassia would get angry when they were young and he and Elias kept her out of their games. The likeness brought on a slash of pity, and guilt, because she was only with Petros now because he'd been foolhardy enough to fight in the first place.

"As it has been since the beginning, eight of my finest gladiators will fight for the chance to defend Deimos."

The crowd cheered again.

In front of Madoc, the Deiman gladiators began to move in a subtle dance, transferring their weight, flexing their fists, tapping their weapons against the armor. Madoc could feel their energy swell, like a wave over the shore. He leaned forward, drawn to it.

"Yes," Narris whispered beside him.

Yes, thought Madoc.

"The Honored Eight begin their trials at dawn. Each I have carefully considered. Each will do our great country proud."

The gladiators began to nod, their weapons louder against the gold plates on their chests.

"Stavos of Xiphos!" boomed Geoxus, and the stands erupted in cheers. "Who will no doubt get his retribution for the interference in the match in Kula!"

The man holding the hammer raised his fist, then left the rank of fighters to move to the stage behind the trainees.

"Raclin of Crixion!"

A woman with thighs as thick as Madoc's chest whooped, and jogged over to join Stavos.

One of them would be getting one thousand gold coins.

One might die in the final round against a Kulan champion.

"Jann of Arsia!"

A man with a bald head twisted his wrist, and with a small flick sent a spiral of sand high into the air. By the time it landed, he was on the stage with the others.

The crowd shouted their approval.

Three more names were called, and with each one, the crowd grew wilder, the remaining gladiators hungrier. A pressure built in Madoc's chest, taking up the room for his lungs. It reminded him of how he could feel Elias's anger, or anxiety, or fear, and how he'd sensed Fentus's fatigue. But this was a thousand times more intense. Stealing his focus. Building pressure beneath his skin. Demanding some kind of release.

He forced his gaze up to the Father God and blinked through the screaming in his brain.

Geoxus was looking right at him.

No, that wasn't right. Geoxus must be looking at the stage, or something in the distance. Why would he be staring at Madoc?

Unless he knew Madoc didn't belong. Unless the rumors about sensing divinity weren't rumors at all.

During the inspection at Headless Hill, Madoc had felt this same awareness rooting in his bones—the sensation of being watched, evaluated, measured for worth. It was ten times stronger now in Geoxus's physical presence—so intense, Madoc could hardly breathe.

Another fighter, two down from where Jann of Arsia had stood, stepped forward and took his place on the stage. Madoc hadn't even heard the man's name called.

One name left. One last fighter. Then the trainees would march back into the corridors beneath the arena. He and Elias would find Cassia, and they would figure out what to do next.

"Our last position, as always, is reserved for a trainee," said Geoxus. "A hungry young fighter, ready to prove their worth to Deimos."

"Finally," muttered Narris, stretching taller. Madoc gritted his teeth, imagining this meathead bringing home a thousand coins. He'd probably buy himself a chariot, like Elias had wanted.

Madoc could do a lot more with that coin.

Though the chances were slim, he found himself hoping to be chosen.

"Madoc of Crixion."

Madoc didn't move.

The crowd quieted. The gladiators looked to each other in confusion.

"*You?*" Narris swore.

It couldn't have been him. Hope or not, Madoc hadn't expected his name to actually be called. He was new. He'd come on three days ago. This was impossible. Narris had misheard.

The entire stadium had misheard.

He sucked in a hard breath. Geoxus was still staring at him, only now he was smiling. It was the smile of the statue in Market Square. It was the smile that had calmed Madoc when he was a child, alone on the streets and afraid. That had convinced him to pray for help.

Geoxus's chin dipped as if to say, *Yes, you.*

"Go." Narris's hard whisper made him jump. "Madoc! Go now!"

Madoc tentatively stepped forward.

The crowd began to cheer again as he took another step through the line of gladiators.

One of the seasoned fighters sneered at him, and he sidestepped into another, then stumbled, catching himself before he hit the ground. The crowd laughed and cheered harder.

All the while, Geoxus smiled.

He knows, Madoc thought. *He's angry. This is my death sentence. As soon as I step onto that stage, someone's going to ram an iron spear through my heart.*

But how did he know Madoc's name?

Because he knows all. Because he saved your miserable life when you were a child, and he gave you to the Metaxas. Because he is a god.

But if that was true, why was he making Madoc, who had no geoeia, one of his Honored Eight?

Madoc could feel the Kulans watching him as he made for the stage, could feel the curious, pointed gaze of the girl with the wild hair. Would he have to fight her? Would he have to *kill* her?

Somehow, he made it onto the stage. On numb feet, he walked across the smooth, shaped earth, passing the other champions, who barely acknowledged his presence. Past a curious, appraising Lucius, to the end of the line, where Petros waited with eyes that gleamed with deceit.

He stood beside the last gladiator, his hands empty without a weapon.

Please don't make me use geoeia, he prayed.

Geoxus was talking. Congratulating the Honored Eight. Saying they would serve Deimos proudly. That their names would live on long after their deaths.

"You look confused, Madoc," whispered Petros beside him. "Don't worry. I told Geoxus how well you've fought in my amateur matches. How you've built your career in the streets. He was willing to forgive you for breaking the law in exchange for what I assured him would be a fierce showing in the arena. He thinks you might be his secret weapon—isn't that something?"

Petros had told Geoxus he was a fighter. That's why Madoc had felt watched at Headless Hill, why Geoxus had chosen him for the Honored Eight. His father was punishing him for what had happened with Cassia, or for beating his hired fighters, or because he'd been born. Whatever the reason, it didn't matter. If he couldn't keep Elias close enough to throw geoeia, Geoxus would see that he was a fraud.

He focused on Cassia's face. He remembered her hand, stretching toward him when they were children, filled with a chunk of dry bread. How she'd sat with him on the temple steps while Ilena had shopped at the market, chattering like a bird about the shapes of the clouds, and how well she could swim in the river. She'd given him all her food, and when he'd gobbled it up, she'd taken his hand and pulled him across the street.

Come on, she'd said. *Let's go home.*

Madoc would bring Cassia home, even if it took fighting. Even if it meant winning.

Even if he had to lie to a god.

SIX

ASH

ASH INSTANTLY REGRETTED telling Tor about Hydra's message.

They stood in the finest viewing box of Crixion's grandest arena, just behind the god of earth and the god of fire. The whole of the city screamed for the eight Earth Divine champions Geoxus had just selected.

One of them was Stavos of Xiphos, and it took every speck of strength left within Ash to not look at him.

"Stop worrying." Tor echoed Hydra's words to Ignitus, but it sounded like a plea to himself.

Rook's jaw worked. "Maybe she didn't mean a direct threat. Maybe the rumor was over something"—he motioned at the lavishness of the obsidian stage below, the rows upon rows of gilded gladiator trainees—"frivolous."

Ash unintentionally followed his pointing finger to where Geoxus's champions now stood. The first, the largest—Stavos. He thrust his arms into the air and bellowed a war cry that stoked a frenzy of screaming in his honor.

The last time Ash had seen his arms lifted like that, they had been lobbing a sword into Char's body.

Heart thundering, Ash's eyes fled to the last Deiman champion. Gods often gave slots in wars to up-and-coming trainees, betting on their determination to prove themselves. Never had one progressed very far, but they always provided a great show in the preliminary fights.

Madoc, though, had been so shocked at his god selecting him that he'd toppled into the other fighters around him. He couldn't have been any older than Ash, but he was slightly taller, more muscular, as Deimans tended to be, with dark eyes that snapped back and forth over the arena. Did he occasionally look at Ash? He shifted so much that she couldn't tell. His nervousness made Ash the most wary of him, out of all of Geoxus's champions. Madoc had to be hiding great skill for the earth god to give one of his coveted war spots to someone who looked terrified to be here.

An announcer started bellowing out a list of the Deiman champions' victories. A few paces ahead of Ash, Geoxus toasted each one, twisting his head back and forth slowly, clearly aware of how the rays from his arena's light-amplifying mirrors caught the opals in the crown of onyx set on his dark, shoulder-length curls. The hem of his black toga kissed the marble floor of the viewing box, one end hooked around his arm as he tipped his goblet at Ignitus.

To anyone unfamiliar with the fire god's emotions, Ignitus would appear disinterested. But that twitch over his eyebrow, the flare to his upper lip—he was furious. Ash could see Ignitus's mind whirling, trying to plan how he could wrest away control for the next public gathering.

Rook had to be right—the only thing a god worried about was an offense to their reputation.

Even if Ignitus could lose Kula's last fishing ports in this war.

"Wine!" Ignitus barked, and a servant scrambled forward to refill his empty goblet.

Ash scraped her palms on the leggings under her gilded reed armor, chest burning as she eyed Tor. Behind them, two of Ignitus's other champions made jokes and pointed at the Deiman fighters.

Tor absently scrubbed his chin. "We have to be sure," he whispered.

Ash stopped herself from wiping her palms on her leggings again. Fidgeting would give away her nerves, and she couldn't afford to show weakness here.

"I could ask him," she breathed.

Tor frowned down at her.

She braced, expecting him to reject her idea. "I could mention rumors I've heard. His worries are my worries, right? I'm one of his champions. I heard horrible rumors of someone who could weaken him. I have to know if it's true, and who might slight my god."

Tor's consideration darkened. A long moment passed before he nodded.

"But I'll be the one to ask him," Tor added on a huff of breath.

Ash tensed. Ignitus was muttering something no doubt contentious as Geoxus slapped him good-naturedly on the shoulder.

No, she wanted to argue. *Let me. I should do it—I cannot lose you too.*

The crowd in the stands cheered as the announcer described the victories of Jann of Arsia. Hawkers sold wine and food, shouting their prices as they walked the rows of seats. Even the Kulan champions behind Ash were jovial, snatching wine flasks from a table in the viewing box.

But Tor set off, focused, crossing the few paces of marble to the railing where Ignitus stood with Geoxus. The Deiman champions remained in that perfect row on the center stage, their backs to an assortment of Geoxus's highest ranking officials.

The announcer moved on. "And, finally, mighty Stavos of Xiphos, who, despite the fire god's meddling, snatched victory from the burning flames of treason!"

Rook cut along behind Tor. Ash stumbled, her body jolting to keep up with them both. Her heart now raced so hard, she could barely fill her lungs against the incessant pounding.

By the time they reached Ignitus, she felt as if her throat had swollen shut, and all she could see was the broadsword sticking out of Char's chest.

"Great Ignitus," Tor started. "If I may request an audience?"

Ignitus took a sip of his wine and scowled. "This tastes like vinegar," he snapped.

Geoxus, in turn, downed a whole glass. "Really? I imported it special from Kula."

Ignitus's face flared red.

"Great Ignitus," Tor said again, louder. "If I—"

"*What?*" A flash of blue fire lit on Ignitus's arms.

Ash lurched, wanting to beg Tor to stop. She was wrong, she had misheard Hydra—

"A moment of your time, Great Ignitus," Tor said. "In private, please."

Geoxus chuckled. "Go—quell your champion's nerves about the war."

Ignitus shifted. A look of calculation passed over his face, and he smiled. "You misread their intention in coming over. Allow me to properly introduce you, brother, to Ash Nikau."

Ash choked. But Ignitus's smile was full and rich now.

Tor shot in front of Ash, his back to her. "My god Ignitus, I—"

"Ash is my newest fighter," Ignitus said. "She was extensively trained by my late gladiator, and it was Ash who took action to stop your gladiator from using his poisoned blade."

Geoxus assessed her face, her neck; lower, lower. Wrinkles at the edges of his eyes dug deeper, and that detail settled oddly in Ash's mind.

Ignitus didn't have wrinkles by his eyes. It was a sign of age, too mortal for a god.

But Geoxus snapped his gaze back to Ignitus and yanked Ash's focus away. "There was no poisoned blade. It is tragic that you have forced this child to be a champion merely to support your made-up claims of sabotage."

Ignitus darkened. "Nikau comes from a line of my most elite fighters. She may be young, but you yourself wasted a champion slot on an untrained street rat."

He batted his hand at Madoc, far below and oblivious.

For the first time, Geoxus lost his composure long enough to scowl. "That *street rat* came from my most trusted sponsor—he's brought me nine war-winning champions, you know. Another of my advisers assures me that he will heap victories at my feet. He's straight from the slums of Crixion. Quite wild, brother. Untamed. He'll tear the limbs from your young champion."

Ash's fingers were in such tight fists that she felt her nails puncture her palms.

Tor slid back to stand at Ash's side. He didn't say anything—couldn't—but with him on one side and Rook on the other, Ash could almost pretend that two gods weren't discussing her like livestock on a farm.

Ignitus cocked his head. "Interesting." He clicked his tongue and grinned at Ash.

She hated him. She hated him, and she feared everything about the look he gave her.

"A proposal, Geoxus," Ignitus said. "Let's give the crowd a taste of the events to come. Your young champion against mine—but without energeia. We'll put true skill to the test, the talents your obscure fighter supposedly has against the training and superior breeding of mine."

Disagree, Ash begged Geoxus. *Cast him off—*

But Geoxus smiled and snapped his fingers.

The viewing box rumbled and a staircase indented from the railing all the way down to the fighting pit. The crowd on either side of the newly appeared path shouted in awe, the exclamation rippling across the stadium.

"Ready the boy," Geoxus told a nearby servant. "Clear a space below."

One servant scurried down the stairs for the stage; others followed and began shooing the trainees back.

A space cleared, a perfect circle on the velvet sands. A fighting ring.

Someone in the sand whooped with excitement. It caught like stray flames, and soon everyone was hooting and cheering. "Fight!" they chanted. "Fight! Fight!"

"Ash Nikau." Ignitus said her name loud. He set a hand on her shoulder and she staggered, fighting a wince. "You will bring glory to Kula."

It was a command. It was a threat.

Ash turned, pulling out of Ignitus's grip, though he hadn't dismissed her. But she couldn't think rationally, could barely see enough to manage one foot in front of the other toward the stairs.

Now. She was going to fight a Deiman gladiator *right now.*

"The gods demand a match!" The announcer's voice shifted, alight with eagerness. "Two of their champions will fight to the surrender in a test of physical strength—no energeia!"

Ash's stomach cramped. The crowd crooned. No energeia meant the fight would be for indulgence—just fists. Just talent.

She could do that. Char and Tor had trained her in every type of combat.

Tor and Rook started down the staircase ahead of her so Ignitus couldn't call them back or argue for them to stay. She focused on their rigid backs as she descended, and when they hit the sand, a path to the makeshift ring through the gladiator trainees waited. Some cheered like the crowd; a few whistled at her.

Ash walked toward the fighting ring, numb.

Tor caught her arm. "Ash." His voice was deep and heavy, and to the people around, it looked as though he was offering her a final tip.

"I'll ask Ignitus," she whispered. It was all she could think to say, her eyes darting between Tor and Rook. "When I win. I'll ask him about the rumors."

"Don't think about that," Tor told her. "Think about the fight. Think about right now, and nothing else. Geoxus's fighter will be sloppy from his limited formal training. He'll likely only know a few attacks. You can learn his patterns. You can—"

"Tor." Rook planted a hand in the center of Tor's chest. "She'll be fine."

But the panic in Tor's eyes stoked the same feeling in Ash's chest.

She was walking into a fight against a Deiman gladiator. Just like Char had.

"Thanks," Ash said to him, and to Rook.

She made her way forward, a knot in her throat, a weight in her gut.

That weight matched the heaviness of the ceremonial armor she still wore. It would be a hindrance, but it didn't seem as though the gods would give her time to change.

Grit crunched beneath her sandals as she stepped into the fighting ring. The empty space around her struck like static.

This ring was for her. The crowd of other Deiman gladiators at the edges, the people thundering in the stands—they would watch *her* fight.

The knot in Ash's throat grew, grew and grew, and she thought she might throw up.

She swallowed hard, hands in fists. She was a gladiator. She was her mother's daughter.

A cheer went up—heckling, too—and the edge of the ring birthed Madoc.

"Show us why Geoxus picked you!" someone called.

The muscles in Madoc's jaw bulged and he ruffled his fingers through his short black hair. His hand was shaking. Was he nervous?

She could use that. She *would* use that.

This was how she would earn her god's trust. Afterward, Ash would go to Ignitus and ask, *Surely there is no one who can worry you, Great Ignitus?*

This victory would bring her closer to finding her god's weaknesses.

Ash took stock of her body and how she was standing—legs squared, jaw set, fingers in controlled fists. She wasn't giving away her own nerves, was she?

Above the fighting pit, Geoxus and Ignitus idly sipped wine, but their eyes blazed. The fingers of Ignitus's right hand were rigid on his goblet, even so far as the viewing box his knuckles visibly white.

Tor and Rook shouldered their way to the edge of the crowd. Tor nodded at Ash, reassuring.

Madoc settled into a fighting stance. His leather skirt wavered around his braced legs, the muscles of his thighs taut. He'd taken off his gilded breastplate at some point—Ash envied him that easy freedom; her armor was one massive piece—and wore only a baggy linen shirt that cut deep down his chest, revealing a patch of dark, sweat-dampened hair. Sweat sheened his neck and face too, and his dark eyes flickered in the mirrored afternoon sun, creating a kaleidoscope of sparking light.

Ash didn't take a fighting stance. Char rarely had.

"Steady, love," came Tor's voice from nearby.

My fuel and flame.

A drum thudded. Silence fell like a boulder into a pond.

"Attack!" Geoxus bellowed.

Ash inhaled, long, deep, centering. She needed to strike before Madoc did, to prevent him from using whatever tactics made him *untamed*. She needed to throw him off.

Ash dived across the ring. She raised a fist, pretending she was going for an overhead strike, and Madoc dropped his weight to lift an arm in a block. The fabric on his shirt went up on the side, revealing tan skin and the arch of his hip bone. Ash released her fake hit and slid to the ground, gliding across the sand, momentum carrying her under Madoc's lifted arm.

She put her hand on his stomach. Even without igneia, Kulans had high body heat, a natural burn that would feel like a lit match to him.

Madoc chirped in surprise. The heat must have been more intense than Ash intended, because as she spun back onto her feet, Madoc crossed his arms over his head and yanked off his shirt as if she'd set the whole piece of fabric aflame.

Scars stretched across his back, a quilt of marks that rippled down his spine. Ash could tell that the ones across the middle had come from a whip.

She scolded herself as she felt an unexpected pull in her chest. Sympathy meant death. Likely Madoc had earned those scars in training—but they were old, long healed, which meant he was more experienced than his nervousness had suggested.

Halfway through ripping off his shirt, Madoc realized she'd tricked him, the fabric tangling around his arms and grim annoyance pinching his lips in a line.

The crowd barked and shrieked. Above them, Ignitus bayed laughter.

Madoc's eyes went from Ash's smugness to his unburned shirt and stomach. "No energeia," he reminded her.

Ash smiled innocently. "I can't help it if Deimans run cold. Want me to warm you—"

"Careful, Madoc," came a voice over Ash's shoulder. "Rules don't matter to this one."

Ash glanced back, unable to suppress the jerk of shock that launched her a full step away from Stavos.

He was here. Of course he'd come down from the black stage to watch the fight. But he was *close*, and he was staring straight at her, one eyebrow arching as his lip lifted in a sneer.

She knew Tor and Rook were across the ring, but she couldn't spot them when she flipped her back to Stavos. She tried to focus on Madoc, who chucked his shirt aside.

Her vision wavered, her hands shaking so hard she knew everyone could see.

"Wouldn't surprise me if she tried to burn us all up here and now," Stavos continued. "But don't worry, Madoc. At the end of it, she isn't really a gladiator—she's a dancer. Give us a twirl there, sweetheart." He clicked his tongue at her.

The fighters closest to him laughed. The sound echoed through Ash's mind, a ricochet of disgust.

Madoc, crouched in a defensive stance, didn't attack. He looked at her anew. "You're the girl who interfered in the fight," he said. "You caused this war."

"I did *not* cause this war," Ash shot back, tapping into her anger and smothering the grief that writhed in her stomach. "Stavos poisoned my mother. He used an illegal move."

She needed to attack. She should go for Madoc's middle again. Maybe—

"Go ahead and keep saying that," Stavos said, chuckling. But there was a tension to it, and out of the corner of her eye, she saw him elbow the men near him, egging them on to boisterous, supportive laughter. "Won't matter. Soon, Geoxus'll make sure everyone gets what they deserve, even your lying god."

Ash winced. Stavos's taunt drove into her chest.

Two voices overlapped. One, Ash recognized as Tor's—somewhere to her left, he started to shout Stavos's name.

But the other voice overpowered him.

"If I need your help, Stavos," Madoc bit out, "I'll ask for it."

Ash felt a wash of surprise—and the smallest, most toxic wave of gratitude.

She glared at Madoc. "I don't need a Deiman to defend me."

She charged, bringing a true overhead strike down on Madoc. He blocked. Her wrist slammed onto his forearm, jarring all the way to her gut.

Stavos pierced the air with a whistle. "There's that Kulan heat!"

The ring of fighters was manic now. They jostled each other and cackled wildly, shouting requests of Ash, the dancer. Ash, Ignitus's pretty flame girl.

She fought to ignore them. She threw another punch, but Madoc blocked that too. Stavos's face merged with Madoc's, and she struck, hard; again, harder. Madoc blocked her attacks, his arms a blur.

One of his hands landed on her shoulder and spun her away from him. Careening, Ash fumbled to stay upright—and stopped in front of Stavos.

He bent closer to her but made sure not to enter the ring, not making the same mistake she had. "You want to know the real reason I won in Kula?" he asked, words low and fast, the stench of his breath like onions and garlic. "My god told me your mother would be an easy kill. And she was. She was weak and lazy, and you'll die just like her."

No one else heard him. Even the fighters closest to him were still drunk on their cheers, so only Ash felt the world tip at the spark in Stavos's eyes, the way he slid his tongue over his teeth.

She lost her senses. She saw Char, dead. Her mother's blood

spreading across the sand, over the arena, darkening all of Igna.

A blur descended on her. Fingers clamped her arm and jerked her, spinning the ring in a wash of faces before Madoc had her knotted against him.

Panic and regret surged through Ash. Stupid, *stupid*—Stavos had been a distraction. Had he and Madoc planned this?

Madoc's grip was unyielding, like being encased in stone. Ash's shoulders scratched on the bristly hairs across his chest, but she couldn't think of any moves to break free. He was probably glad to have her squirming, his arms restraining her against the sharp-cut steel of his muscles, and if she could feel every tendon of his, she knew he could feel the same of her.

"Are Deimans making it part of their training to fight dishonorably now?" Ash growled.

She tried to hook Madoc's leg with her foot, but he bent backward, tilting her. As she kicked wildly, the crowd bellowed.

She couldn't see Madoc's face, but she heard him huff and felt his arms readjust around her. "I wouldn't know," he panted. "I've never trained."

Ash spotted Tor. She almost cried out with relief, but he mimed throwing his head backward.

She did just that, her skull pummeling Madoc's face. He let out a shocked *oomph* and his grip slipped, enough to give her room to free her arm, which she bent upward and slammed into his nose. Bone connected with a solid crunch, and Madoc's grip released.

Ash was the one who held on to his arms now. She landed on the sand, dropped her weight, and heaved forward, propelling Madoc up, over, and down in a brutal, jarring flip. The effort left her breathless and sticky with sweat.

He slammed hard against the ground, grunting with the force. Ash doubled back to plan her next move—but Madoc whirled, kicking her feet out from under her.

Ash crashed down on top of him. For a moment, they were a tangle of limbs, too many arms, too many fingers. She scrambled, trying to aim a fist at his now-bloodied face, but he dodged it by grabbing her waist and flipping them both.

Madoc landed on top of her with his thighs pinning her arms to her sides.

Ash's instincts screamed in fury and revolt. Sweat glossed Madoc's short black curls to his temples, and blood poured from where she'd smashed her elbow into his nose. He lifted one fist back in the threat of a punch, the muscles bunching in his arms, his bare chest a sculpted illustration of Deiman might.

He looked like the gladiators depicted in mosaics and sculptures. Something a god would point at and tell his children, *This is what you should aspire to be.*

"Surrender," Madoc ordered gruffly.

Ash's eyes flicked up to where her god watched, but she couldn't see him over the crowd. He was there, though. He was always there.

Stavos was there too. She could feel his eyes burning her skin.

"You'll have to kill me," she told Madoc. She would not lose unless she was incapacitated or dead. Ignitus would accept nothing less—he would barely accept that.

Madoc looked momentarily horrified at the line she had drawn:

victory or death. He raised his arm higher, but there was a flash in his black eyes that might have been fear. His chest beat in and out in gasping breaths, skin glistening with exertion.

"Show the Kulan dancer her place!" Stavos called. The crowd answered with barks.

Madoc grimaced. He glared up at Stavos.

Ash might not have entirely understood Taro's joke about the Port of Iov's lighthouse looking like a man's *lighthouse*, but she knew that the most sensitive part of her opponent was now directly over her chest.

She bucked her hips to make room and spun onto her side, thrusting her shoulder up into Madoc's crotch.

SEVEN

MADOC

MADOC REACTED BY instinct. His hand sliced down to the inside of the fighter's shoulder, stopping her just before she hit the mark. The heat from her skin immediately scalded his palm and shot through his muscles and the small bones of his hand and wrist. Even without energeia, she was burning. If she had hit him where she'd intended, he'd just as soon be dead.

The girl bucked her hips, throwing his weight forward. His hands slapped against the sand on either side of her head, but his thighs gripped harder. Their faces were close now, close enough that he could feel her hot puff of breath on his jaw and see her smoldering eyes pinch with fury. His shadow cut across her shoulders and chest, highlighting the taut swells of muscle and the wells just above her collarbone. Blood from his lip dripped in a splash on her cheek, sliding down her jaw like a painted tear.

She was a trained warrior. She was better than him, faster than him. She moved like flames, even without the fire energy she so surely loved. If they'd been allowed to use energeia, he never would have stood a chance. But without, their match had come down to physical size, and he had that, if nothing else, over her.

Desperation had her writhing beneath him, her arms flexing within the grip of his knees. It pulled at him like too much gravity. It warred with the roar of the crowd, and the demands ringing through his head.

Fight.

Win.

Do not shame your god.

He hadn't anticipated being chosen for the Honored Eight, but now that he had been, he couldn't waste this opportunity. If he made it to the first match—the first *real* match—and won, he would bring home a thousand gold pieces. Add that to the training money and they'd have most of what they needed to pay off Cassia's indenture.

"Get up, Ash!" called a male voice from the edge of the fighting pit. "Get *up*!"

Ash. Was that her name? It must be, because the girl's eyes rounded and her efforts renewed, every muscle jerking in a frenzied attempt to break free.

Madoc held fast, wrongness tearing through him as he dropped his forearm to the girl's—*Ash's*—throat, careful not to press down too hard. His jaw tightened as the heels of her sandals pushed through the sand behind him. In his mind, he heard Ilena telling him not to use his fists to hurt people, and he swallowed a new gulp of shame.

"Surrender," he pleaded. "We can end this."

Static screamed in his ears over the gallop of his heartbeat.

He had to win.

He had to secure his place in the Honored Eight and get as much coin as he could.

Madoc's breath scraped his raw throat. Disgust rolled through him, hotter than the feel of the girl's skin. His eyes dropped from hers, unable to hold her stare, but he was destroyed instead by the quiver of her full lower lip, and the way it whitened as she gripped it between her teeth.

He wanted away from this girl and her potent, intoxicating fear. He wanted out of this grand arena. He wanted to run until his legs gave up and his vision went dim.

He wanted anything other than to hurt this girl the way Petros might hurt Cassia.

"Well done!"

Geoxus's voice boomed across the stands, and the arena went silent. His applause echoed off the ground, the slap of a hammer against an anvil.

"Come now, Madoc. We don't need to kill her. Leave that for the real match."

Madoc scrambled to his feet. His gaze flew to the Deiman gladiators, his eyes landing on Stavos, now jeering at a gasping Ash. Had he really poisoned Ash's mother? Was that why she'd started this war? Regardless, Madoc fought the urge to shove him out of the circle. He had to remind himself they were on the same side.

The Kulan fighter rose beside him, coughing, wavering as she planted her feet. He didn't chance a look her way. Instead, he focused on the viewing box, where Geoxus beamed and Ignitus glowered.

Maybe Madoc was Kulan too, because his skin was burning. He was half naked in front of a full stadium. People were cheering for him, screaming his name, hurling insults at a girl he'd never wanted to fight. Arkos's earlier demands that gladiators keep their heads high and their backs straight were the only things keeping him from crossing his arms over his chest to cover himself. Never in his life had he wanted to disappear so badly.

But this was what he needed—he had pleased the Father God. He had humiliated his opponent. He had shown he was worthy of Geoxus's attention.

The Father God had to listen to him now.

Beside him, Ash gave a small wince, then dropped to her knees, her back still heaving with each breath as she dipped her head in reverence to her god.

Madoc had no idea if he was supposed to do the same.

"Line up!" From beyond the circle came the shouted orders of the trainers. They were returning to the tunnels beneath the stands. Relief flooded through him; he needed to get out of here and find Elias. He needed a moment to think.

In the box above, Ignitus spun toward his guards, leaving Geoxus surrounded by advisers. Only then did Ash rise.

"Next time we meet, you won't be so lucky," she hissed.

Madoc swallowed. All the lightness in her tone had been stripped away, leaving only anger. He knew he should scoff, or at least pretend he wasn't rattled, but appearances were the last thing on his mind.

"I know."

Her gaze shot to his, a promise of fire in her dark eyes. Her jaw twitched as if she might say more, but instead she tore off toward her people, who were congregating near the mouth of the center tunnel.

Madoc searched for his tunic and armor, but they were nowhere to be found. Someone must have already grabbed them. Sweat dripped down his temples, no longer from the fight but from this new wave of humiliation. Slipping into the nearest line, he forced his chin up and tried to pretend the whistles from the stands weren't directed at him as he marched with the others out of the arena.

He'd no sooner crossed beneath the tunnel's arched entrance than he was pulled aside by a broad, foreboding man in white silk.

"Come with me, Madoc of Crixion." Lucius Pompino's voice ground over Madoc's name, as if the sound of it irritated him. "Geoxus wants to congratulate you in front of Ignitus."

Madoc's stomach dropped. "Now?" He swiped at the dried blood beneath his nostrils with the back of his hand. How could he face his god? He didn't even have a shirt on.

Lucius's glare narrowed. "Yes, now. Where is your attendant?"

"Here, dominus," said Elias, sprinting past the exiting trainees behind Madoc. He'd managed to retrieve Madoc's armor from whoever had taken it out of the arena and was now holding it against his side over one bent arm.

"Clean him up," Lucius snapped, clearly not used to having to explain himself. "Get the blood off his face and put him back in armor. Geoxus will not be kept waiting."

"Yes, dominus," said Elias.

Lucius turned to Madoc. They were matched for height, but equal in no other way. Lucius's shoulders stretched with lean, hard muscle that made Madoc look young and boyish in comparison. The sponsor's face had been chiseled from stone—a polished jaw met a thin, serious mouth, and his slate-colored eyes dared defiance. Even his white toga dripped with affluence.

Madoc could see why he was Geoxus's favorite, and how Petros would never measure up.

"That was pathetic," he told Madoc as Elias shoved a tunic in his direction. "You're a champion now, and champions strike first and strike hard. If I ever see you hesitate again, you'll be slop for the pigs that feed real fighters."

Madoc swallowed and pulled the tunic over his head. "Yes, dominus."

Lucius turned to spout off orders at Arkos, giving Madoc a moment to clean up.

"Better hurry," Elias said. "If this is what happens when you win, I don't want to see what Lucius does when you're late."

Madoc dipped down to check his reflection in the pounded metal of his chest plate, still over Elias's arm. Blood was smeared over his upper lip. Sweat glistened on his forehead, highlighting the tips of his hair. With a grunt of pain, he pressed his fingertips gently to the bridge of his nose, trying to feel if it was broken.

"Get me a cloth," he said.

"Get your own cloth—this is heavier than Geoxus's throne." Elias adjusted the armor to his other arm.

"It's dipped in gold."

"Oh, is that why?" Elias asked flatly.

Madoc grabbed the folds of Elias's tunic to clean off his jaw. His teeth were stained orange with blood, and he ran his tongue along the fronts of them, tasting the copper remains of an earlier wound.

"He made you a war champion," Elias said.

"I know. I was there."

"I thought the Kulan was going to win."

"You're not supposed to tell me that," Madoc said, but Elias was right. Madoc had been thrown into a match with their enemy—a gladiator who, by some stroke of fortune, hadn't been permitted to use energeia.

Suddenly, he wasn't sure how he was alive at all.

"At least you're making more coin," Elias said with weak smile. "If you can take a few more beatings like that, we'll have Cassia home before the war's over."

But the fights to come would be nothing like that, and they both knew it. Madoc wouldn't just be training, he'd be competing against Deiman gladiators for the chance to fight Kula's best champion. The Honored Eight were the most ruthless, skilled killers in the entire country.

In grim silence, Elias helped lift the armor over Madoc's head and then buckled the sides to hold it in place.

"Ready?" Elias asked, his knuckles bumping Madoc's side as he straightened the breastplate.

Nerves trembled through him. He was going to meet Geoxus. *In front of Ignitus*, Lucius had said. Was this a strategy to shame the fire god? Dig the knife of his loss in a bit deeper?

He didn't care as long as it brought Cassia home.

Nerves burned in his stomach as he and Elias hurried toward the line of trainees. There, Lucius and Arkos were lit a pale green beneath the glowing, phosphorescent stones that peppered the ceiling like stars. Geoxus had long ago figured out that the best way to limit the Kulans' energeia was to remove their access to fire. Now these stones were everywhere Ignitus's gladiators might roam—the arenas, the docks, even their lodgings at the palace—so Madoc had heard.

With a somber nod, Lucius departed, his toga rippling behind him as he led Madoc and Elias down a narrow corridor that split from the main hall.

"Thank him for this opportunity, then don't speak further unless spoken to," Lucius said as they came to the stairs where a centurion stood guard. Without a word, the soldier let them pass. "Address him as Honorable Geoxus, or Father God. And stand up straight—you look like pigstock."

Madoc locked his jaw to hide a wince and drew his shoulders together.

At the top was another hall, and across it a stone archway, bright with sunlight. Just outside, Madoc could make out palace attendants in black togas and dresses, city officials and senate members in white. Deiman men and women had more colors on their tunics and gowns than Madoc had seen in the jewel barrels at the quarry.

They'd reached Geoxus's viewing box.

Madoc hadn't remembered there being so many people here during the ceremony or fight, but now that it was over, everyone had flocked around the Father God, seated on a throne made of smoky quartz and amethyst.

His broad shoulders and thick, muscular form filled the entire seat and sent a wave of awe through Madoc. The Father God looked like a man but was immortal—stronger, sleeker, *more* in every way. And when he smiled at the group of men he spoke to, the wisdom in his gaze punctured Madoc's confidence. He wasn't sure what he should say, whether he should even look his god in the eyes, or if doing so would turn him to rubble. They'd told stories of that happening when they were children, but now the concept didn't feel so farfetched.

What if Geoxus sensed he was a fraud?

There was no turning back now.

Lucius led the way, striding across the threshold into the sunlight. On weak legs, Madoc followed, but hesitated when a guard blocked Elias's path with a spear.

"This is champion business," Lucius said. "Your servant can wait in the hall."

Elias's chin jutted inward, but he had the good sense not to speak.

Without Elias, Madoc felt untethered. He didn't belong in this place with these people, drinking wine and eating rich food off ruby-studded plates. He was a stonemason. Pigstock, unable to hide behind Elias's geoeia.

He felt like the boy his father had kicked out all those years ago.

It didn't matter. He was here for Cassia. Geoxus hadn't noticed he was Undivine earlier; maybe he wouldn't now, either.

Madoc gave a quick nod to Elias and followed his sponsor.

Whoever was talking to Geoxus backed away as Lucius approached, tightening the bands of anxiety around Madoc's lungs. He'd thought they might have to stand in line to wait for the Father God. That he'd have a moment more to prepare what he was going to say.

"There he is now. Quite a show you put on, Madoc. You must be starving, yes?"

Madoc's knees turned to water. Before today, Geoxus had been a statue in Market Square, a prayer that came easily to Madoc's tongue. On rare occasions at festivals, Madoc and Elias had seen the Father God from afar, but though they'd clamored for a look like the rest of Deimos had, Geoxus had remained a pinprick at the end of their narrowed gazes, not even close enough to really distinguish from any other citizen. As a child, Madoc had never been permitted to go to the palace with Petros on senate business.

Now Madoc could see every precious stone sewn into the leather bindings of Geoxus's sandals and feel the god's power pulsing across the space between them.

Madoc scratched a hand over his skull, then quickly forced it down. He looked around for Ignitus, but the Kulan god was sulking in his seat, surrounded by servants. His hot glare burned in their direction.

Lucius slapped a companionable hand on the back of Madoc's armor.

Geoxus had spoken. He was now looking at Madoc as if waiting for a response.

"I am. Honorable Geoxus," he added.

"Well, you must eat. You'll need your strength in the coming weeks, isn't that right, Lucius?"

"It certainly is," Lucius promised with a tight, gleaming smile.

"I . . . I look forward to the challenge, Honorable Geoxus."

"Of course you do," said Geoxus, and the pride in his voice gave

Madoc a small dose of courage. A reckless thought kindled in his mind: If Geoxus favored him enough to include him in the Honored Eight, maybe the god would set Cassia free. Maybe he would listen if Madoc told him about Petros's unfair taxes, and how no one in the poor districts could make ends meet.

"Madoc is very fortunate to have been chosen," prompted Lucius.

Madoc was nodding—had he been nodding very long? He made himself stop. "Yes. I'm honored to be here. To be picked for the war." Had he already said honored? He sounded like a fool. "Thank you."

He glanced up and saw that Geoxus had leaned forward in his seat. His face was timeless, jaw chiseled to perfection, cheekbones high and proud. Though he'd lived for thousands of years, only a few small wrinkles lined his eyes—from smiling so much, Ilena used to tell them. His black hair, crowned by the circlet of onyx and opals, hung in fine ringlets to his shoulders. It was no wonder that Seneca, the old bat upstairs, had always said he was prettiest of all the gods. Ilena used to say it was dishonorable to speak of him that way, but blushed every time.

"It's not me you should thank." Geoxus waved a hand, motioning for someone to join them. "Petros spoke very highly of you. There are few mortals whose opinions I value more."

The weight of Madoc's armor nearly dragged him to the stones below his feet.

His father was here. Of course he was. He was a member of the senate, Crixion's tax collector. The box was filled with people just like him. Any thought of asking Geoxus to free Cassia, or of voicing Petros's corruption, dried on Madoc's tongue. How could he explain what had happened with Petros here to refute him? His father had Geoxus's trust. All Madoc had was one nearly failed match without geoeia—and once he was forced to use energeia, he'd lose that slim standing as well.

"Ah, Madoc. I'm glad you could join us." Petros strode up in his fine white toga, cheeks already flushed with too much wine. He smiled at Madoc with yellowed teeth and a glare that said, *Defy me in front of Geoxus, and see what I will do to you.*

"Excellent work in that match," Petros continued. "You drew it out nicely, let the crowd get into it before you won."

I almost lost, thought Madoc weakly. Tension stretched between them, tight enough to snap.

"Yes," said Geoxus. "Deimos already adores its new champion."

"Just wait until you see what he can do with geoeia," Petros said, his eyes gleaming. "The Kulans may surrender on the spot." He laughed loud enough that Ignitus must have heard.

Uncertainty rippled through Madoc's veins. Petros was taunting him, the way he had in the arena and at the Metaxas' home, and just like before, Madoc couldn't stop him. If he refuted Petros's claim, he'd lose his position in the Honored Eight and the money that came with it. Petros would certainly punish Cassia for the humiliation Madoc caused. Even playing at modesty was a risk; to question his position here was to question Geoxus himself.

"I'm sure he's very accomplished," the Father God said with a smile. "He'd have to be, if he's your son, Petros."

Madoc gaped. He half expected to blink and find himself in a different conversation, one in which Petros was still revolted by his very being.

But Petros did not falter. His shoulders drew back, and his chin lifted in what looked suspiciously like pride.

"Your son?" Lucius barked out a dry laugh. "What game are you playing, Petros?"

"An honest one, I assure you," Petros answered. "Had I given away Madoc's lineage, it might have offered him an unfair advantage entering into the war. Young champions must prove their worth to the Father God, not rely on their bloodlines to get ahead, isn't that right, Lucius?"

Beside Madoc, Lucius seethed, the blood rising in his cheeks. His glare slid to Madoc, accusing and disgusted.

"Great-Grandfather," Lucius said between his teeth. "Petros has always been hungry for your attention, but even I don't know what he hopes to accomplish through this claim."

"Petros's intentions favor Deimos," Geoxus assured Lucius. "He only learned of his son's existence recently, once he pledged to train with you. Madoc came to Petros right after—he had waited all these years until he could truly show his worth." Geoxus laughed heartily, but Madoc could only muster a weak chuckle. "What a moment that must have been, eh, Madoc?"

Madoc coughed into his fist, his throat as dry as chalk. He could practically hear Petros laying out this story, feigning his delight at reconnecting with a son he'd never known existed.

"Indeed," he managed. Any lingering doubt that he'd been chosen for the Honored Eight without Petros's interference disappeared. Madoc was only here now because his father had willed it.

Sorrow glimmered in Petros's eyes, as false as his claims at fair play. "Had I known of him, I would have raised him as my own. He certainly wouldn't have been fighting in the streets. It's of great pride to me that you found him worthy to train, Lucius."

Madoc heaved out a breath. Every word his father had said was a lie, from how they'd parted ways to Madoc's supposed geoeia.

And Geoxus believed it all.

He couldn't see that this was an act, meant to humiliate and destroy Madoc, and maybe Lucius by default.

"The fact that Madoc has Petros's blood does not make him qualified to stand in the arena in a war," Lucius said carefully.

Geoxus's smile faded, replaced by a hard grimace. "The fact that you have my blood does not make you qualified to question my judgment, Lucius." When the trainer bowed his head, Geoxus sighed. "I know potential when I see it. Madoc will do great things for Deimos."

"Yes, Great-Grandfather," said Lucius.

"Is there something you'd like to say, Madoc?" prompted Petros.

Anger blanketed Madoc's fear, bringing a sharp, ice-cold clarity. Petros had taken Cassia. He'd lied to Geoxus. He'd pushed Madoc into a war he would certainly lose.

But just because Madoc was Undivine didn't meant he didn't have power.

Petros was risking his reputation, his status, his *life*, just to punish Madoc, and that righteous hate thinned his reasoning. It made Petros weak, and as he had with Fentus, Madoc sensed his point of attack.

Petros would do anything to impress Geoxus, but like so many Divine, he equated worth with energeia. He didn't see his pigstock son as a threat, but he would soon enough.

Madoc was a gladiator now, and once he had the money to secure Cassia's freedom, he could ruin Petros in the only way that would truly hurt him.

He would fail in front of Geoxus. Get the money he needed for Cassia, and then, before he had to risk his neck in a match to the death, lose, and shame his father publicly.

"No, Father," he said, painting a smile on his face as false as Petros's claims. "I'm just grateful for the chance to fight for my god."

EIGHT

ASH

ASH HAD LOST her first gladiator fight. She had lost in front of Ignitus.

Tor and Rook had pulled her into a preparation chamber off the main fighting ring. The world was a blur of color and light, the windowless room washed a sickly pale green in the glow of the phosphorescent stones Geoxus employed. The hue turned Ash's stomach.

When Char had lost a fight, the *only* time Char had lost, she hadn't walked out of the ring. But here Ash was, the thudding of her heart sending pain into every tender bruise and scrape.

If she had lost this fight, how would she fare against a gladiator who could use energeia?

Spark poked Ash's arms, checked her eyes. She dabbed balm on Ash's collarbone and rubbed the smooth cream across her neck where Madoc's forearm had been.

The gladiators Ash had met who worshipped other gods had always been like Stavos, proud and eager and so loyal it radiated out of them. But Madoc had looked like he hated what he was doing. He'd even defended her against Stavos's taunts.

He made no *sense*.

"Nothing broken," Spark declared, twisting the lid back on the jar of balm. "Which is miraculous. Fighting a Deiman without using igneia—it's a wonder you still have all your limbs."

Ash grimaced. "Thanks for your confidence."

Taro pushed forward. "Confidence has nothing to do with it. You got out of there thanks to luck, not skill." Her eyes shifted to Tor, accusing. "You need to increase her training without energeia—"

But Tor ignored his sister and knelt in front of Ash. "You let Stavos get to you," he stated. "Before Madoc took you to the ground. It made you lower your guard."

Ash looked down at her lap.

She hated that she had let Stavos's taunting worm its way into her mind: that she could die just like Char. When she had lain under Madoc, his thighs fixing her to the hot sand, she had realized that if he killed her, she would leave nothing behind. Char would remain unavenged and Ignitus would continue destroying Kula—and Stavos would still be alive.

She wanted Stavos dead almost as badly as she wanted Ignitus dead. She wanted revenge, simple and grotesque, and the desire sickened her like she'd choked down spoiled meat.

Ash replayed Hydra's message in her mind like some kind of desperate prayer, clinging to that goal over the rotten, misshapen desire to bleed Stavos dry.

I have heard no similar rumors. He should stop worrying, and leave me out of his squabbles with Biotus, Aera, and Geoxus.

If Ash thought about the words enough, could she shake the secrets out of them?

Stop worrying. Leave me out of his squabbles with Biotus, Aera, and—

Realization made Ash bolt to her feet. Her head rushed with standing so quickly, and Tor followed her up.

Leave me out of his squabbles with Geoxus, Hydra had said.

"Stavos threatened Ignitus," Ash said, talking fast. She hated even saying his name. "He said, *Soon, Geoxus'll make sure everyone gets what they deserve, even your lying god.*"

Rook, leaning against the wall, frowned. "Those were his exact words?"

"A war insult." Tor shrugged. "He thinks Geoxus will beat Ignitus."

"If that's all he meant, he said it strangely," Ash pressed. "*Even your lying god*, as if Ignitus was an afterthought. Hydra said that Ignitus is in some squabble with Biotus, Aera, and Geoxus. Maybe there's a larger conflict, and it has to do with the thing Ignitus fears."

"And a meathead Deiman gladiator knows about it?" Tor's eyes were wide with disbelief. "We aren't even sure if the threat against Ignitus is credible."

Ash scanned the room, feeling a little manic, until she spotted an unlit candle and matchbox that had fallen out of Spark's medical bag. "I know how we can find out."

This plan was idiotic.

So it was a good thing her brain was foggy from the beating she'd taken; otherwise she might not have gone through with it.

Ash grabbed a match from the box, lit the candle, and stared at the flame.

Tor realized what she was doing. "Ash—stop! What are you—"

"Great Ignitus," she said to the igneia. "I need to speak with you. Now."

Tor seized her arm, but no one in the room dared say more with the fire burning.

A long moment passed.

"Ignitus," Ash said again. "I know you can hear me. I failed you today, but I need to—"

The room burned.

Every crevice filled with a vibrant flash of blue light. Ash spun, instinct jarring her so hard she slammed into the table. Tor, Rook, Taro, and Spark fell to their knees, shielding their eyes from Ignitus's extravagant entrance.

The light faded to reveal their sour-faced god, his arms folded, his glare on Ash. The walls of the chamber bore scorch marks now; this stone was sandy and rough, not the sort of rock made by fire that Ignitus had dominion over. No, this was Crixion—everything was Geoxus's.

Ignitus looked down his long nose at Ash. "Yes. You did fail me."

Shock reverberated through her body. The candle had gone out, and she squeezed the dead wax to ground herself.

"Great Ignitus," Tor said, prostrate on the floor. "The first few fights always bring certain nerves. With time, she will—"

"I didn't lose because of nerves," Ash cut him off. She ran her tongue along her lips. One had split; she tasted blood. "During the fight, Stavos taunted me. He said that this war will be different. That there is someone in Deimos who will give you what you deserve. Is it true, Great Ignitus? Could a person exist who might harm my god?"

Tor sat back on his heels. Rook, Taro, and Spark eased upright.

Ignitus's scowl broke apart. It was so fleeting, his expression imitating a flash of lightning through the blackest clouds. His eyes widened and he sucked in a quick breath.

He was concerned. And it was not the offended concern of his reputation being slighted.

Ash's question had made him worried.

Ignitus huffed a laugh. "What a clever lie he told you. My brother's efforts to undermine me have no bounds. Your concern is touching, Ash." He lurched forward, intensity brightening his eyes, and again Ash found herself thinking of the wrinkles that had creased Geoxus's eyes. Ignitus's skin was smooth—but the hair at the back of his neck, the few gray-white strands, was still there. "In the future, do not let yourself get distracted by what is clearly a vicious, bold *lie*."

He snarled the last word. Ash suppressed a smile at his slip of emotion.

Whatever threat Hydra had told Ignitus to leave her out of—it was real. Real enough that Ignitus feared it.

"Of course, Great Ignitus," she managed. "I will be more discerning in the next fight."

That brought a calculating squint to Ignitus's face. "Yes. Your next fight. I look forward to seeing you shine with igneia tomorrow morning."

Ash's stomach seized. "Tomorrow?"

The other champions wouldn't arrive for a few days. Tor had guessed that she would fight Brand first, the only other champion closer to Ignitus by birth. But if she was to fight tomorrow, then that meant she would fight one of the champions already here.

"At dawn, you fight Rook Akela for advancement." Ignitus nodded at Rook. "Give a good show, but try not to rough her up too much. After all"—his gaze went back to Ash, and he was furious now, his rage returned—"the first few fights always bring certain nerves."

With a sweep of his arm, Ignitus vanished, a column of blue fire launching up from the floor and dissipating into the ether.

Ash staggered in his absence, her mouth open. Ignitus was punishing her for losing against Madoc by making her fight Rook.

Even so, she smiled.

Tor leaped up from the floor and grabbed her arms. "What were you thinking?"

"Did you see that?" She stared at the place where Ignitus had been, now lit only by the glowing green stones. "Did you see his face?"

"He's angry." Rook had stood as well, arms folded, the painted sunbursts on his skin now blurred and faded. "But don't worry. We'll figure out the fight tomorrow. I'll help—"

"No." Ash panted, smiling still. "When I asked him about who might threaten him, Ignitus was *worried*. Which means Hydra's message wasn't a plea to leave her out of something frivolous or petty—it has weight. And Stavos might know of it. We have a lead that could bring him down."

The room fell silent.

"Yes, he was worried," Tor confirmed. Ash beamed up at him. He didn't return her exuberance. "But you were reckless. You can't only focus on this vague lead."

"Let's make it less vague, then. We can push Stavos. Maybe Geoxus has something planned against Ignitus, like Hydra said in her message, some squabble between them. Maybe it could actually *hurt* Ignitus, whatever it is, and Stavos is part of it—he did take out Ignitus's best gladiator illegally. He said—" She swallowed. "He said *my god told me your mother would be an easy kill.* Did Geoxus put him up to poisoning Char? Maybe—"

Someone knocked. "Ignitus's guards," soldiers said from the hall, "here to escort the champions back to the palace."

Tor flinched, giving Ash a pained look. "Stop, Ash. You're fighting Rook tomorrow. You're so focused on bringing Ignitus down that you're losing sight of the immediate consequences of your actions."

Ash wilted. "I'm not losing sight of anything. What more do we have to lose?"

The guards knocked again. "Champions?"

Tor's face flared red. Before he could respond, Rook pressed close to them.

"Ignitus seemed genuinely concerned, which means it's possible that whoever or whatever he fears is in Deimos. We owe it to ourselves to pursue his weakness, Tor. We owe it to everyone we're fighting for back home." He swallowed, noticeably not saying his son's name. "We owe it to Char too. You know we do."

"We'll talk to Stavos, then?" Ash's stomach suddenly shriveled into a knot. "We'll find out if Geoxus told him to kill my mother?"

She didn't want to talk to Stavos.

She wanted to slice his throat.

"Geoxus is likely to have some kind of festivities after the first round fights," Tor said to Rook. He was ignoring her. "Those events are always saturated with wine. We can wait until Ignitus is drunk and press him for information, a more solid lead."

"We have a lead," Ash tried again. "If Geoxus used Stavos to kill Char, he could be—"

"Stavos is a brute," Tor snapped. "A fumbling idiot of a man. He is *nothing*, Ash. Do you hear me? I won't waste any more energy talking about Char's murderer. Stop. We'll question Ignitus. That's it."

Ash agreed with him; Stavos was all the things Tor said. But he could also be the key to figuring out Ignitus's weakness if he was involved in a larger plot.

"Champions," one of the guards called, impatient. "To the palace."

Spark gave an apologetic shrug and answered the door. She and Taro walked out into the group of waiting soldiers.

Ash wilted under the sorrow in Tor's eyes, the fury that was blinding him to a potential weakness of Ignitus's. Or was Ash's own fury blinding her?

The only way to find out was to take the next step at whatever celebration Geoxus held after the first fights. Talk to Ignatus, yes—but they needed to talk to Stavos, too. Even if Ash had to do it herself.

"All right," she told Tor, her head dropping.

Tor spun on his heels.

Rook steered Ash for the door.

"Thank you," she whispered to Rook. "For defending me."

"Don't thank me. You're right about pursuing a lead, but you're wrong too. I know you feel like you lost everything with your mother. But there's always more Ignitus can take from you." He looked at her somberly. "Always."

Ignitus and the Kulans had their usual wing on the twelfth floor of Geoxus's palace. For the first time, Ash had her own room with a canopied bed, chairs and a table with a washbasin, and a balcony ringed by elegant marble statues. Tor and Rook had their own chambers farther down, on either side of Ignitus's room, while Spark and Taro had a room in the hall just below.

Ash lay in the same bed she'd shared with Char a handful of times. With everything that had happened, she'd thought that sleep would instantly seize her. But moonlight made the air a hazy, dreamlike blue, and Ash had to shut her eyes to hold on to her composure.

Having Char had always let Ash ignore her loneliness. When her lack of friends threatened to swallow her whole, Ash had just looped her arm through her mother's and listened to the lull of her voice until she stopped wanting so much.

There was nothing now. No one in this room with her. No one to hold on to.

Ash scrambled for memories, wet eyes squished shut.

"If I had geoeia, I could build a staircase down the side of the palace," Ash had told Char on a previous visit. She couldn't remember how old she had been—young enough to still dream idly of escape. "We could run off into Crixion before Ignitus even knew we were gone!"

Char had been lying on her back under the silky sheets, and Ash had watched her mother stare up at the canopy's translucent drapes. "And where would we run to?" The question sounded broken at first, a sad reminder of the reality of their lives. But Char flipped onto her side and gave Ash a conspiratorial grin. "If we could live anywhere, where would you go, my love?"

"The Apuit Islands!" Ash snuggled closer, planting her head under Char's chin and fixing her arms around her mother's waist. "I want to see a country that's more water than land."

Char hummed, the noise vibrating in Ash's ears. "Are you sure you wouldn't want to go to Itza? I heard they have a type of flower that's the size of a cottage and smells worse than animal dung!"

Ash had gagged, and Char had laughed, and the two had fallen into silence, realizing that even if they could get out of Crixion, the blockade around Hydra's Apuit Islands and Florus's Itza wouldn't let them pass. There was nowhere else to dream of going. There was nowhere that Ignatus could not find them.

Clouds shifted outside the window now, letting stronger moonlight illuminate the room. Ash kicked off her sheets and shrank into a ball, hands over her ears, heartbeat thudding fast.

There's always more Ignitus can take from you, Rook had said.

She knew he was right. But it didn't feel that way. It felt like the worst had happened, so what more could Ignitus do? She had nothing left.

But she did. She wanted to run practice drills with Tor. She wanted to ask Rook if he'd heard from Lynx. She wanted to listen to Taro and Spark banter about which was sweeter, Deiman persimmons or Kulan grapes. But Ignitus had guards in the hall to prevent anyone from trying to leave—which was an unnecessary and annoying display of his power.

Ash groaned at the smoldering coals of fear in her belly. She would fight Rook, but it wouldn't be like she was fighting an enemy. Not like Madoc, his bare shoulders heaving, his dark eyes fixed on her, glistening and afraid. He had had the upper hand; what could he have feared with his arm pressed to her throat?

Ash pushed deeper into the mattress, willing her heartbeats to slow and her mind to empty of thoughts of loneliness, of Ignitus's worry, of Madoc's dark eyes. That pulse of innocent terror.

She saw his mouth form her name. *Ash.*

He became Ignitus, crouched over her, eyes pinched in sympathetic worry. *Ash.*

Sleep pulled and ebbed, and she fell into it, down, down, her only escape.

Char was at the edge of the fighting ring. Dried blood was smeared across her chest and coated her once pristine armor. *Ash*, her lips formed.

In unison, Char at the edge, Madoc—Ignitus—close and heavy. *Where would you go?*

The next morning, after Ash had readied herself—dressed in utilitarian reed armor now—and choked down a handful of breadsticks for breakfast, Kulan guards corralled her into a carriage and out of the palace's complex.

Other elimination fights would occur this week, on Ignitus's side and on Geoxus's, as well as dozens of lesser fights throughout the city to keep the crowds amused. But the current odd number of Kulan champions meant one wouldn't fight until the rest of Ignitus's gladiators arrived from their fights abroad. Maybe Tor would be in the stands when she and Rook fought, cheering for her, and she would know he forgave her for acting impetuously yesterday.

The carriage crossed a narrow bridge. The Nien River glittered in the clear morning, diamonds in blue, before the western edge of Crixion swallowed her up.

Ash didn't know the city well enough to identify its neighborhoods, but they wound through an area that was dirtier than the palace's complex, with clumsy buildings sagging into one another and strands of laundry stretched window to window. People crowded the streets in a flurry of excitement, all heading in the same direction: to the grand arena. Children in faux gladiator outfits brandished wooden shields and retractable rocks on strings; men and women jostled one another good-naturedly, slathered in silver paint with names written on their skin.

JANN arched over one man's brow. Another had *RACLIN* in script down his left arm.

And Ash saw more than one person with *MADOC* scrawled on their bodies.

When the Kulan carriage came into view, a few Deiman people even called out "Ash!" while others shouted "Rook!"

She swallowed hard, her hands in fists on her knees. She hadn't gotten a chance to talk to Rook about their fight. She needed to win if she was to have any hope of earning Ignitus's trust and uncovering more about whatever it was he feared. But would Rook agree? She needed to beat him—but if he won, he would earn a fair amount of gold, money he could use to help Lynx.

Suddenly Ash regretted all the time she had wasted. She needed to talk with Rook.

A lurching left turn, and the carriage swung to a halt near Crixion's largest arena. This area was clearly meant for gladiators, soldiers, and arena workers—it was shadowed and blocked off by a low stone wall. Beyond that wall, farther down the right side of the arena, Ash could see a line of Deiman citizens in stained togas and well-worn tunics.

Some whooped into the air. Another person cried "Bets! Place your official bets here!"

Ash's eyes darted around the rest of the yard, but Rook wasn't here. Maybe he would enter from another tunnel. Or maybe Ignitus had changed his mind and wouldn't make her fight him.

Guards swarmed her when Ash descended onto the dusty road, and she let them usher her into the arena.

The passageway was unlit but for dawn's rays in the entrance yard. It was a short chute of stone with a few closed doors and the golden sands of the arena's fighting pit at the end.

A match raged within between nonchampion Deiman gladiators to warm up the crowd. Ash saw only part of their battle, two warriors hurling each other back and forth with stones.

The crowd above stomped and cheered.

Ash and her escorts reached the end of the hall as one of the Deiman fighters dropped to his knees. He lifted his hands, coated in bloodstained sand, and shouted his surrender.

Most of the crowd booed at his weakness; some cheered for the victor. Regardless, their match was ended, and an announcer's voice cut over the throng:

"Two Kulan champions will take the ring!"

Servants scurried out from other halls and deftly set up for the fight.

Ash couldn't breathe. This was it. Her first arena match. But she wasn't fighting some feral stranger; it was *Rook*, who had always saved the best armor for Char, who had tried to make Ash a chocolate tart for her birthday one year but accidentally swapped salt for sugar. He'd been mortified, but Ash had laughed herself to tears.

Ash curled her hands into sweaty fists and stepped out of the darkness.

The arena's stands were full. A few people milled about the stairways, searching for seats, while a vendor sold hot wine and meat on sticks. In the very center of the pit there was now a shallow brick bowl that held twigs coated with sticky-sweet ignition liquid—Ash could feel the extra intensity in the igneia—and flames crackled hungrily on the fuel. Next to it, a rack of weapons waited, knives and swords and a single shield.

With a relieved sigh, Ash took a step toward the fire, her fingers reaching out to the heat. She had igneia for this fight. She had her fire. Everything would be fine, as long as—

Rook entered the pit from the opposite tunnel.

A trumpet cut through the audience's murmuring. Silence fell.

The final pieces of Ash's resolve slipped through her fingers when blue flames filled a viewing box, so bright they pierced her eyes.

Ignitus materialized out of his fire, flames curling away into his oiled hair, his draping orange-and-blue tunic. The box he had chosen was so close, he'd be able to see every bead of sweat on the gladiators' bodies, and Ash could see just as much of him, his scowling look of anticipation.

Ignitus had come to watch her fight Rook. Or to watch Rook fight her?

Terror ate up Ash's stomach, rose into her throat. Her eyes went to Rook, who watched Ignitus. There was something off about his face—his response to what Ignitus did was usually anger, furious rage that was so beautifully Kulan it lit him up like a flame. But now Rook looked sad almost. His face was red, his eyes swollen.

What had happened?

Ash's mind reeled, her breaths coming in tight gasps.

"Rook Akela," an announcer bellowed, "five times great-grandson of the fire god, will fight Ash Nikau, great-granddaughter of the fire god, to progress in the war. This elimination fight begins"—the announcer paused dramatically—"*now!*"

Fuel and flame. I am fuel and flame.

Ash stumbled forward, her heart a brick in her chest. Her eyes stayed on Rook, expecting some hidden signal from him or a mouthed command.

Rook didn't move, lost in staring at Ignitus. The crowd roared, cheers turning to hisses, and finally he blinked, shaking himself to life.

He and Ash met to the left of the fire bowl, the rack of weapons between them. Rook took a dagger; Ash followed, her palms sweaty, her heart beating so fast it hummed in her chest.

"What should we do?" Ash hissed. "Am I to win?"

"Fight!" the crowd demanded. "Fight!"

Ash's grip tightened on her dagger. She couldn't stand here having a conversation with her opponent. But Rook was staring at the sand between their feet. He hefted the dagger in one hand while his other remained tightly clenched around—was that a scroll?

"Rook," Ash tried. She hated that her voice wavered, but, burn it all, she was terrified, shaking, and she needed him to *look at her.* "Rook, what happened?"

He moved. He didn't draw on any igneia; he just dived at her, thrusting his knife for her middle, and she parried by instinct. He swung again; she dodged. They'd sparred before, and it felt like that, the two of them dancing around each other. Each jab from Rook thundered up Ash's arm, and she blocked most of his blows before he'd completed them.

The crowd rejoiced. Cheering, stomping, an orchestra that multiplied Ash's anxiety and made her miss a block when Rook drove a fist into her shoulder.

She flailed back with a dull yelp, but he hadn't struck her with his knife-wielding hand. Sweat poured down her face and matted the reed armor to her chest and legs.

Rook paused, hands on his knees, face to the ground, wheezing. They hadn't been fighting that long. He couldn't be tired yet.

Had he been poisoned, like Char?

"Rook," Ash whispered, her lungs hollow. "What happened to you?"

At their pause, the crowd's cheering became one collective *BOO.*

Rook swiped his hand across his nose. "Four days. He let me carry on for four days."

"What are you talking about? What's wrong?"

He sobbed once, still bent double. "I wasn't there. Because I was *here*. With him. Great Ignitus, we have to call him. Great *fucking* Ignitus!"

He bolted upright to shout the last words at Ignitus.

The noise of the crowd silenced.

No one—*no one*—spoke badly of the gods, least of all directly to them.

"You need to stop," Ash tried, panic welling. "Please—attack me, and I'll fall. You'll win. Ignitus will be pleased with you—"

Rook whirled toward Ignitus's viewing box. Ash chased after him, coming around the firepit—and there, hands on the railing, Ignitus fumed down at Rook.

Ash grabbed Rook's shoulder. "What are you doing? Remember Wolfsbane—"

He spun on her, slapping her hand away, and pointed his other fist at her, the one holding the scroll. The crowd whooped, urging them to bloodshed.

Blue fire flickered on Ignitus's arms, the tips of his hair.

Rook's lower lip trembled. Ash went motionless, her hands splayed between them.

"Lynx is dead," Rook whispered. "He died the morning after we left Igna."

Ash sucked in a breath.

"My son has been dead for four days, and Ignitus claims he just got the news." Rook opened his fist and let the scroll drop to the sand.

"But he waited to give me the letter until this morning because all he cares about, all he's *ever* cared about, is war."

A howl bubbled in Ash's throat. She fought it down, *willed* it down, because Ignitus watched and already Rook had gone too far and she needed to be the one to save them both.

"Rook," she begged, "I'm so sorry. I loved Lynx too. I'm so—" She swallowed. "Fight me. One more round, we'll fake a win, and we can walk out of here." She lowered her voice. "You'll get your revenge. I swear, Rook. Please."

Sweat, tears, and dust from the arena made a paste on Rook's face, thick streaks of brown across his dark skin. He didn't look angry. He looked . . . tired.

"I should've gotten Lynx out years ago," Rook said. "Char should've taken you too. We all should have run instead of playing his sick games. You deserve better than this life. Lynx deserved better. And I can't—" He coughed, sniffing back tears. "I'm sorry, Ash."

He took off—sprinting away from her, toward Ignitus.

Agony seared hotter than any flame, gouged deeper than any wound. Ash flung herself after him. "No! Stop, please—"

Momentum carried Rook as he leaped into the air and grabbed the wall of the viewing box, kicking the rough edge of the stone to propel himself onto the railing.

The crowd had gone silent again. Shocked, awed, intrigued.

In the viewing box, Ignitus watched Rook come at him, his anger dimmed to disgust. His attendants cowered behind him; his guards held flames in their hands but didn't attack, held in place by Ignitus's two lifted fingers.

Rook balanced on the railing, readied his knife, and hurled himself at Ignitus.

The blade sank into the god's neck.

For a moment, Ash thought it had worked. Ignitus didn't move, as if stricken in the early shock of death. His eyes were frozen on Rook, who gasped for breath before him.

Calmly, Ignitus reached up and removed the knife. A thin stream of blood spurted out of the wound, but before Ash had even blinked, it was closing, mending itself.

She had never seen a god injured before. She had heard about it, dreamed of it, but this was worse. Now she knew, undeniably—the gods could not be killed.

But they *could*. The Mother Goddess was dead. How, *how*—

Rook fumbled against the railing. Ash choked, so far below, helplessly watching him.

Ignitus dropped the blade. In the horrified silence of the arena, it clattered against the marble of the viewing box's floor.

"Mistake," Ignitus growled, and punched his hands palm out at Rook.

Fire blasted like a cannonball. Only Ignitus's fire could burn a Kulan.

A great blue knot shot out of Ignitus's fingers and slammed into Rook's chest, knocking him down, down, down.

His body crashed into the fighting pit.

Ash raced for him, her sandals slipping on the gritty dirt. She dropped to her knees next to Rook, hands hovering over the concave circle burned into his chest. Blackened skin and bone, charred muscle, bulging cauterized veins, all fought to escape.

Her stomach seized, nausea and horror coming out as a sob. "Rook," Ash said, as though he could undo it, as though he could still choose not to leave her too. "Please, Rook, hold on—"

Blood trickled from the corner of his mouth and fell in a perfect circle on the sand.

Blood on the sand. Char's lips moving across the arena. A sword in her chest.

Ignitus, glaring. He was over them right now, scowling in the morning sunlight.

Tears gathered in Rook's eyes. He inhaled, but the air got stuck in the void, and he heaved. The motion rocked a bag out of his pocket, spilling gold, teal, and pink marbles. The toy that Lynx loved.

Ash scrambled to lift Rook, but she couldn't stand and she couldn't run and a scream tore through her that she muffled in Rook's shoulder.

In the stands, the crowd stomped and cheered, stomped and cheered.

NINE

MADOC

MADOC WON HIS first elimination match of the war by forfeit.

After a restless night replaying Petros's bold claims about Madoc's abilities and failing to push Ash's hate-filled eyes out of his mind, he and Elias had fumbled through the morning routine. Breakfast Madoc couldn't stomach. Armor that didn't meet Arkos's high standards for inspection. A wrong turn in the barracks that made him late for the morning roll call. He'd only just found his place in line with the other gladiators when Lucius had announced that in his first fight, Madoc would face Stavos, the giant gladiator who'd heckled Ash in the arena and who favored a broadsword for ramming straight through his opponents.

Madoc had vomited twice on the carriage ride to the small arena on the west side of the city. Even Elias, who could talk his way into and out of anything, had fallen quiet.

But Stavos hadn't shown.

"Probably scared of looking bad when we beat him," Elias had offered weakly.

While the guards had searched the streets, suspicion had gnawed at the edges of Madoc's thoughts. Stavos's forfeit didn't make sense. Madoc had seen him get into his carriage that morning. He'd watched the gladiator mime how he would crush Madoc's face and laugh when Madoc had gone pale. Stavos was a seasoned gladiator; he wasn't afraid of some untrained stonemason who'd barely bested a Kulan fighter without energeia.

So where had he gone?

But when the guards had returned without Stavos, holding a sack of gold coins so heavy Madoc had to use two hands to take it, his worries ground to dust.

He'd won, and it didn't matter how. He was one thousand coins closer to saving Cassia and humiliating his father in front of Geoxus.

"We should take this to Petros now," Elias said. "Offer it as an installment. Maybe he'll let Cassia go once he sees we're going to make good on his demand."

Madoc focused on Elias's voice through the roar of the crowd above them. They were still in one of the exit tunnels, only a short walk from the outside of the small arena. Lesser matches were held here during the week along with plays and livestock auctions, which left the corridor crowded with stage planking and tattered curtains, and smelling vaguely of sheep dung.

"He won't." He couldn't take the edge out of his voice. The crowd was screaming, their stomping feet a stampede one rock layer above his head. Whatever fight had gone on in place of his must have ended quickly, and in a bloody mess.

The crowds always loved those the best.

"Then go back to Geoxus," Elias said. "You've won now. Maybe he'll front you the rest of the money, or grant you a favor." Elias's hands were circling as he talked. "He might free Cassia if you ask."

"And what will I say?" Madoc steered them toward the exit so they could get back into the carriage that would bring them to Lucius's villa. *Hello, Geoxus. I know half of my wins since becoming a champion are by forfeit, but can you do me a favor and set our sister free?* He only chose me in the first place because he trusts Petros."

Elias groaned and pulled at his dark hair, making it stick forward like a wave reaching for shore. The smudges beneath his eyes said that he'd slept about as much as Madoc had last night. Every minute they stayed at Headless Hill was another they risked exposure, and Lucius's training had been particularly brutal that morning following the meeting with Geoxus. Convinced that Madoc had deliberately lied about his lineage, the sponsor had promised to take Madoc's fingers, one by one, should he step out of line. On top of that, rumors had already begun to circulate about Madoc's father, and judging by the heated glares he and Elias had gotten at breakfast, his relationship with Petros wasn't making them popular.

Fifteen hundred gold coins, and then this would be over.

"Madoc! There he is . . . *Madoc!*" A burst of screams had Madoc bracing in defense.

A crowd had gathered near the exit of the arena. Deiman women and men, even a few children, all held back by an arc of centurions.

Madoc's immediate response was to run—these people knew he was a fraud. They were angry at him for his appointment to the Honored Eight, or bitter that he hadn't put on a good show. But their smiles had him hesitating.

"Are you truly a stonemason?" a man called, drawing Madoc's eyes to the mortar stains on his tunic, and his sun-bronzed shoulder, where Madoc's name was etched in black ink.

Madoc opened his mouth, but no words came out.

"Madoc!" came a woman's voice. "Over here!"

He spun in her direction, finding a horde of girls in pale blue-and-gold gowns pressing against a centurion's horizontal spear. They were cheering, cheeks flushed, a mass of bare arms and plunging necklines and laughter, and Madoc found himself completely at a loss about how to respond.

"Was Stavos scared of you, Brave Madoc?" one cooed.

"How many fights have you won?"

"Have you a lover waiting for you in the stonemasons' quarter?"

"You're my pick for champion!"

Madoc's breath lodged in his throat. His blood moved too fast through his veins. A lover waiting for him? How did they know where he lived?

"Why couldn't I be the champion?" muttered Elias.

Madoc tried to smile but only managed a tight grimace. He clutched the bag of gold against his side. He didn't even realize he was backing away until the stone edge of the exit's archway was pressed between his shoulder blades.

"*Madoc.* Elias!" One woman's voice cut through the rest like a pointed knife plunged straight into Madoc's chest.

Pushing to the edge of the crowd was a thin woman with a wrap around her dark hair and a hard stare set to punish. Her tightly cinched dress was made of the plain, worn muslin of the working class. Her skirt was splattered with mud. Madoc suspected this meant she had walked all the way from the stonemasons' quarter.

"Oh no," said Elias.

Ilena waited expectantly, fists on her narrow hips.

Since it was clear he and Elias weren't making it out of here anytime soon, Madoc motioned her through the barricade.

"It's all right," he said when the centurion shot a wary glance his way. "She's my mother."

Ilena pressed between the armored shoulders of the centurions, dragging a frail, hobbling woman behind. *Seneca.* Madoc couldn't think of why she was here, or how she had managed the trip, but it didn't matter, because Ilena was rolling toward them like storm clouds on the sea, and he was not about to get a beating in front of all these people.

He and Elias retreated into the tunnel and were just out of sight before Ilena grabbed both their ears.

"Ow!" Elias howled.

"You're gladiators now? You're fighting in a *war*?" Her voice reverberated off the ceiling, high enough to shatter eardrums.

"I haven't fought anyone," Madoc countered, just as her iron grip began to twist.

Behind her, Seneca chuckled, her voice like gravel shaking in a jar.

"Champion!" One of the centurions from outside had heard the noise and came rushing toward them, spear extended. He took one look at Ilena and then sent Madoc an uncertain scowl. "Unhand him, domina . . ."

"Keep talking and you'll be next!" she hollered, but her grip loosened enough for Madoc to slide free. He waved off the centurion, massaging his hot earlobe and wishing he could melt into the floor.

The centurion waited one more beat before turning.

"That was embarrassing," Elias muttered, wriggling free.

"Your pride is the least of my concerns," Ilena responded. She jabbed a finger at Madoc. "You two leave to get Cassia, and I hear nothing. I fear the worst. And three days later you're one of the Honored Eight? I had to hear it from Seneca! My own sons couldn't tell me the truth!"

"Whispers on the wind," sang Seneca, adjusting a belt around a tunic Madoc was fairly certain had been stolen off their laundry line. "They say you're very impressive, Madoc."

Elias gave her a disgusted look.

"I'm sorry," Madoc said to Ilena, hot shame washing between his shoulder blades. "But . . ." He drew open the pouch of gold nestled in his arm.

The anger ripped from her face, leaving her skin pale and the bones in her cheeks too prominent. "How did you—"

"A thousand gold coins for every round he wins," said Elias. "One forfeit, and we're over halfway to paying off Cassia's indenture."

Ilena hushed him, closing the bag with one hand. She looked over her shoulder, as if fearful that someone might try to steal it. It was almost funny. No one would think of stealing from a champion—not here, anyway.

"It's too dangerous," she hissed. "These aren't street fights, Madoc. These are trained gladiators."

"I know," he said grimly, wondering again where Stavos had gone. As much as Madoc wanted to believe the champion had run scared, he knew that was unlikely. Could it have been illness? Gladiators sometimes fell to pox.

"Does Lucius know you aren't . . ." She didn't have to say the word to make her meaning clear. *Does he know you aren't Divine?*

Madoc shook his head.

"Of course not." Ilena huffed. She inhaled slowly, gaze turning toward the arena, where the crowd had begun chanting, "Burn her up! Burn her up!"

"What's going on out there?" Elias stepped closer to the golden sand at the end of the corridor, the long beam of light reaching the tips of his sandals.

"Ignitus has lost his temper," said Seneca, tightening the knot of silver hair at the base of her neck. "It seems to happen more often than not."

Ilena ignored her and pressed the heels of her hands to her temples. "All right. We need to explain that there's been a mistake. Can you speak to the sponsor—Lucius? Maybe he can help."

Madoc could see her scheming, trying to figure out how to work with what they'd done, and he loved her for that.

Which was why he couldn't tell her that Petros had claimed him as his son. She was more of a parent than his real father had ever been.

"Or maybe you should keep fighting," Seneca clucked, prodding the muscles in Madoc's arms.

"Seneca, please," said Ilena.

"The boy's a gladiator now," Seneca said. "If you'd stop coddling him, we can see what he's truly capable of."

Her words grated on Madoc's nerves. The old woman knew as well as any of them that Madoc was Undivine. It was as if she wanted him to fight for her own entertainment—an experiment that could only last so long.

A commotion came from the entrance to the arena. Three figures crammed into the narrow corridor, seeming to trip over each other in an attempt to get off the yellow sand. It wasn't until they'd crossed the threshold that Madoc registered the silver gleam of the two helmets and breastplates and the broken reed patches of Kulan armor.

Two centurions were dragging a gladiator out of the arena.

Not just any gladiator—Ash.

She thrashed between them, loosening the last pieces of her armor, which fell to the floor in a heap. Now all that remained were the thin binding wraps around her chest, her tattered reed skirt, and the black soot that dusted her legs and smeared over her arms. One of the centurions stepped on her armor as he tried to pull her toward them, but he slipped and crashed to his knees.

With a wail, she lunged at him, but not before the other centurion landed a kick to her gut.

Ash toppled with a dry gasp. The other soldier rose and grabbed her hair. Madoc stepped forward, unsure what he planned to do or say. He could still see her eyes, burning up at him from the ground in hate and fear. He could see her on her knees bowing to her god. It didn't matter why she was fighting now, or if she'd won or lost. She was hurting, and he could feel it searing through his skin like hot coals.

"Let go of her."

Madoc turned. Ilena was standing just behind him, her hands twitching at her sides.

"Stay out of this!" snapped one of the soldiers. "This one's liable to burn you to the ground if she gets near an open flame."

"She's just a girl," Ilena argued weakly.

"She's not *your* girl," said Seneca, and Madoc's panic rose higher in his throat.

Ilena's face tightened.

"I'll meet you at the carriage," Madoc said, passing Elias the bag of gold.

"Madoc," Elias warned.

Madoc knew staying behind was unwise; he didn't need Elias to tell him so.

A scowling Elias took Ilena by the elbow and turned her toward the exit. "Come on, Seneca," he said when the old woman made no motion to follow.

"I'll be right behind you," Madoc told her. The old woman grunted, then followed the other two toward the door.

Madoc turned back to Ash and the two centurions.

He needed to leave. Get in the carriage with the others. Drive away from this place and focus on bringing Cassia home. He was already risking trouble in too many ways.

But it didn't make sense that Ash was being escorted by Deiman centurions. The Kulans were supposed to enter and leave through the east gate.

Ash cried out again, a guttural howl that shook him to the bones, and the centurion jerked her upright. Before she could react, two spears were pointed at her throat.

Madoc's hesitation evaporated. His vision tinged red.

"What's all this about?" he asked, trying to play calm.

"Stay back," one centurion said. "This is arena business."

"That's why I'm here," said Madoc. "Getting a look at the competition. What happened?"

"She wouldn't clear the sand for the next match," said the far centurion between hard breaths. "Wouldn't let go of the body."

Madoc's stomach sank. She'd killed her opponent in a trial? They weren't meant to be to the death, but that didn't mean fights couldn't sometimes go too far.

He needed to back away. If they were restraining Ash, they must have had good reason.

But there was something off about her. A slippery, hot pain sliding across the space between them like a vat of spilled oil. He could feel it wash over his feet and slide up his legs. It coated his chest and throat.

For as long as he could remember, he'd been able to sense what others felt. He hadn't realized it was odd until he'd come to live with the Metaxas, and Elias had caught on to it. *Pigstock geoeia*, he'd called it—a sense that wasn't ordinary but could hardly be called earth divinity. Madoc had assumed he was right. People were different, after all, and sometimes divinity manifested in strange ways. A healer in Kyphus claimed he could hear the ore in a Divine person's blood. One of the priests at the temple could move only sandstone with his geoeia. Madoc's ability was odd, but his father was Earth Divine, and variations in power were not unheard of.

Besides, pigstock geoeia had its uses. Madoc could read the mood of the baker at the market. If he was feeling generous, Elias would beg for the honey cakes that hadn't sold at the end of the day. If he wasn't, they would steal them.

He knew when Ilena had had a good day and when to tread lightly. How to quiet Ava when she had a bad dream. How to sense another fighter's weakness.

But Ash's pain was stronger than anything he'd felt before. He'd never sensed the emotions of someone who wasn't Deiman—that must be why. Whatever the case, he didn't like it.

"Geoxus asked you to escort the victor of the match back to her people?" Madoc scratched his chin, feeling the rough stubble beneath his fingertips.

"Better than her own god, that's for certain." The nearest guard laughed nervously. "You won't see Geoxus burn up his own fighter, I know that much."

Ignitus had killed her opponent? Madoc met Ash's gaze again, and now that oily slickness of her pain was pressing through his pores, weighing heavy in his blood. She blinked rapidly, but it didn't stop the tears. They rolled down her cheeks, carving new tracks in the dust on her skin.

Ash twisted, breaking free. She lunged toward the arena. In a flash, the centurion had snatched a stone from the ground with geoeia and was swinging it toward the back of her head.

"*Stop.*" Madoc's voice echoed in the tunnel. Outside, the shouts of the crowds, already demanding the next match, dropped away.

The centurion lowered the stone.

"Leave her." Lightning raced through Madoc's limbs. "I'll make sure she gets back to her people."

The soldiers both lowered their spears.

"She's calm now," said the closest one. "He'll take it from here."

Madoc could hardly believe the change that had fallen over them.

"You should go now," he said.

The second centurion nodded. "We need to leave."

They departed without another word.

A strange curiosity had him frowning after them. Talking to those guards had felt easy, more so than it should have. They were centurions, and even if he was a gladiator, he should have been more cautious. But they'd listened to him as though he was the captain of the legion.

He had bigger concerns. He was within striking distance of a Kulan gladiator. An enemy of Deimos. A woman he'd bested less than a day before.

Maybe sending the centurions away hadn't been such a great idea after all.

But she didn't attack. Instead, she slumped against the wall, blowing out a shaky breath.

"Are you all right?"

Her chin lifted, dark eyes a sickle of gold and brown in the dim light that came through the front entrance. Madoc deliberately relaxed his arms and hands, hoping she didn't see too much, and focused elsewhere. Her wild spirals of black hair that had broken free from their binding. The thin cloth wrap around her chest that she wore beneath her armor. The slope of her waist, and the small indentation of her navel.

His gaze shot back to her face, and he swallowed dryly.

"I'm sure your people are waiting at the eastern exit. There's a tunnel that runs beneath the stands. It should take you there."

He motioned to the corridor near the arena exit, a cave with a low, arched ceiling. Phosphorescent stones flickered around the bend, bringing a sharp, guilt-coated relief. There were no flames to draw from here. If there were, those guards would be dead. Maybe he would be too.

She pushed off the wall and took an unsteady step toward him, her sandaled feet crunching over the gravel. Her eyes remained on his.

He tried to read her intent, but all he could feel was her wary curiosity, a heavy mantle over his shoulders, and the bitterness of her pain in the back of his jaw.

Her chin lowered slightly—an invitation? She couldn't have meant for him to go with her.

Unless she planned to kill him and cut out her competition. Or maybe she didn't trust that it was safe. She thought it was an ambush of some kind—that he'd orchestrated the centurions to leave so that she could disappear without witnesses.

He stepped into the hallway, telling himself he was doing what any respectable Deiman citizen would do. It was better than acknowledging the small spark of curiosity that lit inside him.

She hesitated. "I don't know what you're trying to do, Deiman. But it would be unwise for you to corner me alone. I told you before, you won't beat me again."

"I know," he said, giving a small and, he hoped, encouraging smile. "I just want to help you get back to your people."

"Why?"

Because I embarrassed you yesterday in the arena. Because if I don't, more guards will come and find you.

Because you're scared, and I can feel it.

He shrugged. "Suit yourself. I'm going this way. Come if you want."

He walked away, and was ten steps in before he heard her following. Soon, she'd come beside him, her wary gaze flicking from his face to his hands.

This space was tighter than the previous corridor, and without the sunlight from outside, it felt too private. Every footstep crackled off the walls. Every creak of his leather armor sounded like the groan of an unoiled hinge. He was as acutely aware of all the places he was covered—his chest, back, thighs, and feet—and all the places she wasn't. There was so much bare skin, he couldn't *not* look. His gaze flicked from the points of her shoulder blades to the cut muscles of her upper arms. It bounced from her tight belly, which disappeared beneath a tattered reed skirt, to her long thighs and calves and the lean tendons of her ankles.

She reminded him of the women painted on the walls of Geoxus's temple—the ones with ample curves and a lack of clothing that Elias and he used to gawk at when they were young. But Ash's back was straighter than the women in those paintings. Her chin was lifted. She might have been wearing a silk gown with a crown of onyx and opals atop her head.

She carried herself like a goddess.

He bumped into the wall. Her stare snapped to his, suspicious as ever.

"What are you doing here?" she demanded. "Are you fighting soon?"

"I won already, actually." He sent her a small grin. "Didn't you hear?"

She gave a quick shake of her head. Of course she hadn't heard. She was busy fighting her own match.

He cleared his throat. "Stavos didn't show."

She paused, her burst of anger like a fist pumping around his lungs. "What do you mean?"

He remembered what she'd said in their fight—that Stavos had poisoned her mother—and he wondered grimly if she had been hoping to face him in the arena.

Madoc shrugged. "No one's seen him. I guess I scared him away."

"I doubt that," she said, making him wince. "Where would he have gone?"

"Back under the rock he came from? I don't know. We weren't exactly close."

The pain he'd felt in her receded, replaced again by wariness. They began walking again.

"What do you want, Madoc?"

It didn't surprise him that she knew his name—she'd probably learned it when they'd fought before—but he was caught off guard by the thrill that came when she said it.

He shoved it down. "Nothing." His shoulder blades knotted as they neared one of the glowing stones set in the wall. "Did Ignitus really kill your opponent?"

He regretted the words instantly. She stopped. Her small intake of breath was like a dagger to his side, laced with bright pain reflected in the pinch of the corners of her eyes.

She wouldn't let go of the body.

Tears welled in her eyes. Her chin quivered the tiniest bit. She seemed suddenly breakable, like a rock wall pressured with just enough geoeia.

Turn back, he told himself. But his feet didn't listen. Instead, his arm lifted, and before he knew what he was doing, his hand was hovering over her shoulder. She didn't see; her face was downcast. He could have pulled away, and she would have been none the wiser. But he didn't.

She was hurting. He could feel the white sparks of pain crackling in the space between their skin. Deep, like a gash in her soul. He didn't know how she still managed to stand, how it didn't topple her over.

It reminded him of the day Ilena had learned her husband had died in the arena. How she'd curled up in a ball on the floor beside the bed, unable to climb onto the mattress. *There's a hole in my chest.* That's what she'd told them. And Madoc had prayed for Geoxus to fill it, the way he'd prayed for help and Cassia had found him on the temple steps.

Now he felt that same hole inside Ash. It pulled at him, and it didn't matter if she was a killer or an enemy or if they were at war. He'd lost Cassia, but this one, small thing he could fix.

Geoxus, he prayed, as he'd prayed all those years ago for Ilena. *Please help her.*

"What are you . . ." Ash sucked in a hard breath.

His gaze snapped to hers. He didn't move. She didn't move. His hand still hovered over her shoulder, fingers curled slightly like he could grab her grief and pull it out of her. Cool breath stretched his lungs. He felt lighter. *Stronger.* Geoxus had heard him—Madoc could feel his power gliding over his muscles. *More*, it whispered, and he complied. His fingers inched closer, hungry now for her grief, for her pain, for the hate that she must have felt for all of Deimos . . .

"Madoc."

He drew back sharply, his hand falling like lead to his side. They were both breathing hard, shoulders heaving. He didn't know what had come over him; this didn't feel like any prayer Geoxus had answered before. Her pain had felt purer than any emotion he'd sensed in the past. It was clear, and potent, and he'd been compelled to do something to ease it.

Something was definitely wrong with him.

"What was that? What did you do?" she snapped.

He needed to get away from her before he made things worse.

"Wait," said Ash as he turned.

He hesitated.

"How . . ." She gave a startled laugh. "How did you do that? I feel . . . different." He turned back to find her shaking her head. "Those guards. You did something to them. They were taking me, but you changed their minds. You made them leave." She heaved out a breath; even her uncertainty buzzed in his veins.

He looked down at his hand, the one that had hovered over Ash's shoulder, as if expecting to see some kind of mark, but there was none.

"I asked for help," he said.

"From who?"

He swallowed, the taste of her pain still fresh on his tongue, and glanced to the stones in the walls around them. "Who else?"

"Your god?" She scoffed. "You asked Geoxus to help me, an enemy gladiator, and he listened? I don't think so."

Panic raced up his spine. He'd felt Geoxus's strength working through him, just as he had all those years ago with Ilena. It couldn't have been anything else.

"What *are* you?" she asked. It took him a moment to register that the light in her eyes wasn't fear but wonder. "You don't use geoeia like an Earth Divine. You don't fight like a gladiator. Are you even Deiman?"

"Of course I am," he said.

"Your gift isn't a Deiman gift."

It wasn't a gift at all, except when he and Elias were stealing bread or fighting. It was pigstock geoeia, some strange manifestation of the Father God's power, but that didn't explain what he'd just done. He wished now that someone could tell him what was wrong with him, but only his family knew of his intuition. He'd never seen a healer for it—Ilena had made it clear that talking about it would put him in danger. When you were Undivine, people saw you as one thing only—pigstock—and acting as if you were anything else made those with real power very upset.

Still, he bristled. Ash called him out as easily as his family, though she'd known him less than a day. "There's sand everywhere. Tiny pieces of gravel you can't even see. I used geoeia."

He wished the arena would fall in on them both, ending this quickly.

"Gravel didn't change the minds of those soldiers, or make me . . ." Her gaze lifted to his, then flicked away. "You used something else. Air energy? Are you from Lakhu?"

"No. I'm not. And no, I didn't." She wanted to argue like children? Fine. He had four siblings. He could do this all day.

"Then do it again," she taunted. "Show me your geoeia."

His cheeks flamed. Warning bells began to ring in his mind. He couldn't risk another prayer now. She had a point—why would Geoxus want him to help their competition?

What if she was right and it wasn't Geoxus answering his prayers at all?

"Sorry. I don't perform on command."

She snorted. "Isn't that why we're here? Because we perform on command?"

He did not like where this was going.

A frown tugged at the corner of her lips. "It's against the rules of war for a god to use another country's Divine."

Doubt tingled at the base of Madoc's brain. Geoxus had never seen Madoc fight before he'd been chosen for the Honored Eight. Even when they'd stood face-to-face, he couldn't see Petros's lies, or that Madoc didn't have geoeia.

Madoc shook the thoughts from his mind.

He needed to laugh. To regain the upper hand.

Instead he stood stone still, speechless, feeling the blood drain from his face.

She moved closer. His back came flush against the wall, but she did not stop her approach. She didn't just look like a god—she was one. Proud and terrifying and pulsing with power.

It was no good lying now. She knew he didn't have geoeia. Maybe she hadn't pieced together the rest yet, but she would soon enough. He was done. He and Elias needed to break Cassia out of Petros's villa and get as far away from Crixion as possible.

Move.

He couldn't. He was captured by her curiosity. The fear of what she would say next.

"Ash? Ash!" A woman came careening down the tunnel. She was tall and broad and bore a strong resemblance to one of the champions Madoc had seen with Ash yesterday.

When she saw them, she stopped.

Ash took a quick step back.

"Please," Madoc whispered. *You can't tell anyone.* He couldn't speak the words aloud.

"We'll talk again soon," she said quietly.

It was as much a threat as a promise. Who would she tell what had happened here? Ignitus? Geoxus? Madoc spun away, walking quickly. He left the warped corridor and entered the long hall exiting the arena. He shoved his way through the crowd outside and headed straight into the waiting carriage, where he told his family the Kulan girl was with her people, and then stared out the window, hoping they couldn't sense his panic.

Ash had him by the throat. How long before Geoxus learned the truth about him? If he ran, he would be hunted and punished for lying to his god. Cassia would never be free. Elias would be charged with helping him. Ilena, Danon, and Ava would all be in danger.

We'll talk again soon.

What did she want? He needed to figure out the price of this secret, and pay, whatever the cost. His family—his *life*—depended on it.

What are you?

He was Deiman. A good Deiman, whose prayers were answered by his god. But as much as he told himself this, he knew what had happened in the hallway with Ash had been different. More intense than it ever had been in the past. When he'd asked for help for Ilena, it hadn't been like this. When he'd made requests of others, they hadn't reacted like those guards.

A quake started at the base of his spine, traveling through his clenched muscles.

If his ability to sense others' fear and pain, to draw it out of them like poison, was not pigstock geoeia, and not the work of his god, then how did he do it?

What was he?

TEN

ASH

ASH GOT TWO gold bricks for winning against Rook.

She stuffed the money into the corner of her room and threw up on the balcony.

The day after, Ignitus was occupied with his other champions, so Tor told the Kulan guards watching them that he and Ash were running drills. They cloistered themselves into the long, narrow training room below Ignitus's wing of the palace, and Taro and Spark snuck in to join them. There, with as much privacy as Ignitus ever gave, they mourned Rook.

And Char. Ash hadn't been allowed to truly mourn her mother.

On the stone floor of the training room, Spark lit three candles. Traditionally, Kulan dead were honored by letting fire reclaim their corpses—once souls had left, their physical bodies were no longer fireproof. But this was as close to a memorial as they could get for Char, Rook, and Lynx, even if Ignitus could be watching. He wouldn't take this from them too.

Taro took Lynx's candle. Tor had Rook's. Ash lifted her mother's candle.

Ash's whole body felt filled with the stones of Deimos. She was exhausted to her bones and she could still feel Rook's blood on her skin, though she had bathed twice. But her grief was . . . softer, thanks to Madoc. Like leather worked from new and stiff to used and supple.

So when she looked at Tor and saw the raw anguish on his tear-soaked face, she felt a tight pull of guilt in her belly. She hadn't told him what had happened in the tunnel, and her excuse to Taro had been that Madoc had shown her the way out of the arena, that was all. Ash should just tell Ignitus, let him call out his god-brother for the unforgivable act of using another god's gladiator in a war. Ignitus would be pleased at the chance to shame his brother, and he'd adore Ash for giving him that ammunition.

But what would Geoxus do to Madoc—and could Ash live with being responsible for it? She was already responsible for Rook's death.

A violent sob tried to claw its way out of her throat. She fought it down, fist to her mouth.

If she hadn't tried to save Char, if she hadn't interfered in that fight and caused this war, then Rook would have been in Igna when Lynx died. He would still have been grief-stricken, but he wouldn't have gotten himself killed trying to murder Ignitus.

Guilt was an even darker abyss than loneliness, one Ash wasn't sure she would survive falling into.

"He was right, you know," Tor said suddenly.

Ash stiffened. It was Taro who prodded, "Rook?"

Tor nodded and jutted his chin at the flames, a reminder that Ignitus could be watching.

"About what we owe to Char," Tor said. The look he gave Ash was full of such intent that the sob she had been holding down broke free. "We owe it to him now too."

What they owed to Char—pursuing the lead that could bring down Ignitus.

Ash's brows pinched. Tor had wanted her to be cautious, to focus on immediate survival, not on long-term goals. But Rook's death was a bitter reminder that they had no control over their lives. At any moment, Ignitus could snap his fingers and break them apart.

"You want to—" She had to speak carefully until they had finished this ceremony for Char, Rook, and Lynx. "You want to keep pursuing our lead? But Stavos is missing." Ash had told Tor already, but she said it again.

"Everyone seems to think he's fallen ill," Taro offered, "and is too ashamed to make it public. Half a dozen Deiman gladiators have died of a similar plague over the past few years. People are already starting to call it the *champions' pox*."

"What are the symptoms?" Spark asked. "How does it only affect gladiators?"

"Geoxus's gossiping servants didn't say," said Taro. "If you ask me, it doesn't sound like a disease at all—it sounds like a convenient way to cover up the fact that Geoxus got fed up with some of his top gladiators and just killed them."

Ash chewed her lip. She couldn't deny that she was glad Stavos was gone, for however long. She hoped Geoxus truly had killed him.

But the facts they had were: Stavos and other top fighters were gone. Ignitus's weakness was no closer to revealing itself. A squabble among Ignitus, Geoxus, Aera, and Biotus was still undetermined.

And now Madoc. He had clearly been planted in this war by a different god—it was impossible that he wasn't involved in the brewing conflict between Ignitus, Geoxus, Aera, and Biotus, the one Hydra had refused to get involved with. What energeia did he have? Aereia, maybe? Ash's chest had felt lighter, thanks to him. Whatever it was, Madoc could even be responsible for the disappearing Deiman gladiators, offing them to make room for spies like himself.

That sort of ruthlessness didn't fit with the man who had lightened Ash's grief. She barely remembered anything after Rook died except a resurgence of the agony she'd felt when Char had died in front of her. Then, a bright spot in the darkness: Madoc.

"We'll figure it out." Tor put his hand on Ash's knee. "I see your mind working, Ash. *We* will figure it out, together. No more losses." His lips curled in on themselves, fresh tears welling.

Ash put her hand over Tor's. The sight of him, broken, stoked the agony in her heart. The agony that Madoc had taken away.

The real reason she hadn't spoken of what had happened with Madoc was that she was grateful to him. If he was involved in the lies and danger surrounding Ignitus's weakness, she knew that whatever he had done to alleviate her pain had likely been a trick to distract her, ease her into trusting him. But a small, bruised part of her didn't care.

He had let her breathe again.

She would find out what Madoc's role in all this was—and then she would tell Tor, if she needed to.

"No more losses," Ash assured Tor, because she needed to tell herself too.

No more losses. No more guilt. She had caused this war—she would make sure everyone else she loved came through it alive.

"Char Nikau," Spark said, pulling the focus back to the memorial. "Rook and Lynx Akela."

"Find your warmth," they said in unison, and snuffed the candle flames into darkness.

The first round of fights ended four days after the welcoming ceremony, once all Ignitus's champions had arrived and gotten a chance to fight. To mark the end of the initial matches as well as the first week of the war, Geoxus held a ball on one of his palace's outdoor terraces.

A long sheet of white and gray marble unfolded from towering doors, with the Nien River and the whole of Crixion spread out three stories below. Columns lined the area despite the lack of a roof, and in the fading sunlight, it took Ash a beat to realize that each column was a mosaic of gladiators. All Deimans—no, actually, that one off to the right was clearly a Kulan, a white flame in his outstretched hand as a Deiman gladiator planted a sandaled foot on his chest in victory.

Geoxus was not subtle. Then again, the gods rarely were.

The Kulan guards who had escorted Tor and Ash sank into the shadows by the door. Phosphorescent stones and mirrors lit the terrace as the sun set. Musicians warmed up in the corner, flutes shrieking and strings plucking, and a banquet table sat opposite them, piled with fragrant smoked pork, dried dates, peeled citrus fruits, and casks of wine. The center of the terrace floor was bare, clearly for dancing later on. For now, the other guests picked at the banquet, everyone wearing opulent togas and gilded gowns, making it difficult to guess who was a fighter and who was not. Ash assumed some of these people had to be the remaining Deiman champions, or other members of Deiman society.

She didn't see Madoc yet.

That realization, and the corresponding pull of disappointment, itched at Ash's mind. She told herself that she only cared whether he was here or not because of the questions she planned to ask him. She had seen the way he'd looked at her during their initial fight, and after Rook's death. She could use that. Fluster him. Lower his defenses.

And milk out the truth about his energeia.

"Remember the plan," Tor whispered to her. He took her arm, the two of them making a slow, circuitous route around the perimeter of the terrace.

Ash bowed her head toward him. They had plotted their own next step just that morning. "We link Rook's attack to Stavos's disappearance and Char being poisoned, and we push Ignitus for more information."

"Subtly," Tor prodded.

Ash lifted an eyebrow. "You don't think I'll be subtle?"

"You like to test the limits. But now is not the time for recklessness."

Impossibly, Ash felt herself smile. "Where's the fun in that?"

Tor gave her a surprised grin, rippling the sunburst painted on his cheek. Ignitus had left explicit instructions regarding their dress for this party. Tor wore blue. The fabric started pale where it hung off one shoulder and bunched at the opposite hip before fading into a long skirt of deepest navy around his feet. Silver sunbursts covered his bare skin, and Taro had spent the better part of the day weaving silver thread into his thick black hair. He looked like one of Ignitus's brightest flames, a streak of star fire or the mesmerizing core at the center of every fire.

"It's good to see you smile," Tor said. "And I must say, Char would be both brokenhearted and proud to see how grown-up you look."

Ash's face stilled. Self-consciously, she smoothed her skirt.

Ignitus had requested that she wear red. This gown was similar to the dancing costume she wore when she played the fire god. The skirt hung low on her hips, held in place by a gold band set with garnets, while the fabric that fell to her sandaled feet was a few layers of sheer crimson. The top cut deep across her collarbone and stopped in a point above her navel, more crimson set with gold-rimmed garnets. The straps holding it in place drooped around her shoulders, all else bare, showing off the gold bangles on her wrists, the thick gold necklace that rose and fell with each breath, her unbound waves of black curls, the way her skin glistened, the gold paint on her lips and the kohl around her eyes.

Tor was the hottest part of a flame, but Ash was the wildest. The red, pulsing fingers that sought and destroyed, grabbed and burned.

The moment Ash had put on this outfit, she'd looked at herself in the mirror and known she could get whatever information she wanted out of Madoc with one sway of her hips. She could draw a confession out of Ignitus with a spin and an arch. She would get to dance tonight, and the hum of the music mixed with the sway of other people would fill up the void of loneliness that Ash constantly teetered on the edge of.

She felt more herself in this gown than she had since Char died.

As they continued to walk, Ash turned away from Tor, her eyes skimming over the terrace. She spotted Geoxus at the edge on a cushioned chair. Ignitus stood at the banquet table with his two other remaining champions: Brand, a year older than Ash but five times as cocky; and Raya, who had traveled here from a fight in Lakhu with her own lavish entourage.

Brand wore orange; Raya wore white. Ash saw the connection between the outfits when she looked back at Ignitus, who was dressed in a flowing tunic of all those colors. Blue. Red. Orange. White. The kaleidoscopic hues all found in fire.

Suddenly, her red gown felt more restrictive.

She and Tor were nearly to the banquet table. Tor lifted his hand. "Great Ignitus," he called.

Ignitus spotted them and turned his back on Brand and Raya.

"Steady, love," Tor whispered.

The crowd continued their conversations, and that kept tempo with Ash's vibrating pulse. She stopped before Ignitus and forced herself to look into his glittering eyes.

It was the first time she had seen her god since Rook's death. That realization chased away her all-too-feeble confidence, and her mind blurred with the memory of Ignitus's hands splayed before him. The fire blasting out. Rook falling, choking in her arms.

"What a tragedy your fight was, Ash," Ignitus said. She was shaking. "I hope you two have had time to collect yourselves? I know you were friendly with Rook Akela."

Ash had to wrestle the disgust off her face. "Yes. We were *friendly* with him."

Tor squeezed her arm. "His betrayal shocked us, Great Ignitus."

Ignitus kept his gaze on Ash. "You are angry," he guessed. "Angry that he failed to kill me?"

Ash gawked and Tor stiffened next to her.

The musicians' volume rose. Couples took to the floor, whirls of colorful fabrics and jewelry that glinted in the phosphorescent stone light. Deiman music mimicked its god in its force; even the flutes assaulted Ash's ears, and the moves she saw were all hard stomps and cutting lurches. The instruments caught up with each other and formed a rollicking melody that made Ash's heart crackle like a forest fire. Her soul ached to sweep onto the floor, to join the dancers, to feel like a part of something, if only for a single song.

"Great Ignitus," Tor started, "Ash is merely—"

"Angry," she said. She stepped out of Tor's arm, closer to Ignitus. "Yes, I'm angry."

She could feel tension palpitating off Tor in waves. She could feel the heat on Ignitus's skin rise, in his eye a gleam of challenge, waiting for her to make a fatal mistake.

"I'm angry at Rook's betrayal. He turned his back on us all when he attacked you. I'm angry that I was unable to stop him before he got so far. And I'm most angry, Great Ignitus"—Ash dropped her voice low beside the party hum—"that this seems to be a pattern. First my mother is poisoned. Then Stavos threatens you. Now something drove Rook to attack you."

Ignitus jerked back. Ash reveled in the surprise that graced his fine features. "I told you," he said, his voice wavering slightly, "there is no threat."

"It cannot be a coincidence." She was pushing the god of fire—she knew how dangerous a line she was walking, but she was trapped on a stampeding horse of her own driving, helpless not to ride it as far as she could. "We are your gladiators. If something's going on, we should fight for you. Let us help."

"My job is to protect Kula," Ignitus said, "which includes protecting myself. I can't have a gladiator involved again—"

"Again?" The word tasted sweeter than the finest honey.

Ignitus glowered at her. "This is the last you will speak of this."

He turned, cutting a path through the dancing crowd without another word.

Tor swung in front of Ash to stop her from running after Ignitus. A dozen questions waited in her throat, things she wanted to scream, but she could only look up at Tor and say, "A gladiator? A gladiator is part of what he fears?"

Tor shook his head, fingers pinched on her arm in thought. His eyes went to the front doors. "Taro and Spark just arrived. I'll get them, and we'll discuss it. Wait here."

He left, shaking out his hands as he walked away. Ash felt the same energy coursing through her body—she wanted to run. She wanted to fight. She wanted to *move*, if only to surge blood into her limbs and out of her chest, where it felt like all of it had gathered, hot and heavy.

A gladiator was part of what Ignitus feared. Could it be a gladiator and not the other gods that was a threat to Ignitus? How so?

Ash's mind seized.

If Stavos's threat had legitimately worried Ignitus, and a gladiator was who he feared . . . then had *Ignitus* gotten rid of Stavos?

She imagined Stavos burning to death in Ignitus's flames and she trembled with an unfamiliar burst of satisfaction. The image felt like justice.

With a shake of her head, she pushed the idea away. She needed more details. She needed fact, truth, no more of this guessing and patchy information.

Tor intercepted Taro and Spark by the terrace's main doors. Not far from them, a movement drew Ash's eye—and her body flared with heat though there was no igneia anywhere nearby.

Madoc was here now. He stood with a boy about his age, and they whispered to each other, pointing at a girl a few paces to their left. She was with a man who was clearly a government official. Madoc noticeably tensed when the man grabbed the girl's arm and barked an order. The girl gave a look that would make the fieriest Kulan proud and reluctantly poured the man a drink.

Madoc's jaw worked, and he shook his head—in doing so, his eyes landed on Ash.

Ash froze, her hands at her sides. For a moment, the music played, and the crowd danced, and Madoc just stared at her, expressionless, calm.

Before she could take a step, he started walking toward her.

The other boy hissed his name, but Madoc ignored him.

He wore ceremonial armor, silver-plated Deiman metal over a pleated leather skirt with sandals that wrapped high up his muscled legs. The breastplate left his arms bare, showing how the muscles bunched as he clenched his hands, and Ash had an odd, disconnected thought: *If he didn't train with gladiators, how did his arms get so big?*

Burn it all, what was wrong with her?

Madoc stopped before Ash. His mouth opened. Shut again.

Ash regained herself. She was in control of their interactions from now on. She had gotten information out of Ignitus; she would find out how Madoc's energeia was part of this.

Ash folded her arms under her chest. "I was just on my way over to you."

It threw him off. Madoc cleared his throat. "What?"

She tipped her head, looking up through her lashes with a soft grin. "You helped me after my fight. Not many gladiators would have done that." She touched his breastplate, pretending to clear away a streak. "I never got a chance to thank you."

Before he could protest or explain his true reason for coming over, Ash hooked her fingers in the collar of his armor and pulled him onto the dance floor. He wobbled after her, shock making him look years younger and sweet, and Ash had to fight down a laugh..

With the reluctance she had seen from him during their fight and his eagerness to help her after Rook's death, she again found it difficult to believe that this man was part of a conspiracy of gods. He was so . . . genuine.

Ash stopped. Madoc's surprise made him stumble, and he steadied himself on her hips. Before he could jerk away, she planted her hands over his, keeping his palms against the curve of her hips.

His fingers were callused but gentle, and she remembered the scars on his back and how the golden hue on his arms glimmered across the rest of his skin. He smelled distractingly of honey and mint, the scent fluttering effervescence down Ash's spine. The sensation wound tighter when she settled her hands around his neck and looked up into his dark eyes.

Pressure built in her chest, something wild and terrifying.

"We shouldn't do this," Madoc said, but he didn't pull away.

The hair on the back of his neck was short and slick with the oils that styled it, and Ash found herself absently stroking her thumb on the warm, smooth skin below his ear. She felt his chest constrict against her, a sudden intake of breath that shifted his breastplate.

"You might not be able to dance," Ash managed, "but I can. I was a fire dancer before I was a gladiator."

Madoc frowned. "I thought Stavos made that up."

His name still plucked at Ash's grief. The pain must have been clear on her face, because Madoc cocked his head questioningly.

She didn't want to talk about Stavos.

The music built; couples twirled past. After tonight, when Ash was back in her room again, loneliness waited. But here, she could be united with these strangers, linked to something warm and strong.

What other chance would she have to dance during this war?

Indulgently, Ash exhaled, eyelids fluttering. She let the music slide across her body. There were more drums than in Kulan songs, less grace from note to note, but she improvised: she arched away from Madoc, swung back. She spun in a full circle without leaving his arms, sliding her body across the front of his armor.

Madoc hardly moved, but something about that felt like part of their dance. He was a stone; she was a flame. He was stillness; she was motion.

When she curved against him, pulling herself up by his neck as the melody rose, she got caught there. His mouth was cracked open, his breath bursting warm against her lips. The smallest moan escaped his throat. It struck a nerve deep in Ash's gut.

She had wanted the unity that dancing brought, a simple connection in a world where everything else was complicated lies.

She had gotten it. Gotten it, and more, stuck with barely a handbreadth between her face and Madoc's, his rough, warm hands splayed against the small of her back. Her heart rolled over, and she felt herself flushing a hot scarlet.

Madoc blinked quickly. "What I wanted to talk to you about—" He sounded in pain. He shook his head. "I mean—you don't need to thank me. I actually wanted to talk to you about that."

The way he looked at her changed. Was that fear?

Good, Ash told herself, but it felt anything but good.

Over Madoc's shoulder, she spotted Tor. He, Taro, and Spark scowled at her. Or scowled at Madoc?

She lowered herself, gently swaying now. "What could you want to talk to me about, Madoc?"

"About what happened in the arena hall, after your fight." He licked his lips, leaving a glossy trail. "That it will . . . get out."

He *was* afraid of her. He was afraid she would tell others about his lack of geoeia.

It should have made her feel powerful, to have leverage over an enemy champion. Ash could break him with a word. But disgust twisted her stomach, the same knot she felt whenever she had to bow to Ignitus. Lies, manipulation, coercion—she hated these games.

But she would win these games. Not murderous gods. Not attractive gladiator spies.

Ash stopped dancing, but she kept her hands on Madoc's neck. "I won't tell anyone," she said. His shoulders relaxed. "If you help me."

He squinted.

She made her face droop with something close to sorrow. It wasn't hard to fake. "I think my god is responsible for Stavos's disappearance. I think a larger threat is looming over this war."

To his credit, Madoc looked honestly confused. "What are you talking about?"

She leaned closer, hoping she looked the part of a scared girl. "I think my god is breaking our holiest of laws by murdering your country's gladiators. I can't say more." Ash sighed. "But I need proof. You can help me get a list of all the Deiman gladiators who have died of the plague that Stavos supposedly has. If they are all former victors against Kula, Ignitus may be to blame. If we can prove even that much, it may be enough to bring before Geoxus. He would be pleased, wouldn't he? If you help uncover his brother's treason."

Madoc gaped, momentarily shocked. The expression receded, slowly, into a small twitch of eagerness.

She had him.

But then he frowned. "You won't tell Geoxus or Ignitus about what happened at the arena and all you want is a list of sick gladiators? What's the catch?"

"No catch," Ash said. "I swear on my mother."

"Your mother." Madoc's eyes narrowed. "What does she think about you sneaking around behind the backs of gods?"

Ash's hands spasmed on Madoc's neck. She knew he felt her flinch, but she gave a small, dismissive shake of her head, as if his question hadn't gouged her heart. "She doesn't think anything of it. Stavos killed her."

Understanding slid over his face. "I forgot. . . . I'm sorry."

His sincerity stole her breath. Again. It was infuriating.

"I've missed something," Madoc continued. "If your god is involved with the disappearance of your mother's killer, shouldn't you be happy?"

Ash's small flash of victory turned against her. She fought not to gape at him; she fought not to rage about how Stavos deserved whatever fate Ignitus dealt him.

This wasn't the purpose of her coercion. She needed Madoc to believe her, or at least feel sorry for her.

Ash swallowed her fury. She had to tip her head back to look up at Madoc, and she thought there might be a small spark in his eyes now, curiosity overriding his wariness.

"I'm not trying to save my mother's killer," Ash said. "I'm trying to make sure that my god isn't breaking our holy laws. There's been too much of that happening lately."

Madoc stared at her for a long, silent moment. Finally, he sighed. "My sponsor." He nodded toward a man at the edge of the terrace. "Lucius is the best trainer in Deimos. He has a records room that his trainees can use. I'm sure there are scrolls that list things like sick gladiators in there. Would that be enough?"

Ash nodded and dropped her arms off his shoulders. Madoc wavered, then cocked his head.

"Now?"

"Yes, now." She waved at the people around them. "Lucius is here, isn't he? So his villa is empty. When will we have another chance?"

Madoc's face reddened. "Fine. We'll need a carriage to get there, though."

He pushed into the crowd. The girl he'd watched was still with the government official, but she was looking at Madoc; and the boy he'd been talking to stared as well. He waved at them both, a signal of *stay put* or *don't worry.*

Ash didn't let herself look for Tor, Taro, or Spark. They'd try to stop her.

But once she got Madoc alone, she knew she could get more out of him. Though he had beaten her in their fight, she wouldn't fear him once they were out in the city, surrounded by candle flames and fireplaces. She would play up her fearful ruse, how she wanted to stop Ignitus from holy treachery. She would even ask Madoc if he was working against Ignitus for one of the other gods and try to place herself as an ally for him.

Madoc could be the gladiator who Ignitus feared.

Ash hurried after him.

Madoc made a quick path across the terrace. Ash's eyes drifted beyond him—the Kulan guards were gone. Deiman guards stood at the main doors.

Would they let her pass, even with a Deiman champion?

They reached the entrance. Madoc started out into the hall, Ash just behind him.

A guard cut a hand over Ash's chest. "No Kulans are to leave."

Madoc drew back. A pause, and his face melted into a cocky smirk. "She's with me," he said, reaching up to twirl a lock of Ash's hair around his finger.

Her mind went utterly blank. She couldn't even play into the ruse.

The guard smiled slickly at Madoc. "Be quick about it."

Before anyone else could protest, Madoc grabbed Ash's hand and yanked her through the door. The moment they were in the hall, he dropped his hold on her, scraping his fingers on his thigh as though she'd burned him.

Her own hand sizzled and sparked. She fought the urge to wipe it off too.

"The stables are this way," Madoc said and started walking to the right.

Ash's eyes lifted. Madoc was the only other person in this towering hall. And they were going to the stables, to leave the palace.

She hadn't connected that part of what they were doing. A childish wish blossomed inside her, to just *run*.

Ash looked to the left, the empty hall stretching on, a beckoning hand she wanted so badly to reach out for. The temptation would be even worse once they were in a carriage, wheels clacking through silent, empty streets.

"Are you all right?"

She spun to Madoc. Behind his wariness, there was honest concern on his face.

"You haven't been a gladiator very long, have you?" Ash swallowed the waver in her voice.

Madoc resumed walking. Ash followed a step behind, so he had to turn slightly to see her.

"A few months," he said. "Why?"

"You're still . . ." Ash hesitated. Madoc glanced back, and she dropped her gaze. "A decent person."

He snorted. "If that were true, I wouldn't be here." He angled them down a set of stairs. "Elias and I started fighting to earn money. It sort of got away from us."

"Elias?"

"My brother—my attendant now, I guess."

Ash tipped her head. Was his brother part of whatever task Madoc had been sent to fulfill? "You were fighting. How? With your fists?"

She watched the muscles in Madoc's shoulders tense all the way up his neck. "It's complicated. We need money to get my sister released from servitude. The man who has her—" The words seemed to choke him, and he shook his head. "It was a mistake," he finished.

Confusion rendered Ash momentarily silent. That was Madoc's cover for being in this war? That he was trying to free his sister? It was such a simple, personal reason, and it had nothing to do with the actual war itself.

None of this information made anything about Madoc clearer.

They came to a door. Madoc pushed it open, depositing them in a wide yard lit by a high, round moon. The air hung heavy with sweet hay and dust, ripe with the first bitter twist of colder nights. To the left sat a grand marble-and-brick stable. Carriages and horses stuffed it now, a few stable hands rustling around, keeping their masters' transports ready for whenever they deigned to leave the ball. The gates of the stable yard sat open on the right, with two centurions standing guard, leaning on spears and idly chatting in the easy assignment.

There was igneia in the stables. Ash could see it flickering in lanterns. She breathed easier seeing it so much more available. Had Madoc noticed the flames?

"And you think this war will free your sister?" Ash managed. "Is she Earth Divine?"

Is she descended from another god, like you? Which god?

What are you really fighting for?

Madoc faced her, the palace at his back, the quiet stable yard feeling expansive around them. His eyes went hard with distrust. "Yes to both. Why?"

Ash matched his stiff-backed stance. She recognized that type of reaction. Many of the other fire dancers had looked at her like that whenever she'd slipped and said something against Ignitus, their features contorting with equal parts disgust that she'd spoken against their god and uncertainty that maybe they'd heard her wrong.

But Madoc's reaction wasn't in relation to his god. It was about his sister, and the difference made Ash's chest swell with the need to explain.

She bit her lips, which made his eyes drop to her mouth.

She hadn't meant to do that.

She *should* have meant to do that.

She shouldn't be worried about what he thought of her, but his eyes were dark and deep and he was standing so close, almost as close as they had been in the dance.

He was so flustering.

"I didn't mean to offend you," Ash said. "I know what it's like for someone you love to be trapped. Not knowing what the next day will bring for them. Forced to watch them suffer. It makes you feel so—"

"Helpless," Madoc finished, studying her.

Ash nodded. "Yes," she whispered, though she barely heard her own voice.

Behind her, the centurions at the gate shouted. "Halt! No beggars in Geoxus's palace!"

"Let me through!" a different voice cried. "I must—I must see—Father God, please—"

Ash whirled at the sound of a fist striking flesh. The centurions had closed together, blocking the open gate, while a lone figure struggled to pass them.

"Father—" The man coughed, gurgled. "Father God—"

Madoc lurched forward, squinting in the darkness. "No—Stavos? Stavos—let him through! He's one of Geoxus's champions!"

Madoc took off and Ash shot after him by instinct, sandals slapping the packed earth.

Her stomach roiled. Stavos was here?

They got to the gate as the centurions pulled apart. Stavos fell to the ground between them.

Blood and bruises covered his body, and each breath came with a quivering gasp, vibrating his ribs, his arms—and the three arrows sticking out of his back.

A knot twisted in Ash's gut. She had wanted Stavos to suffer, but she couldn't muster any satisfaction about this. Only nausea.

A lantern hung in the gate's archway over them, casting the barest light. She grabbed for some of the igneia and flared it into a ball in her hands, bringing brighter light to the ground.

The centurions gasped. One snapped, "Damn Kulans."

Madoc knelt and eased Stavos onto his side. "You, get help!" he shouted at a centurion. "Find him bandages, something!"

One of the guards bolted for the palace, the other for the guardhouse.

Ash moved the ball of fire closer. Her body ached as blood dripped from Stavos's lips. She wanted to pull the igneia from her hands into her heart, infuse herself with strength. That desire grew when Madoc looked up at her and she realized he was just as scared as she was.

If Madoc was part of the plot against Ignitus and the gladiator her god feared, how did he manage to fill his eyes with such raw, honest horror?

Ash balanced the fire in one hand as she dropped to her knees and grabbed Stavos's sweat-stained collar. Her resolve was fraying. If Madoc wasn't part of this, and Stavos was dying—she had no leads. She had nothing.

Her mother's murderer was here, bleeding out in front of her. He was dying at her feet, as she had wanted, as she had *ached* for.

It didn't feel like justice.

It felt like a frayed knot.

Ash bent closer to him, the light in her free hand stabbing into Stavos's bloodshot eyes, widening his pupils. "Did Ignitus do this to you?" she demanded.

Stavos coughed. His eyes spun in their sockets. “No, no, not—” He coughed, blood splattering Ash’s knees. “She took it. She took it from me. Stop—”

And as more centurions came from the palace in a swell of noise and light and party guests, Stavos seized and went limp on the ground.

ELEVEN

MADOC

STAVOS OF CRIXION was dead.

Madoc stared at the body, his gaze darting from the arrows protruding out of Stavos's broad back to the raised welts on his chest and face to his dull brown eyes, open and unblinking. The giant of a man who had threatened Madoc and taunted Ash only days before looked small now, incapable of the many victories he had accrued as a gladiator.

As the ground began to rumble, Madoc jolted upright. Stavos's blood was slick on his arms and hands, and the more Madoc tried to wipe it away, the more it spread, smearing crimson across the bottom of the white tunic that peeked out beneath his armor. It reminded him of the time Ava had spilled honey—by the end of the day it had somehow transferred to Ilena's hair, and Madoc's and Danon's clothes, and Cassia's and Elias's faces. The memory of that laughter was as foreign now as it was sharp, and Madoc hated himself for even thinking of it.

"Be still."

Madoc turned to find Ash staring at a white marble statue near the gate. The figure's chiseled form seemed to be twisting, the stone of his outstretched arms rippling, swelling, as if a hundred snakes were moving beneath stretched silk. The figure's face became distorted, the jaw spreading while the mouth opened in a silent scream. The waist grew thick. The legs divided to make a monster with four sandaled feet.

Madoc fought the urge to scramble back; he'd never seen anything so horrible or exhilarating. His heart pounded with new terror. Around him, the guards had dropped to their knees; in fear or reverence, Madoc didn't know.

Then, before he could draw another breath, the statue split, and Geoxus shed his marble skin, leaving the figure behind him as flawless as it had been moments before.

Madoc gaped. He'd heard that Geoxus could move through stones, but he'd never seen it for himself until tonight. He nearly forgot Stavos lying dead on the ground until the Father God veered toward Madoc and Ash, his black toga rippling in his wake.

"How did this happen?" Geoxus roared, his hands open with lethal intent, the thunder in his voice making the stone wall around the gate vibrate. He crouched beside the body. Behind him, a sea of guards rushed from the palace, the clap of metal and leather armor filling the night. They surrounded the area, blocking the guests who had come to see what had happened.

Madoc trembled, glancing back to the statue Geoxus had emerged from. The god of earth was every bit as powerful as the stories people told, and even though Madoc had had nothing to do with Stavos's death, he felt a sharp bite of shame, as if he should have somehow saved the gladiator, or tried harder to deter Ash from her odd mission.

But he'd wanted to help her. She knew something about the plague that had killed the gladiators before the war—a pox, Remi had told Elias. She wanted Deiman gladiator records—not to use against them in the arena, or so she said. Whatever her true motives were, their goals could align. If he could help her prove Ignitus had something to do with the gladiators who'd fallen ill, surely Geoxus would want to know. He might be able to win the Father God's favor and ask him to set Cassia free.

She was playing a dangerous game, and if nothing else, they had that in common.

He glanced in her direction and found her scowling through the line of soldiers now positioned between them and the body on the ground. He could feel the warmth coming from her, even more than the heat of her skin beneath his hands when they'd danced. Lit torches lined the perimeter walls, the paths, even the entrance to the stables. The phosphorescent stones from the palace did not extend to this area of the grounds—Geoxus must not have thought one of his brother's gladiators would venture so far from the party.

Or that one of his own would have led her here.

They needed to get their story straight before someone asked.

"Honorable Father God!" A centurion, his belt lined with black onyx to denote his high rank, knelt at Geoxus's feet. "Stavos was already wounded when he approached the gates. My centurions did not recognize him. If Madoc had not been here to identify—"

"Your centurions could not identify an honored son of Deimos?"

Geoxus bellowed, nearly knocking the centurion sideways with only the strength of his voice. "One who had been missing for *three days*?" Geoxus made a fist, and for one terrifying moment, Madoc thought he meant to pummel his own guard. Then his hand dropped, and the wrinkles around his eyes, which Ilena had claimed were from smiling too much, pinched with something close to regret. "His life was not meant to end this way."

Madoc's brows drew together. What would happen to Stavos now? Would he still be granted a champion's funeral, his body returned to the earth to become geoeia?

She took it from me.

Stavos's last words plagued Madoc's mind. He didn't know who Stavos could have meant. The warning just as easily might have been the ramblings of a man on the edge of death.

"Apologies, Honorable Geoxus," the centurion said quickly, his forehead now pressed to the ground. "I will find those who denied him entry to the palace and see that their punishment matches the crime."

A shiver crawled between Madoc's shoulder blades. If the centurions were put to death for failing to protect Stavos, what would happen to his actual killer? He didn't want to think of what that would mean for him and Ash, who had found Stavos in a place they had no right wandering off to by themselves.

A nearby guard narrowed his gaze to Ash's hands, fisted at her sides. It suddenly occurred to Madoc that Ash might not have wanted to see Lucius's records at all. She could have been trying to get him alone.

She might have done the same to Stavos before he'd been abducted.

Her curiosity about him might have been a lie—if he'd killed her mother, she had a clear enough reason to want him dead.

But she'd had an opportunity to kill him when they'd been talking, and she hadn't done it.

He couldn't get a clear feel of her emotions. The air was too charged with anxiety, all swirling about the cold void of Stavos's body.

"Who would dare harm one of my gladiators, a hero of Deimos?" Geoxus's voice suddenly fell away. His fingers rose to his temples, and his eyes fluttered closed. When he spoke again, it was no more than a strained whisper. "Where is my brother?"

"I'm here, *Honorable* Geoxus."

Madoc's teeth clenched at the sound of Ignitus's voice. Stavos had told Ash that Ignitus hadn't had anything to do with his murder, but how else could the gladiator's death have stayed hidden from the watchful eyes of Geoxus? Everything in this city was stone. Stavos had to have been kept in wood or water for Geoxus not to hear his pleas.

Why someone would go to such great extents to hide his murder, Madoc didn't know.

He turned to find Ignitus standing behind the centurions, leaning against the side of a marble fountain. People from the party gathered in his wake, some Deiman, some Kulan, all straining to get a look at what had garnered so much attention.

With a sigh, Ignitus pushed off the fountain, the V-cut collar of his tunic dipping down to his waist, leaving his smooth chest bare to the belt. As he sauntered toward his brother and the body, the torches along the perimeter wall throbbed with light and heat.

Madoc glanced again to Ash and found her gaze had dropped

sharply to the ground. She was afraid, and he didn't blame her. Her god had killed one of his own gladiators.

Cringing, Ignitus motioned to the body at Geoxus's feet. "It looks like one of your gladiators might be a bit ill. Is this the pox rumored to be going around?"

"You of all gods should know that it is dangerous to meddle in the rules of war, Ignitus." Geoxus's hands lowered, but as they did, the ground began to rumble, then quake, causing the fire god to stumble and catch himself just before falling. A scream from the crowd slapped off the walls as dozens of voices began talking at once. Sand shifted across the ground, stones from the path pushing out of place. The fountain Ignitus had been leaning against just moments before cracked, and the top half of the stone statue within fell into the water with a splash.

Madoc's pulse stumbled, and he widened his stance in attempt to stay upright. Half the crowd held fast, watching the show, while others shoved past them in an attempt to flee to the palace.

Ash gripped Madoc's arm to steady herself, her palm hot against his clammy skin.

"That was one of my most prized gladiators," Geoxus growled as half the crowd continued to race for safer ground.

"Then for your sake, brother, I hope you have a backup." Ignitus scowled at the ground, as if this would stop the earth from shaking.

Geoxus's lips curled back. His hand twitched, but Ignitus spread his fingers, and every torch from the wall to the palace suddenly went black, the only glow emanating from the blue flames that warped around his long body.

"Yes," the god of fire murmured as more screams erupted. "I can play these games too."

Madoc could hear Ash breathing beside him. Her hand slid down his forearm, the sharp heat of her skin centering him.

"The lights, Ignitus," growled Geoxus.

"Will you be nice?"

A beat passed. Ash gripped Madoc tighter, flooding warmth up his arm into his chest.

With one final groan from the perimeter wall, the ground stilled.

Light rose from darkness, revealing Ignitus, no longer wrapped in blue flames, his arms hanging loosely at his sides.

"I didn't do this, nor did any of my people. We know how to dispose of a body."

All that would be left was a smoldering pile of bones, Madoc realized grimly.

Ignitus's bright eyes shifted across the stable yard, his gaze turning Madoc back to what remained of the crowd from the party—a few pale patrons, the other champions snarling at each other from either side of the broken fountain, and two elegantly clad figures who had shoved through to the front.

Lucius and Petros.

Madoc's gut twisted.

He did not want to be seen here by his trainer—to give Lucius any reason to think he might have had something to do with this, or to question his position in the Honored Eight or the money he'd won by forfeit. Especially not after Petros had embarrassed him in front of Geoxus by claiming Madoc was his son.

"Why should I believe you?" Geoxus asked. "Stavos defeated your best champion in Kula. If anyone holds a grudge, it's you."

Beside Madoc, Ash stiffened. He remembered Stavos taunting Ash during their fight. Again, it occurred to him that she could have had something to do with his death. Ignitus might not be the only one holding a grudge.

"Even so," said Ignitus, "I would not risk losing this war over the life of some Deiman with a knack for throwing pebbles."

Geoxus flinched at Ignitus's casual dismissal of his fallen hero.

Madoc's gaze fell to Stavos—to his dead eyes and his bloated, pale-blue skin—and again felt the urge to clean the blood off himself.

Ignitus folded his hands gracefully behind his back, his sandaled feet barely making a sound as he circled Geoxus and the body. "If I were you, brother, I would question this man's competition. Who stood to gain the most from his fall?"

Ash's grip pumped around Madoc's hand—he hadn't realized they were still touching until that moment—and then she drew back, eyeing him with the same suspicion he'd turned her way.

"You think I . . ." Madoc scoffed. "I've been with you half the night."

Her wary stare was all the answer he needed, and as he looked across the grounds to the other Deiman champions now glaring his way, one word entered his mind: *advancement*.

Stavos was a trained champion. Everyone knew Madoc didn't have a chance at beating him in the arena. Since the forfeited match, speculation had flown that Madoc had poisoned him or delivered some threat that had made the other man run. While the city had cheered the dramatic twist, the gladiators at Lucius's villa had begun to whisper behind his back.

Madoc had kept his head down, focusing on his next chance to earn more coin. But now the missing gladiator could no longer be ignored. He had been found by Madoc, and died in his arms.

Madoc swallowed, his throat making an audible click as more stares turned in his direction. His gaze darted to Geoxus, only to find the Father God already looking his way, his stare as hard and gleaming as quartz. Madoc's bones quaked. He felt the bile climb up his throat.

"How very interesting," said Ignitus, raising one brow at his brother. "Your dead gladiator was discovered by the same man he was meant to battle." Ignitus hummed thoughtfully. "Tell me, Geoxus, how is it that Madoc found your fallen hero? It couldn't be possible that he strayed from the party to clean up his mess, would it?"

Madoc gritted his teeth.

"He wasn't alone," said the centurion captain, now rising to his feet. "He was with a Kulan gladiator."

Ignitus's pointed glare turned to Madoc and Ash, a wisp of blue flame licking over his skin as fury smoldered in his dark eyes.

Ash's sharp intake of breath sent a spike through Madoc's spine. Now everyone was staring at them. The gods. The centurions. The gladiators. Every servant and citizen who remained. Desperately, he searched for Elias, or even Cassia, but if they were here, he couldn't find them.

Fear pounded through his blood. Ash knew he didn't have geoeia—that he had something else. Would she tell the gods now in order to clear herself? If she did—if Geoxus found out Madoc was lying about who he was—all remaining trust in him would be invalidated. They would never believe he wasn't linked to Stavos's death.

Madoc straightened his back. "We had nothing to do with this. I was as surprised as anyone else when Stavos didn't show at our match."

She took it from me.

Who took what? If he knew, he could tell Geoxus. But without any other information he would come off as desperate, hopelessly trying to deflect the blame.

"Liar," snapped one of the Deiman gladiators—Raclin, a woman with a shaved head and a vicious scar through her lips. Her hate slid through the people between them, a stream bending insidiously around stones.

"I swear it," Madoc said. "I did nothing to that man."

"And the enemy you were keeping company with?" Now it was Jann who had spoken, a gladiator Madoc had seen in practice who could move walls with the flick of a finger. He was taller than the rest, and lanky, right down to the spindly braid over his right shoulder.

A centurion stepped closer, the glint of his knife catching Madoc's eye. Another guard joined him, this one stepping in front of Ash. Madoc was suddenly thrust back into the makeshift arena in South Gate, when Petros's bookie had called him a cheat, only now there was nowhere to run.

"Is it against the law for *enemies* to keep each other company here?" Ash asked, the low, sultry timbre of her voice catching Madoc by surprise. She slid closer, tucking herself beneath his arm. The heat of her skin pressed through the thick cloth of his tunic. Each curve of her body fit against him with scalding familiarity, his arm and chest adjusting to her without thought.

Her gaze met his through long, dark lashes, and his heart lodged in his throat.

"We have no such laws in our land," she said. She had the power to destroy him—to let the Father God crush him in front of a despising crowd—but she stayed by his side. There was honor in that, even if she did it only to further her own cause.

Madoc managed a curt nod.

"We do not," Ignitus agreed. "Though Deimos stinks of mud, there are some things it can still offer. Let's leave my gladiator out of this, shall we?"

Madoc looked away as Jann's and Raclin's sneers cut deeper.

"My apologies for leaving the party," said Madoc, searching for whatever words would free him from the Father God's questioning stare. "My loyalty remains to you despite certain . . . fascinations."

He could feel a bolt of heat cut through his side from Ash's fingertips. Lucius's glare intensified, and Madoc knew he would be punished for stepping out of line and upsetting their god, however unintentionally. Still, chuckles rose from the crowd, and Geoxus's gaze softened.

"Centurions," the Father God said, "I want to know what happened to Stavos as soon as possible. Have my servants prepare his body for burial. He'll receive a hero's service."

"Yes, Honorable Geoxus," said the captain.

The guard watching Madoc drew away, and the other centurions followed. Without another look, Geoxus swept back toward the palace, Ignitus trailing him after an amused smile in their direction.

Madoc had to force his hand to uncurl from Ash's shoulder. He sucked in a breath as he detached from her side, the air between them suddenly cold against his tingling skin.

"Thank you," he said.

She nodded.

"I didn't have anything to do with what happened to Stavos." He didn't know why he told her this, only that he needed her to know.

"I didn't either," she said quietly. Her lips pursed in a worried frown, and his eyes dipped to them, lingering too long.

"If it wasn't Ignitus, who do you think did it?" he asked.

She shook her head, brows pinched in worry.

"Ash." A large Kulan gladiator approached. His gaze remained on Madoc, as leveling as the god of earth's. Madoc stepped closer to Ash's side.

"Come," the gladiator said to her, his jaw tight. "You shouldn't be so far from our people."

Wariness worked through Madoc's bones. He didn't like the idea of her getting in trouble for being caught with him.

"Will you be all right?" he asked quietly as she took a step toward her fellow champion.

She hesitated, close enough to hide the brush of her wrist against the backs of his knuckles. Warmth streaked up his arm, knotting behind his collarbones. It was all the answer she could give, and it left a realization he was unprepared to face.

He didn't want her to go. Not just because he didn't want her to be punished, but because he liked talking with her. Being around her. Dancing with her.

This Kulan gladiator who was using him to gain access to Deimos's records.

He pushed the thought from his head as she left with the other gladiator. He had more important things to worry about, like getting enough coin to free Cassia, and not being accused of murdering his opponents to advance.

"A shame about Stavos." Petros came up beside him, his tone mildly disappointed, as if he were talking about a change in the weather. "Though, I admit, he was never my pick to win."

Madoc's disgust was pushed aside as Cassia hurried through the crowd behind his father, her servant's gown clinging tightly to her ribs. Madoc's gaze darted from her warning stare to the edge of a bruise on her shoulder, which she quickly hid beneath her sleeve.

He was going to kill Petros. But he couldn't do it here.

It took all his focus to steady his voice. "I'd guess that meant you'd chosen me, but we both know that isn't true."

"Indeed," said Petros. "You couldn't beat any of these brutes." His grin filled Madoc with cold dread, the same sickening feeling of defeat he'd encountered the day his father had turned him out. "Not without help, anyway."

A buzzing filled Madoc's ears.

"Someone did this to help me?" he asked.

She took it from me. He didn't know anyone was capable of scaring the great Stavos, but there had definitely been fear in the man's eyes.

Petros gave a small shrug, and it was enough to make Madoc feel as if the ground beneath his feet was shaking once again.

"Did you have something to do . . . ?" He couldn't finish. He didn't want to know. He wasn't certain he'd believe Petros even if he admitted to the act—all Petros seemed to do was lie.

But if Petros had had something to do with Stavos's death, the Father God had to be told. Geoxus would never support this. He'd loved Stavos.

Why was the Father God blind when it came to Petros?

Elias's words in the arena corridor scratched to the surface of his mind.

"Enough of these games." Madoc moved close enough that those who passed couldn't hear. "I have a thousand gold coins for Cassia's indenture. It's yours if you give her back."

"*Madoc*," Cassia hissed, but Petros silenced her with a raised hand.

"Quiet," he reminded her. "Or we'll have to use the shackles again, won't we?" When she dropped her chin, he smiled at Madoc. "I believe our price was fifteen hundred gold coins."

Madoc mirrored Petros's confidence, hiding the hate searing through him. "I thought the price went down when you lied to Geoxus about my impressive geoeia. I could expose you at any time, *Father*."

"You could try. But the truth comes with a heavy cost." Petros laid a hand on Madoc's shoulder, bringing an involuntary flinch. A pocket of memories broke free—Petros's fist against his jaw, the whip against his back. *Power waits inside you. If you won't set it free, I will.*

Madoc faltered. His only leverage was the truth, and that would condemn them all.

"Let her go," Madoc said, forcing his shoulders back. He wasn't a child anymore. He didn't have to answer to his father. He didn't have to bend to his demands.

Around them, patrons headed for the palace, observing the damage done by the gods. Centurions were standing by, gladiators from both sides close. Too many people. Too much power.

Petros's brows lifted, a strange light in his gaze. "Come now, Madoc. Is that all you've got?" Behind him, Cassia leaned closer, her brows drawn as she strained to listen.

Madoc's thoughts shifted to the guards who had taken Ash, to the way they had bent to his wishes with only a simple request. If he could do that now, he could end this. Get Cassia back. Then, once she was safe, he could make a pitiful showing in the arena to get himself out of this war, and humiliate his father in the process.

He shook his head, trying to clear it. Trying to remember what he'd said to the guards to make them leave Ash alone, but all he could remember was her fighting.

Her pain, sliding over his skin.

The rush in his blood when he'd taken it away.

The crowd around them seemed to slip away as a cool breath filled his lungs. A quiet rustle filled his ears, a whisper of wind from far off.

"Let her go," Madoc said again.

Petros's brows lifted, though his gaze grew unfocused. "That's a good idea," he said quietly. "I could let her go. . . ."

Madoc was reeling. This strange power was working; Petros never would bend otherwise. Ash was right. Madoc was different. Not Earth Divine like his father, but something else.

More like his mother, maybe. Petros had always said she was pigstock, too, but he was a liar. Madoc could be like her.

"Now," Madoc said. "Tonight."

"Tonight . . . ," Petros began, but just as he opened his mouth to say more, Cassia jerked behind him, drawing Madoc's gaze to the soldiers who heaved Stavos's body off the ground and lifted him to their shoulders.

The breath in Madoc's lungs deflated.

Petros blinked.

Panic shot through Madoc as whatever connection they'd formed severed. He tried again to concentrate, to draw his father's attention, but Petros was staring at him with new clarity, amusement rounding his cheeks.

"No, tonight won't do," Petros said. "What am I saying? We have too much work to accomplish before then."

"We can do whatever you like after you let Cassia go." Madoc's gaze flicked to two centurions now watching them.

"That's no way to do business, son," said Petros. "When you have what someone wants, you can't give it away."

Madoc felt whatever hope he'd grasped moments ago slipping through his fingers. The strange power he'd sought to use was gone now. He could no more control Petros's mind than move the rocks beneath their feet.

His father tilted his head toward the palace, and they began to walk, Cassia a few steps behind. "I need an heir, Madoc. I've built an empire in this city, and I need someone worthy to leave it to."

Madoc wondered if it was too much to hope that Petros was dying. "You want me to take over your legacy." That wasn't possible. Petros would never give it up so easily.

"Of course not," said his father. "But it's what you want, isn't it? To get out of the stonemasons' quarter? To have a home with servants to attend to your every need? *Power.* It's what everyone wants."

Madoc wanted Cassia. That was all he would ever want from Petros.

His father turned to him before they reentered the palace, resting a hand as deadly as Stavos's hammer on Madoc's shoulder.

"Win this war, and the Metaxa girl is yours to do with what you will. I'll name you my heir. You'll have whatever you like."

It hit him with the force of a punch. *Win this war.* Petros said this like it was easy. Like it didn't involve defeating two experienced Deiman champions, and then facing—*killing*—a Kulan gladiator, equally deadly if not deadlier, in an arena in front of thousands of people.

His mind flashed to Ash—would he be matched against her?

"If I can't?" Madoc could barely choke out the words. He didn't look back at Stavos. He didn't have to—the dead man's blood was still smeared on his hands and clothes.

Petros stepped closer.

"I'll sand Cassia's slender hands to the bones. And then I'll find her brother, *Elias*, yes? And Danon. And little Ava. I won't touch their mouthy little mother. I'll let her wait, alone, for you to tell her how you couldn't save her family. How you let them die, one by one."

Madoc couldn't move. Too late, he remembered his determination to regain the upper hand over his father. He thought of the soldiers in the hall outside the lesser arena, but it seemed impossible now that he had persuaded them to leave, or pulled any of Ash's pain from her body. Whatever strange power had afflicted him was gone. He was weak. A shell. Nothing.

"Why are you doing this?" he breathed. "Why now? Why me?"

But Madoc already knew. His only value to Petros was in his victory—the esteem the house of Aurelius would boast with Madoc's name. Now that Petros knew he was a fighter, he expected him to win, and Petros would ensure that victory by holding the only things Madoc loved beneath the point of a knife.

"We have a deal," Petros said. No other answer was necessary.

With a hearty pat on the back, he left Madoc outside the entrance of the palace.

Cassia closed in on him instantly.

"What was that about?" she demanded.

"I . . ."

Elias darted out of the crowd entering the palace. "Did that Kulan kill Stavos?" he whispered, loud enough for the line of guards behind them to hear.

"Quiet," Madoc cautioned. "No. We found him with three arrows in his back." He focused on Cassia, his gaze dipping again to the hidden bruise on her shoulder. "Are you all right? What has Petros done?"

Cassia dismissed his words with a wave of her hand. "What did you say to him?" Her tension combined with Elias's, prickling over Madoc's skin. "You threatened him. You scared him, didn't you? That's why he looked like he might keel over."

Madoc opened his mouth, but the words stayed trapped in his throat. Petros's threat was still ringing in his ears. *Win this war, and the Metaxa girl is yours.*

If he couldn't win, the entire family would die.

"What did you say? Did you tell him we'd pay him what we have?" Elias asked.

"I didn't, I mean, I did . . ." *I'll sand Cassia's slender hands to the bones.* He pressed his thumbs to his temples. He couldn't tell them what had happened. Not now—here, in this palace surrounded by guards who reported to Geoxus. If questioned by the Father God, Petros would surely refute him. Geoxus had already made it clear where he placed his trust. If Madoc went to the god of earth for help, he'd have to admit that he was Undivine, and what would Geoxus do then?

He needed to think.

"We should go inside," he said. "We look suspicious standing out here."

"You looked suspicious sneaking off with a Kulan gladiator," Elias countered. He jabbed Madoc's shoulder. "What's going on? What aren't you saying?"

Petros will kill you if I don't win this war.

Panic and hate gripped his throat. He knew what would happen if he told Elias. His brother would want them to run, and he wouldn't be wrong. But centurions would hunt them. Petros's guards would come for Ilena, and Danon, and Ava.

"It was nothing," Madoc said. "Petros drank too much, that's all. Half this party already thinks I had something to do with Stavos's death; let's not give them reason to question me more."

"You're lying," Cassia said, pursing her lips. "If you think I don't know it, you're a bigger fool than you look in that costume."

He pulled anxiously at his armor. He had to give her something. "Ash wants—"

"Ash?" Elias balked. "So we're on a first-name basis now?"

Madoc ignored him. "She's looking for gladiator records—champions who've beaten Kula and died of the plague. She thinks Ignitus has something to do it. If we found something, Geoxus might be interested. We could use it to bargain for your release."

"Hold on," Cassia said. "If she's trying to commit treason, why would she tell an enemy gladiator about it? Use your head, Madoc! She means to trap you in some scheme—get you locked up or killed so she can secure Kula's victory."

It seemed possible when Cassia said it out loud. Maybe Ash had been lying to him all along.

Madoc shook his head. She'd stood by him in front of their gods. She'd found Stavos with him, and her shock at his murder had been genuine.

"She knows about me," he said.

"I'd say she knows enough to get what she wants," Elias huffed.

"Knows what?" Cassia was more pointed.

Quickly, Madoc explained what had happened with the guards in the arena—how they'd left Ash alone, and how she'd surmised that he wasn't Earth Divine.

"You can control minds?" Elias asked. "What am I thinking right now?"

"It doesn't work like that," Madoc said. "Look, it was probably nothing. I just know she could have told Ignitus, and Geoxus, and anyone else that I'm Undivine, but she hasn't."

"Do you trust her?" Cassia peered at him the way Ilena did when she caught any of them in a lie, and just like with their mother, Madoc buckled.

"I do."

"We're doomed," Elias said.

He had no idea.

Cassia glanced over her shoulder, into the hall. "Petros has a library at the house. It's where he keeps all his tax records. I'll see if there's something there that can help."

"No," Elias said. "It's too dangerous."

"You're right," she snapped. "Maybe I'll sign up to be a gladiator instead. That's much safer."

Elias winced.

"I have to go," Cassia said, her jaw growing tight. Madoc followed her stare to one of Petros's guards, stalking toward them, and fought the urge to step between them. That would only make this worse.

"Be careful," she cautioned. "Be smart."

"Watch yourself," Madoc told her as she hurried away. He didn't have to warn her what a monster Petros was. Based on her shoulder, and the way she'd flinched when Petros had mentioned the shackles, she already knew.

Madoc watched her go, hoping she'd be safe. Hoping she would find something, and that Ash's suspicions had been warranted. If not, the fate of his family would fall to him.

He'd entered this war to save his sister. Now he'd have to win it to save them all.

TWELVE

ASH

"AND WHAT DO you do if Brand takes all the igneia from the firepit before you can get any?"

Ash finished buckling her armor's shoulder strap and fought a groan, keeping her eyes on the preparation chamber's dusty floor. Above her, hundreds of feet thundered in the stadium; hundreds of voices cheered. A handful of Deiman gladiators were out stoking the crowd with a fight as an announcer listed the day's matches. His muffled words didn't make it through to the arena's tunnels, but Ash knew what he was saying.

Ash Nikau will fight Brand Pala to advance as Ignitus's champion.

Madoc Aurelius will fight Jann Moisides to advance as Geoxus's champion.

Tor had fought Raya yesterday, two days after the ball, and won. Geoxus's other champions had fought as well, elevating the gladiator Raclin to one of Deimos's two remaining positions in the war.

Did Madoc know Raclin personally, like Ash knew Tor? Was he in another of this arena's preparation chambers, adjusting and readjusting his armor, worrying not about how he had to win his fight today, but how winning would mean facing off against someone he knew? And worse, that he would have to do all this without energeia. At least Ash didn't have that worry.

She flinched, realizing Taro was still watching her, waiting for an answer.

"Keep the fight close," Ash said. She rose from one of the benches that filled the windowless room. The only light came from those stones Geoxus loved so much, their glow sickly green-white. "Use knives. Go for his side. Taro, I *know.* Tor's been relentless these past two days."

This preparation chamber was smaller. A pump at the back brought in fresh water while a cracked mirror sat over a table of bandages, rags, and medical tools. Taro stood next to that table, glaring at Ash.

"He's been relentless," Taro said, "so you don't get yourself killed."

Ash wilted and looked away. After the debacle in the stable yard, Tor, Taro, and Spark had instantly set upon Ash in the palace. She had finally confessed how Madoc had affected her grief in the arena's tunnel, that she thought maybe he'd used air divinity to fill her lungs, soothe her tension—but that whatever he'd used, it hadn't been geoeia. She told them how she'd blackmailed Madoc into getting her to his sponsor's records, which was where they had been going when—

The memory of Stavos's corpse still hovered at the edge of Ash's mind. He had been shot in the back. He had been shot running *away.*

Days ago, Ash would have reveled in that. But now, reality overshadowed any satisfaction.

The official investigation into Stavos's murder had turned up empty so far, and most people seemed to have shrugged off the incident as a cost of war. But Stavos's words echoed in Ash's mind, his dead eyes watching her, his chapped lips moving. *She took it from me.*

He had said that Ignitus hadn't done this to him. Could Ignitus have paid someone else to do it, though? He would have been smart to stay out of it himself, and get rid of the gladiator through someone else. Someone like the mystery *she.*

Who could it be? Was it someone Ash didn't know, an assassin Ignitus had hired to dispose of Stavos? Or was it someone larger—maybe Aera, the goddess of air from Lakhu, who was one of the warmongering gods who Hydra had mentioned in her message to Ignitus?

But what had this mystery woman taken from Stavos?

At least Ash knew that Madoc wasn't involved. He'd been so sincere about everything, not just Stavos—the only thing linking him to any of this was her own assumption. Whatever Madoc was, he wasn't involved with a gladiator who Ignitus feared or with the other gods poised against Kula. He was just trying to free his sister.

Ash's chest warmed. It was such an honorable goal to have. There was far too little honor in these wars.

Taro slammed a fist onto the tabletop. Ash jumped.

"You're distracted," Taro snapped. "Get your head straight. Tor hasn't been able to talk to you about it, he's been so distraught, but he's been hard on you because you left the terrace to go out, alone, with an enemy gladiator. And then another champion turns up dead?

Do you know how easily that could have been you? Do you have any idea what that gladiator could have done to you, and none of us would have been there to help?"

Ash's mouth dropped open. Taro had never snapped at her before. She was usually the one who winked at Ash when Tor or Char reprimanded her.

But she knew Tor had been furious with her. He hadn't let her out of his sight for the past two days. Mornings of drills in the training room, afternoons running laps through Geoxus's gardens.

"When you fight Brand," Tor had told her, "you must be ready. You won't get lucky again."

Brand was the only other champion to outrank Ash in blood. He was young, and virile, and brutishly confident, with a reputation for only being satisfied with a win if it ended in death.

You won't get lucky again.

Tor hadn't meant her fight with Rook and how she had won because he got himself killed; Tor would never speak ill of Rook like that. He had been talking about Madoc.

"Madoc wouldn't hurt me," Ash fumbled now. The statement burst out of her, so obvious that she didn't hear its stupidity until Taro's eyebrows went up.

"Ash." Taro's voice was heavy with exasperation. "Every move that fighter makes in this war, he does at the behest of his god. We don't even know what god that *is*, do we? Maybe Aera. Maybe someone different entirely. We don't know what kind of energeia he used on you. And we have no idea who killed Stavos. That's exactly the point—*we* don't know. We're in this together, the lot of us, and you're young, but I'd have thought you'd learned not do something so stupid as to get tangled up with an *enemy*."

Ash shot closer to Taro. "I am *not* tangled up with him."

Taro's face went red, but she straightened, her broad shoulders stretching. "Take a second to center yourself. You can't go into a fight like this."

She stomped across the room, threw open the door, and slammed it behind her.

Ash stood in Taro's wake, her mind thudding. She knew Taro was right—she *wasn't* in this alone. Each day she felt the weight of guilt of this war, the chafing horror that she had caused this conflict. Rook was gone—because of *her*.

Which made her try harder, fight longer, beat herself ragged to figure out the riddle of Ignitus's weakness. The actions she took to bring down Ignitus would ripple out to Tor, Taro, Spark, and others back in Kula if she failed, or if Ignitus found her out beforehand. And in a few moments, she would have to fight Brand. She couldn't afford distraction. She couldn't—

The door to the preparation chamber opened. Ash closed her eyes with a soft sigh.

"Taro, I'm not ready for—"

"We need to talk."

Ash's eyes flew open. A girl stood inside the room, her back to the door. When Ash looked at her, she threw the bolt, locking them in.

Ash's muscles hardened, but she didn't move.

The girl's lips flickered. "I'm Cassia. Madoc's sister. I don't have a lot of time. My guard is right outside—I told him I needed to use the facilities."

She pulled a scroll out of the pocket of her linen shift and tossed it into the air. Ash caught it, the aged parchment crinkling in her hand.

"I'm in the household of Crixion's tax collector," Cassia said. "He's also a senator. I grabbed this out of his office—it's one of the records all senators have. 'Results of Wars with Kula.'"

Ash's confusion didn't abate. "Did Madoc tell you to bring me this?"

"He doesn't know I'm here, but he did manage to tell me that you wanted him to get you a list of gladiators who've fought against Kula and have the champion's pox. This lists those gladiators and what became of them." Cassia bristled. "You aren't going to blackmail my brother. You aren't going to drag him into some conspiracy against your god. This is all you'll get from us, and now you're going to forget about him."

The emphasis she put on the last word was heavy with all the things unsaid.

"He isn't a spy, is he?" Ash asked, her voice soft. "He isn't working against Ignitus."

Cassia's face contorted with honest confusion. "What? Of course not."

Ash's heart squeezed. In her mind, she heard Taro chastising her. If associating with Madoc made Taro fume, then so would being here with Cassia. So would *trusting* Cassia.

Ash unrolled the parchment. Sections had been added to it over time, with the ink at the top a faded brown while the entries at the bottom were vibrant black.

Kepheus Ptolamy, one record started:

FIRST WAR, YEAR 894:

STAKES: FISHING RIGHTS OVER VORES BAY, WESTERN KULA

FINAL WAR MATCH: FOUR-HOUR FIGHT, GEOXUS VICTORIOUS

SECOND WAR, YEAR 895:

STAKES: KULA'S CLOTH TRADE WITH LAKHU

FINAL WAR MATCH: NINE-HOUR FIGHT, GEOXUS VICTORIOUS

TITHED: YEAR 898

DEATH: YEAR 899

Ash squinted. "What does it mean when a gladiator is tithed? We don't have that in Kula. Is it some sort of donation they get?"

Cassia pursed her lips. "I've heard people say it's like retiring."

"Retiring? Gladiators don't retire. They die."

"Maybe in Kula. In Deimos, Geoxus lets gladiators retire when they've fought for him well. He's benevolent."

Ash's skin prickled. *Benevolent.*

Before Ash could ask more, Cassia snatched the scroll back from her. "That's enough. These records are yours only if you promise to forget what you know about Madoc."

Ash's eyes dropped to the scroll. Would this information be useful?

I can't have a gladiator involved again, Ignitus had said.

Maybe the other Deiman gladiators who had disappeared in the past were connected to Kula. She could still look for those ties. She could still find something that could help.

Ash sighed, defeated, and took the scroll. "Fine. I won't tell anyone about Madoc."

She scanned the parchment with bleary eyes. She didn't know how she would begin to—

Amyntas Fulvius, another entry said.

FIRST WAR, YEAR 886:
STAKES: TWO HARVESTS OF KULAN WHEAT
FINAL WAR MATCH: TWO-HOUR FIGHT, GEOXUS VICTORIOUS

SECOND WAR, YEAR 888:
STAKES: THREE YEARS OF KULA'S MEAT TRADE WITH CENHELM
FINAL WAR MATCH: NINE-HOUR FIGHT, GEOXUS VICTORIOUS
TITHED: YEAR 894
DEATH: YEAR 898

More—

STAKES: KULAN LUMBER EXPORTS. GEOXUS VICTORIOUS.

STAKES: KULAN MEDICINAL IMPORTS FROM LAKHU. GEOXUS VICTORIOUS.

More and more. The stakes, Kula's dwindling assets; the victor, Geoxus.

At the very bottom, outlined from old faded ink to crisp black, was a record of Kula's resources, laid out like a shopping list that a servant might take to a market. Some items had notes beside them—*Won by Aera; Won by Biotus*—while more than a dozen items had lines through them, all the things Geoxus now owned from Kula.

Ash had never seen Kula's losses laid out so succinctly before. It was infuriating, her country's reality scratched on parchment as though it was just some footnote in history.

But three items were not yet struck through. Kula's rights to the Telsa Channel; their two remaining fishing ports; and their glass trade.

All the resources that were at stake in this war.

Ash's chest seized. "They're bleeding us dry," she breathed.

"Who?"

"Geoxus." Ash frowned up at Cassia. "Biotus. Aera. The other gods."

Leave me out of his squabbles with Geoxus, Biotus, and Aera.

This wasn't a *squabble*. This was a targeted effort to strip Kula of resources.

Cassia made a noise like a laugh. When Ash didn't relent, she squinted like she had thought Ash was telling a joke. "Geoxus is a peaceful god. Or he would be, if he wasn't surrounded by warmongering siblings. Ignitus has caused all the wars Geoxus declares against him, and the other ones were started by Aera and Biotus. Ignitus deserves everything he gets."

"Yes," Ash said by instinct. But—

She glanced over the entries again. She remembered a few of these wars. One, Ignitus had definitely caused—he stole a cargo of goods bound for Deimos. But years ago, a fleet of passing centurions raided a coastal village in Kula, and when people fought back, Geoxus declared war for the offense of murdering his elite soldiers. In a second instance, a landslide decimated a mountain town in northern Kula—while Geoxus just happened to be in Cenhelm, Kula's northern neighbor. When Ignitus had accused Geoxus of causing it, Geoxus had declared war, aghast at the offense to his reputation.

Ash would have been able to reason it away like she always did, the gods just being petulant children. But her eyes went back to the list.

When Ash went to Lakhu, Cenhelm, and Deimos for arena fights, those countries were prosperous, their people cared for, even though warmongering gods also ruled them. Why were Kula's resources the only ones running out?

She thought again of Hydra's message. *Leave me out of his squabbles.*

Was it possible that Ignitus had been asking Hydra for *help?*

Ash dropped to a seat on the bench, the scroll held limply, horror stabbing her in the stomach so hard she gagged.

A horn bleated through the arena. Her fight would be starting soon, another bloody match she would have to devote herself to in order to please Ignitus, to get close to him—to destroy him.

From the look of it, Geoxus, Biotus, and Aera were trying to destroy Ignitus too. But their version of destroying Ignitus meant destroying Kula.

Could there truly be a larger conspiracy that Geoxus, Biotus, and Aera were playing out against Ignitus that could actually *kill* him? Or was there only a mystery woman killing Deiman gladiators, a rumor that made Ignitus tremble, and a gladiator he had mentioned offhandedly?

Ash let her head loll between her slumped shoulders, her chest deflating. Dead end after dead end. She was so tired.

The bench groaned as Cassia eased onto it. Ash jumped. She had forgotten Cassia was even here.

"We're done," Ash said to the floor. "You brought me the records. You should go."

The crowd erupted above them. The warm-up matches must have been ending.

"Is your country struggling?" Cassia asked.

Ash huffed. "You could say that."

"You blame your god for these wars," Cassia said. "That's why you tried to get Madoc to help you pin Stavos's disappearance on Ignitus."

Ash whipped a look up at Cassia. No one else had been able to so easily see through her lies before—the default with most people was devotion to the gods. No one would think to accuse someone else of disloyalty.

Curiosity surged through Ash's veins.

After a long pause, Cassia spoke again. "My father got sent to debtor's jail, but when he couldn't keep up with the work, the tax collector who arrested him sold him off to an arena. A gladiator killed him. In a practice fight."

Ash's knee bounced.

"I was so angry," Cassia whispered. "I blamed Geoxus for the longest time. But my mother took me to one of his temples, sat me down before his statue, and asked if I knew what Geoxus was thinking at that moment. Of course I didn't. She said we can't know what the gods are thinking, but we have to believe they know best. The gods aren't to blame." Cassia landed a hand on Ash's shoulder. "*People* are to blame. Every choice the gods make, they do so trying to give us a good life. Corrupt people are the ones who mess it all up."

Like Stavos.

Ash's body heat spiked, and she knew Cassia felt it when she drew away with a jerk.

Ash was glad Stavos was dead for what he'd done to Char—but it was Ignitus who had caused Char's death. Ignitus who bore the most blame.

And no matter what Cassia thought, it was Geoxus who had caused her own father to die in an arena. Geoxus, like the other warmongering gods, was the one who kept the arenas active.

Ash felt a line draw between herself and Cassia, like it always did, a stark reminder of her fate: to be alone in a world where most people worshipped the gods instead of hating them.

"Thanks," Ash managed, her teeth welded together. "I'll try to see it that way."

Another horn blasted. Cassia stood. "I'll need the scroll back. I should be at the next war celebration. Get it to me then." Her voice was softer now. "And . . . good luck today."

She opened the door. It squealed against its frame, letting in a rush of cheers before it shut in her wake.

Ignitus didn't make decisions to try to give Kula its best life. Ash was holding a list of all the resources he had gambled away. For every instance where Ignitus *might* have been justified in dragging Kula into a war, there were a dozen where he had done so frivolously and lost greatly. Char had died because of his choices, because of his selfishness and manic pride and petty temper.

And he *was* responsible for Char's death. Her blood was on his hands. Rook's blood, too.

These records changed nothing. Cassia's devotion to her god was no different from the loyalty Ash had seen in the other Kulan fire dancers, and in other gladiators, and in everyone else besides Tor, Taro, and Spark.

She shouldn't have felt disappointed, but the flicker of hope that had lit at Cassia's words now smoldered angrily in Ash's belly. Between Madoc and now Cassia, the Metaxas seemed determined to reignite the void in her soul, the loneliness that ached and throbbed. She had almost managed to drown it out with grief, with guilt, with focus, with a dozen other things she'd stuffed into her mind.

Like why it looked so much like Geoxus, Aera, and Biotus were trying to drive Ignitus into destitution.

Ash rubbed the scroll, her jaw working.

Why had they targeted him? It made her feel the smallest, dimmest flicker of solidarity—with Ignitus.

Body coiled, she launched herself to her feet and hurled the scroll at the door.

THIRTEEN

MADOC

"JANN'S BEEN FAVORING his right side since the first match." Elias fastened Madoc's breastplate, pulling the metal flush to his chest. "When you make your move, go for those ribs." Elias jabbed him in the spot he meant, which reminded Madoc too much of Stavos's body and the puckered wounds around the arrows in his back.

Madoc focused on the slashes of light streaming through the small barred window farther down the stone wall. The breeze that swept through the corridor from the arena carried the harsh bite of woodsmoke.

Ash was fighting outside. He'd heard the announcement before they'd made their way to the corridor near the south entrance. Her opponent was someone named Brand, and it had taken extreme force of will not to go to the window to see who was winning.

Ash's fight was her business. The Metaxas' lives didn't depend on her advancement.

"He'll see it coming," Madoc said, rubbing the side of his unshaven jaw, where Narris had landed a punch in training that had knocked Madoc on his back just yesterday. One of his heels bounced against the floor.

"It won't make a difference if you can get there faster," Elias told him, moving to the other side for the final adjustments to his armor. "He's from Arsia—the ground is softer there, so he'll think that he'll be able to pull up more of it than he can."

Madoc pictured the northern province, circled on the map pinned to the wall in the barracks by Jann. *Arsia has the finest dirt and the finest lovers*, he'd declared all week. Madoc hadn't thought that information would actually prove useful.

More smoke wafted in on the breeze as, outside, the crowd erupted in cheers. Had Ash pinned her opponent or had Brand defeated her? Madoc didn't know if he wanted her to win or lose. A victory might secure her safety a little while longer, buy her favor with Ignitus. But her victory also meant that Madoc might have to fight her in the final battle.

And Madoc had to win that final battle.

A high cry stabbed through his concentration, weakening his resolve not to watch the event outside. Pulling away from Elias, Madoc stalked to the window. *Please let her fight be over*, he found himself thinking, even as he wished it would go on forever, just so he wouldn't have to face Jann.

He spotted Ash immediately. Her armor was charred on her left hip and her long hair was slicked back with sweat. She'd lost her sword in the sand and her hands were open, pulsing with deadly balls of orange flames. With another cry, she launched herself across the arena toward Brand—a young, thick-shouldered gladiator carrying a shield and a spear. Fire hurtled from Ash's hands, barely blocked by Brand's shield. Just before she reached him, she dropped to the ground, kicking out his feet in a spray of sand.

Madoc's pulse tripped as Brand fell to his knees. The spear landed just out of reach, and as Brand stretched for it, Ash pounced on his back.

"Good," Madoc whispered.

Brand rolled, releasing his shield. Ash straddled his chest, hands curling around his throat. Her face and arms glistened with sweat. Even from outside the fighting pit, Madoc could see the hard planes of her shoulders.

Brand shoved at her forearms, but Ash didn't falter.

"You have him," Madoc muttered. Now that he was watching, he wanted Ash to win. She was more skilled. Faster. She deserved this victory.

"Having a good time?" Elias asked beside him. Madoc had been so consumed with the fight that he hadn't noticed his brother approaching. "If it's not too much trouble, maybe you could stop drooling and get your head in your own match."

He wasn't drooling—he was a fighter watching another fighter, that was all. But when the announcer called Ash's name, Madoc's fist pumped against his side, and his lips curled into a small smile.

Elias pulled sharply on the breastplate belt, and Madoc's breath exhaled in a huff. He turned away from the window as Ash raised her hands in victory.

He had bigger things to worry about than Ignitus's gladiators.

"Jann's got it in for you," Elias said, returning his focus to the match. "He, Stavos, and Raclin were close. They've trained together for ten years."

Ten years ago, Elias and Madoc were eight. While they'd been nothing more than skinny boys catching lizards and playing pranks on Cassia using Elias's geoeia, Jann had been learning to kill.

"He thinks you had something to do with Stavos's death," Elias said.

Madoc's jaw flexed. It didn't matter if he shouted from the top of the palace that he was innocent, the other gladiators believed what they wanted—that Madoc, untrained and unheard of before this war, had rigged the fight to advance.

"All this helpful information wouldn't be coming from Narris's attendant, would it?" Madoc snorted. *"Remi."*

Madoc had seen the two of them together around the barracks and in the dining hall during meals. Maybe others hadn't noticed the way Elias perked up when Remi entered a room, but Madoc had.

Pink blossomed on Elias's cheeks. "All I do, I do for our cause."

"I'm sure."

But the tilt of Elias's head revealed the edge of a bruise along his temple, previously hidden by his hair. When he saw Madoc looking, he combed it down over the mark.

"Who did that?" Madoc asked quietly, grateful for the anger sliding over his queasy stomach.

"No one," Elias muttered. "Doesn't matter."

It didn't. That was the problem. Madoc might have taken his blows during the day, but at night the champions had their own rooms at the barracks. The attendants slept in a community room near the kitchen, and Madoc's lack of popularity had bled through to his brother.

"You'll stay in my room tonight," Madoc said.

Elias glared at him. "Why don't you focus on Cassia instead of on me?"

"I am," Madoc said, throwing a glare Elias's direction. "It's *all* I'm focused on." Cassia. Elias. Ava. Danon. Ilena. All of them.

"Could've fooled me."

"What is . . ."

Madoc bit back his retort as two Deiman arena workers raced down the hall, their arms filled with blackened torches. Outside, the arena was being cleared and prepared for the next fight.

It was almost time.

"What is that supposed to mean?" Madoc muttered once the workers were gone.

Elias spun away from the window and kicked a wave of sand against the far wall. "It means this was supposed to be about getting the money and getting out. The past two days you've been different. Waking up before dawn to practice. Studying records in Lucius's library. The way you gave that speech to those donors Lucius brought you to see yesterday—about your 'humble beginnings in the stonemasons' quarter' . . . I almost bought it myself."

"Because it's true." Maybe he embellished a little, but it had earned Lucius five hundred gold coins and Madoc a break from his sponsor's irritation.

"That's what I'm worried about," Elias said. "This is a job, nothing more. Keep your eyes on the prize: as soon as we have the money we need for Cassia, we get out. Or you're either going to end up in the finals or with an arrow in your back like Stavos."

Madoc hushed him. They couldn't be talking about that here. Too many people suspected Madoc's involvement, and they didn't know who was listening.

He tried to brush off Elias's words, but they clung to his skin. It didn't matter if he didn't want the attention. He couldn't slow down or give in. Each day his father's promise carved a wider divide between him and Elias, but as much as Madoc wanted to, he couldn't tell his brother what Petros had threatened.

"I don't have much of a choice," he said, avoiding the truth. "Lucius already despises me because of Petros's games and Stavos's death. I need him on our side to get the money for Cassia."

"*We* need him, you mean," Elias muttered.

Madoc could feel his brother's desperation, a cloak of lightning, clinging to every jerky movement. He felt the sudden urge to touch Elias's shoulder. To calm him, the way he'd calmed Ash after Ignitus had killed her opponent.

For a moment, the urge stole every bit of his concentration.

His strange perceptions were getting stronger. He'd been convinced after what had happened with Ash in the hallway that they had some kind of connection, that he was more aware of her emotions because of her igneia, or even because of the way she commanded his focus. But it wasn't just her. He was becoming more aware of everyone—Elias, the other gladiators, even Lucius, who'd worked him twice as hard since Stavos had been found dead.

Something was changing, or maybe he was losing his mind. It didn't matter if worries about it felt like a closing fist around his throat—he couldn't deal with it now.

"We need to go to Petros," said Elias. "Give him the thousand coins and tell him we'll make good on the rest."

Madoc blinked, steadying himself. "We can't go back to Petros."

Elias's chin shot up. "Why not?"

Because I tried talking to him and it didn't work. Because if I don't do what he says and win this war, he's going to kill you and the rest of the family.

"Because he'll report us to Geoxus for cheating—you know that."

Elias kicked at the ground. "Are you sure it has nothing to do with those crowds cheering your name?"

Madoc's hands fisted. How could Elias think this was about glory? It was about *survival*. If Madoc told Elias that the Metaxas' lives depended on Madoc winning this war, Elias would do something stupid, give Petros an excuse to react.

Madoc refused to have his family's blood on his hands.

Outside, the crowd had begun to chant for Jann. He must have just been announced.

"It's time," Madoc said.

Elias crossed his arms. "Well. Don't die."

Madoc flinched. Elias's narrow gaze turned toward the bright afternoon sky beyond the window. *I'm sorry*, Madoc wanted to tell him, but the words were locked behind his chattering teeth.

This was no time for nerves. No time for weakness.

He had to defeat Jann to advance. To save Cassia, and Elias, and everyone he loved.

Madoc took his place at the mouth of the arena, just as Arkos had told him to. Jann, his breastplate glowing gold, was already standing by his rack of weapons on the far end of the sand oval. The grand arena might be vast, but Jann was close enough for Madoc to see his brows lift in amusement.

"Madoc of Crixion!" the announcer called.

Madoc's throat knotted.

"I mean it," said Elias, just behind him in the shadows. "Don't die."

Madoc nodded and then stepped onto the sand. Heart galloping, he raised his right hand. The audience, seated on steep steps two stories high, screamed in delight. Sweat dripped down his brow, and the breath he swallowed tasted of fish.

Beat Jann.

Madoc spotted Lucius and Arkos in a box in the center of the stands—no doubt ready to tear apart his performance. They moved down the row as two figures slid in beside them.

Petros, in a fine white toga, and Cassia.

His blood surged at the sight of her. Petros had brought her here to taunt him. To remind him of what he could lose if he failed in today's match.

Her gaze met his across the arena, and all he could think of was her as a child, taking his hand. *Let's go home.*

Madoc looked away; he must not be distracted now. He made his way toward the weapons rack and grabbed the gladius—a short, curved blade halfway between a knife and a sword—that he'd begun to favor. His father wanted to see him fight? Fine. He would get this victory, and all the rest, if that's what it took for Petros to leave him alone.

Madoc glanced once more back at the arena exit, but Elias was not standing there as planned. Nerves rose in his chest as he turned back toward Jann. Elias was nearby. He had to be. Madoc couldn't see him, that was all.

Instead, he spotted a girl who had changed into a simple white tunic, her long, dark hair knotted at the base of her neck. She stood just above the exit in the first row of stands, her arms folded across her chest, a few bandages pressed to her fresh wounds. Her stare was as steady as Geoxus's had been when he'd chosen Madoc to fight in this war.

Ash.

His heart gave an unexpected lurch.

"Champions, take your places!" the announcer called. Madoc homed in on the voice—a tall man in a white-and-silver toga standing at a podium above the spectators' box. He couldn't think about Ash now. He needed to secure his placement in the next round.

Madoc evened his steps as he walked to the center of the arena. The sand slipped between his soles and the hard leather of his sandals. He adjusted his grip on the gladius's handle and tried to shut out the cheers.

"You offend me, boy," Jann said as they drew closer. He'd chosen two knives Madoc recognized from training, and they gleamed in his equally lethal hands. This match was to submission, but that didn't mean it wouldn't end in death. "You learn you're fighting Stavos, and he doesn't make it to the arena. But here I am. Are you not afraid?"

Madoc ignored him.

"The fight begins now!" shouted the announcer.

But Jann only lowered his stance, turning the knives in his hands so the sunlight danced in Madoc's eyes.

"You know why I moved to Arsia?" Jann asked. The long braid over his shoulder was fastened with rubies the color of blood. "I was born in Crixion. Me and my four brothers."

He began to make a slow circle, and Madoc countered, one hand lifted, the other gripping his weapon. He looked for a weakness in his opponent's side, as Elias had said, and found a slight hitch in Jann's gait.

"I left because the taxes were too high, but then you'd know nothing of that, would you? *Petros's bastard.*"

In the blink of an eye, Jann dropped the knife in his left hand and scooped his fingers into the dirt at his feet. A storm of gravel slashed across the arena, and Madoc lifted his forearm to shield his eyes as the small rocks pinged off the blade of his gladius. The other man sprinted toward him, half hidden by a curtain of sand. Madoc raised his gladius just in time, deflecting Jann's windmilling knives, and threw himself to the side.

The larger bits of gravel fell, but the dust did not settle.

"He came to my house," Jann continued, as if he had not just attacked. "I was only nine, but I remember as if it were yesterday. He took my mother as payment—a servant for debts we didn't even owe. And when my father objected, Petros's men stoned him to death."

Madoc swallowed, grains of sand gathering as grit between his teeth. He needed to remain focused. He needed to win.

He glanced back, but Elias was still not in the doorway.

Jann had snatched up his second knife, one for each hand, and begun circling again.

"My oldest brother was next," Jann said. "Beaten so badly he would never walk again. All thanks to your father."

Madoc didn't care. He wouldn't. He needed to attack with Elias's geoeia to land a powerful enough blow. Jann was so busy talking, he wouldn't see it coming.

Madoc tapped his thigh twice.

Nothing happened.

"We had to live with a cousin in Arsia," Jann said. "Which is more than Raclin can say. Did you know she grew up on the streets? A few of the other fighters too. All thanks to your father."

Madoc tapped his thigh again, but to no avail. Sweat poured into his eyes, mingling with the dust coating his face. Panic raced through him. Where was Elias?

With a roar, Jann dropped to one knee, the ground beneath Madoc's feet quaking hard enough to knock him backward. He scrambled away as Jann flew toward him, leaping through the air, knives slicing downward.

Madoc twisted aside, clearing the jump, but not before Jann spun on him. Madoc swiped his leg low, tossing the other gladiator onto his back. He raised his weapon but was hit hard in the gut by a punch of geoeia. His gladius fell to the sand as he gasped for breath, white frames ringing around his vision.

Jann charged, one knife scraping Madoc's breastplate. Madoc dropped and threw his weight forward, tossing the taller, thinner man back onto the sand. His fist connected with Jann's right side—the space between his breastplate and his back shield—once, twice.

With a grunt, Jann dropped his knives, and dust flew into Madoc's face, blinding him. He swung at where he thought Jann's face would be, but the gladiator had twisted and elbowed Madoc hard in the side of the head.

They grappled, fists thudding against metal and meat, the roar of blood in Madoc's ears louder than any crowd. Then Jann was kneeling over him, his hands closing around Madoc's neck. Madoc could feel the thick tar of Jann's hatred clogging his throat as he struggled to get free.

"You're no better than him." Spittle flew from Jann's split lower lip. "You have no honor."

Elias, where are you?

Madoc's frantic gaze shot from Jann to the shadowed south entrance of the arena, to Ash, now leaning over the edge of the railing, to the box where Lucius, Arkos, Cassia, and Petros sat. But Elias was nowhere to be seen.

He shook his head, sweat burning his eyes. His family depended on him. He might not be a gladiator by training, but he was a fighter at heart.

As Madoc's vision dimmed, he clung to Jann's hate. As with Ash's pain, Madoc breathed it in, gulping it like bitter wine. He grasped it with both hands and climbed out of the pit of his own failing body.

The Metaxas were his family, and no one would harm them.

He blinked up at Jann, but the rage in his eyes had turned to white-ringed fear. Madoc could feel Jann's hands scratching at his throat, but there was no longer pressure—it was as if Jann was trying to choke a stone column using only the strength of his fingers.

With a heave, Madoc twisted, and Jann fell to the dirt at his side. This time he was the one scrambling away, and Madoc pursued—Jann was no longer the gladiator who'd beaten him in training but an obstacle between him and his family.

Jann was just like Petros.

Madoc felt his muscles swell with power. He focused on the glistening sweat on his opponent's brow, and the tick of the vein in his forehead. Jann's fear was hot, and sweet, and Madoc wanted it the way he thirsted for water after a long day at the quarry. He imagined drinking that terror the way he would a bowl of broth, swallowing it down until his stomach felt like it would burst, and Jann was no more than a shell.

You are weak, Madoc thought at him.

Jann dropped to his knees. His mouth gaped. He looked down at his legs, as if shocked they could no longer support his weight. He fell forward onto his forearms, quaking.

Madoc had done that. Just as he'd turned away the guards with Ash. He'd failed with Petros, but he wasn't failing now.

You are nothing, Madoc thought.

Jann gave a cry, and when he looked up at Madoc, fear pulled his features taut.

Madoc stepped closer.

You can't hurt me. You can't hurt my family. You won't hurt anyone ever again.

Jann curled into a ball at Madoc's feet, a giant man, whimpering. Rocking.

The dust from his attack was beginning to settle, but Madoc hardly noticed. His skin felt cleaner than it had ever been.

Beat Jann. The words echoed in his head, but now seemed inconsequential. Jann wasn't a difficult opponent. He was a stone in the road that needed to be kicked aside. His hatred had been fuel, and Madoc had drunk it up.

Surrender, Madoc thought.

Jann raised one shaking hand, and over the quiet in his ears, Madoc registered the announcer's voice.

"The victory goes to Madoc of Crixion!"

Madoc blinked. The air rushed from his lungs, and he staggered to one knee. The arena was spinning, or maybe he was falling. He couldn't distinguish up from down.

Before him, Jann gasped, staring at him in terror. He crawled away, then rose and sprinted toward the edge of the arena.

Madoc's thoughts were muddled. He searched for Elias but still didn't see him in the mouth of the tunnel.

Ash.

She was at the edge of the stands, watching him with wide eyes and parted lips. He clung to her gaze, desperate for something to steady himself. The rest of the crowd would see the dust and assume he'd used geoeia, but Ash knew what he'd done.

She could go to the gods, now with proof that he was different.

No. She wouldn't do that. She'd stood by him when Stavos had died. She'd pressed herself against his side, unafraid of this strange power lurking inside him.

Would she fear him now?

It didn't matter. He'd won. He'd saved his family, at least for one more day. But as he rose unsteadily, he felt no joy or even relief.

There was thirst. He longed for Jann's hatred, for Ash's pain, for Ilena's grief. He was parched for their emotions. Now that he'd had a taste, he wanted more.

Madoc shook his head. He didn't know what was happening. This was different from the fight against Fentus, or any opponents before him. Madoc hadn't just sensed Jann's weakness; he'd made him weak without even touching him. He'd willed Jann's submission, just as he'd willed those centurions to leave Ash alone, just as he'd willed the pain to leave her body. He'd taken an invisible step, and the change rippled through him, powerful and undeniable. Siphoning the hate from Jann's soul had made him something more—something terrible and dangerous.

A champion.

Slowly, he raised his hands over his head, and the arena screamed his name.

FOURTEEN

ASH

WHEN ASH WAS eight, she was obsessed with aereia.

It had been shortly after she had learned that her birth father had been from Lakhu, and so Ash was part Lak. She was certain that that meant she could learn to control air energy too, though Char told her repeatedly that mortals could only hold one type of divinity in them.

On visits to Lakhu, while Char and Ignitus's other gladiators warred against his god-sister's fighters, Ash studied the Air Divine. They moved deliberately, in contrast to the sharp ferocity of Fire Divine. When they used aereia, there was a ripple in the particles around them, dust disturbed by the funnels of air they pulled and directed.

Ash had taught herself to move like them. She put all her focus into imagining the air swelling and puckering—but she hadn't wanted to be Air Divine, not really. She had started to understand the awfulness of Ignitus, the growing poverty from scarce resources in Kula, and she had just wanted something else, *anything* else, to link her to a different god.

So she knew what it looked like when someone used aereia. And she knew what it did *not* look like.

The crowd in the arena was hysterical. Madoc's opponent scrambled for the exit, his face the ghastly gray of someone who had seen death. But Madoc hadn't touched the man. The air hadn't moved; all the dust, the geoeia from Jann's attacks, hadn't so much as twitched.

What had Madoc done to him?

"You said you thought he was Air Divine," Tor whispered next to her.

Every muscle in Ash's body, tense already, wound so tight that she started to see stars. Madoc having aereia had been a wild guess. "What else could it be?"

"Water, maybe?" Taro leaned around Ash to frown at her brother, one hand clasped in Spark's, who watched from the end of the aisle. "He could've manipulated the water in Jann's blood. Hurt him in ways we couldn't see."

The crowd's voices had meshed into one steady cheer. "Madoc! Madoc! Madoc!"

They thought Madoc had used geoeia somehow. It wouldn't occur to anyone else that he *hadn't* used his god's divine gift.

"But how would hydreia have affected me after Rook's death?" Ash asked. "And Hydra's people are peaceful."

Tor's arms were crossed over his chest, his face bowed in thought as Madoc lifted his hands to the audience. "Are they?"

Ash could see his mind working, connections weaving together.

Hydra had sent the message that Ash had intercepted, assuring Ignitus that his worries about an unknown threat were invalid. Had she lied? Could she have planted one of her people in Deimos to fight for Geoxus? Was that the gladiator Ignitus feared? But that meant then that Hydra was part of the stripping of Kula's resources. That she was no longer a peaceful god.

Four gods had united against Ignitus, then? *Why?* And hydreia didn't explain the way Madoc had soothed Ash's grief after Rook's death. The easing of her pain. The . . . sweetness.

Ash swallowed the memory, her body heat amplifying. Attendants ushered Madoc into the tunnels, and the arena crowd began to disperse.

The people seated around Tor, Ash, Taro, and Spark had been eyeing them the whole fight—here were Ignitus's two remaining champions, as close to gods as a mortal could get. Now Ash watched some Deimans linger in their departure, tittering to themselves when she glanced their way.

Tor grunted, frustration bunching his shoulders. "Either that gladiator infiltrated the war at another god's behest in order to weaken *both* Geoxus and Ignitus, or Geoxus is involved and allowed another god's descendant to become his champion." Tor looked not at Ash, but at Taro. "Whatever the case, someone's working against Ignitus. Maybe . . . maybe he could be useful."

"Could Madoc be the gladiator Ignitus mentioned?" Taro whispered. "The one he might fear? It makes sense."

Everything kept pointing back to Madoc. But nothing about him fit this conspiracy, the vicious, merciless warrior he would have to be if he was truly planted here by another god.

Unless Madoc was a far better actor than Ash had given him credit for.

She hoped not. She hoped so hard it shocked her, a childlike wish that he not be hiding his true intentions. She wanted him to be genuine, to be sweet, to be everything he had seemed to be—because *she* wanted so badly to be that freely innocent herself.

Ash shook her head. "I don't think he's part of this. He said he's only in this war to save his sister. That's all he wants."

Tor dropped his hand to his knee, his knuckles white in a fist. "You're certain he wasn't lying to you? If either of us goes into the final war match against him and he truly is part of a scheme against Ignitus—"

Tor flicked his eyes to the emptying arena, the blood-streaked sand. Ash fought not to follow his gaze.

An image fell over her of confronting Madoc in an arena, her face frozen in the look of horror that Jann's had shown before his surrender. Only she wouldn't get to surrender.

"I've already looked into him," Ash managed. "He isn't part of this."

"Is he truly innocent?" Tor stood, looking down at her. "Or do you just want him to be?"

Ash gaped. Tor had so quickly plucked out her truth.

She turned her shock into a scowl as Tor brushed past her, toward the stairs. Taro and Spark fell in without giving Ash a glance.

They thought Tor was right. Truthfully, it made sense—Ignitus had alluded to a gladiator being part of what he feared. And here was a gladiator with mysterious powers.

Maybe Ash's judgment was clouded and she had missed the signs of his guilt.

The last time her judgment had been clouded, she had run into an arena's fighting pit and started a war.

Ash shoved to her feet and followed Tor, her arms shaking.

The departing crowd headed for the main exit, which left the path down to the preparation chambers free. The guarding centurions gave Tor and Ash stiff nods and let their group pass without issue into the phosphorescent-stone-lit halls.

The preparation chambers for the Deimans were on the northern side of the arena. Only one of the doors was shut in the hall, and Taro and Spark took stances on either side of it. To keep watch, Ash realized—centurions wouldn't hesitate to come to Madoc's defense if he cried out.

Tor knocked.

Ash held her breath, pulse racing, when the door swung open.

It was one of the women who had been with Madoc after Rook's death. The barest wrinkles around her eyes tightened, and a few lines of gray in her dark hair caught the stone light from within the room.

She recognized them. Ash only knew because the woman tried to slam the door shut.

Tor stuck his foot into the threshold, keeping it open a crack. "We just want to talk," he said, his hands lifted in submission.

The woman scowled. "Unlikely."

"Ilena? Who is—"

The voice died as the door opened wider.

Madoc had removed his breastplate, leaving a sweat-stained tunic matted to his side. Dust and blood clumped along his hairline; the skin under his left eye was already yellow. But for all the ferocity he could have harnessed—a victorious champion, fresh off a fight—the expression on his face was one of narrow-eyed confusion and suspicion.

"We'd like to speak with you," Ash said.

Madoc's face paled. He shook his concern off with a frown. "It'll have to wait. I have somewhere I need to be." He turned to Ilena, his voice lowering. "I'll find him. I promise."

Ash blinked, startled. "Find who?"

Madoc wouldn't meet her eyes. "My brother."

The sight of Madoc's slumped shoulders would have been enough to stab Ash through her chest, but the pain in his words made her wheeze. "What? He's gone too?"

"He disappeared during my fight," Madoc said. "I don't have much time before my sponsor comes back. I have to go."

He touched a bag at his waist that clinked gently—those were his winnings from the fight against Jann. Geoxus paid his Deimans in coins, while Ignitus would have Ash's gold bricks for beating Brand delivered to her room.

Ash cast her eyes to Tor, pleading. *See?* she wanted to say. *A spy from another god wouldn't be trying to pay a ransom with coin—he'd know he could only pay in blood.*

Tor refused to meet Ash's eyes, but she saw his jaw tighten. "We know there is another god involved in this war," he stated. "And we know you aren't Earth Divine."

Tor's abruptness yanked a gasp from Ash's throat. A look of betrayal jolted across Madoc's face, and seeing it was as good as a slap to her face.

"You need to leave," Ilena snapped. A dimple punctured her eyebrows. "Now."

"Wait." Madoc put his hand on her shoulder. His jaw worked for a moment, his eyes on Ash, unreadable.

Did he hate her for telling his secret? Did he hate her for letting Tor use it against him?

After a long, agonizing pause, Madoc backed away from the door. "Let them in," he said.

Ilena pointed a threatening finger at Tor. "Champions or not," she said to him, and included Ash with a tight glare, her nostrils flaring, "if you touch my son, I will kill you."

"I believe you," Tor said.

Only one other person was in this small room: a white-haired, blue-eyed woman sitting on a bench. She had also been with Madoc after Rook's death, and she was old enough that very little seemed to rattle her.

Ash and Tor slipped inside. Ash pushed the door shut behind them, holding her back to the solid stone, hating that there wasn't even a candle flame of igneia that she could pull on to calm her nerves. It was better, of course, that Ignitus wouldn't be able to hear their conversation. Could Geoxus, though? They would have to take that risk.

Ash willed herself to grab control of the room before her resolve broke completely. She could feel the tension palpitating off Madoc even as he leaned against a table across the room from her, his ankles crossed, his arms folded.

"We'll be quick," Ash said. "And then I can—I can help you look for your brother."

At Ash's words, Tor cut a glare at her. This was a clandestine meeting between enemies. She couldn't show mercy.

Tor eased down onto a bench, elbows on his knees. "The energeia you used to defeat Jann was not geoeia," he started when the silence stretched. "And that could be useful to us."

"What do you mean?" Ilena demanded. "Why would you think Madoc used another type of energeia?"

Ash eyed Madoc, whose gaze had dropped to the floor. Had he told this woman what he'd done to Ash in the arena tunnels—or would that be another secret she would have to reveal?

She hesitated, willing Madoc to fill in the gaps for Ilena. When he didn't, Ash exhaled slowly. "After Ignitus killed my opponent during my first fight, Madoc took my grief."

"He took nothing," Ilena said immediately. He must have told her. But some of the strength had gone out of her voice. "He comforted you. That's all."

"It isn't all," Ash said. "My grief was *gone*. And he made the centurions leave me alone—they just left. Whatever he did to Jann was the same."

She didn't want Madoc to hate her. She didn't know what else to do. This situation hurt—this room *hurt*.

But she had to be sure of who he was. *What* he was.

Finally, Madoc looked at Ash. His face was a mask. "If I did take your grief. If I did make the centurions leave. *If* I did these things. Do you know how?"

Ilena's folded arms slipped apart to her sides. She grabbed Madoc's hand and he wilted under her touch.

"Do *you* know how?" Tor pushed back at him.

Madoc looked away. He didn't respond.

"What god are you descended from?" Tor's voice was softer. Cautious.

Madoc sank back more heavily against the table. "My father is Deiman. Earth Divine."

"And your mother?" Tor gave a questioning look to Ilena.

Ilena's face turned pink. She was looking at Madoc, but the old woman spoke up.

"She isn't his mother."

Ilena threw a glare at her. "Seneca—"

"Not by blood, anyway." Seneca pulled herself shakily to her feet. "Doesn't know his birth mother."

Tor held for a beat. He shifted back to Madoc. "You don't know your birth mother," he echoed. "So you truly don't know what your energeia is?"

Madoc hesitated, his eyes flicking, once, to Ilena. He shook his head.

Tor looked up at Ash from the bench, a tangle of annoyance and doubt on his face. So far, what she had told him about Madoc had proven true, and she could see Tor's options dwindling. He couldn't approach this conversation sternly, as he might have intended, through coercion or blackmail—not if Madoc wasn't involved with a plot against Ignitus, as Ash had said.

But he was *something*. Something different.

"It is rare, but not unheard of, for people with other divinities to live and grow under different gods," Tor said. "The gods and their retinues travel. Children happen. But the odds of one being made a champion in a war are . . . impossible. The gods choose their war champions with more care than they show about anything else."

Ilena bristled. "It sounds like you are accusing Madoc of something. It sounds like you are accusing *Geoxus* of something." She waved at the stone walls.

"If your god is listening," Tor said, picking up on her implications, "then I would be glad to have him make his presence known, to explain this to us. Because making someone from another god one of his war champions breaks every war law the gods hold most dear—and Geoxus has been quite protective of those laws recently."

Tor didn't look at Ash, but she felt his meaning: that her involvement in Char's fight had broken the holy laws and given Geoxus fodder for this war.

My fault, her guilt trilled. *All of this, my fault.*

The room paused, everyone waiting for Geoxus to respond to Tor. No god who heard such an obvious dig at their pride would have stood by without confrontation.

So when a long moment passed and Geoxus didn't appear, Ash exhaled. She heard a few other held breaths release too.

Tor looked back at Madoc. "What did it feel like? When you fought

Jann. Did you feel the blood pumping through his veins? Did you feel the air grating in his lungs? Was there a plant poison?"

The muscles in Madoc's arms bulged. Ash thought he wouldn't respond until his lip curled. "It felt like I feel talking to you—*angry*." But a muscle in his face twitched. Was that relief? Maybe he was glad to be talking about this. To not be lying. "I felt Jann's anger," Madoc clarified, less defensive. "His fear. Pain."

"And with Ash." Tor's voice noticeably hitched. "What did that feel like?"

"Sorrow." Madoc's eyes slid back to Ash. He didn't glare or sneer or anything she expected. He looked tired. "It felt like . . . a breaking heart."

"You felt their emotions?" Tor pressed.

"Emotions?" pressed Seneca. "Or their *souls*?"

"Souls?" Ilena huffed. "That's absurd. No one can control souls."

But Tor looked up at Ilena, his eyes tight. "That's not entirely true, though. Or it wasn't always."

"What?" Ash pressed. "What is—"

But she couldn't finish her question. *Souls*. Soul energeia.

Tor rose, brushing his hands on his tunic, and Ash realized he was nervous. Scared, even. "The first goddess. The Mother Goddess, Anathrasa, was the goddess of souls."

The silence that fell over the preparation chamber was thick with sweat, sand, and iron.

Ash went slack. "You're saying he used energeia from the goddess who the other gods *killed*?" She was overcome with the desire to smooth away the anxiety that had turned Madoc's face gray. She could see his chest fluttering, his brow pinched, his lips twisted in confused disgust.

"I'm not listening to this. I have to find my brother." Madoc took a step forward.

"Some gods say Anathrasa endured." Seneca clucked her tongue and grinned. "A horror story the gods tell each other. *She survived! Shudder in fear!*"

Her words hit Ash, flashing unavoidable light over the shadowed pieces she had been fumbling to connect for weeks.

Hydra's message to Ignitus. *I have heard no similar rumors. Stop worrying.*

She took it from me, Stavos had said with his dying breath.

"The message. The person Ignitus fears. A mystery woman," Ash said, her head ringing like a struck gong. She looked at Tor through a blur of wonder.

A god who had helped kill Anathrasa would be right to fear her.

He would be right to shudder at the mere *rumor* of her.

"It's her," Ash wheezed, lifting her hand to her mouth. "Tor—it's her. Isn't it? She's back. Madoc—" Ash looked at him, sagging. "She's his god. The goddess of souls."

"Wait." Ilena spun, her posture hard. "Ignitus mentioned her in a message? Does he know about Madoc?" Her face paled, but her eyes blazed. "What exactly do you want from us?"

"We thought a god planted Madoc in this war to rig it against Ignitus," Ash said. "It seemed too convenient that Geoxus selected Madoc—a gladiator without geoeia—to become a champion without someone having an ulterior motive, as Tor said. And we've been tracking a person Ignitus fears—maybe . . . maybe he fears Anathrasa? But that's impossible. She's been dead for centuries."

Ash's euphoria fizzled out, a storm leaving behind a hot, muggy dawn.

If the Mother Goddess truly was back, and she was at the center of all of this—she had captured Stavos, murdered him; she had planted Madoc in this war—then the gods *hadn't* killed her hundreds of years ago, like they'd said. And there was no proof that gods could be killed.

"You think the Mother Goddess is alive? And what—she intentionally put me in this war?" Madoc gawked. "If she survived, why would she wait until now to show herself? Not even show herself—just interfere with a war between Geoxus and Ignitus? I don't think so."

It was a stretch—and Ash breathed a little easier in it. "That's true, I guess. If Anathrasa had survived, she would have brought down a reckoning on the other gods for turning on her. They killed her because she almost destroyed the world—it doesn't make sense that she would have survived for hundreds of years without making herself known. Maybe she truly is dead and only a line of her descendants survived?"

Tor nodded, grim. "But if she or her line did survive, the world would not have endured this long. That kind of energeia control brought such chaos that it united all six gods, and we know how volatile they are."

Ash chewed her lip. But who was the *she* Stavos had mentioned, then? Could it be as simple as an unknown assassin hired to kill him? Maybe Stavos wasn't tied to this at all.

And if Anathrasa was truly dead, then it meant it was still possible to kill a god.

Tor bobbed his head in thought. "We can look into it. Maybe press Ignitus for—"

"I'm not descended from a soul goddess." Madoc whirled on Tor. "Why do you even care what I am? Why not turn me in and reap the reward?"

Ash stepped closer. She had laid Madoc's secret bare; it was only fair she reveal hers too.

Her fingers trembled. She had never told anyone this before, outside her little group. It was such a nourishing sensation, the truth of her motives waiting on her tongue, ready to spill free.

"We want to kill Ignitus," she said before Tor could stop her. "We want to stop him from hurting Kula any more."

She felt giddy. She felt light. She even managed to ignore the look of confused horror on Madoc's face, too high on saying these things out loud.

This is who I am. This is what I want.

She had never been more raw.

"We think Ignitus fears a gladiator for some reason—that he fears *you*," Ash said. "And it makes sense, if you can control souls."

Ilena and Seneca stared at Ash, and she felt Tor's disapproving glare.

"You bring dangerous ideas here." Seneca's glassy blue eyes were narrow.

"I'm not part of any plot," Madoc croaked. "I can't help you. I can't control *souls*."

"Are you sure?"

A new voice came from the door. Someone had opened it. Ash

spun around to see Elias stagger past Taro and Spark.

Elias ignored Ilena's cry of relief. His dark hair barely covered a bruise on his temple and another, fresher one on his cheekbone.

Madoc surged toward him.

"You can control souls?" Elias pressed.

Madoc ignored the question. "Are you all right? Where were you?"

"I'm fine." Elias yanked out of his mother's grasping hands. The abruptness of it sank into Ash's heart, making her aware of how he *wasn't* fine. "*Stop*—I said I'm fine. Petros's guards grabbed me. They wanted to make sure I was occupied during your fight." He gave Madoc a heavy look. Ash remembered—Elias had geoeia. Was he the reason Deimos thought Madoc was Earth Divine? Was he using his power to assist in Madoc's fights? "It seems like Petros thinks you can control souls too. He wanted to see what you could *really* do."

Madoc's face paled. "I don't—"

Seneca grunted in impatience. "I've watched you grow up, Madoc. You've always been far more sensitive to other people than most. If this is what you are, you could take down all your opponents like you did with Jann. Drive them mad by playing with their emotions, or weaken their geoeia until they were ordinary, or just pull their souls out like draining the milk from a coconut. You helped that girl without even thinking about it." Seneca waved at Ash. "Imagine what you could do if you *tried*. You could take out any mortal. Or even, maybe, a bigger target."

A bigger target? Ash felt her body grow light.

Could Madoc even affect a *god's* soul? Was that why Ignitus feared him—not only because he was descended from a goddess who should be dead, but because Madoc could hurt him?

Ash's mind spun with a mix of excitement and terror.

Madoc threw up his hands, cornered. "What happened with Jann was an accident, all right? The same with what I did for Ash. It was a *fluke.*" He looked at Elias, imploring. "Petros shouldn't have touched you. That wasn't the deal—"

He stopped, eyes closing on a wince.

"Deal?" Ilena twisted to Madoc, cutting in front of Tor and Ash as if they could have this conversation in private. "You made a deal with Petros?"

"Petros changed the cost of Cassia's indenture," Elias said. His bloodshot eyes never left Madoc. "He won't accept coin now—the only way he'll give us back Cassia is if Madoc wins the war. That's what Petros's men told me. When were you going to let us know about that, Madoc?"

"I had it handled," Madoc bit through a clenched jaw.

Elias's shoulders slumped. His eyes slid to Tor, then Ash. "Is that what you're doing here? You want to make a deal with him too?"

"No," Madoc said. "I won't—"

But Elias grabbed Madoc's arm. "Would you just shut up for a second and listen to them? Whatever they want can't make things worse. If you stay in this war, you're going to die. Petros already took Cassia. We can't lose you."

"Elias," Ilena hissed, but Ash noticed how she looked from her son to the Kulan champions, waiting. She wanted to hear what they said too.

Tor stepped forward. "Earth Divine and Fire Divine together could easily free a servant. We'll rescue your sister—if you try to use your powers on Ignitus."

Ash gaped at Tor. She had never heard him say anything like that before, willingly putting himself—and Ash—in a dangerous situation for enemies.

But he returned her stare with a firm nod, resolution straightening some of the worry lines around his face. Seeing that change in Tor made all of this suddenly, shatteringly real to Ash.

Madoc had energeia they had never seen before. He could be the person Ignitus feared.

He could be the very thing she had been looking for to save Kula and bring down a god.

Madoc's nose curled, disgusted, horrified. "You want me to try to affect a *god*? Do you have any idea what would happen to my family if I got caught doing something like that?"

"Madoc." His name slipped between Ash's lips. "Geoxus is just like Ignitus, only he hides it behind wealth and prestige. He has a list of my country's resources, and he checks them off every time he wins one, as if he's collecting them. We aren't even asking you to turn against your god. Just ours. We have no idea if your powers can affect gods, but—we'd ask that you *try*."

Madoc was silent long enough that hope welled in Ash's throat. But when he shook his head, the flurry of it dissolving stabbed her like knives.

"And get my whole family killed in the process? What do you

think Ignitus will do to them if I fail? This conversation—" He swept his eyes over the room, waving his hands wide. "This conversation never happened."

Madoc pushed past Elias and Ilena. He yanked open the door and shouldered around Taro and Spark, the slapping of his sandals echoing up the hall.

Ash bit her lips together so she wouldn't call after him. The way he had looked at her seared her mind like hot iron, the repulsion she had feared since she'd revealed his secret. Since she'd revealed her own.

He hated her. She had laid everything bare, and he hated her.

Ilena started to go after him when Seneca put her hand on her arm. "Take me home, Ilena," she said. "This is too much excitement for my old bones. Let the boy sulk. He'll come around."

Ash stiffened. "He doesn't have to come around," she said, and she realized no one had said anything like that through all of this. "He has a choice."

Even if he chose not to help Kula. Even if Ash ended up back where she started, with no leads on how to destroy Ignitus or how to keep her country from slipping away into starvation.

Tor glared at her. Ilena shot her a look of surprise before it darkened into suspicion.

Ash continued, mouth dry. "I'll speak to him. I can . . . I'll make sure he knows that he has a choice."

In truth, she wanted to see what he thought of her now. Maybe she had been right to always hide her true feelings about Ignitus. Maybe she had been right to sulk in loneliness rather than show her true self and hope that someday, someone would see her and understand.

"There. The girl will get through to him," Seneca declared as though it was her idea.

Elias grunted, exasperated, and mumbled something about having to load Madoc's armor. He left, stomping away.

Ilena gave Ash a weighted stare. "He's scared," she said. "Be patient. Please."

That narrowed her focus. She could help Madoc. He didn't deserve to deal with this immense burden alone. He didn't deserve to feel like some plaything of the gods when all he wanted was a soft life, safe with those he loved.

Ash's throat swelled.

Char, singing her old Kulan songs as they cooked supper. Tor, rustling her awake so the two of them could watch the sun rise. Rook, Taro, Spark—and even Madoc, looking at her the way he had when they'd been standing side by side after they'd found Stavos's body. As if her presence was comforting.

She shot out the door, racing through the dusty arena after Madoc.

FIFTEEN

MADOC

WHEN MADOC HAD left the preparation chamber, he'd wanted to go home to the quarter. To sleep off his thunderous headache in his own tiny bunk, and wake a stonemason again—a pigstock nobody whose only concerns were mixing mortar and ranking the chariots driven in by the master architects. But when he'd reached the main exit of the arena, a crowd had gathered to celebrate his victory, so he'd stolen a guard cloak near the weapons depository and gone out a side exit.

He hadn't intended to come to the temple, but it wasn't the first time he'd ended up here when he'd been lost.

Soul energy. Anathreia.

Each thought kicked against the base of his skull as he climbed the stone steps past the beggars in their worn tunics. He kept replaying what he'd done to Jann in the arena—the swell of his own veins, the rightness of Jann's surrender. Madoc still couldn't remember fully what had happened, and it worried him, but not nearly as much as having his skin sanded off by Geoxus if he learned Madoc had used an energeia not sanctioned by the rules of war.

Madoc pulled the hood of his cloak lower as a group of children raced by, fighting with wooden swords and handfuls of pebbles.

Cassia. Petros. Elias. Ash.

They were all pulling him in different directions. A month ago, no one had cared who he was or what he did. Now it seemed like the whole city knew his name, and most of them wanted him to kill someone.

He didn't know if he was capable of that.

He didn't want to find out.

The temple was open to the air, two dozen pillars hoisting up a sloped stone roof. The east side made up the closed sanctuary, the walls the priests lived within separated from the arena by a single road that transported gladiators and their training entourages to a private entrance that led to the facility's preparation chambers. Madoc walked that road now, skirting the edge of the sanctuary, until he reached the steps that led into the temple's main atrium, and the door that held the offering box.

This was where he'd come as a child when Petros had kicked him out. Where his frantic prayers to Geoxus had led him. Where he'd eventually met Cassia. How many times had he prayed here since then? The location had hardly been necessary—Geoxus was part of the earth, this city's foundation, and he heard Madoc's words wherever there was stone. But Madoc had come to the temple again and again, drawn by the quiet, and the sense of safety that always put his mind at ease.

How little he'd prayed since this war had begun. It was different now, harder. Seeing Geoxus up close had made him real in a way Madoc hadn't previously been able to fathom. And the Father God's blindness to Petros's deceit had been a bitter disappointment. It had made the god of earth seem almost human, and if Madoc had learned anything from Petros, it was not to worship mortals. Sooner or later they would always let you down.

Not that it mattered anymore. Geoxus might not even be his god.

People milled about inside the atrium, lighting incense and placing their hands on the sacred stones in the walls. Some carted baskets from Market Square, on the west side of the temple. Others begged for food or coin, shooed away by the centurions posted at each corner. But it was movement near the three-story statue of Geoxus that caught Madoc's attention. A woman stood near a pillar, her long cloak dark against the stark white marble. He should have kept walking to the offering box—the purse was heavy on his belt, and it was foolish to think he wouldn't be recognized if he stayed too long. But when she stepped forward, the light slanting through the open atrium caught her face and a wild curl that escaped her cloak's hood.

A knot formed in his throat, but he swallowed it down, searching for the Kulan guards who surely would be nearby. He didn't see them, but that didn't mean they weren't close.

"Do you want to be alone?" Ash asked as he finished climbing the steps to meet her under the shelter.

Yes. No.

"Did you follow me all this way to ask me that?" His tone was gruffer than he'd intended. As he moved closer, he gripped the satchel of coins against his side to keep it from jingling. Again, he looked for her guards, but either they were well disguised among the other patrons or she'd lost them between here and the arena.

It wouldn't be the first time she'd snuck away unattended.

"Are you all right?" she asked.

He laughed dryly. He'd just been told he wasn't fully Deiman, but instead might belong to the dead seventh goddess who'd been killed by her six children hundreds of years ago. Seneca thought that he could drain souls like a coconut. And his own brother was convinced he'd die before the war was over.

"I'm great."

Her lips pulled to the side, as if trying to hide a smile, and when she knotted her fists in the long fabric of her cloak, she looked younger, more girl than gladiator.

"Me too," she said, her gaze flicking to the nearest centurion, standing on the steps that led to the market. She turned her back to him, and Madoc did the same.

"Are you here to pray?" she asked. The breeze teased a loose strand of hair across her forehead. He waited for her to tuck it inside her hood, behind the half-heart-shaped shell of her ear, but she didn't.

He shrugged. Could he pray here if Geoxus wasn't his god? He didn't know where to start to pray to Anathrasa. "To think. Maybe to hide."

"Good luck with that," she said, scowling up at the giant statue before them. "What are you going to do? About Cassia, I mean. Are you really going to try to win this war?"

Her questions filled the space between them, filled his lungs until he felt like he would choke.

He didn't know how to answer. He'd barely known how he beat Jann; he had no idea how he was supposed to face a seasoned opponent trying to kill him with fire.

Especially if his opponent was her.

"I can't help you," he said instead. If she'd come here to change his mind, she'd made a needless trip. "I don't know how I do what I do . . . it just happens."

She didn't move.

Neither did he.

"My mother . . ." She hesitated. "My mother used to say energeia listens to the heart, not the mind."

He wasn't exactly sure what this meant, but he knew power didn't come from will alone—if it did, it would have manifested when Petros had tried to force it out of him as a child.

As it had in the tunnel, her grief misted around her, palpable and familiar. This time, though, he did not try to take it. Instead, he pictured Stavos and Ash's mother in the arena—him cheating, Ash rushing to help—and rage spiked on her behalf. Madoc would have interfered in that fight too if Ilena, or Cassia—any of the Metaxas—had been in danger. Even if it had started a war.

It struck him just how brave Ash actually was. She hadn't just defended her mother, she was defending her people. Facing a god's wrath if her intentions were discovered. Somehow, amid the lies and bloodshed, she had found honor, and it made any war their gods fought feel small and petty.

"Do you miss her?" He didn't know why he asked. They were opposing gladiators, both fighting their own battles. But he knew what it was like to be told your mother was dead, and even if he'd only been a child, he felt the kindling of likeness between them.

"Yes," she said, a small line forming between her brows. "Do you miss yours? Your birth mother, I mean."

"I never knew her." He sighed. "It would be nice to talk to her. Petros is Earth Divine, so this . . . anathreia must have come from her side. Maybe she could tell me how it works."

She watched him, all long black lashes and deep-brown eyes.

"My mother taught me how to use igneia. At home, before I started training." She kicked at the bench in front of her. "She never wanted me to fight."

Her words cut off, as if she suddenly remembered who she was talking to.

He didn't want her to stop.

"Ilena doesn't like me fighting either." He'd felt her fear and desperation in the preparation room after the fight. Whether she admitted it or not, what he'd done to Jann had scared her, and that made it so much worse.

Ash nodded. "My family has been gladiators for generations. It's in our blood, according to Ignitus." Her jaw clenched over his name, but softened with a small smile. "My mother pushed me to do other things."

"Fire dancing?" Madoc asked.

A flush blossomed on her cheeks. "Yes. I loved it, but I was still born to fight and had to train for the arena. It was just a matter of time before the dance was real."

Her pain shifted to a softer kind of grief, and he felt his own regret mingle with it. Dancing made her happy. He would have liked to see her that way.

"If what I saw at the ball is any indication, you must be pretty good."

"Well, I don't usually dance like *that* at ceremonies." She snorted. "Fire dancing isn't quite so forward."

Madoc shrugged. "I didn't mind."

She smiled.

He did too.

"What's it like then?" he asked. "Fire dancing, I mean."

A light filled her eyes. "It's heat and hunger and life. It's a celebration of everything good about igneia."

Longing pulled at him. Elias had once told him geoeia was a necessary part of himself, like his lungs or his heart. Madoc had never imagined energeia feeling so crucial, but hearing the passion in Ash's voice gave him a strange hope that anathreia wasn't all force and power. That it might have an upside.

"It must take a lot of practice," he said, realizing how much control she employed to use igneia. In the arena with Jann, Madoc hadn't even felt like himself.

"It does." She hiccuped a laugh. "Once I was in the galley of a ship on the way to Lakhu—we were always traveling for the next war. I was practicing a twist with igneia." She leaned to the side, turning her wrist to emulate the path of the fire. "I went a little too far. I nearly set the ship on fire."

Madoc winced. "I don't imagine that went over well."

"Everyone was meeting with Ignitus," she said. "Taro found me covered in soot and corn flour—I'd grabbed the first thing in reach to put out the flames, but that just made it worse. She doused the fire before anyone knew what had happened. She called me Corn Cake for a year after that."

He wasn't going to laugh.

It happened anyway.

"I'm sorry," he said, getting himself under control. "You don't exactly look like a corn cake."

Ash was trying to hold her lips in a straight line, but they twitched with the effort. "*Madoc* isn't much better. Unless you're an angry bird. Ma*doc*. Ma*doc*."

He gaped at her. "That hurts, Corn Cake."

She covered her mouth with both hands, stifling her laughter. Her joy lifted his shoulders. It smoothed the rough edges inside him. He wished she would put her hands down so he could hear the full force of it.

"Not as much as watching you flail around the arena," she said, humor in her eyes. "You were serious about not training."

He snorted and she laughed again. "I'll have you know I won four matches before this war."

"Using anathreia?"

"Using deception. And Elias. The anathreia . . . we didn't know much about it." It was strange confessing this to her—to anyone. But she knew more about him than most people.

She seemed impressed. Was it wrong for him to hope she was?

She bit her bottom lip. His gaze focused there, on the dip made by her teeth in the soft, pink skin. "So that's how champions are made in Deimos."

His grin faded. His head dipped lower, and he pulled at his hood to keep his face hidden. Here he was with a gladiator who was trying to save her country from her warmongering god, while he was risking the fate of Deimos for one person—*Cassia*.

Not even the money he'd earned to save her would help.

"I'm not a champion," he muttered.

"You're fighting, aren't you?" Her gaze met his, steady and brighter than the gold gleaming beside them. "For your people. Your family. Where I'm from, we call that brave."

She saw through him like he was made of glass. Like she wasn't afraid, or disgusted by what he'd proven capable of.

It was she who was brave.

Her hand dropped to her side. He wished she had reached for him.

"That's good," he said with a dry laugh. "Because I may have to move to Kula when this is all over."

Her smile started small, then rose like the sun, the heat of it warming his skin. He became aware of the distance from her arm to his, and the delicate, lethal shape of her fingers, and the flecks of gold in her irises.

She was *beautiful*.

He swallowed, his throat tight. He shouldn't have been thinking this way about her. He shouldn't be alone with her, laughing, either. They were enemies.

Who were both on the same side against Ignitus.

"You would love it in Igna," she said. "Our capital city. It's quiet enough that you can hear the sea if you're anywhere near the shore, and the crackle of wood from all the fires. There's glass everywhere, rainbows of it. And the food . . ." She sighed. "You've never had anything as good as our cacao pies."

He could see her there, listening to the sea. Laughing with her friends. For a moment, he imagined her reaching for his hand, dragging him through a garden of glittering glass sculptures.

"Maybe I'll visit it someday," he said quietly.

She nodded, but her eyes were sad. "If the gods don't tear my home apart first. Ignitus has lost most of our resources. If this doesn't stop, there will be nothing left for me to go back to."

"I'm sorry," he said. And he was. But that didn't mean he could help her kill her god. He was just a cheat from the stonemasons' quarter with a power he didn't fully know how to use.

"Madoc?"

At the sound of his name, Madoc startled, wincing as the coins against his side jingled. A man in a priest's robe approached from behind the statue, where the covered sanctuary extended along the length of the market. He looked as ancient now as he had been when Madoc was five, and moved slowly, with a slight limp.

"Tyber," said Madoc, calming Ash's worry with a smile as he strode to meet the temple priest. Tyber's robe was stained with gruel from the morning charity line, though he didn't seem to notice.

"Is it true?" Tyber asked. "We heard a rumor that you'd become a gladiator. . . ." He tapered off as his gaze landed on Ash, whose hands were wringing before her waist.

"It's all right, Tyber, she's a friend."

Ash's arms lowered. "Hello."

Tyber nodded slowly. "Any friend of Madoc's is a friend of the temple."

Madoc felt her curious gaze warm the side of his face.

"Tyber and I have known each other a long time," he explained. "Ever since I was five, when he caught me stealing from the offering box."

Tyber gave an amused snort. "He'd gotten his arm stuck in the slot in the door. The poor boy had to wait until morning for me to fish him out."

Ash didn't laugh; instead her lips parted in surprise. Maybe it should have embarrassed him for her to know he'd been poor, but it didn't. She already knew his other secrets.

"He let me stay in the sanctuary for a while," Madoc explained. "It was softer than the streets."

"Petros threw you out," Ash said.

He nodded. "I was here for two years until Cassia found me."

"Thanks to several anonymous donations over the last few months, we have many more beds for little thieves these days," Tyber said, his eyes glinting with a humor that took Madoc by surprise. "Don't think I haven't seen you and your friend sneaking around the temple at night."

"You're up awfully late, old priest." Heat climbed over Madoc's jaw. He hadn't considered that Tyber would have caught him and Elias. When they'd earned the fighting money, Madoc had wanted only that the coin Petros had wrongfully taken be returned to those who needed it. The only credit Madoc had dreamed of accepting was the fury on Petros's face when he'd discovered what his son had done.

That hadn't worked out as Madoc had hoped.

"There is more work to be done than there are hours in a day." Tyber straightened his back with a soft groan. "Besides. Someone needs to set free any children our hungry offering box grabs in the middle of the night."

Madoc snorted, but Tyber's words pulled at him. The priests would never be able to help everyone in this city. Not while Petros and people like him terrorized families like Jann's and Raclin's, and could break apart the Metaxas out of spite.

"Well," said Madoc, "I hope you have even more beds soon." He pulled open his cloak and untied the heavy purse from his hip. Carefully, he handed it to Tyber, who gaped at the gift.

"Madoc," he whispered. "This is . . ."

Madoc waved a hand. "I don't need it." Whatever lightness he had felt with Ash was slipping away. The coins were a reminder of Cassia, and the failed plan he'd made to save her. At least now he knew this money would help someone.

Ash was staring at him, respect lifting her chin. It brought on a new wave of uncertainty. This coin would feed a few hungry mouths, that was all. It wasn't as if he was taking down a god to save his people like she was.

"Thank you." Tyber shook his head in wonder, clutching the purse against his chest. "When his people are in need, Geoxus provides."

"If Geoxus provided, his people wouldn't be in need," Ash said.

When Tyber's brows lifted, Madoc coughed into his fist. "She's a skeptic."

But he couldn't help thinking she had a point.

"The Father God's strength flows through his children," Tyber said. "Their works are his works."

It made Madoc think of Stavos, and the arrows in his back. After what Petros had told him at the palace, Madoc was sure his father had had something to do with the murder, and yet Petros was a child of Geoxus. If strength came from Geoxus, where did deception come from?

Tyber patted Madoc's arm. "He will bless you all the way to victory, I'm sure of it."

Madoc glanced to Ash, who gave a tight smile.

"I'll see you soon, then," Madoc said.

"Champion!" All three spun to the steps that led to the market, and the crowd that had gathered. The children Madoc had seen playing earlier were among those gathered, their eyes wide with wonder.

"Madoc!" called a woman standing with a basket in her arms near the statue. "Is it really you?"

Shoved forward by her friends, she moved closer, frowning as she tried to decipher the face beneath Ash's hood. Wordlessly, Tyber went to usher the woman away.

"I should leave," Ash said quietly. "It's not wise for us to be seen together."

She was right, though he regretted it all the same. If two champions from opposite sides were seen talking, it could be construed as plotting.

"We could both go," he said.

A flicker of amusement crossed her face, bringing a lightness in his chest. "Where would we go?"

"Anywhere." He didn't care as long as it meant a few more minutes with her. But a shadow crossed her face, and her back rounded.

She stepped nearer, and his skin warmed at their closeness. "I'm sorry for what was said earlier. You have your own people to fight for. We shouldn't have dragged you into our trouble."

He wanted to tell her not to be sorry—that anything someone loved that much deserved defending—but how could he say that when he was here, and Cassia was still locked away?

"I understand why you tried," he said, then added, "Corn Cake."

She smirked. "Goodbye for now, Madoc."

He watched her go, stealing past the centurion on the steps with her hood pulled low. Her absence was as broad a force as her presence had been. The air was cool now, and smelled like olives and baked bread and too many people from the street gawking at him.

As he stared at Ash's back, he thought of her fight against Rook, the gladiator who'd tried to kill Ignitus, and Ash's dead mother, and a land far away that she would kill a god for.

She was sacrificing everything for her people.

Maybe it was time he did too.

He might be a cheat from the stonemasons' quarter, but he was here, like Ash had said. He wasn't a coward—he'd made himself a champion, whether he'd earned it fairly or not.

Elias was right; without doing what he'd done to Jann to someone else, he would never win this war, which left him one last play to convince Geoxus that Petros was corrupt so he could bring Cassia home.

It was time for the Father God to know the truth about his trusted tax collector. And to tell it, Madoc would have to lie.

SIXTEEN

ASH

THE DEIMAN CENTURIONS in the temple glowered at Ash until she slipped between the pillars and back across the road to the arena. *You shouldn't be so far from our people*, Tor had said the first time she'd snuck off with Madoc—but neither Tor nor Ash had realized the similarity until now. Maybe because this time felt starkly different from before.

Maybe because Tor's mind was just as loud with panic as Ash's, drowning out all sense.

Ash darted into the arena's servant entrance and returned the cloak she'd swiped from a laundered pile. She took a turn down the yellow-green halls, winding her way toward the arena's more opulent exit, where her carriage would be waiting with Tor. The sandstone floor was rough under her shoes, the hem of her white tunic softly brushing the tops of her knees with every step. She folded her arms across her chest, her eyes downcast, a headache pounding from her temples into her neck.

Either the Mother Goddess was still alive or a line of her descendants had survived. Madoc could be one of many Soul Divine, or he could be the only one. It seemed unlikely there were others like him, or word would have surely spread, the same way word—or vindictive carnage—would have spread if Anathrasa were still alive.

So it made the most sense that Madoc alone could manipulate soul energy. Anathreia.

And he hadn't known until today.

Madoc had to be the gladiator Ignitus feared. But whatever plot was unfolding, Madoc didn't know about it. *Someone* had to know, though. Geoxus? Was Madoc an unwitting player in his targeting of Kula? What did Geoxus, Aera, and Biotus have planned for Madoc, then?

Honestly, it didn't matter. Madoc wouldn't do what they wanted him to do. He wasn't driven by petty revenge like they were, or swayed by glory like other gladiators. He wouldn't play along with the gods' scheme.

But he also wouldn't help Ash kill Ignitus. He didn't want to be involved in their treason.

Though he wasn't repulsed by her treason either. He'd looked at her openly, softly, even with all her truths laid out before him, and the memory of his teasing smile played itself over and over in Ash's mind.

She lifted her fingers to rub small circles into her temples. The key to Ignitus's undoing, the answer to all the riddles she had been beating herself ragged to solve, was Madoc. And she was walking away from him.

How foolish was she? What would Tor say about this? That she was unerringly stupid and so obviously childish for not coercing Madoc to help simply because, with him, she didn't feel so alone anymore? Because he was the first true friend she had made in . . . a lifetime?

Ash stopped walking and fell back against the rough wall, needing a moment to collect herself. This day had exhausted her to the core of her being, and all she had to show for it was the gold bricks that would be delivered to her room, a few new bruises from Brand's attacks, and the position as one of Ignitus's two remaining champions.

She could use that. Her god would trust her, now more than ever. She could go back to the beginning. Poke him for weaknesses, again.

If Anathrasa truly was dead, there was still hope that Ash could kill Ignitus.

The reassurance only exhausted her. She wanted to sink to the floor and sleep. She wanted to go back to her room in the palace and slip into a scalding bath, the kind Char would heat for her with igneia until the water bubbled.

A pang of missing Char rocked through Ash. She wanted to talk to her. To lay her head on Char's shoulder and let her mother take her weight, just for a moment.

"The arena is empty?" a voice rumbled from the hall to Ash's right.

"Yes, dominus. A guard saw your son heading for the temple. Shall I fetch him for you?"

Ash straightened. *Your son?*

She edged closer to the corner, keeping her breathing shallow, her body stiff.

A slow peek around, and she spotted Petros and a guard, their backs to her.

Cassia wasn't with them.

"No." Petros flicked his hand. "Prepare my carriage."

"Yes, dominus."

The guard marched off, taking the hall opposite Ash's. She sank back regardless, keeping her eyes wide, muscles rigid.

Only she and Petros were in this intersection of halls now. She knew enough of his treatment of Madoc, Cassia, and Elias to know that this situation would not result in her favor, especially with the hall absent of igneia.

Lungs burning, Ash slid to the side, readying herself to retreat the way she'd come—

"I am alone," Petros said.

Ash froze. The hall hung silent, the press of the empty arena above feeling suffocating.

After a long stretch of nothing, someone else spoke.

"You let Stavos escape," the male voice snapped.

Ash ground her fingers into the wall. She thought she recognized the voice, but it was muffled, as though whoever was talking did so from behind a door.

She started to peek around the corner again when her heart seized.

Wait—had the voice meant that *Petros* had abducted Stavos?

"I started rumors that his behavior was from a fever," Petros replied, ripe with confidence. "People already believed he'd fallen ill with the champions' pox, like the others. Now they say he was delirious with fever, roaming the streets, and attacked an innocent family. Centurions had no choice but to shoot him down."

"You are getting sloppy. First, Stavos. Now, your son."

Ash bit her lip. Luckily, Petros asked the question she wanted to shout.

"What about Madoc?"

"He knows more than he says. Too much."

"What he does or doesn't know is of no consequence. I have his sister. He entered this war. He will do whatever we ask of him with her life at stake."

"I'm losing faith in your ability to—" The voice cut off in a sharp drop.

Ash waited, sweat slicking down her back, her heart thundering against her ribs.

Then the voice spoke again. And Ash retched.

"Our conversation is not private."

She shoved herself off the wall, sprinting back up the hallway. She didn't stop to look back, to see if Petros was gaining on her.

He was Earth Divine; they were in a tunnel of stone. She had to get *out*.

Ash's heart lodged in her throat, galloping pulses that made her wheeze. She slammed into a corner, shoved off it; she took a turn, barreling on. She didn't know where she was going, only that she thought she was heading back toward the temple.

Petros was behind this. All of this. He was the one who had planted Madoc in this war, knowing about his anathreia. He was the one who had abducted Stavos.

Why? How did Stavos's abduction tie in with Madoc?

And who had Petros been talking to? There was no one else there that Ash could see. Just the stones—

The answer throbbed in Ash's mind. *Geoxus. He was talking to Geoxus.*

Ash had to find Madoc.

She bolted around another corner—and went sprawling through the air.

The floor rose up in a sharp wall that sliced right at calf height. Ash tucked her head before she hit the ground, rolling across her shoulders at the last moment. The flip rounded her onto her feet facing the way she'd come.

There Petros stood. His cheeks were red from chasing after her, his hand extended as the floor sank back to normal beneath him.

All thought left Ash's mind. The only thing that broke through was terror.

She was panting, her body shaking. She had no weapons. She had nothing.

Petros scowled at her, his stout face turning purple with rage. "The Kulan. You—"

"Champion!"

Ash flung herself around. Up the hall, a trio of Ignitus's guards were running toward her, flames in their hands.

She almost wept. When she opened her mouth, she heard herself croak out a trembling whimper, but she couldn't muster enough shame to care.

The faces of the Kulan guards were fuming when they stopped before her.

"Ignitus has been asking for you," one snapped. They were likely angry that she had been difficult to find. "He requests you join him for dinner with his other champion."

Ash pulled the igneia out of the guard's palm. He started, grimacing at her until she pressed that hand to her chest and moaned with gratitude. Heat filled her heart, searing and strengthening, calming her twisted nerves.

The guard cocked his head at her. "Champion? Are you all right?"

Ash nodded. "I am now."

She turned, pulling the igneia back out and into her open hand—

But the hall behind her was empty. Petros was gone.

Ash staggered, her firelight wavering off the bare sandstone walls. Each crevice looked like eyes in the shadows, watching; ears, listening.

Petros knew she had overheard him. Geoxus knew too.

"Champion?" one guard pressed. "The carriage is waiting for you. The other champion is as well."

She swung back to the guards. "Take me to Tor. Now."

The guards led Ash to the arena's outdoor stable yard, the one used by the gladiators and their attendants. Only two carriages remained: the one for Ignitus's champions, with Tor, Taro, and Spark seated in the high, open-air compartment; and one that Ash didn't recognize at first. It bustled with servants loading weapons and armor.

One of the servants was Elias. That was Madoc's carriage.

Ash scanned the people around it, but Madoc wasn't there. He hadn't come back from the temple yet? Where was he?

The Kulan guards broke apart, two climbing into the driver's seat of the carriage, one mounting a horse. Ash lingered on the ground, her fingers clenching and unclenching at her sides.

When Tor met her gaunt eyes, he instantly leaped over the carriage railing and closed the space between them. "What happened?"

But Ash turned back to Elias. He was handing up a load of wrapped swords. He felt her watching him and turned.

His eyebrows bowed, a question, before he stuffed his hands into his pockets and took slow, easy steps toward them. None of the other servants noticed; even the Kulan guards, who had been so impatient to leave, were distracted by something that had broken on the carriage.

"Petros is behind this," Ash hissed when Elias was within earshot. "I heard him in the halls. He was talking to someone about how Stavos escaped from him. I think *he's* the cause of the champions' pox, the gladiators disappearing. I think he does something to them. And they talked about how Madoc knows too much, and Petros has Cassia so he can keep Madoc in line." She looked up at Tor, breathless. "I don't know what he's planning, but he put Madoc in this war. He knows what Madoc is."

"That rat," Elias cursed. He ground his jaw. "I have to get Cassia out now. This ends today."

He turned away, hands in fists as though he intended to march up to Petros right then.

Tor grabbed Elias's shoulder, causing the boy to go utterly slack. But he dropped his hand when a few of the Deiman servants by the other carriage looked over.

They had to be careful. They had to be quick. Even out in the open, there was stone under their feet, in the building behind them.

Nowhere was safe.

"We can help you get Cassia," Tor said, low. "She's being held at Petros's villa?"

Elias nodded, dumbstruck. "You'd help? Because you think Madoc will help you."

"Because if Petros is behind this, then he's the person we need to focus on," Tor said. "If he's poised to move against Ignitus—"

But Ash couldn't bear thinking that they'd have to *ally* with Petros to bring down Ignitus. Everything about Petros felt oily and stained.

"You need to find Madoc," Ash cut over Tor, talking to Elias. "I left him at the temple, but—you need to tell him."

Elias nodded. His face went pale. "If Petros is the one who killed Stavos, he could go after Madoc next. What's to stop him? He's murdering gladiators." Elias slid a hand through his short hair, pulling it up at the front. "I'll find him. I'll warn him."

"Good." Tor looked up at the Kulan guards. They were adjusting a bolt on the rear axle while Taro and Spark took up an idle conversation with them, keeping them occupied. A small grin of pride spread across Tor's face, but he turned back to Elias.

"Find Madoc and meet us tonight outside Petros's villa, just before midnight," Tor said. Ash had heard this tone of his so many times—it had ordered Char through training drills, had reprimanded Ash for taking foolish risks. "The four of us—two Fire Divine, one Earth Divine, and a Soul Divine—should be able to sneak into Petros's villa. We'll split up, find Cassia, and get her out first. Ash and I—" He glanced at her. His face softened. "We'll investigate on our own, after she's safe. We'll find out what Petros has been hiding."

Elias nodded. Again. "Okay. Yeah, that sounds good." He shook his hands out by his sides, his body humming with pent-up anxiety. "Tonight. Before midnight. Petros's villa is in the Olantin District in South Gate. You can't miss it—it's the only big, rich house there. I—" He started to turn back to the carriage. "Thank you," he whispered over his shoulder before sprinting away.

"The Kulans tried to pass a threat from me to Madoc!" Elias shouted as he rejoined the servants. "They're so scared of him, they can't even threaten him themselves!"

The servants broke out in a chorus of laughter.

Ash gave a brittle smile, but it froze on her face.

"Champions—the carriage is ready now," one of the guards called.

Tor took her arm and led her to it. "Who was Petros talking to?" he whispered.

The carriage rocked as Ash pulled herself up. She looked down at Tor, her insides shifting with the carriage.

"Who do you think he was talking to?" was all she could say in response.

Tor swallowed, hard, and gave a curt nod.

Geoxus. Petros may have been the one making the moves, but Geoxus was giving the orders. Which meant it was all connected: Madoc, his anathreia; the target painted on Kula by Geoxus, Aera, and Biotus; even Stavos using the poisoned blade on Char. Had Geoxus told him to do that in order to get rid of Ignitus's strongest gladiator and Geoxus's biggest threat?

The only pieces that still didn't connect were why Petros had captured Stavos, why he was dead, and what had happened to the other missing gladiators.

Ash sat next to Spark and let the healer check on a cut Brand had slashed across her thigh. Her mind was far away, poking at the lingering uncertainties.

Part of her felt like these final questions, and the waiting answers, would be worse than all the other revelations. Like the dark green-gray hue the sea would take before a punishing typhoon.

So Ash sat up straighter, watching Crixion roll past, and thought about how tonight, she would help Madoc get his sister back.

The moment Ash and Tor returned to the palace, servants swept them away to get ready for the dinner Ignitus had requested. He wanted to strategize about the final battles, they said.

Ash found it hard to care about the war when so many other dangers stalked around it.

As night fell, guards led them to Ignitus's personal chamber. They reached an entryway with flames whipping in braziers on either side of two towering white doors, making the area smell of earthy burned pine.

"Wait here," one guard said, and slipped inside. The other took up a stance before the doors.

Tor idly stepped away from him, his arms folded over his beige tunic. Ash followed, the two taking a slow stroll across the wide, empty marble floor. Her hands shook, built-up energy begging for release, and she fought to keep from breaking into a run just for some way to expel the unbearable emotions reeling inside her.

"We need to excuse ourselves from this dinner at the first opportunity," Tor whispered. "It'll take about thirty minutes to get to Petros's villa."

"How will we evade the guards?" Ash eyed the one by the door. "How—"

She stopped and planted her hands over her mouth.

Tor swung on her, eyes twisted. "What? What's wrong?"

"I forgot to tell you and Elias that Petros knows I heard him. Oh *no*." She dug her hands into her loose curls. "He knows, so he'll be expecting me to do something like this. And if it was Geoxus who was talking to him, then Geoxus likely was spying on us in the preparation chamber, even though we tried to get him to show himself. He knows we talked with Madoc—"

Tor touched her shoulder. "Calm, Ash. You were right to take risks. You were right to push for a better future. What Madoc is changes everything." He exhaled, face slack, and bent close to her, his voice a brush of whisper. "You have shouldered so much since Char died. Most of that is my fault, for being so shortsighted. I'm telling you I see it now, the possibility for a *future*, and we can't let that possibility escape. We'll take this opportunity—we'll free an innocent girl and find out what Petros and Geoxus are planning against Kula. And we'll use that to take down Ignitus."

"What if Kula still gets hurt?" Ash breathed. She fiddled with the hem of the tunic she had changed into, a weave of treated Kulan leaves that left one arm bare. "What if in defeating Ignitus, we open Kula up to being conquered by Geoxus or some other god?"

"If we have the power to destroy one god, all gods will fear us."

"What I meant was—" Ash licked her lips, but she couldn't get the words to come out.

These words that had been swelling in her heart since Cassia had brought the records detailing Kula's lost resources.

These words that had been choking her since she'd wondered if Ignitus had sent a message to Hydra asking for help.

Is killing Ignitus really best for Kula—or is it just best for our revenge?

Anxiety skittered through Ash's chest. Horror. Disgust.

"How many wars has Ignitus fought in your lifetime?" Ash asked instead.

Tor watched her, his eyes narrow, curious, and cautious. "Thirty-one."

"And how many of those did he start?"

"Does it matter? Good Kulans suffered either way."

"But the other gods sometimes harm Kula to instigate wars. Ignitus couldn't just let them get away with it. Could he? He had to respond." She looked at the striated marble under her sandals. "I just want to be sure that this is right. That he is the monster we think he is."

"Ash." Tor took a step closer, his eyes darkening. "Where is this coming from?"

She fought against the instinct to reach for the igneia in the braziers, knowing Tor would feel her nervously pulling strength. "Have we ever *talked* to him? Have we ever tried to understand what—"

Tor seized her shoulders. Ash gawked up at him.

The guard didn't flinch. He might have even been smiling at the sight of Ignitus's two champions scuffling before their coming battle.

"There is nothing to understand," Tor said, the veins bulging around his eyes. "That monster killed Char and Rook, and we are close to bringing him to justice."

Tor's fury pulled Ash's awareness to a fine, sharp point.

Char had been Ignitus's *best*. She'd constantly defeated his other gladiators during training fights. Her control of igneia was unprecedented, deliberate, and smooth.

If Kula's resources were at risk, who else should Ignitus have gambled on?

Tears gathered in Ash's eyes. She couldn't bear the deluge of thoughts that broke free, things she had never in her life predicted she would think.

Behind Tor, the door opened.

"Remember who killed your mother," he told her in a rumbling whisper. "These questions disgrace her memory, and Rook's too. You've come so far, Ash. Don't back down now."

Tor spun away—but not before Ash saw his bloodshot eyes, the pain on his face.

She had broken his heart with her uncertainty. She had broken her own too.

This was why she had shoved down thoughts like this for as long as she had. They would destroy her.

Ash trembled. Tor entered the room at a servant's beckoning, and the absence of him made her feel cold under the high, exposed ceilings of the hall. She wanted to tell him how sick her own questions made her, how much she hated the doubt twining around her heart.

She wanted to be angry again. She wanted to fume with vengeance.

But she could only step forward, her shoulders bent, and enter Ignitus's room.

The wide, well-lit chamber appeared to have many uses. A ruffled bed on a short dais filled one corner. On a table in the center of the room, food waited, steaming plates of roasted chicken and spiced orange slices and charred peppers arrayed before three chairs. To the left, shelves of scrolls and books peered down at a desk strewn with papers and quills.

Ignitus sat at that desk, forehead in his hands, body hunched over a stack of papers. He didn't seem to know Tor and Ash were here. A servant poured wine into three waiting goblets on the table, and when the guards shut the door with a thud, Ignitus still didn't react.

Tor curled his fingers into fists. He didn't eye Ash in question as he usually would have—their conversation had cracked something between them. Nausea gripped Ash when she realized that what had broken was trust.

Ignitus launched himself from the chair and swept the papers off the desk. "*Damn it!*"

As the papers flurried through the room like leaves off a tree, Ignitus covered his face and took a slow breath, clearly gathering himself. This was the most disheveled Ash had ever seen him. Scarlet wrappings tangled around his hips, brushing the tops of his feet, his chest bare. His hair, unornamented, erupted around his face. The gray strands were prominent now, looped into a single coil that fell down his shoulder.

That wasn't a chunk of silver thread woven into his hair. Why did he have it?

"Wine," he barked, and the servant dashed to bring him one of the goblets from the table.

"Great Ignitus," Tor started, "we can leave, if you wish."

Ignitus snatched the goblet from the servant and downed the

whole thing before chucking it across the floor. He blinked at Tor, frowned, and looked at Ash.

"Nikau." There was tangible relief in Ignitus's voice. "That champion of my brother's—Madoc. His latest win was . . . troubling." He glanced at the stone floor and walls with a grimace. Geoxus could easily spy here—it was his palace, crafted of his stones. "You were with him the night of the ball. Tell me—what have you noticed about him?"

Now you want my help? Why? she wanted to ask. She wanted to beg him for an answer.

Ash's throat was raw from holding back tears. She felt Tor watching her, waiting.

Judgment and wariness from Tor; eagerness and hope from Ignitus.

The emotions made no sense, and churned the already confusing thoughts in her head.

What would Ignitus do if she told him the truth: that Madoc might be descended from a goddess Ignitus supposedly helped kill long ago? How would he react if she dropped to her knees and told him how much Kula was suffering, about the poverty and disease? Had anyone ever brought their concerns to him before? Or had they stayed silent out of fear rather than working with him to better their country?

Ash's eyes fell to the ground. Her heart beat so hard it ached.

Remember who killed your mother.

Stavos had killed her. But Ash remembered the way Char hadn't even noticed Ash in the hall before her fight. Her stilted conversation, the loss of focus as she bore unimaginable burdens.

Ignitus did that.

Ignitus did that.

Rook had sobbed on the arena sands, his pockets heavy with marbles he would never get to give to his son. Ignitus had chosen to tell Rook about Lynx just before that fight.

Ignitus did that.

Heat sparked in Ash's chest. It sent feeling into her numb limbs.

Good intentions or not, misunderstanding or lies, Ignitus was still a monster.

Ash gulped in the air, tinged with the scent of crackled chicken skin and grape wine. "Actually, Great Ignitus, I overheard Madoc tell his attendant that he would be meeting someone in one of Crixion's poor districts tonight. As you said—he is troubling. There is more going on with him. With your permission, I would like to follow him and find out what."

Ignitus puckered his lips. "I do not like the idea of my champion venturing into this pit of a city alone. I'll send one of my guards to follow Madoc."

He started to snap for his guards when Ash's chest bucked.

"If Madoc sees them, they will have no good reason to be following him," she said. "But if he discovers me, it won't be unusual. I already have a rapport with him."

Ignitus hesitated.

Tor stepped forward. "I will go with her, Great Ignitus. Surely your two strongest champions can handle the dregs of Crixion."

That earned something that was almost a smile. "Indeed." Ignitus held for another long moment. Finally, he nodded. "Report to me as soon as you are back."

Ash exhaled and bowed her head. "Thank you, Great Ignitus."

Tor took Ash's arm and guided her to the door. His face was awash with desperation, wanting to get out before Ignitus changed his mind—but Ash's eyes dropped to the papers Ignitus had thrown in his anger.

Remaining Wheat Holdings, one read. The list beneath was painfully short.

Another. *Alternative Fishing Ports*. Only three locations were listed on that sheet.

Ash looked up at Ignitus.

He too was staring at the papers on his floor. His hand was on the back of his neck, rubbing out a kink in an exhausted motion that was far too human.

Tor pulled the door open and dragged Ash into the hall. Guards started to follow when Ignitus shouted from within, "Let them pass!"

For the first time in Ash's life, she walked away from her god with only Tor by her side.

"Good thinking," Tor told her. "Are you all right?"

She clenched her jaw. Bunched her hands into fists.

Ignitus killed Char. Rook. Lynx. Ignitus desecrated our country.

"Yes," Ash said. She couldn't look Tor in the eyes. "Let's go meet Madoc and Elias."

SEVENTEEN

MADOC

THE HIRED CARRIAGE rocked to a stop at the palace gates. Inside the cab, Madoc turned a gold coin over his knuckles, hoping that Geoxus would agree to see him without Lucius or his suddenly supportive father.

"State your business." A palace centurion stuck his head through the window of the carriage, and after inspecting Madoc, flushed in surprise. "Apologies, champion," he muttered quickly, then motioned the carriage through, a messenger charging ahead on horseback to announce his presence.

By the time Madoc had gotten out and paid his driver, his heart was in his throat. He clung to the dim hope that Geoxus would show him mercy. That since he hadn't known Madoc wasn't Earth Divine, he might not sense the deception in what Madoc was about to say. That Lucius, who he'd bypassed by taking a carriage straight from Market Square, had not already informed the Father God of Madoc's strange tactics against Jann.

Madoc tried to keep a steady pace as he walked between the rows of palace guards that lined the path to the entrance, but everyone was watching him, and without the distraction of other party guests, he felt on display.

The glow from the pulsing white stones lining the path danced off the archway mosaic of Geoxus reaching an open hand toward the small people of Deimos. For some reason it made Madoc think of how Ash had said Ignitus was stripping Kula's resources, and how Petros was wringing the Undivine dry.

If Geoxus provided, his people wouldn't be in need.

He shook Ash's voice from his head. Geoxus did provide. The Divine had everything they could possibly want, and the Undivine could too if men like Petros didn't twist the Father God's intent.

Geoxus wasn't like Ignitus.

Madoc was asked to wait in the atrium, where he again found himself overwhelmed with the grandness of the enormous painted columns, and the fountains, spraying crystalline water over white marble figures. He stared out toward the terrace where he and Ash had danced before the gods and party attendees, and he straightened the decorative armor he'd changed into for this meeting.

He was still a champion. He needed to look the part.

The guard returned not long after and escorted Madoc into a long corridor that ran the length of the front wall. They stopped at a small room with a planked wooden floor that Madoc eyed with wary curiosity. He had not seen another room in the palace like it.

"The Father God will meet you in his chambers," said a servant, an old man with wrinkles around his eyes. He motioned toward the room.

Madoc's mouth went dry.

He stepped into the room. It seemed significantly smaller now that he was inside.

"You may wish to take hold of the railings," the old man cautioned. "The movement can be jarring."

Madoc wasn't sure what he meant, but as his eyes lifted, his jaw dropped. The top of the room had no ceiling, only a wooden crossbeam. A twisted chain was fastened to the center and extended up into the long stretch of tunnel overhead.

Another smaller rope hung from the ceiling, and as the attendant gave it a sharp pull, the ground beneath Madoc's feet lurched.

"What is this?" He'd been wrong. Geoxus *was* going to kill him. This unique torture device was just the start.

"A pulley of sorts," said the old man as Madoc gripped a railing. "Someone at the top loads stones onto a neighboring box, and when it's heavy enough to counter our weight, we rise."

The floor lurched again, along with Madoc's stomach. Then they began to lift, as if the room were floating.

Slowly, the corridor began to disappear below them. The entrance to the small room became a smooth, solid wall, slipping by faster and faster as they climbed.

"How . . ." Madoc adjusted his white-knuckled grip on the railing. Cold sweat dripped down his chest. "How high does this go?"

The attendant smiled. "To the very top."

Higher they climbed. Faster, until Madoc's stomach felt like it was in his sandals, and he was sure they had poked a hole through the clouds. When he looked up, the small flickering lights had grown larger, and a ceiling came into view. Fear gripped him. If they kept on at this pace, they were going to slam into it.

"Shouldn't we be stopping?" he asked.

"Yes, just about," said the old man.

Madoc's knees bent. He hunched, making himself smaller.

A moment later the pulley slowed, and the doors that appeared before them opened up into another room, this one just as grand as the rest of the palace, with a high ceiling glimmering with onyx and opal like stars in a night sky, and walls painted with bloody gladiator victories in the arena. Books lined the shelves on one wall, and a bed pressed against the other, three times the size of the one Ilena shared with Cassia at home.

Geoxus's personal chambers.

With a tilt of the old man's head, Madoc stumbled into the room, glad to be on solid ground. From behind came a creak, and when he looked back the doors were closed.

Before him, the balcony was open, and standing against the railing, looking out over the Nien River and the flickering lights of his city, stood the Father God, draped in black silk.

"Madoc." Geoxus didn't turn but motioned Madoc toward him with one hand.

On shaking legs, Madoc approached, moving carefully around a stout pillar shaped like two lush stone bodies wrapped around each other. The breeze from outside was stronger as he approached the balcony, the curtains dancing like smoke, teasing his ankles.

They were higher than Madoc had guessed. Stories upon stories in the air. He could see the ports at South Gate from here, and the line where the lights at the port at Iov met the black sea.

"Honorable Geoxus," Madoc said, voice unsteady. He hesitated at the edge of the balcony, feeling an odd tugging sensation pulling him closer to the brink.

Geoxus turned, and Madoc felt the urge to look away. Waves of black hair stretched to Geoxus's shoulders. The cut of his toga showed the gleam of his smooth, muscled chest. Power radiated from him, not unlike the anxiety that had crackled off Elias before the fight with Jann, and Madoc fought the odd impulse to touch the Father God's arm, just to see if he could feel that power.

"Thank you for seeing me," Madoc said.

"Of course." Geoxus smiled, and guilt splashed over Madoc's resolve. This was the Geoxus who had brought him Cassia when Madoc was alone in Crixion. Without his crown, he seemed more mortal than not, and Madoc felt a new wave of sickness over what he had to do.

Petros took Cassia, he reminded himself. *Petros has hurt countless people in this city.*

He had to break Geoxus's trust in Petros, even if it severed his faith in Madoc too.

"I always make time for my champions," Geoxus added. "You give our people so much."

Madoc dipped his head.

"How are you faring?" Geoxus asked. "This must be quite a change for you. The life of a stonemason is quite different from the life of a gladiator."

Madoc glanced at the luxury of the room behind him. There were servants he hadn't noticed standing beside the bed, and a door beside the bookcase. They were so still, they'd blended in, like the statues around the room.

"It is very different," he said.

Geoxus chuckled and leaned back against the railing, causing Madoc's chest to constrict. "You look well."

"I am, Honorable Geoxus," Madoc said, but the questions had begun pressing against his teeth. *Are you my god? Am I truly a son of Deimos?*

Or am I something else?

"Still glowing from your latest victory, no doubt." Geoxus grinned.

"That . . ." Madoc swallowed. Without thought, he pulled his breastplate away from his sweating chest, then stopped himself. How many times had Lucius told him that gladiators did not squirm? "That is what I came here to discuss with you, actually."

"Yes, tell me all about it. I wanted to attend but was tied up with war proceedings. Petty details Ignitus wants accounted for." Geoxus waved a hand dismissively, and Madoc frowned, reminded of the seaports that Kula stood to lose, and Ash's words in the preparation room.

He has a list of my country's resources, and he checks them off every time he wins one, as if he's collecting them.

He could not think of Ash now. He had to think of Cassia. He had to be *her* champion.

"I only fought Jann today because Stavos forfeited our earlier match."

Geoxus grew grim. "Yes?"

"I believe Petros may have had something to do with that."

Geoxus stepped closer. "You believe your father was behind the murder of my gladiator." His gaze darkened. "That is a very serious accusation. What proof do you have?"

Madoc felt as if his organs were vibrating. "None, Honorable Father God," he said. "I only know that Petros would do anything to gain your favor."

"And why would you say that?"

"Because I didn't win today using geoeia."

Madoc waited, braced for Geoxus to sand him raw or throw him over the edge of the balcony. An urge of self-preservation stirred the strange power in his blood, but it was trapped in place by a cage of doubt.

He had said the worst part; there was no going back now.

"I know Petros told you I went to him after I'd pledged myself to Lucius, but that wasn't the truth. It was the will of my father that I submit myself to Lucius Pompino at the start of this war. Petros said I wasn't to tell anyone who I was, and that I couldn't use geoeia." He deliberately left out any mention of soul energy, preferring to avoid territory he couldn't navigate his way through. "He demanded this of me, and I had no choice but to comply because he'd taken my sister, Cassia. She isn't his daughter. I thought if I could do what he asked, he'd give her back, but then I was chosen to be one of the Honored Eight . . ." Madoc shifted, aware of the fine line he was walking between accusing Petros of a war violation and accusing Geoxus. "I do not mean to question your judgment, but cheating caused this war. I do not want Deimos to be accused of the same due to my behavior."

Madoc felt another tremor rip though him. *Speak*, he urged Geoxus. *Say something.*

Geoxus's knuckles absently traced the line of his smooth jaw. "It is a weighty thing to turn against one's father," he finally said.

Madoc's stomach churned. His god or not, Geoxus was still the ruler of this land.

He focused on Cassia. He would say whatever he had to in order to free her.

He would sacrifice, like Ash, to bring his sister home.

"Petros has turned against our people," Madoc said, Jann's words from the fight rising like knives in his memory.

Geoxus stepped forward slowly, and Madoc trembled as the Father God's hand came down on the back of his head.

He did not feel a burst of strength or power. He did not feel *seen*, his mind on display for his god. He felt nothing but the gentle pressure of a kind touch.

"You'll speak to no one of this," Geoxus said.

"Of course not, Honorable Geoxus."

"Good." Geoxus sighed. "After all this time, few things surprise me, but you have. You've made me very proud with your efforts in this war."

Madoc's heart stuttered.

He should have been honored. Humbled. Geoxus was proud of him. But Madoc had fought in the arena—in a war—using a power other than geoeia. Such a thing was treason, upheld by the highest law. If Geoxus was pleased with Madoc's win, it meant that he was allowing such treason, and that was something Madoc didn't understand.

Geoxus was fair, and just. He was defending their country against the warmongering Ignitus—a god whose own people wanted him dead.

But Geoxus was saying Madoc did well, that he'd achieved greatness. By *cheating.*

That couldn't be right.

"Forgive me," he said. "I will withdraw from the war immediately. If you could ask Petros to return my sister . . ."

"Withdraw?" Geoxus huffed. "Why would you do such a thing?"

Madoc balked. "I told you. I didn't use geoeia. My father . . ."

"Your father is under control. You have no need to worry about him."

No need? Petros was torturing the people of Crixion with his debt collection and holding Cassia against her will.

"But my sister," Madoc tried again. "Her name is Cassia Metaxa—"

"Tell me about the anathreia," Geoxus interrupted. The wall of the Father God's emotions faltered, giving way to the slick, hot pulse of intrigue.

Anathreia. Soul energy.

Ilena and Tor had been right.

"You know?" Madoc asked.

"Of course I know. Why do you think I chose you for the Honored Eight?"

Madoc's bones turned to salt, fizzing as his blood rushed against them.

Geoxus didn't just know who he was, the god of earth had chosen Madoc *because* of what he was. It had been a deliberate choice.

Madoc had thought he could come here and discredit his father by playing to Geoxus's honor, but he'd been wrong.

Before he could find his bearings, Geoxus grasped his shoulder, leaning close. "Can you extract soul energy?"

Madoc flinched. Wariness drew his shoulder blades together.

"I don't know," he said slowly, panic igniting in him as he thought of the preparation room where Ash and Tor had talked about killing Ignitus, and Seneca had brought up the Mother Goddess. They'd thought Geoxus wasn't listening, but he must have been—that's how he knew about the anathreia.

A moment later, his fear was coated with dread. "Why are you asking me this?"

There could only be one reason: he wanted Madoc to use it in the arena. That's why he'd been chosen for the Honored Eight.

"Not yet, eh?" The Father God's voice thinned. "I suppose it was prideful to think you'd learn so quickly. Not to worry—we have time before the final match."

Madoc felt as though he were back in the moving room, only the floor had been torn away, and he was falling, nothing to cling to.

"Am I a descendant of the Mother Goddess?" he managed. "Are there more like me? How am I supposed to—"

"I know this must be a great burden on you," Geoxus told him, somber again. "If I could ease your suffering, I would. But Deimos is depending on you, Madoc. We cannot show weakness now. One crack in a foundation is all it takes to crumble a tower."

Madoc avoided the god's gaze, ashamed of all the cracks in his own foundation—all the questions and doubt poking through his gladiator facade.

"This is only the beginning," Geoxus continued. "I'll explain more when you're ready. All you need to know now is that great things are in store for our people because of you." He straightened and snapped his fingers to summon the servant from the bedside. "Get our champion something to eat. He must be famished."

Madoc had never been less hungry. Everything about this was wrong.

Geoxus already knew of Petros's corruption and had him "under control." The Father God was cheating at war. He wasn't even Madoc's god, not fully.

The intuition that Madoc trusted in every fight, the anathreia that told him when to stall and when to attack, was sending a warning through his soul.

Be ready, it said.

He would be.

EIGHTEEN

ASH

ASH AND TOR changed into old leather garments, grabbed weapons from their training supplies, and rushed out of the palace.

When they came to the bridge over the Nien River, Ash grabbed Tor's arm. She nodded at a fishing boat docked a few paces away, the oars tucked under a faded tarp.

"Energeia" was all she said, with a quick look at the stone road under their feet.

If Geoxus had been listening to their conversation with Ignitus, he might know what they were planning. He could be tracking them through the rock of this path. But if they took a boat across the river instead of the stone bridge, he couldn't follow them through the hydreia. They could dock far down and rush off into the city while Geoxus scrambled to locate them again.

Tor and Ash worked their way down the riverbank and leaped into the boat. They shoved off, rowing hard for the opposite side of the river.

Did the road groan when their feet left the rocks? Did a stone crack somewhere, sounding more like a bark of frustration?

Ash rowed hard and fast. The air smelled of chalky grit and crisp chill, of mildew-streaked river water and salted fish. She willed herself to believe that Hydra wasn't involved in this when the current of the river tried to push them off course.

Straining and sweat drenched, Tor and Ash reached the eastern bank of the Nien. They pushed the boat back into the water, hoping it would find its way to the other shore and whoever they had stolen it from.

Then they sprinted into Crixion.

Though they kept their weapons hidden, they still must have given off an air of aggression, for no pickpockets accosted them and passing groups of drunk revelers gave them wide berth.

The streets got progressively narrower, the buildings shabbier. Ash and Tor turned a corner and saw a short, manicured path leading up to a massive closed gate that was lined with precious gems, all of it dripping wealth even in the night's shadows. This villa's shuttered walls were opulently out of place, a jewel lodged in muck to remind the impoverished of what they would never have.

This was Petros's villa. Ash and Tor simultaneously slowed to a walk.

"How will we find them?" Ash whispered. The street was nearly abandoned; only one building showed signs of life, two up from where Petros's villa capped this street. It had a gauzy red curtain draped across the window and a sign over the entrance with a picture of an embracing, half-naked couple.

"Patience," Tor said. "Walk with purpose."

Don't stick out, Ash translated. She focused ahead, subtly scanning the edges of the road for Madoc. Her stomach tightened, but not in anxiety or fear—she was, somehow, excited.

She hadn't gotten to save Char. But she would help Madoc save Cassia.

Ash bit the inside of her cheek. If nothing else came of tonight, that would be enough.

Before they got to the end of the street, a figure pulled out of the shadows around the corner.

Elias jogged toward them. His face was gaunt, and it only intensified when Ash glanced behind him.

Madoc wasn't here.

"He never came to the carriage at the arena," Elias said. He bounced on the balls of his feet, sticking his hands deep into the pockets of his knee-length tunic. "He didn't come to Lucius's villa, either. I waited around for him as long as I could, but—what if Petros got to him first?"

Ash blew a fast breath out her nose. Guilt and panic squeezed her throat. "Petros knows we're coming. He's prepared."

She refused to let herself think beyond that. But the image of Stavos flashed through her mind. The arrows in his back. His look of horror.

If Petros had Madoc, and was doing to him whatever he'd done to make Stavos afraid . . .

The world tilted. Ash balled her hands, grounding herself.

Elias looked just as rattled, but also determined. "We need to do this anyway."

Tor rubbed his jaw, scratching the rough bristles. His eyes were distant on the walls of the villa. "We'll scout the villa first. See what's waiting for us." He looked at Elias. "Can you lift a section of the outer wall for us to slip inside? Something small, discreet."

Elias exhaled a hard grunt. "Yes. Am I coming in too?"

Tor considered. Elias still bounced from foot to foot. His nerves were as untamable as Madoc's—neither of them had been bred for fighting, and Ash realized Elias was weaponless. She almost called him on it—how much use would he be with only his geoeia?—but she realized he likely hadn't brought weapons because he couldn't get any without arousing suspicion.

She lifted a knife out of her sheath and extended it to him, handle first, keeping the blade hidden under her arm and out of sight of any passersby.

Elias eyed her, then the blade. He took it, scrubbing the back of his other hand across his nose. "Thanks. I—" He dug into his pocket again and handed something to her.

Two small stones and a knuckle-sized knot of downy fibers.

"We use those rocks to start fires, and the fiber as a tinder," he explained. "I thought you'd need igneia, but I realized halfway here just how much fire we already have in this city. You Kulans could burn us all to the ground, couldn't you?"

The tension in Ash's chest alleviated at Elias's gesture.

No Deiman worried about having igneia out in the city, not so far from an arena. It was ripe for the picking, torches lighting streets, lanterns hanging outside doorways.

She tucked the fire starter into her pocket. "To be fair, rocks are all over Kula too. You could just as easily decimate our country."

Elias grinned. Ash felt a tightening of cameraderie.

"The knife is only for desperate situations," Tor said. "Without Madoc, the situation has changed. I don't like being short a fighter. Elias—Ash and I will scout the villa for Madoc and Cassia first. The two of us will be less to worry about than three. If we find them, we'll get them out. You stay out here and hold the wall open in case we need to make a quick getaway."

Elias looked noticeably relieved. "Yes. Of course. Whatever you need me to do to get this done as fast as possible. My family's packed and waiting."

Ash's chest bucked. "You're leaving?"

Elias shook his head. "Just them. Madoc and I are staying." His face solidified. "We have to make sure Petros can't use our family against us anymore."

"Let's go," Tor interrupted, and he started off, drawing them closer to Petros's villa.

Ash tripped along behind him, her nerves easing back up. Walls towered three stories over her head. Beyond them, firelight speckled the night with orange here, there. Voices lifted—guards giving orders, servants out of sight calling commands to one another as they settled the villa for the night.

Tor angled Ash and Elias to the right, keeping to the shadows that crowded the wall's edge. Ahead of them, the villa's wall bent to run along the eastern side of Petros's complex.

Ash reached out, senses scrambling until she found igneia pulsing in a nearby lantern. Whoever had lit it would think the wind had blown it out as she pulled, the entirety of the fire soaking into her like water into a sponge. She pulled another lantern, a flickering candle;

more and more, until she was saturated, her body scalding.

"Good luck," Elias whispered.

Ash gave a small smile.

A moment passed. The earth under their feet trembled, rocks skittering around their sandals before the rough wall scraped against their shoulders. Ash bit down a chirp of surprise when a short arch appeared in the stone, so low she would have to squirm through on her belly. But it showed the villa's courtyard beyond, with Petros's soldiers and servants moving about, unaware.

Tor dropped to the ground and wriggled through first. When his feet disappeared into the hole, Ash flattened, using her elbows to work her way across the ground. Only when her body was half under the arch did she realize she was entirely dependent on Elias being able to hold this open if one of Petros's guards tried to close it over her.

She scrambled on and heaved herself through the other side. Tor was waiting in the shadows, his eyes glinting in the moonlight as he took in the villa's layout.

The main house was a grand structure of marble columns and silver lit by a few torches, a single firepit in the front courtyard, and the full white moon overhead. A few plain stone structures with shuttered windows sat around it—the stables and outbuildings. Two guards moved toward what was probably a barracks while a servant carried a basket loaded with laundry toward the backyard. Nearby, a small cluster of citrus trees made the air acidic with mingled orange and lemon oils. Some of them had gone rancid, and the stench tickled Ash's nose.

"You take the main house," Tor whispered. "I'll take the outbuildings. Look for Cassia and Madoc, and keep an eye out for anything that could lead us to Petros's true plan. Letters, documents, maps. But at the first sign of trouble, you run, Ash." He flipped his eyes to her, imploring. "You get yourself out, no matter what."

Ash nodded stiffly. She was operating on momentum and thoughtless action—if she paused too long, doubt and worries would obliterate her.

She didn't give Tor another chance to speak. She took off, ducking in and out of shadows as she made her way to the main house.

Ash yanked igneia from torches along her way, giving her more shadows to move through and building her strength. By the time she reached the house, her pulse was a hum.

She slipped along the wall until it ended in the open-air columns of a veranda. A hall stretched to her left, and a tall, narrow staircase lifted to the right; she headed for the stairs, ears straining for any shuffling servants or the clank of centurion armor.

The chill of the marble flooring penetrated Ash's sandals. A shudder rippled between her shoulder blades and she pulled free her remaining knife. Moonlight cut through windows and spilled over the white tiles, but that was the only light—no torches, no flames, not even any of those phosphorescent rocks. The igneia Ash had stored in her chest felt flimsy suddenly, a dying flame choking for oxygen.

She forced herself on, edging step by step onto the second floor landing. One side had balconies every few paces that showed a courtyard below; the other had three doors. Farther on, another staircase led back to the first floor.

If Cassia or Madoc were in this house, Petros would keep them close so they wouldn't be tempted to run. If one of these rooms was his, then the others might be theirs too.

Sweat slicked Ash's palms. She took a step forward, crossing the empty hall, her shadow playing on the ornate ivory walls.

She headed for the door on the right. No—the middle one. *No*, definitely not the middle one—that door was overlaid with a scene of wailing figures beseeching Geoxus alongside . . . was that Petros? The moonlight blurred the image.

Ash backed away from that door, her hackles rising.

She grabbed the knob on the leftmost door and twisted.

It didn't budge. Locked.

Breath a painful knot in her throat, Ash closed her eyes. This could mean death. This could mean a senseless end.

"Cassia?" she whispered into the doorframe. "Madoc? Are you there?"

Silence. Ash held her breath.

"Who are you?" a high voice whispered from the other side.

Ash choked on her relief. "Cassia! It's—it's Ash. You brought me records in the preparation chamber the other day."

"Why are you here?" A pause. "And why did you ask for Madoc too?"

"Is he with you?"

"No—did Petros get him too?" Panic rose in Cassia's voice. "What's going on?"

Ash started to shake, but she couldn't lose herself to questions now. She pushed on the door. "The door is stone—can you manipulate it?"

"If I could, I would've gotten out of here a long time ago. Petros had this whole room lined with wood. Listen, I'm not sure why you're trying to free me, but I—"

"Wait. Did you say wood?"

"Yes?" Cassia's voice twisted in question and worry.

"I'm going to try something. Stand back."

She heard Cassia shuffle away.

Ash backed up a step too. She sheathed her knife and shook her hands out by her sides. The igneia she'd drawn into herself would have to be enough.

The stone door on this side had a small iron lock. Ash focused on it, exhaling, relaxing.

A ball of fire filled her palms. She remembered the dance of the Great Defeat, the fire rope she twisted high into the arena. She made one now, lengthening the fire as thin as she could hold it. Sweat popped along her forehead with the effort, but she gritted her teeth together and slithered the fire snake for the lock. It eased into the hole, and Ash closed her eyes, swaying with each small, sparking flame and pulsing with every sizzle on the iron lock's grime.

That tumbler. Her flames pressed on it. *Click*. Another. And another.

The exterior lock released.

Ash pushed her flames on. They met the wooden interior and crackled hungrily, burning away the connection that kept Cassia imprisoned. She knew when fire burst into the room by Cassia's startled gasp. A pull, and Ash sucked the igneia back into her heart.

She opened the main door. The wooden one swung inward, leaving the lock in the frame, and Cassia gaped at Ash as she stepped into the hall.

Ash half smiled. "We should go. Elias is waiting at the east wall."

The moonlight shifted. Cassia's eyes weren't on Ash.

Ash looked over her shoulder to see a hulking form in the middle of the hallway.

Petros.

"You seem to have a habit of inserting yourself where you don't belong," he snarled.

He heaved his arms, ripping two massive chunks of marble from his own floor. As he threw them, Ash swung around and tackled Cassia, landing them flat just before the boulders sailed over their heads.

"Go!" Ash ripped Cassia to her feet and the two of them took off, sprinting around the rocks and down the opposite staircase. Petros thundered after them and the floor shook, the ceiling raining dust, the walls groaning as geoeia shifted and re-formed and—

Instinct seized Ash with white-hot panic. She hit the first floor and spun around in time to see a wave of razor-sharp rocks slicing through the moonlight toward her. A cry, and Ash washed a wall of flame up the stairs. She couldn't see anything through orange and shadow, but she heard the clatter of stones hit the steps and the sharp wail of Petros taking the hit of fire.

Outside, a horn sounded, calling Petros's centurions to mobilize. Alongside it, the earth rumbled, and a narrow window showed the walls of Petros's villa stretching taller.

A failsafe.

Even if Ash, Cassia, and Tor got to the wall, Petros likely had Earth Divine guards stationed all around, holding it secure. Elias would be unable to keep the small opening for them.

And where was Madoc?

Horror shredded Ash's resolve and she kept running. She skidded on the slick floor, a beat behind Cassia as they spilled into an atrium. They raced across it, leaping over a bare firepit and empty banquet tables.

The doors at the front end banged open and centurions surged into the room.

Cassia flung out her arms, catching Ash, the two of them gasping.

Before Ash had time to gather her wits enough to blast igneia, Cassia stomped on the stone floor. A violent crack trembled the room. Hands out under hovering stones, the centurions lurched at the unexpected quake. Cassia wasted no time—she grabbed the collar of Ash's armor and dragged her toward a smaller door set in the side wall.

They flew out into the night and stumbled to a halt at the top of a set of stairs.

Cassia panted in recognition. "The soldiers' barracks," she said as Ash's eyes adjusted to the shadows.

Centurions raced across the side yard, hefting weapons, barking orders. The villa door banged against the wall and drew the attention of one soldier, two, three—

A dozen centurions faced Ash and Cassia, spinning rocks with geoeia, poised to throw.

Reaching for Cassia's sleeve, Ash took a step back—but she bumped into someone.

Her skin prickled when she looked up and saw Petros, surrounded by centurions.

With one hand, Ash shoved Cassia down the steps; with the other, she washed flame in an arch that provided a cover. Her igneia was dwindling and all torches had been extinguished; she would be defenseless soon, but Ash pushed her fire hotter, heavier, with everything she had left.

Hands clamped her throat.

Ash lost the hold on her igneia, the fire snuffing out, throwing the courtyard into darkness but for the heavy, brilliant moon. It made Petros's eyes look ghostly and faded, his snarl feral, his fury potent.

It was impossible that this man was Madoc's father.

Ash clawed at his hand on her neck. His grip was relentless, but her legs were free—she managed a solid kick to Petros's stomach that bent him double.

Petros hurled her to the ground and she gasped on the surge of air. The centurions behind him moved, but he waved them off, grinning at Ash from his slumped position.

"I can see what my son finds so appealing about the young Kulan champion," he rasped.

Fury raged in Ash's stomach. She couldn't catch her breath, couldn't piece her thoughts together. And in the yard, she saw the centurions heave and pull the earth.

Cassia was fighting them, stones flying, and—flame. Tor was with her.

The world shifted and Ash tumbled down the steps to land in the yard at Tor's feet. He scooped her up, clamping her to him in a gruff, brief hug.

A few paces away, Cassia whipped away from having moved the step.

"I'm out of igneia," Ash gasped at Tor.

He grimaced. "You go in low and—*down!*"

The moon vanished.

Too late, Ash realized that a boulder hovered over her head.

She looked up at it. Pieces of dirt drifted off and brushed her cheeks.

The whole of the night slowed. The centurions, bent on blood; Tor spinning on Petros, who stood now on the edge of the side door's step, his arms lifted.

And Cassia.

She eyed the boulder. Then, dust flying under her sandals, she ran and urled herself into Ash.

Ash flew backward and rolled across the ground. A centurion spread his arms wide and snapped them shut, simultaneously opening and closing a solid mass of earth around her body.

She writhed, pinned, helpless as Cassia took a wide-legged stance under the boulder.

"Cassia!" Ash squirmed, tasting earth and rocks, grit in her eyes. "Get out! Just *get out*!"

Cassia's arms stayed lifted, bracing the rock over her head with geoeia.

Tor advanced at Petros with flames, but centurions blocked, three of them—four of them—*five* surging at him, finally taking him to the ground.

Cassia was alone against the centurions and Petros.

Ash bucked, but the soldier holding her bore down. She sank deeper, only her head staying above ground, her arms trapped and her legs twisted in stone and mud. Panic swarmed her with the delirium of drowning.

"Surrender, girl," Petros barked at Cassia. His raised arms bulged, strain showing on his sweat-glistened face as he pushed down while Cassia pushed up. "You're useful to me alive, but your death can be useful too."

Her feet shifted, slipping, but she held. "*No!*" Cassia screamed.

That scream moved the rock infinitesimally toward Petros, the force of Cassia's geoeia shoving him back, grinding his feet against the marble step.

"Take her!" he bellowed. "Take her *now*!"

Movement pulsed from the door. A woman stepped out of the shadows, the moonlight caressing her small, bent frame.

Ash blinked. Squinted.

Cassia gave a cry of recognition. "Seneca!"

Hope tangled with horror. What was Seneca doing here? Had Petros captured her too? If she was here, was Madoc? *Where was he?*

Take her, Petros's plea echoed in Ash's ears, jarring loose a memory. *She took it from me*, Stavos had wept before he died at Madoc's feet.

Seneca smiled, stretched out her hands, and pulled.

Cassia bucked from her head to her toes. She dropped to her knees, gaping at her palms.

"What—" She flared her hands. Nothing budged, no stones or rocks or dust. The boulder over her head remained, only held by Petros now, who grinned wickedly.

"It's gone." Cassia launched herself to her feet, teetered, and went back down in a weak topple. "My geoeia—it's gone. Seneca, *what did you do?*"

"Stop!" Ash begged. Tears rushed down her cheeks. "Stop it! Petros—let her go!"

He ignored Ash's cries, Tor's snarling curses, Cassia's look of terror and brokenness.

"Keeping you imprisoned didn't get through to Madoc," Petros snarled. "Maybe this will."

He dropped his arms with a savage grin.

The boulder, hovering over Cassia, crashed down on her.

"NO!" Ash screamed. "No—Cassia! *Cassia!*"

Sorrow cracked her chest. Only Cassia's arm could be seen reaching out from beneath the boulder, motionless.

Petros walked into Ash's line of sight, blocking the ivory moonlight. He lifted another stone, smaller but sharp and pointed at her skull.

"Ignitus will kill you," she snarled through her tears. "He'll kill you for murdering his champions, and Geoxus will have to let him."

Petros hesitated. But he dropped the stone, and it smacked the dirt next to Ash's head.

"Your god has no idea what's coming for him," Petros told her. To his centurions, "Bind them in my atrium and summon the Father God."

The soldiers moved. Petros retreated to the now-empty steps of his villa.

Seneca was gone, as though she had never been there at all.

NINETEEN

MADOC

BEFORE HE CROSSED the Nien River in a carriage borrowed from Geoxus's palace, Madoc could see the smoke rising in plumes from Petros's villa.

When news had come of the attack, Geoxus had gone still, placing one hand on the fitted stones of the wall. His head had tilted slightly, his eyes closing as his fingers spread and grew white at the knuckles.

I must go, he'd said quietly. *Kulans have attacked the house of Petros.*

Madoc, raw and still trying to make sense of Geoxus's knowledge of his anathreia and Petros's corruption, did not have time to ask what had happened, or if Cassia was all right, because before his eyes, Geoxus changed. The pale color of the stones seeped into Geoxus's hand, over his skin, and even his robes, until his chest matched the sandstone sculptures in the courtyard. The color climbed his throat, painting his face and even his dark eyes.

Then Geoxus, a moving, breathing statue, stepped into the wall and was gone.

Madoc had seen Geoxus move this way during the last party, when they'd found Stavos outside, but he still couldn't wrap his mind around it. In shock, he stumbled toward the moving room, and soon was in the carriage, cursing the slow pace of the galloping horses as they crossed the Nien River into the Olantin District where Petros lived.

As he reached his father's villa, Madoc fought off a punch of unwelcome nostalgia. In the thirteen years since he'd been turned away from these doors, the memories he'd earned within had become tainted, and then so marred by hate that he'd had to stuff them deep inside. Stored there, they could seem not to exist, as if he had been born a stonemason and lived with Elias his entire life. But now Madoc remembered every night he had dreamed of coming back to this place and burning it to the ground.

His gaze lifted from the crowd that had gathered in the street. The stone walls that surrounded the estate stretched twice as high as he remembered in his youth. It was a protective measure, but though the outside seemed unharmed, that could only mean that the real trouble was locked within. Fear throbbed as his eyes lifted to the smear of gray smoke across the black sky.

Ash and Tor couldn't be responsible. He'd told them he wanted no part of any plan.

Telling himself this did not ease the tension between his temples.

"Make way!" a centurion trumpeted as the palace carriage approached the opening gate. Inside, Madoc could make out a courtyard four times the size of the Metaxas' house, lined with potted plants and orange and fig trees, and the stone fountain of Geoxus, water pouring from his outstretched hands, that Madoc had once dipped his feet in on hot days. It was broken now, into chunks of marble strewn across the charred grass.

Questions and shrieks of surprise sliced through the cool night air.

"What happened here?"

"Is Petros dead?"

Through the shouting, Madoc heard a familiar voice.

"Madoc! *Madoc.*"

He searched the crowd, spotting Elias behind the row of centurions as the carriage entered the villa grounds.

"Elias!" Relief flooded Madoc but froze before it reached his heart. Elias should have been at Lucius's villa with the other attendants. Even if word had traveled quickly to the training barracks, it would have taken Elias a half hour by carriage to get here.

"Wait!" Madoc called to the driver, but they were already inside.

By the time Madoc stumbled out, the front gates were sealing with a screech of metal and rock. The crowd outside was muffled, and Madoc couldn't tell if it was due to the partition between them or the sudden rise of energeia in his blood. It swirled like an angry tempest, needling the back of his skull with dread.

Slowly, he turned, gaping. The front wall of the house was still aflame, attended to by half a dozen servants carrying buckets of water. A team of soldiers were dismounting outside the stables, where silver mosaics of twin horses rearing up on either side of the barn entrance glimmered through the smoke.

A warning throbbed in Madoc's temples. Too many conflicting emotions waited inside the house. He sensed them like sound, like smell. Like the bright flash of colors at the market. Fury and rage warred with despair and the sharp pitch of fear had his back straight as an arrow.

There was something else too. Something he didn't recognize. A void. A bleak, empty space, beckoning him closer. It felt wrong, and he wanted no part of it, but he couldn't turn back.

Willing his anathreia down, he charged up the house's steps and into the smoke, leaping over the scattered stones and burned bits of rubble and sprinting past a corridor lined by dark sconces on the wall. Madoc tripped over his own feet at the sight of it. His bedroom had once been down that hall. A space all to himself, with a bed twice as large as the bunk he squeezed into in the stonemasons' quarter, which he used to hide under to escape his father's wrath. He found Geoxus just beyond, in the atrium where Petros worked and took his meals. There were parties here, Madoc remembered. Food and drink. Music.

He'd forgotten about the music.

Now the table was overturned, the chairs were in pieces, and the moon shining through the open ceiling was the only light in the room.

Cassia, where are you?

"He's safe!"

At his father's cry of relief, Madoc stopped cold. Petros swept toward him, arms outstretched. For a moment, Madoc wasn't sure if he meant to embrace him or crush him with geoeia.

"Where's Cassia?" Madoc demanded. His own hands rose in defense, bringing Petros to a halt.

"Madoc!" A female shout sounded from the thick shadows on the far side of the room, cut short by the harsh crack of a slap against skin.

Madoc rushed past Petros toward the sound, ready to fight, ready to pull the energeia out of every god and mortal in this villa.

But as he approached, he didn't find Cassia.

Five armed guards surrounded a block of stone, their weapons drawn as if expecting someone to burst through. Madoc thought part of the wall must have collapsed in the battle, but as he peered through the dim light he caught a tremor of movement—the twist of shoulders, of a person struggling to get free—and he realized the stone was a deliberate creation of geoeia. A prison encasing not one, but two people. The man, facing sideways, was trapped from the neck down, his jaw flexing with the effort to break out. One of his heels extended out the side of the rock, frozen, as if he was in the process of kicking free.

The woman beside him was stuck just below the shoulders, her arms and legs disappearing into the stone, her long curls stuck to her cheek, hiding half her face.

Ash.

Fear solidified into a ball of ice in Madoc's chest.

Ash had come here to get his sister out, just as they'd discussed.

Petros came beside Madoc, a puff of dust rising from his toga as he batted it clean. "I feared for your life, son. They were so angry. So *furious* with you."

Madoc flinched. "Where is Cassia?"

Ash's face fell.

Panic skirted along the edges of his focus. *Why are you here? What did you do? Where is my sister?* He wanted to shout, but he had no voice.

The anathreia. He could make her tell him. He would pull it out of her.

But it had quieted again. Receded into that hole in his chest.

"What happened?" he managed.

"They came for you."

Madoc tore his gaze away from Ash to a scowling Geoxus, barely distinguishable from the shadows just behind him. A glow began to emanate from his hand, a phosphorescent rock for light. Its growing brightness cast an eerie gleam over the damage as Geoxus pressed it into the wall.

"Me?" Madoc's brows furrowed.

"No," Ash shouted. "Madoc, that isn't true. You have to listen—"

"*Quiet*," Tor warned as a guard raised the blunt end of his spear to strike her.

"It was fortunate you weren't here!" Petros motioned to the damage around them. "The Kulan gladiators climbed over my wall. We were shocked, caught completely off guard!"

Madoc could feel Ash's eyes on the side of his face. When his gaze flicked in her direction, tears were glistening in her eyes, gathering dust as they trailed down to her jaw.

Ash and Tor couldn't have come to kill him. They wanted his help—they'd said they needed him. Madoc had helped Ash. He'd held her grief in his hands, and when she'd seen the real him, she hadn't looked away. She wouldn't have betrayed him.

But here she was, with Tor, and his sister was nowhere to be seen.

"They set fire to my villa in search of you, Madoc." Petros heaved a breath, head shaking. "They kept asking for you—*Where is Madoc? Where is your beloved son?* They seemed to think you would be with me, not training with Lucius Pompino."

"That's not what happened!" Ash cried.

Madoc shook his head. This was wrong. It was as wrong as Geóxus placing the weight of his war on Madoc's shoulders.

"What is the meaning of this?" Madoc spun to find Ignitus materializing through a haze of gray smoke. His white robes offset the pale blue glow above his skin—the igneia just waiting to be set loose on anyone in his way. "My gladiators are caught outside the palace and I am the last to hear of it? This is an outrage. Where are they?"

Madoc slunk back without thinking. He didn't need to be Soul Divine to sense Ignitus's fury—guards and servants jumped out of his way as he approached his brother.

"Encased in stone," Geoxus growled, pointing to where Ash and Tor were trapped in the corner. "Which is more than they deserve for attacking a prized son of Deimos and trying to kill my top champion!"

Ignitus bared his teeth in anger. "Set them loose immediately."

The ground beneath Madoc's feet began to rumble.

"Tell me you had no part in this," Geoxus responded.

Ignitus's eyes pinched around the edges. "If I did, what would you do, brother?"

Madoc's pulse raced as the gods faced off. He remembered what had happened last time they'd argued. The quaking earth in the stable yard under Stavos's body. The plunge into darkness.

"Would you claim it a violation of the rules of war? Say I cheated?" Ignitus asked. "Maybe you'd use this as an excuse to double the stakes and sink your greedy claws into even more of my country."

Madoc braced for what remained of the walls to come toppling down. Without thinking, he glanced at Ash, whose teeth were clenched in horror.

"As much as your happiness means to me, no," continued Ignitus. "This was not my doing, and as such, I will see that my gladiators are punished accordingly."

Without looking away from Geoxus, he motioned to the guards. "Set them free."

Tension arced across the room, as brittle as burned sugar.

Petros charged between Ignitus, Ash, and Tor. "Do you think the Honorable Father God will let this offense slide so easily? Your gladiators have broken the rules of war! Attacked an innocent citizen and tried to murder another champion! They should be handed over to the Father God and sanded in the city center."

Madoc's muscles seized.

"We meant Madoc no harm, Ignitus!" Ash called. "We must speak to you. *Please.*"

"Shut up!" snapped a guard.

"The girl was so reckless in her rage, she destroyed my favorite servant." Petros's voice was lower now.

"Liar!" Ash screamed. "You did it! You and—" Her words were stopped by a fit of coughing. Dust sputtered from her mouth, sent there by a flick of Petros's geoeia.

Madoc's blood slowed, along with his heart.

Petros's favorite servant.

Destroyed.

He swallowed a hard breath, pulling at the ceremonial breastplate still clinging to his chest. It seemed to grow tighter by the moment.

They couldn't be talking about Cassia. He was jumping to conclusions. Petros had many servants.

Ash would have come here to protect Cassia, not destroy her.

Again, Madoc became aware of the void in this house, the empty space that filled him with a sense of wrongness.

Geoxus was talking. Madoc couldn't make sense of his words. Something about deceit and punishment. About war.

Ignitus had raised his hands and was shouting back.

Madoc's eyes found Ash's.

Where is Cassia? He didn't have to say the words. She knew what he wanted to know.

She shook her head, still unable to speak for the mouthful of dust. It didn't matter. Tears were streaming from her eyes. The tremble of her shoulders punctuated each shallow breath. Her grief was a physical thing, and it stretched toward him, painting him with poison.

Madoc couldn't breathe.

He didn't want her tears. He wanted Cassia.

"Be sensible, brother," Ignitus was saying. "No harm was done to your champion. We cannot forfeit this war based on one baseless accusation of attempted murder!"

"*Accusation?*" shouted Geoxus. "This man's house is nearly razed to the ground!"

"And at least some of that is his own doing," Ignitus shot back, pointing at the stones and rubble. "Any wrong done here was not by my will, I assure you. Let us end this war. *Tomorrow.* We'll forgo the final round of audition fights and be done with this, your best against mine."

Madoc turned away from them. The void was getting wider, a black pit in his gut, dragging him away. The voices became muffled in his head.

"Tradition says there are still four days until the final war battle. You offend me, then try to change the rules?"

"See reason. Chaos has haunted this war. Let us finish it."

"Fine—but you'll fight the girl. Not that big brute. He'll sit out."

Ash, finally able to speak, called Madoc's name again and again. He didn't listen.

He followed the sense of emptiness, his hands numb, his mind blank. He turned toward the side door that led to the guards' barracks, picking his way through debris. The fire at the front wall was now out; a servant girl sat on the ground, heaving, her hands wrapped around a bucket. The smoke had mostly dissipated, but the scent was still strong in the air.

The emptiness widened, filling his lungs.

There had always been a boulder near this exit. He remembered climbing it when he was young to watch the guards and the servants mingle over the wall. Someone had moved it closer to the main gate.

This was the center of the void. The absence that had felt so wrong since he'd first come. He'd thought his anathreia had silenced, but it had been calling him to this place the entire time, beckoning him like a nightmare he was trying to forget.

As he approached, terror gripped his limbs. He could see a figure lying on the ground beside the boulder—a girl. Her tunic was torn and dusty, her dark hair matted with soil and blood. She was still, and well before he reached her, Madoc knew that she was dead.

Even as the void drew him forward, part of him fought to pull away. Still, he kept going. She was lying in a hollowed-out area. The indentation created by the boulder now beside her.

He fell to his knees. Crawled closer.

"Cassia."

The emptiness. The utter lack of energeia. He could feel no soul inside her. It was gone, and he had been too late.

He took her hand in his, her cold fingers fragile and lifeless. He bowed his head to the back of her wrist. *I'm sorry. I'm sorry. I'm sorry.*

He rocked, elbows digging into the earth. Every muscle in him seized. Every part of him hurt.

Let's go home, she whispered in his mind. She was introducing him to Elias. To Ilena. *This is my new brother*, she'd said.

Behind him, he heard movement. People running, shouting to each other.

Ash's voice. "Madoc!"

The girl was so reckless in her rage, she destroyed my favorite servant.

Petros's words were lies. Cassia had no burns on her clothing or skin. She'd been crushed by rock, by this boulder beside her.

But maybe she wouldn't have been if Ash had never come.

The gates at the front of the villa opened. More movement, and the sudden roar of voices waiting outside.

The gates closed.

He couldn't let go of Cassia's hand.

He would find out what had happened to his sister, and those responsible would suffer.

Madoc didn't know how much time had passed, but soon he

became aware of a man standing beside him. The familiar disappointment and irritation scraped at Madoc's skin.

"When you were a child, you used to feed a stray dog in the street, do you remember?" Petros asked.

A scrounging gray mutt with a half-torn ear. Madoc remembered.

"You were so determined to make it a pet. Every day you brought it scraps from the kitchen, and every day, it came a little closer, until one day it was close enough for you to touch. What happened then?"

Madoc gritted his teeth, the faint scars on his forearm tingling.

"It bit you," Petros said. "The guards had to crush it with stones to loosen its jaw." He inhaled slowly. Exhaled on a sigh. "You are still that same boy, trying to coax the loyalty out of a wild animal, and shocked when it betrays you."

In Madoc's mind, he rose. His hands closed around Petros's throat. He squeezed until the life was gone, and the void belonged to his father.

But Madoc didn't rise. He didn't let go of Cassia's hand.

"A father's duty is to teach his son the hard lessons of life, even if that means taking away the things he loves." Petros patted Madoc's shoulder, not noticing how Madoc flinched away. "Get some rest. At dawn, you need to put the Kulan girl down."

With that, Petros turned and walked away.

Cassia was smaller than Madoc realized.

Even when she was young, she'd been loud—banging pans together or shouting for attention. When her geoeia had manifested, she'd become a nightmare. Madoc would walk headfirst into dust storms of her making or have to catch stones she hurled his way. When she was happy, everyone was happy. When she was mad, everyone needed to hide.

But as Madoc wrapped her in a blanket that a servant had brought out to air, he realized it had been her soul that had taken up so much room. Without it, she was no more than the bones that had carried her.

With trembling hands, he bound her arms to her sides and smoothed down her hair. Fighting the bile that clawed up his throat, he covered her face and the marks on her legs. He needed to take her home to clean her up; then they could bring her to the burial fields outside the city, where her body would reunite with the earth over time. But the thought sickened him.

He longed for the void to take him over so that he could feel nothing, but it denied him. With every breath, he swallowed glass. Each brush of her cold skin burrowed ice through his bones. She was broken, and pale, and bloodied, and everything about her was wrong.

And it *hurt*. It hurt to touch her. It hurt to look at her. It hurt not to find Petros and siphon the life out of him. It hurt not to chase Ash down and demand the truth about what had happened. It hurt because maybe he was too much of a coward to do any of that. Maybe that was why he hadn't gotten Cassia sooner—not because he'd put his faith in Geoxus, or because he'd thought incriminating Petros would set her free, but because he'd been weak.

He wouldn't be weak now. She needed him to tend to her, so he would.

When he was done, he felt as if a hand had closed around his throat. His breath came out in a fractured sob.

He forced swallow after swallow until the tension subsided. He would not cry here.

He removed his armor and left it on the ground.

"All right," he said. "Let's go home."

He picked her up, rested her fragile head against his chest. She weighed practically nothing, but still his arms and lungs trembled with the effort.

Petros's guards didn't stop him. They opened the gate without a word and closed it behind him. The crowd was gone now; only a few servants remained to clean up the mess.

At dawn, you need to put the Kulan girl down.

Ash.

Ash had come here when he'd told her not to, and now Cassia was dead.

He crossed the street, stopping when someone stepped into the light of a nearby torch.

Elias took one look at the bundle in Madoc's arms and caved forward, arms around his waist. He shook silently, and tears streamed from Madoc's eyes.

"Get up." His voice broke. "We're not doing this here."

Elias got up.

They walked home, taking turns carrying their sister.

By the time they reached the stonemasons' quarter, the ache in Madoc's chest had stretched to his arms. No one had bothered them on the roads—it was too late for most to be out, and those who were seemed to recognize that they should be left alone.

He and Elias hadn't spoken, but there were words Elias wanted to say, Madoc could tell. Every so often, Elias's breath would grow rough. He'd punch his thigh, swallow a sob. Maybe it was better that he didn't speak. Their failure had cost Cassia her life.

The taverns and brothels were beginning to close as they made the final turn down their alley. Elias led the way, head bowed, and when they entered the courtyard, Madoc was surprised to see the lights in the house still lit. As if expecting them, Danon rushed outside, Ilena on his heels.

They were dressed strangely—wearing too many clothes, maybe all they owned. Ilena had a bag over her shoulder, and it fell with a clatter on the ground, baskets and utensils rolling free.

Were they leaving?

A sharp pain jabbed at his empty stomach.

He looked to Elias, wondering again why he'd been at Petros's—but Elias only shook his head, the hair falling over his eyes, and rushed toward their mother.

"No," Ilena said, and all the questions died. "*No.*"

She turned to go back inside. The bag was left on the doorway.

"Is that . . ." Danon's gaze bounced between them, horrified. "What happened? You said we were all leaving!" Elias ignored him, pushing by to follow Ilena inside.

Through the window, Madoc saw her crumple against the side of the table and fall to the floor.

Steeling himself, he carried Cassia into the house. He took her to the bedroom and laid her on the bare mattress.

He was right—they *had* been leaving. The blankets were gone.

Why? Would they have told him?

He felt something tear open inside him. The hot spill of shame and guilt and loss. He was alone. Even when he'd wandered the streets, searching for help, he'd never felt this alone.

The next moments were a blur. Danon's relentless questions. Ilena's wail of grief. Ava was crying. Elias, for once, tried to keep them all calm.

Ilena came and lay beside her daughter on the bed. Madoc, now curled in a ball in the corner, wanted to lie beside them, but he couldn't let go of his knees. The void had reached him, finally, and it was sucking in every emotion, screaming with hunger. There was too much here to feed it. Too much pain. Too much grief.

"You didn't listen," Ilena whispered. Her words weren't for Cassia, they were for Madoc, and he crawled to her, pressing his forehead against the edge of the mattress. "I told you we'd handle this as a family. But you didn't listen."

Her pain was like a noose around her neck, closing off her words. Madoc couldn't stand it. He could take it. He would, for her.

He rocked onto his heels. Her back was to him. Tentatively, he placed one quaking hand on her shoulder and opened himself up to her pain.

Instantly, he tasted her bitter despair. It was like Ash's grief, but more potent, and even as he hated himself for the rush it gave him, he hoped it gave her peace.

"*No.*" She shook him off. Sat up. Faced him. "Don't you do it, Madoc. I will feel every bit of this."

He was disgusted with himself.

He rose and left the room. He shoved by Danon, still holding a packed bag on his thighs, and Elias, carrying Ava around the kitchen.

No one stopped him.

He wanted out of this house. Out of this district—this entire city. He wanted to run so far no one would ever find him. Anger rose up in him, as harsh as Ilena's pain. He wished Cassia had never found him on the temple steps. That he had stayed an orphan, unwanted. Unattached.

Unable to hurt anyone.

He was done fighting. Done pretending he was a gladiator. He pushed out through the Metaxas' front door, his last view of their home the floor above, where Seneca watched him from her balcony, a candle in one hand, a cat curled in the other. He walked, the minutes turning to hours as he passed the quarry and the aqueduct, winding through the alleys toward South Gate. And as the sun glittered over the golden water, he skirted around the crowds on the streets that headed toward the arena in their black and gray paint, ready to cheer him to victory.

He wouldn't be there.

TWENTY

ASH

THE SUN HAD barely risen, but already it scorched the arena. The logical part of Ash's brain whirled. *Heat is good. It will slow my opponent.*

She braced one hand on the arched entryway that would spill her out into the fighting pit. The warm, gritty stone was all that kept her from dropping to her knees.

That, and the Deiman centurions standing guard at the end of the hall, there to make sure she didn't run. She wouldn't show weakness in front of them.

If she won this fight, Kula would keep the fishing rights in the Telsa Channel, the stock in their glass trade, the two valuable seaports. The vital resources Ignitus had staked on this war.

If she lost, Kula would slip even further into poverty.

Madoc's life or fishing ports. Madoc or Kula.

Cassia. Saving Ash's life. Once—by pulling her away from Petros.

A second time—by shoving Ash aside and taking the weight of the boulder meant for her.

Because of Seneca. Ash still couldn't process what she had seen. Hints of connections threatened to tie the remaining pieces of the mystery together, but she refused to think about them now. She couldn't unravel yet.

The look of disgusted shock that had paled Madoc's face in the villa's main room would forever be branded in Ash's mind. Where had he been? Petros obviously hadn't captured him.

Ash wanted to talk to Madoc. She wanted to apologize. She wanted to bear the weight of the blame she knew that she deserved from him.

She and Tor had failed. Not just failed—they had gotten an innocent girl killed.

Just like Rook. My fault, my fault, all of it—

Ash gagged, her fist to her mouth. She had lost count of how many times she had vomited since centurions had locked her in a chamber in Geoxus's palace last night. Getting to this moment—the roar of the crowd and the heat of the sun and the wide, waiting glitter of sand—had been a blur of grief.

Drums rumbled across the arena. The crowd thundered, pushed to hysteria by the unorthodox detour from the usual structured wars. They wouldn't have more parades and parties; they wouldn't get the final audition fights. This was it. This fight would end the Kulans' stay in Deimos.

This would end everything.

"Ash Nikau will fight on behalf of Kula," an announcer bellowed.

Ash hobbled out of the tunnel. Sand slid over her feet, velvet soft and warm, and she lifted her eyes to the cheering crowd. People wore elaborate costumes, mock armor and full body paint and signs that read *Death to Kula!*, *Geoxus Prevails*, and *Glory, Glory.*

To her right, bodies packed the grandest viewing box. Untouched food weighed down a table while around it, upper-class Deimans mingled with Kulans.

Ash spotted Tor, Taro, and Spark. They were at the edge, watching her, faces gaunt with sleeplessness and strain. They had prepared her for the battle, but centurions had kept a close watch the whole time and escorted them out as soon as they'd finished. She hadn't gotten a chance to ask what she should do.

In the viewing box beside Tor, clutching the railing just as tightly, stood their god.

Ignitus hadn't spoken to them until they'd returned to the palace. There, Ash had been too grief-stricken to say more than that Petros was plotting against Ignitus—*Your god has no idea what's coming for him.*

Tor had scrambled to apologize. Geoxus had every right to execute them for what they had done.

But Ignitus had shaken his head. "Tell me what happened tomorrow," he had said, "after you defeat my brother's champion."

He had shown restraint. He had shown—dare Ash even think it?—kindness.

Ash lifted her hand to the viewing box. Tor nodded at her, solemn.

Ignitus lifted his hand in return. "Ash!" he cheered, though there was no joy in it.

Tor glanced at him, then caught the cheer. "Ash! Ash!"

Soon, all the Kulans in the box were chanting her name. Beating it alongside the heavy drums.

Ash dropped her head, tears welling, heat streaking through her in stabs of sorrow.

"Fuel and flame," she whispered. "I am fuel and flame."

"Madoc Aurelius," the announcer said, "will fight on behalf of Deimos."

The crowd, being mostly Deiman citizens, made such a noise that Ash fought to keep from covering her ears.

She turned, slowly, and faced the archway where Madoc would emerge.

It was empty.

A moment passed. The crowd's cheers grew.

Why was he delaying? Was Geoxus making him wait in order to build anticipation?

Ash cut a glance at the other half of the viewing box. Geoxus had his arms crossed over his broad chest, flicking his scowl back and forth from Madoc's archway to Ignitus, a few paces to his left. Geoxus's people applauded—one of them was Madoc's sponsor, Lucius.

Another was Petros, smugly gazing down at the tunnel.

Ash fought not to tear the igneia from the firepit that waited for her and hurl it all at him.

The cheers faded; the crowd was confused.

Ash's eyes flipped back to the archway to see a man striding across the sands toward her. Her heart seized before she realized it was Elias, not Madoc.

And he was wearing Madoc's armor.

"What trick is this, brother?" Ignitus's voice broke the edge of Ash's awareness.

"Stop the fight!" Geoxus boomed. "Find my champion!"

Commotion filled the stands, but Ash didn't look away from Elias. She matched his pace, holding her breath against the sizzle of wariness that compelled her to turn back. Why was he here? Why was he outfitted to fight?

Where was Madoc?

They met in the center of the pit, Ash's bowl of raging flames to one side, a pile of boulders that she knew were just for show on the another, and a rack of weapons between the two.

The moment she drew close enough to see Elias's face, Ash's chest bucked. He was seething at her, shoulders rising and falling in tight breaths.

"Elias," Ash said slowly, "where is Madoc?"

Guilt wrung her veins until black spots danced across her vision. Madoc hadn't been able to face her, so he'd sent his brother in his stead?

"He never should've been a gladiator," Elias told her. A bead of sweat darted down his face. "It always should've been me. I hid behind him and let him take the hits—" He hiccuped and scrubbed the back of his hand across his nose, giving his head a jerky shake.

The crowd started to boo. They wanted blood. They wanted

Madoc to charge out and destroy the Kulan gladiator.

Back in Elias's tunnel, centurions were talking ferociously, giving orders, shouting. They sprinted into the darkness, no doubt searching for Madoc.

"Where is he?" Ash tried again. "He can't want you to do this."

"He never showed." Elias gave a shrug, calm despite the tears in his eyes. "I told the centurions he just didn't want to be disturbed, but truth is, I haven't seen him since last night. This isn't his fight anymore."

Madoc had left?

Guilt piled on guilt, regret clacked atop regret, until Ash couldn't pull in a breath for all the agony clogging her body.

"Elias—"

"I failed Madoc," he whimpered, eyes on the sand. "I failed Cassia. I was going to take her home and our family was going to leave the city and they would've been safe—"

Elias's eyes shot up to meet Ash's.

And she buckled, faltering back a step under the raw fury that punctuated his glare.

"But now she's dead," Elias snarled. "She's dead because I trusted *you*."

He clenched one of his hands and the boulder pile next to him shifted. One rock rose above the others, and Ash dropped into a defensive stance.

"Elias—Elias, *stop*!" She held a hand out to him, one toward the rock. "I'm sorry." Anguish pinched her words. "I'm so sorry about Cassia."

His face turned scarlet, then purple. "Don't say her name. Don't even *talk* about her."

The rock flew.

Ash flattened to the ground a beat too late. The rock tore across her shoulder.

Pushing the pain to the back of her mind, she twisted to her feet, pulling igneia to fill her palms with open flames.

Elias circled her, slow, meticulous steps, his eyes watchful and intense.

Around them, the crowd had resumed their cheers as though Elias was, in fact, Madoc. But surely the gods were still fuming. Surely Ignitus was crying foul on this breach of war rules. Surely someone would stop this.

"I'm so sorry. I don't know how to fix this!" Ash straightened, snapping the flames into her heart. "I don't want to fight. I won't."

Elias stopped. Sand mounded around his ankles. "I will."

More rocks flew at her. Ash batted away the first one, but the second caught her in the temple and she hit the ground, sand spraying in her face. She spat it out, but the world spun and flickers of light played over her eyes.

"You were supposed to *save her*."

Rocks clacked, shifting in the pile, and though Ash couldn't see them, she scrambled forward, elbows dragging through the unstable grit.

A stone crashed into the back of Ash's head. She rolled over, clutching the spot, pain like white lightning shooting down her spine.

Madoc or Elias—it didn't matter who was attacking her. She couldn't fight either of them. She wouldn't.

She had gotten their sister killed.

Just like she had gotten Rook killed.

She had failed in so many ways, and this felt like that reckoning, all of her mistakes come to demand recompense here, now.

Ash sobbed and shifted upright, one hand braced behind her, the other holding her blood-dampened head. "Elias," she begged. "Stop—please—"

"Stop? *Stop?*" Elias bent double, the remainder of the rock pile rising behind him like a wave of death. "You have no right to ask me for anything!"

He flung out his hands.

Dizzy, Ash managed to get to her feet.

The crowd was wild with bloodlust. Jeers of *Kill the Kulan!* echoed across the stands. Ash wanted to look at the viewing box for some burst of support, but the images beyond the fighting pit were a blend of color and shape, movement and fog.

She ran. She ran and ran, and when she tripped, she hit the ground with a jolt of memory.

Char, looking at her across the arena's pit in Igna.

Mama, don't do this. Mama, he'll kill you.

Rook, his body smashing into the fighting pit.

Please, Rook, hold on—

Shadows speckled the sand around Ash. She stiffened and looked up.

A dozen stones hovered over her, poking holes in the morning sunlight.

The crowd bleated. "Kill her! Kill her!"

The first stone dropped with a jarring thud onto her spine. Something cracked in her chest, and she cried out—behind her, Elias pushed the rock deeper, harder. It twisted, cutting into skin and muscle.

Ash screamed. She tried to claw her way out, but the rock anchored her, and she knew—she would die here.

Let me take your place, Mama.

She had begged her mother to let her be a gladiator. *I can handle it*, Ash had thought.

But she couldn't. She couldn't handle this pain—she wanted to cleave her body apart to escape it as the rock burrowed into her back.

Another rock dropped, smashing into Ash's head, pinning her skull to the ground. She had been helpless many times throughout her life, but *this* type of helplessness broke her. She whimpered and writhed, half hearing the muffled pleas spilling out of her mouth. She didn't want this. She didn't want to die like this.

The sand wavered in the heat; the crowd's noise was a dull roar. Ash was fading, flickering, a candle pulsing in a raging storm.

Across from her was an archway. Far away, too far for her to reach, someone staggered out under it.

Madoc?

The stone on her head pushed down, down—

There was light.

Bright, all-encompassing light, as though the sun had dipped down to escort one of its daughters to the afterlife. It flooded every space in Ash's body, expanding her broken ribs, soothing her cracked skull.

Ash fell into it. If this was how life ended, she didn't know why she had ever feared death.

Death was calm. Death was safe.

Death felt strangely like energeia.

Ash's eyes flew open. She was standing, her body humming with power and might and *burn it all*, she had never felt this good. Every muscle stretched and relaxed, ready for use; every bone was whole and strong; every nerve tingled with alertness.

Her body reacted, moving as more stones descended. Speed let her dodge left, right, left, cutting around the rocks as Elias jutted his arms to direct the geoeia.

"No!" Giant tears tumbled down his face. "No—I have to do this!"

Behind him, through Ash's tunnel, Kulan guards stormed the fighting pit. They sped toward Elias, who didn't notice their approach.

The first guard hurtled into him, taking him to the ground. His hold on the geoeia dropped and the remaining stones crashed to the sand around Ash like so many raindrops.

The noise of the stands came back to her. Someone—Ignitus?—was shouting, "Arrest him! He interfered with this war—arrest him!"

Others: "How did she survive? What energeia is this?"

Ash whirled toward the archway.

Madoc stood there, his hands out to her, palms up.

He swayed and dropped to his knees.

The Kulan guards wrestled Elias into submission. He sobbed, heaving against them.

"I'm so sorry," she told him.

Ash sprinted away, toward Madoc.

He leaned against the sandstone bricks, sweat sheening his face, his eyes closed.

Above them, the crowd's cheering became murmurs of confusion—had the war ended? What had happened to Geoxus's real champion?

Ash threaded Madoc's arm around her shoulders. It was far easier than it should be to support him.

"You came back." It was both a question and a statement.

He lifted hooded eyes to her before he nodded down the hall. "Preparation chamber. Before—"

Footsteps pounded on the stands, through the tunnels. At any moment, centurions would storm after them, following the orders of two no-doubt-furious gods.

Ash dragged Madoc for the closest room. She kicked the door shut and heaved her hip into the bolt to lock it. It would only buy them a little time.

This preparation chamber wasn't for public use—it was opulent and pristine, worthy of a final war match. Ash had been vaguely aware of the gaudiness of her own that morning, the blue silk covering the walls, the padded chaise and table spread with food and drink.

This one looked just the same, only with heavy onyx silk accented by white lace. Phosphorescent stones glowed in the walls, but for once Ash didn't seethe with the lack of igneia—her body was awash with color and light from Madoc's anathreia.

In the corner a cushioned pallet sat on a raised dais, and Ash eased him onto it before turning to the supplies spread on the table. She poured minted water from a pitcher into a ceramic bowl. There was a sponge too—she dipped it and turned back to find Madoc lying on the pallet, one arm thrown over his forehead, his eyes split open enough to watch her.

His attention immobilized her. Water dripped down her fingers, splashed on her feet, perfuming the air with the sharp, cool scent of mint.

"What happened?" she whispered.

Madoc's arm slid off his forehead. "I tried to leave." His voice wavered. He sat up, legs folded under him, looking down at his hands in his lap. "But I heard the crowds in the arena. People running past said that Geoxus's champion hadn't shown—and his attendant had taken the ring." Madoc glanced up at her, unspeakable sadness in his eyes. "Elias blamed you for Cassia. Why?"

Ash tossed the sponge to the floor and dropped to sit at the end of the pallet. She gave Madoc a brief summation of what she had overheard in the arena's tunnel after she'd left him at the temple, Petros admitting to Geoxus that he had killed Stavos. She told Madoc how she had looked for him, how Elias had looked for him too. And how they had decided to free Cassia—and that when Elias had been unable to find Madoc, they had all feared Petros had taken him.

"I was with Geoxus," Madoc said quietly. He winced, rubbing the skin between his brows. When he spoke again, his voice was thin with tears. "I was trying to get him to free her."

Ash twisted one leg between them on the silk blanket. Tears pricked her eyes as she grabbed his wrist. "I'm sorry. We shouldn't have gone into Petros's villa at all."

Her words tumbled into themselves.

"Seneca was there," she forced herself to say. The final missing piece. The mysterious *she* Stavos had mentioned. "She can control anathreia too. She took Cassia's divinity."

Madoc whipped a horrified look to her, bloodshot veins running through his eyes. "Seneca is Soul Divine?" He paused, gaping. "That's how she knew so much about it."

Or she's something far worse. But Ash couldn't say more without disintegrating.

A brittle sob racked her. "Everything's so wrong," she managed. "It's too much. You shouldn't have come back. You were right—you should've just run while you had the chance."

"But then you'd be dead," Madoc whispered.

Ash thanked the blur of tears in her eyes that she couldn't see the look on his face. She didn't think she'd be able to handle it.

"You should know," Ash started, "that Cassia saved my life. She was so strong, and she fought so well. She died protecting me."

Madoc gave a weak chuckle. "That sounds like her. She was our protector—kept us in line, at least. She always did what was right. If Petros had wanted Elias or me, she'd never have let us get taken in the first place." He scrubbed the heel of his palm into his eye.

Ash's heart cracked. "I'm so sorry."

She was still touching his other wrist; she could feel his pulse beating under her fingertips. And when he twisted his hand to grab her arm, gripping her imploringly, Ash couldn't breathe.

Madoc kept his head bent. "It wasn't your fault."

Ash jolted, relief trying to push its way through the heaviness of sorrow and the intensity of sitting here next to him. But she had carried guilt for so long in other forms—she didn't know how to peel it off, even with his absolution.

She started to stand. "Thank you for saving me. We should—"

Madoc's fingers tightened around her arm. They were callused on the tender skin of her wrists, and that touch kept her seated. "You didn't fight back. Against Elias."

"Of course not."

"He would have killed you." His eyes lifted to hers, intent, heavy. "I thought he had."

Ash felt timid under his gaze, though she was covered in dried blood and sweat and sand. "I'm an enemy gladiator. Losing me shouldn't matter to you."

"If it didn't matter to me"—Madoc's voice was husky—"I wouldn't have stood in that entrance hall, watching Elias hurt you, thinking, *Not her, too.*"

Ash's body vibrated so fast it hummed. It seemed impossible that he was saying this to her, that he *cared*, after everything that had happened.

But he wanted her.

He had seen all her truths and scars and failures, and had still rushed back to save her life.

Ash's lips parted, her eyes darting over his, searching for some sign that this was all a ruse. But his sincerity was as pure as it had always been.

After a lifetime of fighting to keep herself out of the yawning chasm that was loneliness, Ash let it rise up over her. She didn't have to fear it.

A dam broke in her chest. Madoc's hand was around hers, but suddenly that small touch of his fingers on her skin wasn't enough. She wanted his arms around her. She wanted to feel his body's warmth against her own heat. She wanted to comfort him and let him comfort her and feel something *good* in all this *bad*.

"Madoc." His name tumbled out of her mouth, a plea, a promise.

His eyes fell to her lips. Light spun through Ash's mind.

But footsteps stampeded up the hall, breaking her out of the spell.

She flew to her feet. Madoc pushed himself up beside her and gave her a firm look.

Unable to speak, she took his hand. He squeezed her fingers.

A heartbeat later, centurions kicked in the door and backed away to reveal—Geoxus.

Unease roared in Ash's chest. But he wasn't alone. As he stepped across the threshold and his guards retreated, two figures followed him into the room. Petros, and—

Ash's blood went cold. "Seneca."

TWENTY-ONE

MADOC

MADOC'S GAZE SHOT from the god, in his sweeping black silk, to Petros's jewel-studded robes, to the hunched woman in the baggy gray tunic who clung to his father's arm for support.

What was Seneca doing here? Ash had said she was Soul Divine. Maybe the old woman was here against her will—Geoxus had been interested in Madoc's anathreia as well. But that didn't explain why Petros was touching her so gently.

"Well done, Madoc!" Geoxus stepped over the shattered door and placed his heavy hands on Madoc's shoulders. "I admit, I was surprised to see your attendant try to step in and take the glory, but you put a stop to it, didn't you? I assumed you wanted to kill the Kulan yourself, but I see that's not the case!" His low chuckle rumbled in the room. "The things mortals will do for love never cease to surprise me."

Wariness churned in Madoc's stomach. Geoxus wasn't upset that Elias had taken his place. He was *praising* Madoc.

"Rumors are already circulating that the Metaxa boy was tired of living in his champion's shadow," said Petros, petting Seneca's hand. "That his jealousy became uncontained. The drama has only built the people's anticipation—they're calling for the true main event now. We'll delay, of course, for another day or two. Make them purchase a new ticket in order to see my son."

My son. The words chafed Madoc's skin.

Nothing about the scene before him made sense. He hadn't fought, and still Geoxus was delighted. Petros had threatened to kill Madoc's family if he didn't win the final match, and yet he seemed relieved. Seneca's smile appeared more pleased than confused, and no one seemed to notice Ash at all.

With a lurch, the wrongness of the situation caught up with Madoc, and everything within him screamed to tear the man who'd killed Cassia limb from limb. The rage was so intoxicating, he could barely breathe.

Ash's grip on his hand held him steady.

"Madoc is the hero Deimos needs," Geoxus said proudly. "The time of gladiators is ending. The old crone said you'd be worth the wait, and she was right!"

The old crone must have been Seneca, but why Geoxus was calling Madoc a hero didn't make sense. The last time he had seen the Father God, he'd been sure Geoxus wanted him to use soul energy to win this war, but now he seemed just as pleased that Madoc had used his power to save the enemy.

Geoxus's smile, lit by the pale green phosphorescent glow of the stones in the walls, filled Madoc with dread. "The Kulan was as good as dead, but you used anathreia to bring her back. Do you know what this means? Do you have any idea what you're truly capable of?"

Madoc slid back another step, trying to put more distance between them. "No, but I'm guessing you do."

Geoxus's laugh was booming. "I'm talking about a world with no war. Where the wealth of our great capital city will spill out into the neighboring countries, and nowhere, not even Kula, will suffer under the greedy hands of my siblings." The god began to pace, a strange, frantic energy crackling off him.

Ash had warned him of this. *Geoxus is just like Ignitus, only he hides it behind wealth and prestige.*

"Madoc, we have to get out of here," she hissed, her wary eyes still locked on the old woman.

But Madoc couldn't focus on Seneca, or even on Ash's concern.

"How?" Madoc heard himself asking. It felt wrong—Geoxus's words were slick, his meaning hard to grasp. How did any of this have to do with his saving Ash in the arena?

Geoxus threw his arms wide, not seeming to notice the way the stones in the walls on either side of the room were punctured by the force of his geoeia. "If you can bring her back from the brink of death, think of what you can do for our people—for *all* people. What mortals could accomplish without the lines drawn between them."

Wariness clenched Madoc's shoulder blades together. "Are you talking about the Divine and Undivine?"

Geoxus waved a hand, as if batting the worry from Madoc's mind. "Forget the Undivine. They need much and give little."

Madoc almost laughed. This had to be a joke. The Undivine were the backbone of Deimos. The city wouldn't stand without their labor, their farming, their *taxes*. If he hadn't mixed mortar at the quarry, the Divine architects might actually have had to use their own muscles. If he and Elias had been paid the same wages as those working jobs requiring geoeia, they would have had the coin to pay off Cassia's indenture. Madoc never would have joined this war in the first place.

There was no humor in Geoxus's eyes, only a wild, greedy light.

"Think bigger, Madoc. Imagine a Deimos where these petty wars were a thing of the past. Where Air and Water and yes, even your little Fire Divine, could live equally, peacefully, under a single god."

"How exactly would that work?" Madoc managed, his eyes flicking to Ash. "The gods have fought for hundreds of years. You're going to stop now?"

"That's exactly what we're going to do," said Geoxus. "With your help."

"Impossible," Ash said. "Ignitus will never submit to you."

For the first time since entering the room, Geoxus's gaze shifted to Ash.

Icy spindles of dread filled Madoc's lungs. He edged in front of her. He could not shield her from a god, but if it came to it, he would try.

"He won't have a choice," Geoxus answered, his stare returning to Madoc. "Just like Jann didn't have a choice when you defeated him in the arena."

Madoc pulled at his tunic, now stuck to his chest with sweat.

He could still see the fear in Jann's eyes as Madoc took control of his mind. How easy it had been to make the stronger, more seasoned gladiator succumb to his wishes. "You want me to control Ignitus with anathreia."

It was almost what Ash and Tor had asked him to do, and Madoc couldn't help thinking that Ash must have hated having that in common with Geoxus, now that his true nature had been revealed.

He felt as if everything he knew had been turned upside down. Geoxus, Petros, Seneca. They were all in on this together—part of some grand plot to overthrow the gods using a power he'd only just discovered.

Geoxus's smile cut through Madoc like knives. He stepped closer, forcing Madoc to raise his chin and meet his stare. "I want you to strip the fire from my brother's veins. Then I want you to give it to me."

Now Madoc did laugh, a strangled sound without humor. "I don't know what my father's told you, but I can't take energeia from a person, much less a god."

"Yet," Geoxus said. "You will with practice. It's what you were made to do."

"Make you the god of fire?" Madoc shook his head. "What's next? Air? Water?" Grim realization settled into his bones as he imagined feeding on gods the way Ash had said Seneca fed on Cassia. "Just because I healed someone doesn't mean I can give energeia."

"Why not?" Seneca asked.

Madoc's gaze shot to the old woman.

"It is what the Mother Goddess did, after all," she finished, her lips curled into a cold grin. "Pushed energeia into the gods. At least what she used to do before her children diminished her powers." Her gaze narrowed, briefly, on Geoxus before returning to Madoc.

He thought of her words in the preparation chamber after his fight with Jann and shuddered. The Mother Goddess had made the six gods by pushing pieces of her soul into them, and in turn, they had destroyed her.

"You want me to make you Soul Divine," he realized, focusing on Geoxus. "You want to have the power of six gods."

Geoxus smiled, somber now. "I want you to think of a world without weakness or war. Kula, Cenhelm, Lakhu—every country will fly the flag of Deimos and live in peace."

"And what if Kula objects?" Ash asked.

Geoxus inhaled. "Then you will be crushed within the fist of your new god."

Behind Madoc, Ash shivered. This wasn't just Ignitus losing their land or trade routes. This was the utter destruction of her people.

Madoc grasped for reason through the roar of defiance in his blood. "What's to stop me from keeping the gods' energeia for myself?"

Geoxus offered a condescending chuckle. "Mortal bodies are weak. It would destroy you."

Beside him, Seneca's arm slid free. She approached Madoc, her hand cold and dry as she slid her fingers around his wrist.

"Strangle your doubt," she said. "It has no place in the heart of a weapon."

Her words resonated through him, their true intent slicing his confusion. What was she doing here? Last week she'd been their neighbor, an old woman who gave too much advice and stole people's clothing off the line, yet she was Soul Divine, and keeping company with a god and his trusted adviser.

As he grasped for understanding, all he could think of were times he and Elias had caught her spying from her upstairs balcony, or coming over for meals without an invitation, or prodding his arms with her spindly fingers and asking where his energeia was.

She'd been around the Metaxas as long as he could remember.

Not around the Metaxas. Around *him*.

He jerked his hand free from Seneca's grasp. "Get away from me."

Petros jabbed one finger toward Madoc.

"You'll treat your mother with respect," he warned.

Madoc laughed coldly. "My mother?" Seneca had to be at least thirty years older than Petros. How did they know each other? Madoc tried to imagine their meeting during a routine tax collection, and the thought of their courtship was less than comforting.

But the anger pulsing off his father was lightened by something softer that Madoc couldn't immediately recognize.

Love.

Petros was in love with Seneca.

For a brief moment, he wished Elias could hear this. Another time, they would have laughed about it for days.

"My mother is dead," Madoc said, but before the words were out of his mouth, anger tore through him. When he'd been a child, he'd wanted a mother—someone to protect him from Petros. Where was she when Petros had beaten him? When he'd thrown Madoc to the streets?

No, this wasn't his mother. Ilena was his mother.

Even if she'd never forgive him for Cassia, he wouldn't let another fill her place.

"You were too young to know the truth," Petros said. "And undeserving anyway. Had you shown earlier signs of energeia, I might have been more inclined to share, but you appeared to be pigstock. I knew she'd never come back to me if you were worthless."

Hatred scoured Madoc's insides. Petros had taken Cassia. He was responsible for her death. And now he admitted to withholding news of Madoc's mother just because he'd assumed Madoc was Undivine?

But when Seneca patted Petros's shoulder, Madoc saw how eager to please his father had become. It was as if all the beatings, all the times he had torn Madoc down for showing no sign of energeia, had been done by a different man.

"My Petros is so impatient." Seneca's proud gaze turned cold and unfamiliar. "And yet look at what Madoc has become. A marvel. A living tribute, carved in my likeness."

Madoc froze.

"He's the offspring of a goddess, not a god himself," Geoxus reminded her. "You bred him by mating with one of my Deimans. That makes him mine to use."

The god's words stabbed into Madoc's brain.

Offspring of a goddess.

Bred him.

Mine to use.

Madoc would have laughed if the situation had not been so dire. "So now I'm the son of a goddess? Is there anything else I should know?"

"Madoc," Ash hissed, and when he glanced her way, he watched her lips form a single word. "Anathrasa."

Seneca cackled, and cold shivered down Madoc's limbs. She looked like the old woman he'd known all his life, but there was something different about her now. It was as if her top layer had been shed like the skin of a snake, revealing the slick and poisonous soul beneath.

"I told you," Petros said quietly to Seneca. "You are not forgotten, Goddess."

Madoc raked his fingers over his skull. "Anathrasa is dead. The other gods killed her hundreds of years ago."

"There are many ways to die." Seneca's hard gaze flicked to Geoxus. "And there are many ways to live. When stripped of most of one's powers, one has to become *resourceful*."

"Come now," Geoxus told her, annoyance dragging at his tone. "Pity looks poor, even on you. I give you tithes. I feed you for your services."

Beside him, Ash flinched. "He feeds you?"

"Gladiators, dear." Seneca's lips tilted in a wicked smile. "They are quite sustaining. Stronger than your average Divine. Stavos was particularly hearty."

She took it from me.

Ash fell back with a wince. Her fear slashed against Madoc, hot and uncontained.

"I saw a record that said some of Geoxus's top gladiators had been 'tithed' before their deaths," Ash said. Her gaze flicked to Petros. "And

I heard him talking about how he'd had to cover up Stavos's escape. It was all because of you." She pointed to Seneca, new horror dropping her voice. "You've been taking the energeia from gladiators. Stavos. How many others?"

"It's hard to say," said Seneca, her brow scrunched. "Dozens? Hundreds?"

"People thought I killed Stavos to advance," Madoc said. He trembled, remembering the arrows in Stavos's back. Remembering his last, strained breaths.

"We did it for you," Petros said. He turned to Seneca. "I told you he was ungrateful."

Seneca chuckled.

Madoc glanced to Geoxus, remembering the god's despair over his champion's murder. Now there was only self-righteous greed.

His grief, his love for Stavos, had only been an act.

"It's a pity the Kulan champions travel in packs," Seneca continued. "I would have liked some time alone with your mother, Ash. I hear she was very powerful."

Ash jerked forward, but Madoc blocked her path. Seneca was baiting her.

He stared at the fragile old woman. The seventh goddess—*Anathrasa*. She could harness the power of souls and had tried to cleanse the world of anyone, god or mortal, who she couldn't control—or had, before her god-children had risen against her and drained her power. But before that, could she do the same things as Madoc? Convince Jann to surrender. Draw out Ash's grief.

What else could she do?

Push energeia into gods.

He shuddered as this understanding worked its way into his bones. As much as he didn't want it to be true, he thirsted for more. Something was cracking inside him, tearing open. Questions he'd suffocated long ago.

Who am I? What am I?

Anathrasa had answers.

"You're fortunate, you know," Geoxus said, smiling a little. "She might have killed you. Broken open your soul and emptied it, like she did with so many before you."

Like draining the milk from a coconut. That's what Seneca had said in the preparation room.

"It is all I seem to be able to do now," Anathrasa said tightly.

"There are others like me?" Madoc's stare locked on Anathrasa, hope surging through him at the prospect of not carrying this burden alone.

"There were, in the past." She batted a hand at him. "I could not put all my hope in one fragile mortal. They crack like eggs. One slip, and their skull is broken. Weak bones are truly the flaw of human design. Weak bones and saggy skin." She pinched the wobbling flesh beneath one arm. "Soul energy is not so easily released. It matures over time. It builds by feeding on emotions."

Madoc's stomach turned as he recalled the beatings he'd taken in his childhood—how Petros had tried to force the power out of him at a young age. Pain or not, there was a strange satisfaction in knowing his father had been wrong.

"Some died as their powers came to be. Weak constitutions,"

Anathrasa continued. "I used to think absorbing the soul energy of the stronger ones would bring my powers back, but alas. They, too, eventually faded. But you, Madoc, have matured nicely. You will be a true champion."

"You killed your own children," Ash breathed, horrified.

Madoc could see why the gods had turned against the Mother Goddess in the old stories. She was a monster.

But so was Geoxus.

He didn't want Madoc to make Deimos equal. He wanted to build an indestructible country.

Geoxus. Petros. Anathrasa. They all wanted the same thing: power.

Ash's words returned, streamlining the chaos in his brain into one singular thought.

Seneca was there. She took Cassia's divinity.

Cassia was dead because of Anathrasa.

Pain wrenched Madoc's muscles around his bones. He saw Cassia lying in the indentation of earth, the boulder beside her. Had she been trying to lift it when it had fallen? Had it been flung her way by Petros, or one of his guards, and she'd found herself unable to stop it?

Anathrasa had made her powerless, but Petros and Geoxus were just as guilty of her death.

Madoc stalked forward, fury raking through him, but was stopped by Ash. Her arms wrapped around his shoulders, her chest drew flush against his back.

Her anger flooded him, potent and scalding and edged with ferocity.

She meant to protect him. He could feel her intention, truer than any words. He grasped it with all he had, his anchor in the storm.

"Enough of this!" Geoxus growled, still driven by a frantic energy that scraped Madoc's paper-thin resolve. "Take Ignitus's gladiator to the jail—we may find use for her in the future. The rest of us will return to the palace. There's much to do, Madoc. Much we must prepare."

"No."

Geoxus, heading toward the door, froze. He turned toward Madoc. Behind him, Petros's face was red with fury.

"No?" Geoxus asked.

Madoc felt as if his bones would shake apart. His breath came in rapid pulls. Fear burst inside him, hotter than his anger, more desperate than his will to survive.

He might be the son of Anathrasa, but he would not be a weapon. He would not tear souls away like she had done to Cassia and Stavos. He would not fill gods with energeia just so they would turn and invade countries like Ash's.

Determination quieted the raging of his soul. For the first time since Cassia had been taken, he knew what he had to do.

He had to fight for Deimos. Not Geoxus's power-hungry ideal. Not Petros's corrupt reality. The Deimos that had raised him, that pressed gemstones into its doorways, and always smelled of olives and fresh earth, and stained his clothes with gray mortar and his heart with laughter.

The Deimos that had given him the Metaxas.

"*No?*" Geoxus asked again, incredulous. "Perhaps you have misunderstood, Madoc. This isn't a choice. You are my champion. You belong to *me*."

The floor began to shake with Geoxus's temper. Sand sifted from the ceiling above.

Ash released Madoc. He glanced her way, and when her stare met his, hard and ready, he felt a piece of his soul slide into the palm of her hand.

There was no igneia here, but she would fight with only her bare hands, like the first time they had met. And if they died, they would die together.

"No," Madoc said. "I don't."

Geoxus raised his arm, and Madoc braced for the onslaught of stone that was sure to come. He raised his hands before him, unsure what he would do, only knowing that a great storm of energeia was swirling inside him, begging to be unleashed.

"Guards!" Geoxus called. "Take my gladiator to the palace!"

In an instant, a swarm of silver and black shoved through the broken door, weapons drawn. They cut across the room, knocking over benches and chairs in their path.

Ash lowered to a crouch, hands outstretched. Her eyes narrowed to slits. Her ferocity fed him. Soothed him. Silenced his fear.

He inhaled, slowing his heart, and wrapped his mind around a single word.

Stop.

The guards at the front of the attack froze, those behind tripping over them.

Stop.

Those on the floor scrambled up, confusion on their faces. They looked at the weapons in their hands as if they couldn't remember why they'd drawn them.

Power pulsed in Madoc. *Finally*, it whispered over Geoxus's howl of anger.

But to his left, out of the corner of his vision, he caught movement. The subtle flick of Anathrasa's wrist.

He realized, one moment too late, what she intended to do.

Dropping his hold on the guards, Madoc yanked Ash toward him, pivoting to place himself between her and Anathrasa, but it was too late. Ash bucked in his arms, her spine bowed taut, her head thrown back. Her mouth opened in a silent scream.

"Stop!" he shouted at Anathrasa, gripping Ash tighter. "Leave her alone!"

"I will not play these games," the Mother Goddess hissed. "When I'm done, there will be nothing for you to bring back, Madoc."

Ash's teeth began to chatter. "Madoc?" Her voice was strained.

Her fear pumped into him, and he took it, transforming it into his own usable power supply. He would make the guards destroy Anathrasa—he didn't care who she was. He'd turn the entire city on Geoxus and Petros.

Madoc spun, still holding Ash against his side. The glow of the stones in the walls was too bright. The scent of the food was too rich and turned his stomach. His anathreia roared, hungry. He lifted his hand, but Ash screamed and slumped against his side.

"Get them!" Geoxus shouted. "Take them both!"

The guards were on him before he could react. One struck him in the side, the sharp jab of pain thrusting the breath from his lungs. His knees were swiped out from behind, and he fell hard to the ground. He grabbed at Ash's arms as a kick landed against his side, but they slid through his hold, cold and limp.

"Ash!" Panic seared him. He scrambled across the floor toward her, but they were already dragging her away.

"Don't listen to them!" she screamed, her voice thin with pain.

The metal hilt of a knife came down hard on the back of his head, making the room go dim and black around the edges. All sounds muffled as if he were underwater. He blinked, but Ash was gone. There was only Geoxus, standing over him, and the silver glint of centurion metal wavering on the edge of his focus.

"If you fight me, I will kill her myself," the god thundered.

Rage roared through Madoc's blood. He would get Ash back. If she was hurt, he would heal her again. Then they would stop Anathrasa, Petros, and Geoxus, even if he had to pry their souls from the cold shells of their bodies.

But if he and Ash were going to fight, they had to survive.

He thrust one shaking hand into the air as gladiators did in the arena, and surrendered.

TWENTY-TWO

ASH

IN THE CENTER of Igna, there was a well.

Char would sometimes stop at it, take a coin out of her pocket, and pluck handfuls of the short, spiky grass that grew at the well's base.

"Make a wish," she would say as she wove the grass around the coin. A flick of her fingers, and she set the grass aflame. "If the fire stays lit all the way to the water, your wish will come true."

Ash had laid out her wishes carefully when she was very small. Creamy custard-filled pastries from the market; a hoop and stick game she had seen other children playing.

But there was one day, when she had been about eleven or twelve years old, that Char had wrapped the coin and lit it on fire and held it out over the well.

A week earlier, Ash had watched her mother spend three days fighting Ignitus's new recruits in training exercises. It was routine, but this particular round of exercises had come when Char had been so ill she'd spent every break heaving in the corner. What should have been quick training matches turned to bloody scrambles as the new recruits saw the opening to dethrone Ignitus's champion.

But Char had bested them all, and afterward, Tor had had to carry her out of the training arena. Delirious with fever and pain, Char had mumbled into Tor's shoulder, "But she's safe. Ash is safe? Don't let him fight her—"

Ash had been next to Tor. She'd heard her mother's question, seen the wince in Tor's eyes.

At the well, Ash had stared at the flaming coin in her mother's palm. "I wish," Ash started, "I wish I wasn't Fire Divine."

Char had cocked her head.

"I wish I was ordinary," Ash whispered. "So you wouldn't have to worry about me, Mama."

She hadn't truly wanted to be ordinary. She loved igneia, the sizzle it left in her heart, the heat that felt like the very essence of life. She loved that it connected her to Char in a visceral, scorching way. They were both made of embers and passion, and no matter what Ignitus did to them, they would always have that connection.

But Ash knew that her Fire Divine abilities were one of the biggest sources of strain in her mother's life—the fear that if Char failed, Ignitus would turn his attention to Ash.

The flame snuffed out in her mother's hand and the coin sank, unlit, into the vast black abyss of the well.

Char had snatched Ash into a hug. "Never wish that. Don't let my concerns worry you. You are perfect as you are. *Perfect.*"

Ash had become that well now.

She was a long, endless chasm, cold and desolate and echoing with the sluggish *thump-thump* of her heartbeats like the distant *drip-drip* of water on stone.

She was that coin too. A soot-streaked wish plummeting down, down, down.

The air stank of mildew, straw, animal dung. Hands released her and she dropped face first onto a straw-covered stone floor. Horses whinnied; a hoof stomped.

She was in the arena's stables.

"Ready a prisoner transport!" ordered one of the Deiman guards. Others were around her, more than the two centurions who had hauled her out of the preparation chamber.

"We sent the last metal carriage off with that Metaxa boy. All we've got are these wooden ones—"

"Wood is fine."

"But she's *Kulan*, sir."

"The Father God said she's been drugged. She won't give us any trouble."

Ash tried to push herself upright, but her arms wouldn't support her, the muscles rigid with cold.

She was so cold.

Mama. Her throat scratched with whimpers. *Mama*—

Anathrasa had taken her igneia. She had taken Ash's fire.

Her vision spun, seizing on the sandaled centurion feet standing nearby and—a lantern. Another. A third. Flickering and pulsing around the stables, orange and red and hazy, delicate gold.

Ash shifted. Her fingers crawled across the straw, picking through stone and mud to reach for the igneia.

The lanterns didn't heave toward her. The firelight didn't waver.

Please.

She stretched, fingers bobbing.

Please. Mama.

A sob fell out of her mouth. It was as though her last, feeble memory of Char had snuffed out, plunging Ash into a desolate reality.

Her mother was gone.

Ash was gone.

Everything she cared about. Everything she loved. Everything that made her *her*—it was all gone. What was left if she wasn't Fire Divine? This shell of a girl, sobbing on the dusty stone floor.

The lanterns heaved at the blurred edges of her vision. The only thing remaining in her was something she had never done. Something she had shied from, feared, hated.

She looked at a lantern flame. Willed her vision to focus.

Ignitus.

Would he hear her if she prayed? She wasn't Divine anymore. She was nothing.

"Ignitus," she said out loud. "Ignitus, help me—"

A centurion hauled back and kicked her in the stomach. "Shut up! You, there—get a move on, will you? Gotta get this one locked up. Geoxus's orders."

Wheels rumbled across the stone, sending vibrations up Ash's body. She twisted, coughing blood down her chin, and saw a windowless, boxed carriage harnessed to two horses.

Her teeth chattered. Numbness prickled over her fingers, her toes, and her mind was starting to spiral. She was cold and tired—but she could not get into that carriage.

Ash drew in a breath and held it against the shivers that tried to break her apart.

"Get her up!" a centurion ordered.

Rough hands grabbed her arms. Ash went limp between the guards, her eyes on the transport, its open door showing a black abyss within.

If she got in there, she would never come out of the darkness. And she needed to be *out*.

Purpose surged through her, a thin rope she grabbed onto and held squirming to her chest.

She would stay out of that carriage. She would focus on nothing else.

The centurions dragged her forward a step.

There were four guards in these stables with her. It was likely that all of them were Earth Divine.

Ash's head dipped between her shoulders and she saw a short sword at one centurion's hip.

She let her body weight, what little remained, fall heavily.

The guards cursed. "What'd the Father God do to her?"

"Damn it—get her up!"

One of her arms dropped free as the guard bent to grab her waist—and she moved.

Ash grabbed his sword's hilt, drew it, and swung it back. It sliced into the man's thigh and he shrieked.

Orders flew. Armor clanged, stones jostled into the air, but Ash lost her body to momentum. She deflected a centurion's raised stones with her blade. She ducked under his lifted arm and hurled the sword with all her remaining strength. The blade twisted through the air and caught another soldier in the arm, eliciting a sharp yell that riled the now manic horses.

An arched doorway stood at the rear of the stables—it would lead back into the arena. Ash scrambled for it.

Her knees gave out. She slammed forward, head jarring as her chin struck the stone floor.

It took a full breath before she felt the heaviness of stones encasing her ankles, holding her down.

"Put her in the gods-damned carriage!" The lead centurion's furious yelp rattled the walls.

"That's strange," another voice said. "I don't remember damning a carriage."

Ash knew that voice. Why did she know it? Her body spasmed, involuntarily curling in on itself but for her trapped legs. She was fading, darkness, ebbing into a void—

Flame swelled into the stables, rising higher, stronger, brighter.

The centurions screamed. Horses bleated—in fear, not in pain, Ash noted dazedly—and hooves clapped the stone as the beasts fled. The fire must have freed them of their restraints.

Another surge of fire; another screech of men in pain.

And then Ash was *warm*.

Something scorching encased her from head to toe. She inhaled as though she hadn't managed a full breath in hours. Her muscles relaxed; her fingers unclenched.

She looked up.

Ignitus knelt next to her on the stable's floor. Scarlet robes wrapped around his body and rippled over the straw. A braid holding his hair back had come loose, but his mind was clearly roiling with thoughts, a simmering rage twisting his face into a scowl.

One of his hands was out over her, washing fire just above Ash's body. It wasn't close enough to burn her skin but it disintegrated the stone imprisoning her ankles and warmed every frozen crevice, trapping heat under her fireproof Kulan reed armor.

He looked down when he felt her watching him.

"You didn't fight them," he noted with a scowl. "Not with igneia. And you're shivering."

Ash didn't speak. That was her explanation, her wail of agony—just silence.

The scowl stayed on Ignitus's face, and Ash realized that he wasn't angry at her, but *for* her.

He dropped his hand and the fire went out. She still didn't feel whole, and numbness fogged her thoughts, but she was no longer unbearably cold.

She managed to push herself upright.

Only the stone floor, walls, and ceiling remained. All the wooden dividing walls and storage closets were burned away, and a pile of cinders that must have been the carriage lay in the middle of the room—next to four bodies.

"You killed the centurions." Ash's voice was gravelly.

Ignitus huffed but said nothing.

She looked at her god. He sat with his hands limp on his thighs, jaw working and eyes distant in a way that said he was calculating.

Even weak and spent, she found that she no longer feared him. Maybe because there was nothing left that he could take, and far worse creatures than him had shattered her.

Ignitus didn't look at her. "Anathrasa did this to you." It was a question she didn't have to answer. "I can't give your igneia back to you," he continued. "Putting energeia straight into a mortal could kill you."

Ash was too numb to even feel disappointed. "You knew she was alive. You've known all this time."

Ignitus stiffened. "I suspected a lot of things that I could never prove, and neither of my so-called peaceful siblings could ever just take me at my word." He grunted. "I knew Geoxus wanted something else out of these wars—he's been such an aggressive pain in recent years, and he got Aera and Biotus to turn against me too." He cut his eyes to Ash, his jaw twitching with contained rage. "She's working with Geoxus. Isn't she?"

"Yes."

"And that gladiator? Madoc. He saved you by using anathreia."

Ash was silent too long.

Ignitus frowned. "Have you sided with her, then? Anathrasa? Even after—" He motioned at Ash, referring to her lack of igneia.

"No," Ash instantly said. "I didn't side with her. And neither did Madoc."

"Intriguing. I suspect that will really inconvenience her and my brother."

Ash wilted. "Why didn't *you* side with her?" The question gathered others as it came out. "Why has Geoxus targeted Kula—it's because of her, isn't it? But why aren't you on his side? Aera and Biotus are part of it. Aren't they?"

Why, she wanted to scream. *Why Kula, why us, why—*

Ignitus was quiet a long moment. "I first told Geoxus my fears about Anathrasa not being dead. It was right after we'd defeated her. I kept asking him about it over the years. He's always known how I felt about her and that I would never side with her. So he's been whittling Kula away to nothing, making sure I won't have any resources to fight back with, it would seem." He sighed and bit the inside of his cheek. "But you should know that I didn't want this for any of my children."

"Didn't want what?" Ash asked with more bite than she had ever given to her god. "Death and pain? You may not be on the side of a deranged goddess, but that doesn't absolve you of the suffering you've inflicted on us."

Ignitus closed his eyes.

"You sent my mother to her death." She said this because she had to. Because she wanted this monster to feel it. "You waited to tell Rook about Lynx's death. You—"

Ignitus's eyes flashed open. "I told Rook about Lynx's death as soon as I got word of it. The infirmary staff didn't tell me through fire—they sent a letter, and that letter took days to reach me. I reprimanded them for that slight, you know. I told them from now on—"

A growl built in Ash's throat. She didn't want his excuses. "You still told Rook about Lynx before our fight. And then you killed him."

Ignitus gave her an offended look. "Rook stabbed me."

"You're *immortal.*"

"With Anathrasa seeking revenge, I couldn't be too careful."

Ash's chest bucked wildly. Was he implying that there truly was a way to kill him? And Anathrasa knew it?

Ash shook her head. "No—you don't get to make this about you. You've killed endless numbers of us. How can you claim to want anything better than our deaths?"

"You have every right to hate me." There were tears in his eyes now. "But I've been trying to make things better. My siblings keep staging wars against me. I fight, not just for glory, but for Kula. I have to push my gladiators, because if they fail, *thousands* suffer."

To see Ignitus heartbroken would have once made Ash sing with joy. Now, though, she wanted to weep herself—she understood the pain in his eyes. Worry for Kula. Guilt that he had tried his best and still gotten people killed.

It was an intimate, wrenching connection, and Ash realized the truth that had been knocking at the door of her soul for days:

Ignitus was a monster, but killing him wouldn't save Kula.

Anathrasa was alive. Which meant she had survived her godchildren's attempt on her life, and if she could regain her power, she would no doubt seek to restart the butchery she had wrought on the world centuries ago. How had she done it then? Had she manipulated the anathreia in mortals and warped them into an army that slaughtered those who resisted her control? Could gods be defeated at all?

How could anyone possibly stop a force like her? She was weakened—but could she be *killed*?

"This isn't just about a war anymore," Ash managed. Her throat swelled. "Madoc can control anathreia. Geoxus wants to use him to enhance his own powers and invade the other countries. He had Anathrasa threaten to take Madoc's energeia if he doesn't obey."

Ash didn't mention the rest of Geoxus's plan—that he thought Madoc could take a *god's* energeia too. She didn't want Ignitus to see Madoc as a threat.

Ignitus rolled his eyes skyward. "That damn fool. No one can *use* Anathrasa. Geoxus is so power hungry, it probably wasn't difficult for her to manipulate him."

Ash stiffened. "She can take energeia, but that's the extent of her powers."

Ignitus dropped his eyes to Ash with an exhausted smile. "Anathrasa was once queen of all the gods. She was manic and controlling and wanted to force the world into obedience—she could, with some of the weaker-willed mortals. We tried to kill her—we thought we had. But, obviously, we failed. And she's had centuries to plot her revenge. Whatever Geoxus thinks he'll get out of her is, I fear, a ruse that will only feed into something far worse."

Dread hollowed Ash's belly. No matter what Anathrasa's true plan was, Madoc stood at the center of it.

She tried to get up, wobbling onto her knees. "We have to go to the palace. We have to—"

She pitched forward, the room spinning. Ignitus caught her shoulders.

"Steady now. We can't do—"

"Let her go."

Ash blinked and saw Tor framed in the stable doorway. Flames danced up his arms, highlighting Taro and Spark on either side of him. Tor glared at Ignitus.

Who had his hands on Ash's shoulders, her body wilting in his grip.

Ignitus sighed and released Ash, who wavered but managed to kneel upright on her own.

Tor dropped to the ground and grabbed her. "Are you all right? He said he heard a prayer from you here. What happened?"

He clearly meant the scorched stables. The burned bodies. Ash alone with Ignitus. How the last time he had seen her, she had been racing out of the arena after Madoc.

"It doesn't matter," she said, because she couldn't lie and tell him that she was fine. Even the thought made her stomach sour. The void inside her throbbed, aching, empty hands grasping for igneia that wasn't there.

She had thought loneliness was a void. *This* was a void. Loneliness had been a chip in a vase.

Ash touched Tor's shoulder until he pulled his focus away from Ignitus. "I know you'll hate me for saying this," she whispered, "but right now, Ignitus is our best chance of getting out of Deimos alive. He's on our side."

Tor's face went gray. "What are you talking about?"

Ash told him everything that had happened. How Madoc saved her life. Geoxus's plans to subdue the world. Anathrasa, revealing herself and taking Ash's igneia.

Tor jolted at that. Behind him, Taro and Spark gasped.

Ignitus beat dust from his robe as he stood. "I've sent messages to my other god-siblings about Anathrasa before. It always bothered me that there was nothing left when we defeated her—they all thought her body vanished with her anathreia. But then Geoxus, Aera, and Biotus started targeting Kula, and Geoxus, especially, was so *smug*. More than normal. Something changed, has been changing, but Hydra and Florus ignored my worries because there was no proof. *This* is proof now, I'd say."

"How did you defeat her last time?" Ash asked. In all the stories of their victory over Anathrasa, there were no hints as to what exactly the gods had done.

"Anathreia is the combination of all six energeias—fire, earth, animal, air, water, and plants. That was how she made us, at the beginning; she took a piece of her soul and split it apart. We knew we could never defeat her individually, as she'd always be stronger than any one of us, and we couldn't risk all six of us attacking her at once. She'd only give us one chance to fight her. So"—Ignitus gave a grim smile—"we decided to make a single vessel just as powerful as she was. One vessel, one shot, one fight. We took the strongest mortal we had and each put pieces of our energeias into her."

Ash's eyebrows shot up. "You created a Soul Divine mortal?"

"In a way. She was more of a vessel for our energeias. Our fighter lured Anathrasa into what became the first arena—and so that fighter was the first gladiator. She managed to drain the Mother Goddess of her anathreia. Or most of it."

Ash wheezed. *I can't have a gladiator involved again.*

Ignitus had said that to her when she'd confronted him about letting her help.

"The threat you feared wasn't a gladiator—the *solution* was a gladiator," Ash said, breathless.

Ignitus scowled. "I don't think such a solution will be possible this time, though. That gladiator was still mortal in the end—she's been dead for centuries. We'd need all the gods to put pieces of their energeias into a vessel again, and if Geoxus thinks Anathrasa is his to control, he'll never rise against her."

"Wait." Ash's heart kicked up. "You *can* give me igneia back?"

The fall of sympathy on Ignitus's face was sudden and soft. "It isn't that simple. Putting pieces of our energeias into a mortal proved . . . costly. Many mortals died before we found one who could withstand a god's direct energeia. And as for us—" Ignitus pulled his hair to the side, tugging free the gray-white strand. "We were not made to break apart our souls like Anathrasa did when she made us. She's the goddess of souls; we are not. Giving away our energeia is to give away our very beings. It started to kill each of us. We had to stop, or—"

"Or become mortal," Ash finished.

Ignitus's gray hair; the wrinkles around Geoxus's eyes. Putting a part of their energeias into another vessel had started to weaken the gods' immortalities.

So there was a way to kill Ignitus—by taking away or giving up his energeia. Now that Ash no longer wanted to kill him, having that answer felt cruel.

Ignitus clapped his hands together. "We need to return to Kula. Geoxus isn't the only one who can gather an army. We'll be ready for him and for whatever Anathrasa tries to do, and we'll get the other gods to stand against them too."

Tor gaped up at Ignitus. Ash recognized the shock on his face—it was the first time he had heard Ignitus say something in defense of Kula.

She understood the discomfort of listening to Ignitus speak and realizing that she agreed with what he said. It was a foreign sensation.

"He's going to help us," Ash told Tor. "All the wars, the arena fights—he's been trying to protect Kula's resources. I don't forgive him." She looked pointedly at Ignitus. "But he can help us now."

Ignitus sulked. But he flinched when Tor pushed to his feet, eyes studious. Ignitus returned the stare before shifting and dropping his gaze.

He deferred to Tor.

Ash's lips parted. The whole world felt like it fractured and remade itself anew.

Tor's breath grated as he lifted his hand and pointed a finger at Ignitus, trembling. "Things will be different," he said. "When we return to Kula, we want to be involved in its governing."

Ignitus straightened his shoulders. "I'm the god of Kula. It's my job to rule it."

"You've done a shit job," Tor said.

The surprise that painted Ignitus's face was one of the most satisfying things Ash had ever seen.

"Kula is our country too," Tor continued. He was close to tears.

Ash grabbed Tor's hand and used it to pull herself to her feet. She felt stronger now, filled with the sensation of something long broken coming together. "What he's trying to say is—you aren't alone in ruling Kula. We all want to help make our country safe."

Ignitus started. His eyes shifted back to Tor, and after a long moment, his eyelids fluttered.

"I'll consider making some changes," he whispered.

Tor nodded. A tear slid down his cheek, but he looked back at Taro. "We need to get all the Kulans to the docks. Our ship shouldn't take long to prepare. The sooner we leave, the better."

Ash braced herself. "I have to go to the palace. I'm not leaving without Madoc."

Tor whipped a look at her, but she held up her hand.

"If we leave him, Geoxus and Anathrasa will force Madoc to take away other gods' energeias and give them to Geoxus so he can invade the world. I won't let them do that. We need to save him."

"Ash—" Tor bit off whatever he'd been about to say. He looked her up and down. "Can you fight?"

He didn't mention her lack of igneia, but it was heavy in his eyes.

She ground her teeth and nodded—though she truly didn't know if she could fight. She had managed to fend off four centurions, but that was only thanks to Ignitus's assistance. What would she do against Geoxus, Anathrasa, Petros, and even more centurions?

"I'll have my guards head for the palace," Ignitus said. "Brand and Raya haven't yet left—they can help too. You just worry about getting Madoc. Leave the fighting to us."

Ash bowed her head in thanks. She wasn't sure she could speak.

What would Char say about this alliance?

Their god swept away, making for the corridor and his soldiers in the arena beyond. Taro and Spark shot aside, and once he left, they closed in on Ash, wrapping her up in a shared hug.

But Tor turned away, his eyes on the ceiling.

Ash pulled herself out of Taro's arms. She took a wobbling step forward, surprised when she was able to catch herself and stand upright.

"I know this isn't what you wanted," she said.

He flinched but didn't face her.

"I know you hate him," she pressed. "I know you blame him for my mother and for every other horrible thing that has happened in Kula. And I know you probably hate me now too, for putting us in a position where we have to ally with him. But I'd do it all again, Tor. I'd relive you hating me over and over, if it meant bringing about what just happened—because talking with Ignitus, I felt all the horrible things I let happen start to heal—the war, Rook's death." Ash coughed, tears falling. "I felt hope."

Ash didn't have a chance to scrub her eyes clean before a blur of darkness and muscle grabbed her into a hug.

"None of this was your fault, Ash," he whispered into her hair. "And I don't hate you. Never. You're so like your mother—but *better*, as she used to tell me. I'm prouder of you than I can say—and I know Char and Rook would be too."

Ash sobbed, clinging to him, absorbing the feel of his lungs expanding and the pounding of his heart under her forehead.

Taro and Spark moved in from behind. And though she had no

igneia, though more bloodshed no doubt stood between them and leaving Deimos, Ash relished this moment of calm.

In the comfort, she felt Char's love.

She felt Rook's strength.

She felt all of Kula swell with possibility.

Whatever Anathrasa truly wanted, whatever misguided invasion Geoxus had planned—none of it mattered.

Ash had peace in Kula within her grasp, and nothing would stop her from seeing it through.

TWENTY-THREE

MADOC

MADOC SPAT BLOOD onto the smooth sandstone floor. The taste of it was bitter copper in his mouth, and as his tongue prodded a gash on the inside of his cheek, the bright spark of pain centered him.

"Get up," Geoxus snarled from his twisted onyx throne. The glossy black spikes that made up the back fanned behind him like the tail feathers of a deadly bird. "Get him up."

Madoc was hoisted to stand by two centurions. The metal plates of their armor pinched his sides, cold against his sweat-slicked skin. He swayed, unsteady, when they left him.

"I'm losing patience," Geoxus said between his teeth.

Madoc blinked at Petros, standing before him in the throne room. His father doubled in Madoc's hazy vision, a pair of furious gazes circling in a slow dance. They'd been at this for the better part of an hour—Geoxus ordering Madoc to give Crixion's tax collector igneia, to prove that Madoc had control of soul energy. Madoc refusing to even try.

A centurion or two punishing his insubordination with their metal-coated fists or the weight of a stone wall on his back.

Giving Petros igneia was only the first step of Madoc's training, Geoxus had told him. Soon, Geoxus would summon Ignitus and the real work would begin.

Draining a god, infusing another with his power.

"Where's Ash?" Madoc stumbled a little, then caught himself.

The end of a spear whipped through the air and struck him hard across the middle of his back. Pain seared through his flesh, the bruise instant and deep. With a grunt, he fell to one knee.

Madoc could make these guards do what he wanted—he was confident in at least that aspect of his anathreia now. But what would that accomplish? If Madoc turned the guards against Geoxus, Geoxus would kill them, and then the god of earth would call more guards, and when those ran out, he would stone Madoc himself.

Refusing Geoxus until he was sure of Ash's safety was Madoc's only play. He could take a hit—that's what Elias had always said.

The reminder of his brother brought a new stab of pain. Elias would have been taken to the jail after his arrest. He would be safe there, at least for now.

Madoc hoped.

"Give Petros igneia," Geoxus demanded. "You are Soul Divine, Madoc. Your anathreia is composed of the six energeias. Did you think Jann surrendered simply because you willed it? Or that the Kulan gladiator was healed by your good intentions? You manipulated their muscles, the air in their lungs and the iron and heat in their blood.

You used aereia and hydreia and igneia, all at once. Now weed it out. Give Petros fire energy and show me you can control your powers. Do this, and I'll call for Ignitus's gladiator." He sighed through his teeth. "I don't expect my guards have been too lenient with her, now that she's unable to defend herself."

Disgust lodged in Madoc's throat. Every prayer he'd ever uttered burned in his chest. Every stick of incense he'd lit shriveled in his memory. He'd needed something to believe in; he realized that now. He'd needed a father, and the Father God had become his answer. Without any proof, Madoc had sunk his belief into Geoxus, and in turn, Geoxus had been there. Guided him to take the money he'd won from Petros's fights to the temple, where priests like Tyber could care for those in need. Let Madoc convince himself that he was worth something, even though he was pigstock.

But that was all a lie, a story Madoc had told himself to get through the long, lonely nights when the power whispering through his veins had made the emotions around him too loud to ignore. He hadn't survived because of Geoxus; he'd survived because he'd refused to die. Elias, Cassia, the Metaxas, their home in the stonemasons' quarter—it had all been chance.

The god of earth looked like Petros now, threatening pain and fear to force the energeia out of him. How small Geoxus must have felt to need Madoc's power, the way Petros had needed him to win Anathrasa's approval. Looking at them, Madoc couldn't believe he'd ever thought one would be his salvation from the other. God or man, they were both carved from the same clay.

They would get nothing from him.

A guard raised a stone in his fist, but as Madoc braced for the impact, a gritty female voice cut through the stagnant air.

"Enough."

Madoc's gaze was drawn to the hunched woman standing at the edge of his vision. Anathrasa watched him with a scowl from a bench below a massive painting of Deimos. The other countries of the world were scaled smaller around it to appear meager and unthreatening.

Hate shivered down Madoc's spine. He could still feel the coolness of Ash's skin beneath his fingers. *Empty*, he'd overheard Anathrasa tell Geoxus as they'd dragged him from the room. *Not a drop of energeia left inside her.*

His birth mother had taken Ash's igneia. Had *fed* on it.

Ash's panic replayed in every clenching breath Madoc took. She'd known what was happening to her, felt her power being ripped away, and he'd been unable to stop it, just as she'd been unable to save Cassia.

His pain was silenced beneath a suffocating blanket of rage.

"He needs to feed." Anathrasa rose and walked closer, stopping between him and the guards. She moved more easily than before, her back straight and her steps light, and he couldn't help thinking that it had to do with the strength she'd gained from consuming Ash's energeia.

Dark thoughts swirled inside him. Geoxus had said he could take a god's power—not for long, but maybe long enough to leave the god of earth defenseless.

To turn Geoxus's geoeia on him.

Madoc didn't even know if that was possible, much less how he would control a god's power.

"I told you he's too fatigued," Anathrasa continued when Geoxus groaned in frustration. She'd been arguing this since they'd arrived. "He's not going to be able to do what you want when his soul is starving."

"Ignitus is in Crixion," Geoxus said. "He's got only a small group of guards to defend him. If he returns to Kula, he'll have half the country rising to his defense. This needs to be done quickly. You told me he'd be ready. These exercises are becoming a waste of time."

"This is how divinity works," she answered calmly. "Your Deimans do not move mountains without first deriving strength from the earth." She tugged at a white whisker jutting from her chin. "The boy needs a tithe."

Madoc flinched.

"He needs pressure," Petros growled. "He is willful. We went through this when he was a child. I tried to force the energeia out of him, but clearly I didn't push him hard enough."

"The Kulan girl did not force his anathreia free," Geoxus mused, his fingers tapping on the arm of his throne. "He gave it willingly." With a sigh, the god straightened, eyeing Madoc with paper-thin patience. "Very well, Madoc. You want the girl? You can have her. If that's the cost of giving Petros this power—"

"I will never give Petros anything," Madoc spat, realizing a moment too late that he should have first secured Ash's safety. "He doesn't deserve the power he has."

He didn't deserve to live. Madoc saw that clearly now. Petros had tortured innocent people—the Metaxas, Jann's family, the Undivine in the poor districts. For a while Madoc had thought it would be enough to punish Petros by taking his money, but now he could see that would never hurt him. All Petros did, he did with Geoxus's approval. As much as Madoc tried to cut him, he would never draw blood.

The only way to stop Petros was to destroy him, and Geoxus, too.

Madoc was starting to sound a lot like Ash.

Petros scoffed. "Defiant to the end."

Madoc's glare narrowed on his father. It may have been pride that straightened his back, but it was hate that curled his hands into fists.

Geoxus shifted to the front of his seat, his brows raising as he looked from father to son. His sudden interest felt like needles piercing Madoc's skin.

"So there is something else you want," he said quietly.

Madoc's mouth grew dry.

"We have been applying the wrong methods," said Geoxus. "It seems a tithe is precisely what he needs."

Anathrasa smiled.

"If you see a desirable tithe here, Madoc," Geoxus said, motioning to Petros, "by all means, take it."

Petros's laugh fell flat. "That wasn't what we discussed," he said.

Greed blossomed deep in Madoc's gut. *Take the energeia*, his soul whispered, bringing a pang of hunger.

"I don't need your approval to change plans," Geoxus told him.

"The boy is harboring a grudge," Petros said. "He means to see me humiliated. Surely you aren't actually considering—"

"Think carefully before you question a god," snapped Anathrasa.

Petros blinked at her in surprise, then dabbed at the sweat beading on his brow. "Madoc's going to *give* me power, not take it. Father God, how am I to lead your charge across the six countries if I'm nothing but pigstock?"

"There will always be others," Geoxus said, his stare still set on Madoc. "If this is what my champion needs, this is what he shall have."

Petros glanced at Anathrasa, but she, too, was looking at Madoc expectantly.

The tension in the room thinned, scraping at his resolve. The anger, the frustration, had given way to support and understanding.

Madoc tried to shove it off, but their expectations clung to his skin.

They wanted him to take a tithe. To do what Anathrasa had done to Cassia, and Ash, and Stavos, and countless more. The thought repulsed him. It fueled his hate.

"I don't need anything from you." The words scratched his raw throat. "Any of you."

Petros's shoulder jerked in a shrug. "See? There you have it."

"But you do need it," Anathrasa insisted to Madoc. "You want his energeia. I feel it in you. You are a vessel, thirsting to be filled."

He shook his head, sweat stinging his eyes. As soon as Anathrasa mentioned it, Madoc felt the deep well inside his chest. The empty cavity that held the memories he didn't want to keep.

"Let it expand inside you," she whispered. "Don't fight it."

He did fight it. He tried to close his mind to the sudden abscess inside him, but it was already there, waiting. A void, like Cassia's void, in his own soul.

"There is nothing to be afraid of." Anathrasa moved closer. "It is as simple as breathing. In and out. That is the way of energeia."

"Anathrasa!" Petros started toward her, betrayal creasing his face, but was stopped by one of Geoxus's guards. "Anathrasa, look at me. Please!"

"Stay back," Madoc warned Anathrasa, but she kept steadily creeping toward him, ignoring Petros, who was now attempting to shove past the guard.

"You sense emotions the way others hear or see. You taste their longing and anger, and it gives you strength. That's the anathreia in you. It hungers for the souls of others. At first a sip would do, but now you need more to sustain yourself. You'll need to drink from those with powerful energeia for your anathreia to thrive. Divine, like champions. Like Petros."

"Let me through!" Petros shouted as a second guard held him back.

Madoc's hands flexed, then fisted. She was talking in riddles, trying to get into his head. "Everyone's soul is the same. Energeia doesn't make a person's soul stronger."

"What is a soul but the collective will of the heart? Intention is power, Madoc, whether it be a storm of rage or a whisper of regret. Energeia amplifies that intention, turns it to action." She pressed her fingers just below her collarbone. "You know what your heart wants, Madoc."

Energeia listens to the heart, not the mind. Ash had told him that when they were in the temple. He could feel connections forming in his brain—links between his intuition and hunger, between emotions and life. To take a person's energeia was to open their chest and rip out their beating heart.

It was a good thing Petros didn't have one.

He shook his head to clear it. He couldn't listen to Anathrasa. He refused to make himself like her in any way.

But when he breathed in, his veins were tingling. He glanced at the guards who had beaten him, now holding back Petros, awaiting their Father God's command. At Geoxus, watching him with anticipation. At Petros, arms crossed, glaring at Madoc with the same smug superiority that had haunted Madoc all his life.

"Petros hurt you, didn't he?" murmured Anathrasa. "He took your sister away."

Madoc flinched. Petros hadn't killed Cassia alone. Anathrasa had made it possible.

"He wanted to frighten you," she said. "Great power comes from fear. He planned on taking the mother—he knew you were fond of her—but the girl got in the way. You remember . . . that day he came to ask about the street fights."

Don't listen, he told himself. But his anathreia was already swirling to life, and his throat was parched for a taste.

"He hurt her to incentivize you," Anathrasa whispered. "She was begging for death in the end."

Petros had taken Cassia because of him.

Petros had killed her because of *him*.

"What are you doing?" Petros now faced Anathrasa with his arms open, pleading. "Anathrasa, you condemn me? I have given you everything!"

Madoc's hands were shaking. His jaw flexed. He could see Cassia's face, twisted in pain.

A burning, poisonous anger raced down his limbs. His sister's death demanded vengeance. Elias had known it. Elias had tried to act on it.

Now it came down to Madoc.

Petros's arms dropped to his sides. A sneer curled his lips as he lifted his gaze from Anathrasa to Madoc.

Madoc tried to shove away the panic now blaring inside him, but memories were clawing to the surface. Things he didn't speak about or even admit existed. He'd locked it all away, but it was spilling free now, like his anathreia, no longer able to be contained.

Madoc closed his eyes.

He was hungry. It was dark. He was in his bedroom, where his father had thrown him after he couldn't lift a rock in the garden. He swept the dust and small bits of dirt into the center of the room with his hands and tried to move them. He tried and tried and tried, but he was still hungry, and it was still dark.

He was on the street. Starvation gnawed at his stomach, as if his belly button and spine were chafing together with nothing in between. He picked the pieces off fish bones that someone had thrown out. But a growling dog stole the carcass from him before he got enough.

Elias was at the table, spinning a clay bowl of broth lazily with the twist of his finger. *You can have some if you can get it*, he said. Madoc tried to pull the bowl his way with geoeia. He focused all his efforts. In the end, he slugged Elias in the shoulder, and the broth spilled on the floor, and they were both hungry.

Three brutes with rocks in their hands attacked him on his way home from the market. *Pigstock*, they called him. They stole the wheat he'd bought for Ilena. The beads he'd gotten for Cassia. They kicked him and pummeled him until his vision went dark. That night, he heard Ilena tell Elias never to leave Madoc alone again. He wasn't strong like them. He wasn't safe. And he was ashamed.

He lifted the heavy stones at the quarry. He hoisted them overhead again, and again, while Elias mixed the mortar. If he couldn't have geoeia, he would be so strong that no one would challenge him. The other Undivine laughed. *Don't bother. You'll never be enough.*

But he'd tried anyway. He'd taken the beatings in the arena while Elias threw geoeia from the safety of the crowd. He'd done what he could to pay their debts, to protect the family.

In the end, they were right. It was never enough.

He was never enough.

But now he would be. Now he had anathreia—not a single energy, but six combined.

"There it is," the Mother Goddess coaxed. "Now I want you to open your eyes and take what you need from Petros."

Madoc's eyes opened. Hunger surged inside him, teeth as sharp as knives. A buzzing filled his ears.

Behind the Mother Goddess, Petros paled. "He needs a tithe. Very well. We'll find another. These guards will do fine."

At the flick of Geoxus's wrist, the centurions holding Petros back from Anathrasa stepped away. Not even Petros's personal attendants were willing to cross the floor to assist him.

Petros stalked toward Geoxus. "I'm his father. This will never work!"

Madoc raised his hands. His anger had an appetite, and he was done starving.

"Stop," Madoc said.

Petros stopped, controlled by Madoc's command.

"What . . . what is this? Geoxus?" Petros's gaze shot to Madoc. "*You?*"

Madoc thought of Cassia as a child, forming clay figurines with a swipe of her hand.

Begging him and Elias to bring her along to the river to play.

Laughing at something stupid Danon did, tears streaming from the corners of her eyes.

"Turn around," Madoc told his father.

Petros did, twitching, fighting the pull of Madoc's order.

"Stop this at once, Madoc!" Petros shouted, but his words were thin with fear.

Anathrasa moved closer to Madoc's side. "Feed, my son."

A tempest was building inside Madoc's chest. Chills raced over his skin. Petros had hurt Cassia. Petros had tortured him. Elias's father was dead because of this man. Raclin, Jann, so many lives ruined because of one person.

It ended now.

Madoc inhaled and felt a cool rush in his blood. It soothed his wounds. His muscles relaxed, infused with relief. His stare held Petros's.

You're done hurting people, he thought. *You'll never hurt anyone again.*

"This isn't right. This isn't—Madoc!" Petros's voice cracked as he fell to one knee and clutched his chest. "Anathrasa! My love, you can't possibly . . ." His words gave way to hacking coughs. Panic contorted his features. Madoc tasted the hot bitterness of it and swallowed more.

"That's it," Anathrasa urged.

Petros fought through the pain and staggered toward him. The stones trembled around Madoc's feet but didn't rise. Hate lashed across the space between them, but Madoc took that too.

He grew stronger. Untouchable. He didn't know how he'd survived so long without this. Now that he'd taken the edge off, he could feel how truly empty he was. This was only the start. He needed more. He needed to drink, and drink, until the pain was gone.

Petros's strangled scream became a lullaby, calming Madoc's last frayed nerve.

"Yes," Anathrasa said, pride brightening her tone. "He deserves this."

Deserves. The word pressed through the rush of blood in his ears. Madoc wasn't just draining Petros—he was punishing him. The way Ash and Cassia had been punished by Anathrasa.

This wasn't right.

It *felt* right.

"Stop," he whispered.

He couldn't. He didn't want to.

"Stop," he said louder, trying to get ahold of himself. "*Stop.*" He was taking too much, too fast. His anathreia was working against his will, swallowing gulps of soul energy on his behalf. He had to slow it down. There had to be a way to shut it off.

He was becoming just like those he most hated. If Ash saw him now, she would look at him the way she looked at Anathrasa. In fear. In disgust.

Ash. He held her name in the grip of his teeth. She was fighting him in the grand arena. Smiling at him in the temple. Touching his hand after he'd saved her from Elias's wrath.

His outstretched hands jerked, severing his invisible hold on his father. Madoc staggered back, his heart kicking against his ribs. Before him, Petros lay motionless on the floor.

Trembling, Madoc crept closer. Panic warred with a heady pulse of power inside him, twisting his stomach. He reached for Petros with anathreia, searching for hate, for life.

With a jerk, Petros scrambled drunkenly to his knees. He pressed his palms to the marble floor like he was trying to lift a stone with geoeia, and hissed out a breath.

"Excellent." Geoxus was clapping. "He's fed. Now let's see if he can give power in addition to taking it. Guards! One of you, step forward!"

Anathrasa nodded her approval as one of the guards lifted a hand.

Sickness speared through any victory Madoc had earned. He'd nearly killed his father. He'd nearly *become* his father.

But Petros would never hurt another person with his energeia again.

Madoc shuddered. His anathreia was barely contained. He felt like he could punch through a wall. Break bones with the clench of his fist.

But there was something wrong about it too. Tainted. An anger that wasn't his own moved through his veins, heating his muscles.

Petros's energeia was powerful, as Anathrasa had said, but it was slick and tasted like rusted metal. Madoc wanted to be rid of it, but he didn't want to give it to anyone else. If there was a way to destroy it, he would do so.

At the flick of Geoxus's hand, a guard rushed toward Petros and assisted him to his feet. Madoc watched his father struggle, saw the deep lines around his eyes and mouth and the bow of his spine. Anger warped his every feature, as if the ugliness inside him had finally risen to the surface.

"Should have killed you when you were a baby," Petros spat. "Should have let the birds pick the flesh off your bones!"

Madoc recoiled. Petros's smooth front had vanished. Fury was all that remained, and it smelled like death. With one last burst of strength, Petros grabbed the spear from the unsuspecting guard, then wrenched back his arm, prepared to hurl it at Madoc's chest.

Without a second thought, Madoc lifted his hand.

"No."

Petros's arm arced down, plunging the spear into his own belly.

With a gasp, Madoc lunged forward, terror ripping through him. Petros staggered, then fell back with a grunt, his eyes wide, both hands curved around the pole protruding from his body. Blood stained his tunic, spreading to the floor beneath him.

A few gasping breaths, and then Petros went still.

Madoc's anathreia screamed in his ears.

His father was dead. Had he done this? He'd meant to stop Petros, that was all. To protect himself.

But he'd wanted Petros punished too.

He was vaguely aware of movement. The guards, leaving Petros in a puddle of his own blood. Geoxus's tightening frown. Anathrasa, closing in beside him.

"You've done well," she said, for only him to hear. "You're ready."

Madoc was reeling. "I didn't mean . . . I didn't think he would . . ."

From the hall outside the throne room came a thunderous crash, and the sound of moving footsteps. All eyes turned toward the entrance, where four centurions came rushing beneath the silver-plated archway.

"Honorable Geoxus!" one shouted, bowing before the god of earth. "We told Ignitus to wait, but he insists on seeing you now!"

"I told you, no interruptions!" Geoxus bellowed.

Madoc could not take his eyes off his father. He'd done this. He'd done it, even though he hadn't held the spear. Even if he hadn't told Petros what to do. *Intention is power.*

The next crash shook the floor and had Geoxus sweeping toward the entryway.

A strong grip closed on Madoc's forearm, dragging his gaze away from the horror before him to the old woman at his side.

"Forget Petros," she said, more urgently now. "Your purpose is far greater than anything he could have accomplished."

His eyes flashed to hers as a new dread overrode the churning anathreia in Madoc's body.

"What are you talking about?"

Her mouth warped into a severe smile. "It's time to do what you were made for."

He shook his head. Jerked out of her hold. "I won't help Geoxus." Not if it meant more of this.

"No—we have to stop him. Otherwise, he'll destroy everything." Anathrasa kept her gaze on Geoxus as he spouted orders to his guards. "I can't take the energy from other gods after what they did to me—he was right about this, at least. You can."

Her words took a beat to sink in.

"You want me to drain Geoxus." His gaze flicked back to Petros. She seemed as unaffected by his death as she would be a spider she'd accidently crushed beneath her sandal.

She nodded.

"He thinks he's humoring me, tossing me these gladiators to feed on in exchange for a Soul Divine heir. A child who can use anathreia at his master's bidding. He thinks that I believe him when he says I'll stay at his side as we march on the other countries. But he forgets that I'm the one who made him, and I see that all he truly wants is power." Her fingers dug into Madoc's wrist, her yellowed nails pressing into his skin. "Unless you want the death and destruction he craves, we must take his energeia now and make him mortal."

We.

Madoc was trembling. There would never be a *we* between him and Anathrasa.

But the truth punctured through his defiance. Now that Geoxus had seen what Madoc could do, he would use him to bring destruction to the world. Petros was only the beginning. Madoc would be forced to use hundreds more as tithes, and eventually give others energeia. Deimos was in danger. Kula would be next, and then there would be no stopping Geoxus.

Anathrasa was right. He had to end this.

And then, if he still breathed, he would end her too.

Madoc's stare landed on Geoxus. He didn't know if he was strong enough to take a god's energeia, just as he didn't know what it would do to him if he was able to complete the task.

A god's power did not belong in his body.

It would kill him.

But if it saved a thousand more families like the Metaxas, he had to try.

With Petros's slippery energeia still sloshing through him, Madoc reopened the void, the pain tearing up his throat as he focused on Geoxus's back. He reached for Cassia, an image of her to hold in his mind, but landed on Ash instead. She was walking beside him in the hallway alongside the arena, just after Ignitus had killed her opponent. Grief was falling off her in waves, but still she'd walked tall, as though even death would not bend her spine.

He grasped that strength now.

But before he could act on the hunger in his soul, another crash came from the corridor. Guards swooped through the door, shoving Madoc out of the way in their drive to surround Geoxus. Anathrasa howled in anger as she was pushed behind a row of centurions.

". . . a fire in the atrium!" someone was shouting.

"Kulan gladiators with him . . ." came another voice.

Madoc could barely distinguish their words over the grind and clap of metal armor, too loud in his ears, and the slice of anxiety through the air. Had the Kulans come for Ash? If they had, he would make sure Geoxus did not stand between them.

He grabbed the nearest centurion by the shoulder, shoving him aside. Another turned, but Madoc only shook his head, and the man scrambled away with a cry. He peeled the guards back, like layers of an onion, but still ten centurions blocked his path to Geoxus.

A great rumble shook the ground, and Madoc's gaze shot to the throne room door, where the ground punched up through the stones, a quaking wall of gravel rising to seal the exit of the room.

"They're here!" a woman screamed. *Anathrasa.*

A knot twisted in Madoc's throat as he searched for the old woman among the centurions. The last he'd seen her was near Petros, but his father's body was now hidden by a sea of armor.

The exit barrier was turning black, and then red in the center. The temperature of the room shot up, raising panic in the air. What were the Kulans doing here?

The wall gave a crack and burst inward, splinters of rock flying toward the hive of centurions with the speed of loosed arrows. Debris pinged off metal armor and shields. Gargling screams echoed off the ceiling.

Madoc's gaze landed on Ignitus, bathed in blue flames, surrounded by his guards. Tor with an orb of fire in each hand. A gladiator with a spear lifted overhead.

Ash.

Ash was here.

Madoc's blood surged as Ignitus carved a path in flames toward his brother.

Chaos gripped the room. From all around him came the clang of metal and the crack of breaking bones. Shouts rang out in horror and fury alike as Ignitus's guards clashed against the centurions.

Madoc breathed it in, his muscles tense and ready. His heartbeat came in hard kicks to his ribs.

"Ignitus!" Geoxus roared. The floor gave a hard lurch, and Madoc was tossed to his hands and knees. A centurion fell on top of him but didn't move.

Madoc didn't have to reach out to feel the void of the soldier's soul.

He shoved off the soldier and rose, searching for Ash. He couldn't see her. He didn't understand why she was here, but it didn't matter. He had to get to Geoxus.

"You side with Anathrasa and you bring death to the world, brother." Ignitus's voice rose above the screams. "Did you think I'd let you pick Kula apart until nothing remained? That I would stand by while the two of you finished what she started all those years ago? You're a fool if you thought I wouldn't fight back."

Fire whipped in a ring around the room, a snake eating all those in its path. Madoc dived just as it singed a tapestry on the wall above. Still aflame, it ripped free with a crackle and landed on several centurions.

"The time of gladiators is over," Ignitus said. "Now we fight our own battles."

Geoxus laughed, the sound sending terror down Madoc's spine.

"Finally, we agree," the god of earth roared.

A rumble thrust through Madoc's chest, shaking his organs. He fell backward as the far wall of the throne room exploded outward, revealing the blinding white light outside. The courtyard beyond was coated in dust, plants and trees crushed and knocked down by the blow. Half of the mortals in the room dived for cover. The others clashed, guided by a fevered, desperate need to survive.

A hundred stones rose into the air around the newly carved exit and hurled toward the god of fire in the center of the room. With a hiss, Ignitus thrust his hands out, creating a wall of fire to block the attack.

The ceiling groaned as a section gave way to Madoc's left. He threw himself clear as giant hunks of stone fell, crushing centurions and Kulans alike, but bounced harmlessly off Geoxus's shoulders as he charged toward Ignitus. The gods collided with a deafening boom that shook the entire palace from the roots to the tallest tower.

Outside, Madoc could hear faraway screams as giant sections of the building began to topple.

There was no time left. The palace would be destroyed, and when it was, Madoc would die, and no one would be able to stop Geoxus.

Wiping the film of dust from his eyes, he rushed forward, shoving two fighters out of his way. He lifted his arms, calling on the pain inside him, demanding it feed on the figure in black standing in the center of the room.

It began like a whisper. A soft breath against his neck.

Then it took hold like a hurricane.

His body jerked, a puppet on strings. He pulled and pulled on Geoxus's soul, unable to stop each huge gulp that filled him. His bones pressed outward. His skin stretched to the point of tearing. In his head, he could hear his pulse like the galloping of a monstrous horse. He could feel the cold chafe of sand against his heart.

It was going to kill him. Taking the soul of a god would tear him apart.

Still, he thirsted.

"No!" Geoxus's scream filled the room. Filled Madoc's head. Burst in his ears.

He squeezed his eyes closed in concentration. He wound his fingers around the invisible threads of the god's soul and pulled harder.

But something inside him twisted, shuddered. *Heated.* This was wrong. There were no more rough edges. No heavy weight on his bones. The soul energy had changed. It was lighter now, harder to hold on to.

It *burned.*

He couldn't let go. He sucked air through his clenched jaw, trying to control it, to release the reins, but the god's soul had wrapped its tendrils around his limbs, his chest, his throat. He couldn't peel free.

He gasped, his heart pumping harder, at the point of overflowing.

"Madoc, stop!"

He heard Ash's voice to his left. But his gaze locked on Ignitus, standing before him. The god's head was thrown back, his mouth gaping. His arms hung loosely at his sides.

Behind him, holding his brother's body as a shield, was Geoxus.

It took Madoc a moment to make sense of the image.

Ignitus and Geoxus had switched places.

Madoc had drained Ignitus's power, not Geoxus's.

The god of earth tore his gaze from Madoc's shocked face and reached toward his onyx throne. A crack resounded off the walls as one of the spikes on the back broke free and hurtled through the air toward his waiting hand.

He twisted and rammed the pointed end into Ignitus's chest.

Beside Madoc, Ash screamed.

TWENTY-FOUR

ASH

EVEN IN ASH'S most twisted imaginings of Ignitus's death, she had never dreamed she would feel pain.

The missing outer wall of the room threw late-afternoon light over the scene before her. The onyx spike from Geoxus's throne sparkled in the glow, the polished black edges glinting with blood.

Ignitus's blood.

The gods did bleed, but they always recovered—they were immortal. He would heal. He would turn and rage at Geoxus for being so stupid as to—

Geoxus twisted the onyx and Ignitus bucked, his mouth agape in desperate shock. A push, and Ignitus crashed to his knees, his gaze falling to the stone protruding from his gut, open hands hovering around it like he could rip it from his chest.

But he pitched to the side, slumping to the marble floor.

Ash shrieked, fingertips to her mouth, only half aware of what she was feeling, watching him lie on the floor before her.

Ignitus had been willing to save Kula. When they got back home, their god was going to work *with* them to improve their country. No more living in terror. No more senseless death. No more hatred and corruption.

All that hope drained out of Ash when Ignitus didn't rise from the ground.

"Kula, Ignitus is dead!" Geoxus bellowed. He opened his arms in triumph. "Bow to your new god!"

Ash slipped to the floor and crawled across the ground. The fight resumed around her, Deiman centurions demanding Kulan guards submit; the Kulans refusing in washes of flame.

She grabbed Ignitus's shoulder. Shook him.

"Ash!" Madoc dropped beside her. His eyes were wide with apology. "I didn't mean to—I thought he was—" He stopped, swallowed, and touched her arm. "Are you all right?"

He was the one who looked far from all right. His body twitched and rocked as though he had taken a lightning bolt straight to the heart.

"You took Ignitus's energeia." Awe socked Ash in the gut. Awe—and horror.

Madoc's face paled. "I was trying to take Geoxus's."

Ash cupped Madoc's jaw in her palm. He shuddered, and she swore she could feel the igneia churning in him, the energy of a god now trapped in his body.

"Can you do it again?" she whispered.

Madoc's lips parted. He nodded.

Ash looked past him.

They were kneeling in a battlefield, bodies strewn around them, blood smearing the smoke-gray marble floor. A spike of rock suddenly jutted up from the floor to her right, spraying gravel across her torn gladiator armor. Geoxus stood in the epicenter of the chaos, yanking boulders from the ceiling and lifting shards of rock from the floor.

"Submit, Kula!" he demanded. "There is no victory for you now!"

Something in Geoxus's own words struck him, and he whipped toward Ash and Madoc, kneeling over Ignitus's body.

All the stones he had pulled free swiveled with him, aimed at Madoc. "You, traitor," Geoxus said, "give me my brother's igneia."

Madoc braced an arm in front of Ash, as though he might be able to take the brunt of the projectiles aimed their way.

Crouched behind him, Ash slowly pulled a knife from her thigh sheath, determination heating her from her head to her toes. It wasn't igneia, but it was powerful all the same, and she used Ignitus's corpse to push herself to stand.

Geoxus flinched. The stones he had raised reared back, poised to strike.

Ash took a step forward, hiding the knife by her hip.

"Nikau. My brother's champion." He grinned. "Stand aside and I might let you live once I am the god of fire as well as earth."

Madoc rose slowly beside Ash. She could feel the tension in him, half from Ignitus's energeia, half from his own trepidation.

Ash stepped over Ignitus, putting more space between herself and Madoc. Geoxus's smile tightened, his stones poised and ready, waiting for her to submit. With every step, she was pulling his attention away from Madoc, who panted, eyes flicking from her to his crazed god.

Ash stopped when Geoxus had to turn away from Madoc to see her. Beyond, Kulans still warred with centurions; she heard Tor cry her name from somewhere in the fray.

But she held Geoxus's eyes. "Kula is not yours. We will never bow to you."

"Careful, Nikau." Geoxus's arms drew up. The wave of rocks swelled behind him, chunks of marble peeling from the floor to grow the threat. "Remember how easily your mother died. One poison-tipped blade, and she snuffed out like a flame."

Ash's eyes widened.

Geoxus beamed. "I had my gladiator poison his knife to bring down Ignitus's champion—she cost me far too many fighters. But I have no reason to kill you, Nikau. Bow to me."

My god told me your mother would be an easy kill, Stavos had taunted her during the opening ceremony.

Ash had guessed that Geoxus had ordered Stavos to poison Char. Hearing it confirmed from Geoxus himself cracked her concentration, a fragment of shock slipping through.

Geoxus had had Stavos cheat in his fight with Char just to get her out of the way. Because Geoxus had known his fighters could never best her, not in war or any other fight, and he'd never be able to thoroughly weaken Ignitus with Char at his side.

Unexpected pride flooded Ash's being. Pride in her mother, who had threatened a god just by living.

"Bow, Nikau," Geoxus ordered, "before you do something foolish. Mortals die all too easily."

Ash tightened her fingers on the hilt of her knife. Her body was still weak and battered, but she had never felt more certain of her abilities.

She was a gladiator. She was Char's daughter.

And she had always known that, one day, she would fight a god.

Geoxus thrust his arms toward her—but froze. The rocks behind him hesitated, stuck in the air.

They clattered harmlessly to the floor.

He frowned, eyes going from Ash to his own body to Madoc.

Who stood next to him, fingers splayed, chest heaving with exertion.

Geoxus realized his mistake and Ash's trick.

"No!" he boomed. "*No!*"

Ash moved.

She dived at Geoxus and thrust her knife forward and up, planting it under his rib cage. It sank home, and he gave a wheezing, husky grunt of pain.

"Gods die as easily as mortals now," Ash whispered to him.

She yanked the blade free. Blood surged down Geoxus's black silk robes. His hands went to the wound, mouth bobbing open in helpless shock.

He looked at Ash, fuming. "You—you can't—"

He lunged at her but only succeeded in slamming to the floor. There, he writhed once, body jerking, before he went limp at Ash's feet.

The whole of the palace trembled, ceiling and floor and stories upon stories of rooms.

Geoxus had been holding this room in place. With his geoeia

gone, the stone supports were too brittle, the foundation too shredded, for it to hold.

Deiman centurions, aghast at the sight of their dead god, began screaming mixes of threats for revenge and pleas to run.

Ash dropped the knife on the marble floor. Her hand was sticky with Geoxus's blood, and she stared at it as dust rained down on her.

She had killed a god.

A wild, wicked laugh cracked from the side of the room. Ash looked up, her vision throbbing, and spotted Anathrasa, smiling at her beside the gaping exterior wall.

People streamed past them, centurions and Kulans alike, all clawing for the safety of the terrace outside.

Ash blinked, and Anathrasa was gone, pulled into the chaos.

"We need to go!" Tor was upon her, grabbing her wrist. "The room is collapsing!"

Ash spun, reaching—but Madoc was on the ground, his shoulders heaving.

She bent over him and put her hands on his back. Just that touch, and she could feel the tension winding through his body; she was half shocked that sparks didn't leap off his skin and ignite the air around him.

"Tor!" she shouted. "He can't walk."

Ash looped one of Madoc's arms around her neck. Tor did the same, and when they stood together, Ash teetered, dizzy with her own lack of strength.

But they would get out of that throne room.

Taro shot ahead of them, fending off any centurions who chose to attack rather than escape. Step after hobbled step, they made their way across the marble, dodging spikes of rock and falling chunks of debris that shot stones like arrows.

The broken wall showed the terrace beyond, its beckoning marble columns and twisted stone fountains and benches that had once been for easy lounging.

Ash pushed on and on, gasping in the dusty air.

A grating screech chased them across the room. It rose to a crescendo, and Ash dared a look back to see the far end of the throne room cave in with a mighty crash. A billow of dirt plumed into the air.

Ash shot back around and redoubled her efforts, tongue rough with grit.

They burst out of the throne room and dived behind a short stone wall seconds before the dust cloud rolled behind them. The thunderous roar of the ceiling collapsing deafened Ash to any other sounds, bringing the situation to her through sight alone. Even with the deaths of Geoxus and Ignitus, their energeias endured: Deiman centurions were using geoeia to keep the destruction contained to the throne room; Kulan guards were hunched behind this wall and another, sending fire blasts at other centurions, who returned with stones.

Ash and Tor dropped farther behind the wall, with Madoc slumping to the ground next to them. Ahead, Spark was tending to the wounded. Taro fell on her with a relieved cry.

Behind their hiding area, the edge of the terrace revealed the palace's outbuildings, far below. To the left, a staircase opened, and Kulans were racing down it, fire flaring as they fought off the centurions on lower levels.

Across the terrace, over the short wall, a voice bleated. "Return Geoxus's champion!" Anathrasa demanded. "The Kulans stole him and murdered Great Geoxus! Thieves! God killers!"

A fresh wave of stones hailed down. Ash cupped her arms over her head, bending into Madoc to shield him too.

"What are we supposed to do now?" barked a Kulan guard. Brand. Ash shot him a glare.

Ignitus had told his guards most of what awaited them before the attack on the palace. That Geoxus intended to invade. That he had a weapon capable of decimating Kula. That Anathrasa had returned, and her survival could mean the destruction of the world.

They didn't know what Madoc could do. Who he really was, or what had truly caused two gods to die.

"We get to the ships," Tor told Brand. "We return to Kula. We need to rally our people now more than ever."

"Without our god?" Brand's face pinched. Ash hadn't thought him capable of looking so forlorn. "What chance do we have of holding off the mother of the gods?"

"I can stop her," Madoc wheezed.

Brand frowned at him in confusion.

"Not now, you can't," Ash told him and took his hand, half holding him down, half trying to plead with him to stay quiet. Even if Madoc was at his full strength, the moment he tried to take Anathrasa's energeia, she would do the same to him, as she had drained her other mortal offspring.

The thought cored Ash. She wouldn't watch Madoc go through that. She wouldn't let his mother strip him to nothing.

"We need help," Ash started. "Now that both Geoxus and Ignitus are dead, all Anathrasa has to do is tell her other god-children that *we* are the threat to them. We need to get to the other gods before she does."

"We can't just abandon Kula!" Brand shot back. "Deimos will attack out of revenge, gods or no gods."

Ash sank against Madoc. Her gaze went to Tor, whose lips twisted. She knew that look, that conviction in the wrinkles around his mouth, the spark of intention in his eyes.

Stones continued to fly. Guards returned with fire.

Back up the terrace's staircase, a Kulan shot out. "The exit is clear!"

"You go to Kula," Tor told Brand. "Take the other champions, the guards. Rally an army. We'll go to the other gods, tell them what's happened"—he nodded at Ash—"and gain allies."

Brand's face went utterly white. He thought for a moment, his focus drifting back to the collapsed throne room, to Ignitus's body now crushed by rubble.

"For Kula," Ash said.

Brand looked at her. "For Kula. We'll be waiting for you."

Some guards were helping the injured shamble for the exit. Others, still holding off the centurions with fire and flame, shouted at them to go, run.

Tor seized Ash's arm and included Madoc with a glance. "Make for the docks. Stop for nothing."

They nodded. Ash helped Madoc stand. He waved off Tor's offer to help support him again, and when he tried to do the same to Ash, she wedged herself under his shoulder, her arm around his waist.

"You're stuck with me," she told him.

Madoc's lips pulsed. "I can accept that fate," he whispered.

Ash managed a weak smile as he leaned into her, and the two of them hobbled toward the stairs, Tor behind, Taro and Spark ahead.

Down they went, the sounds of fighting echoing from above and shuffling bodies from below. The stairs gave a view of Crixion, the city nestled in the setting sun's vibrancy, its citizens unaware that their world had forever changed.

The staircase deposited them onto the palace's main road. People clogged it from every angle, servants and centurions and palace inhabitants fleeing for safety. Most would have no idea what had happened, merely that a room had collapsed—which likely meant Geoxus was in danger.

Ash panted in the chill air, clinging to Madoc—or maybe Madoc clung to her now, she couldn't tell—and focused every muscle on pure movement as they crossed the bridge over the Nien River.

Ignitus was dead. And though the hope she had felt at his alliance had flickered, a new hope flared strong again, driven by Brand's support. By Tor and Taro and Spark and how they would convince the other gods of what Ignitus could not: that Anathrasa was back and out for revenge.

Ash should have been terrified. And she was; she was exhausted and sore and still harrowingly empty from her lack of igneia. But there were no secrets in her world anymore. No hiding thoughts of revolution from her murderous god. Her goal was laid out for all to see, her dreams unmasked and raw.

That realization felt like it honored Char more than Ignitus's death had. Freedom over vengeance.

Ash began to recognize the area Taro and Spark led them through. The grand arena was on the left; Market Square to the right. And ahead was the temple, its high columns and wide marble floor showing worshippers within, like normal. News hadn't reached them yet.

Ash tripped along, willing her body to keep moving. Taro took the stairs two at a time, cutting across the temple floor, her face set with determination. The fastest way to the docks was down the road ahead.

Madoc tightened his hold on Ash, and when she looked at him, her heart quaked. He was barely holding himself together, his brow furrowed in intense pain, his eyes lifted to the temple's roof.

He looked like he was saying goodbye to it.

"Madoc!" A voice broke Ash's concentration. Again it cried his name, frantic, "Madoc!"

He went rigid. Recognition struck him, and his lips parted in an exhale of disbelief. "Ilena!"

TWENTY-FIVE

MADOC

THE WORLD FLASHED by in fractured moments. The soot on Ash's skin. The slick blood on her hand as it slid beneath his arm. Slices of roaring sound and intolerable brightness that gave way to black.

He blinked, and Ilena was there.

"Look at me," she said sharply. He was leaning against a wall. A man stood behind her—Tyber? Were they in the temple sanctuary? He didn't remember coming here. "What's wrong with him?" she snapped.

"Too much energeia," Ash told her. "It's a longer story than we have time for."

Ash was there. He clung to her voice as a thousand needles drove through his brain, and the darkness loomed again.

"I'll get water," Tyber said, and was gone.

Ilena cupped his cheek. "Madoc."

His name on her lips nearly broke him.

"I'm sorry about Cassia." His words were a strained whisper over the roaring in his ears. He needed to get it out before it was too late. "I'm sorry I didn't get her in time."

He siphoned in a quick breath of pain.

Anathrasa had known he was capable of taking a god's power, just as she'd known it would kill him to do so.

He didn't want Ilena to see him die, not after Cassia.

Ilena's hands were on his face, her tear-filled eyes in front of his. She'd been crying. He hated it when she cried.

"I don't want to hear you say that again, understand?" Her voice broke. "I'm the one who's sorry. I never should have said those things. I didn't mean them. She was your sister, and none of this is your fault."

His throat twisted into knots.

"Petros is dead," he told her. "Geoxus and Ignitus—they're all dead. But Seneca—she's not who you think. She's dangerous."

Ilena huffed in surprise, then muttered a curse. Her gaze lifted as a burst of shouts echoed outside the sanctuary walls.

"We have to go" came a deep voice from behind him. Was that Tor?

"Come with us," Ash said to Ilena.

Hope whispered through him. Even that hurt.

"It won't be safe here anymore," Ash added. "People will be angry about what's happened tonight. They'll come for Madoc's family."

"I need to get Elias out of jail." Ilena's voice went thin. "I can't leave my other children."

"Then I'll stay." Madoc would hold out a little longer. He would give them time to hide.

"No." She smoothed a hand over his head. Over his cheek. Tears streamed out of the corners of her eyes. "Madoc, it's time for you to go."

He shook his head. He didn't know what to do. He couldn't think straight.

"Yes," she said. "I'm going to take care of the family, and you're going to take care of yourself, and we will meet again, I swear it on my life."

"I can't leave you here." He forced himself off the wall to stand on his own, but his body was quaking. Knives sliced through every breath.

"You will," she said firmly. "You'll stay alive, whatever it takes. And when it's safe, I will find you."

He dipped his head against her bony shoulder, and she squeezed him tightly. But Ash and Tor were already dragging him away.

"Mother." He struggled, but the shouts were growing nearer. He could feel fear prickling on the breeze. He could hear the chafe of metal from centurion armor somewhere in the distance.

"You've never called me that before," Ilena said with a small, sad smile. She kissed his forehead. "You're my son, and I love you. That's what I meant to say before. I love you, Madoc. Now go."

He blinked, and she was gone.

"Madoc."

He startled at the sound of Ash's voice. She'd come up beside him on the deck of the ship, but he hadn't heard her approach. How that was possible he didn't know. He could hear everything else with crystalline clarity—the wind filling the sails. Tor urging the captain to veer south to avoid Deiman fishing crews. The creak of every board and the slap of the waves against the siding.

It all pulled at him, demanding equal attention with the too-bright gleam of the moon and the rough, splintering wood of the ship's siding beneath his hands. The only way he'd managed to stay conscious was by holding perfectly still. He could still feel the pulse of the gods' energeia in his veins, the warring strength of his muscles with the mortal frailness of his bones. He couldn't hold a single thought in his head.

Ilena.

Elias.

Anathrasa.

Petros and Geoxus and Ignitus. *Dead.* Dead because of him.

"Madoc." Ash's voice was softer now. He turned slightly toward her, finding she'd changed into a clean, white tunic and braided her long hair over one shoulder. Her mouth was a knot of worry, and the lines that creased her brow brought a jagged edge to his breath.

She had lost too much to be worried for him.

He set his gaze back to the black water. It stretched on and on, blending with the night sky in the distance.

"I can't see Crixion anymore," he said, voice cracking.

Her gaze stayed on him, warm, even without her igneia. "That doesn't mean it isn't there." She placed two fingers on his temple, stilling the punch of his thoughts. "Or here."

He tried to focus on home. On the good parts. On Ilena's promise. But he couldn't hold on to them.

Her fingers drew away, and he tilted forward, wishing she was still touching him.

His shoulder twitched. Would this energeia ever subside? It had been hours since the ship had left the mainland, and still he felt like lightning encased in flesh. He had to get this under control so he could go back for the Metaxas. Ilena was in more danger now than ever. Elias needed him. If anything happened to them, Danon and Ava would be alone.

For a brief, weak moment, he wished Anathrasa was here to teach him how to shut this down. But he didn't know where she was, or if she had survived the riots that had taken the city as they'd run.

Maybe it was the energeia inside him, but something told him she lived, and that the next time they met she would be stronger, more deadly.

"You need to rest," Ash said quietly. He tried to cling to her voice, but it was swept away in the current of sound and sights. He blinked, trying to steady his breath. Trying to will down the fear of what he'd done, what he *could* do. What he might do next.

Strangle your doubt. It has no place in the heart of a weapon.

He wasn't Geoxus's weapon. He wasn't Anathrasa's either. But he was more lethal than either of them, because he could take their power away.

Where did that leave him?

What did that *make* him?

"I can't . . ." He gave a dry, pained laugh. "I can't let go of the side of the ship."

Ash's gaze dropped to his hands, and his followed. His knuckles were white, his fingertips tinged purple from the effort.

"What happens if you do?" she asked, her voice on the edge of the pounding in his head.

"I don't know."

The slight pressure of her fingers against his shoulder made him jerk. She went to pull away, but he quickly shook his head.

Her touch slid slowly down his arm, gentle and steady, and quieting each flexing muscle it passed. He focused on the cool feel of her fingertips, on the tiny muscles that bent each knuckle as her hand closed around his.

His breath came out in a hard pull.

"What if you hold on to me instead?" she asked.

His gaze shot to hers, and then back to his hand, where she'd softly begun to pry loose each of his fingers. Longing cut through him with the sharp point of a knife. He wanted to press his face against the groove of her neck. Fan his hands over the small of her back. Disappear in the scent of her skin.

But she was different now, and so was he. He had to be careful.

"I don't think that's a good idea."

Still, she worked at his grip, until his right hand was free and his fingers were weaving with hers. Smooth skin met hard calluses; then her hand tightened around his.

The ship rocked. His breath came out in a shudder.

"I'm not going to break," she told him.

He wasn't so sure. He was barely holding himself together.

"Come with me," she said.

The low beckon of her voice had him releasing the railing with the other hand. He followed her, aware of Tor's narrowed gaze tracking him from the upper deck, and the swinging lanterns, and the unevenness of his own steps. Of the energeia searing through his chest, and his frantic efforts to keep it trapped inside so he wouldn't somehow use it to hurt Ash.

The wind pulled strands of hair free from her braid, and they whipped across her straight back. Even now, she walked like a goddess. Even after she'd lost her igneia. Her mother. Her home and her god.

She had never been more divine.

His scowl eased as she led him to the steps below deck. He felt too big for the narrow corridor, clumsy, but her hand stayed in his and he did not let go. He held on to her as tightly as he dared. She had come for him in the palace when she should have run. She had fought for him when she had no energeia to fight with.

His head began to quiet, though his heart did not.

They came to a series of doors, latched so they wouldn't swing with the movement of the ship. At the last one, Ash slid the bolt free, revealing a small chamber with barely enough room for the bunk against the far wall.

With a hard lurch, it reminded him of home—the bunks he shared with Elias and Danon—and he knew that even when he went back for the Metaxas, things would never return to the way they'd been.

Ash locked the door behind him and reached for the candle on a small table against the wall. Her hand paused over the blackened wick, and a pained grimace crossed her face as she reached for a match.

His chest heaved.

When the candle was lit, she tugged him toward the bed.

With a dry swallow, he followed her and sat on the edge of the thin mattress. She sat beside him. The brush of their knees sent a spark up his thigh that had nothing to do with energeia.

The porthole gave just enough light to soften the high bones of her cheeks and the wisps of her hair. He reached for one now, intending to tuck it behind her ear, but hesitated.

His hand was shaking. He dropped it into his lap.

Her cheek indented, as if she were biting it. "Stop trying to control it," she told him.

He huffed. "Control is all I have."

"No," she said simply. "You have me."

She moved closer—close enough for him to see each long lash around her eyes, and the soft slope of her nose. Her thumb pressed to his eyebrow, smoothing away the tension.

It loosened something inside him.

"Energeia listens to the heart, not the mind," he said, thinking of how he'd nearly lost control taking Petros's energeia. How quickly his father had plunged a spear into his gut with only a word.

That power was still inside him, and if he couldn't stop himself, he might kill her.

"What does your heart want?" she asked.

You.

He didn't look directly at her, afraid he wouldn't see the same truth on her face.

"That's not a simple question," he lied.

"It's guided you before. Why don't you trust it now?"

Because I don't want to hurt you. Because I am capable of terrible things.

But her words nestled beneath his skin and took root. His anathreia had not always listened to him, but when it had, it wasn't because he'd ordered its compliance. It was because he'd felt something too strong to ignore. Ash's grief. Jann's hate. His love and fear for Cassia.

His love and fear for Ash.

All blanketed by a new terror taking the shape of the small woman who'd lived above him for eleven years.

He opened his eyes to meet Ash's gaze. "I won't be like her."

Anathrasa.

He didn't have to say the name. Ash knew.

"You won't," she said with certainty, her thumbs now pressing against his temple in a way that elicited a soft groan. "You healed me, remember? You wouldn't have done that if you were like her."

He wasn't as sure as she was, but he remembered the force that had driven him toward her broken body. He hadn't thought of what he would do in that moment. He'd only wanted her to be alive and unhurt.

When Petros had died, Madoc hadn't thought to kill him; he'd only wanted to protect himself. When he'd stopped from taking his father as a tithe, it had been because of Ash's face in his mind.

Intention is power, Madoc, whether it be a storm of rage or a whisper of regret.

He understood now what Anathrasa had meant. If the soul was the will of the heart, then he could never do Ash harm, because even with this strange, dangerous power, his heart belonged to her.

He leaned closer, and when her hands skimmed past his ears and traced lines down the back of his neck, he knew, finally, what he had to do.

"Can I kiss you?" he murmured.

Her lips parted. She nodded.

He lifted his hands, no longer shaking. His fingertips brushed her cheeks. As her eyes closed, a new power took hold inside him. He would not break this trust she laid out before him. He would honor it, and her, however he could. However she would let him.

Her pulse fluttered beneath her skin, beating like the wings of a butterfly, and his tunic pulled tighter across his back as she fisted her hands in the hem at his waist. She might have had her energeia taken, but she had more power over him than any mortal or god.

He closed the small space between them. His mouth found hers, a gentle sweep from side to side, the barest pressure. A question she answered with a sigh and a curve of her shoulder.

He leaned closer, finally moving that stray hair behind her ear, and kissed her, taking her full lower lip between his. As their knees brushed, the scent of honey water invaded his senses. His heart was pounding, but as his anathreia spread across his body, his mind quieted, and he could feel the different strands of energeia braiding together inside him.

The breath of aereia from air divinity. The strength in his muscles and bones—bioseia and geoeia, he now knew. Hydreia flowed through him like water in his blood. Growth, floreia, came from plant divinity.

And finally, he found the warm pulsing glow of igneia.

He summoned the heat in his veins, drawing it behind the paper walls of his ribs. He parted Ash's lips, and the sweet taste of her brought a rush back to his ears. He pulled her closer, his hand trailing down her back, to the side of her waist. He kissed her more deeply, with everything he had. Every speck of fear. Every drop of joy. He kissed her until Deimos disappeared, and the arenas were empty, and the pain gave way to that steady ache of fire. She gasped for breath, and his mouth found her neck, a spot just below her ear that made her shudder and dig her fingers into his shoulder blades.

And then he let go of his control.

The energeia swirled through him, warm now, a soft pulsing glow. It pushed through his hands and his fingers and his lips. Through his breath. Through her skin.

What does your heart want?

You.

Her hands were warm against his back, leaving trails of heat straight to his bones. Then she was kissing him with a fevered passion, sliding onto his lap, her hot thighs bracketing his hips. Her fingertips heating through his shirt.

Burning.

She gave a staggered gasp, and he stopped at once, unsure what the sound meant. She jerked back, and he caught her around the waist before she fell, so intently trying to read the wonder in her round eyes that he missed the blue flames flickering from the palms of her hands.

"Look!" she cried. "Madoc, look!"

He was looking. He was grinning. The light from the candle was out now—it was inside her, dancing in the palms of her hands.

"You did this," she said in wonder.

It is as simple as breathing. In and out. That is the way of energeia.

He'd given a piece of his soul to Ash, and in doing so returned her powers.

He wanted to shout in excitement, and weep, and punch a hole through the black night sky. He wanted to kiss her mindless and rush home to save his family. He wanted to sail on and find allies in the other gods and unite the world.

He gave a small shrug.

In an instant, she had him wrapped so tightly against her that he could hardly breathe. He didn't care. If this was how he died, he would die happy.

She pulled back. "Are you all right?"

"You're asking if I'm all right?"

But he was. The ache in his head was gone. His muscles no longer twitched. His bones didn't hurt.

"I'm fine," he said, surprised. He was alive, severed from his home and any god who tried to claim him, and it didn't matter, because for the first time in his life, he felt whole.

He didn't need Geoxus or Anathrasa. He didn't need Petros, whispering in his ear that he wasn't enough. He didn't need to hide behind the curtain of Elias's power. He had his own power, and he could trust himself to use it.

Ash hugged him again, and kissed his neck, and as the moon crossed the sky, the ship rocked, carrying them farther from the chaos in Deimos and closer to a wild, uncertain future.

Together, they would survive this war. They knew what it was like to be broken. They knew what it was like to be remade.

They were strong. And now, they would be ready.

ACKNOWLEDGMENTS

Set Fire to the Gods has been six years in the making.

The first spark of an idea started at the 2014 RT convention in Dallas. Everything we are now, everything this book became, originated there, where we were eating cake in a hotel room and went, "Hey, we should write a book together." It was a game at first, but over time and a few (thousand) emails, we fell in love with the characters and created something neither of us could have imagined all those years prior.

A massive *thank-you* goes out to our agents, Mackenzie Brady Watson and Joanna MacKenzie. This book underwent many concept shifts, and your careful reads and guidance are the reason *Set Fire* became what it is today.

To Kristin Rens, who became "Editor Kristin" and who we adore even though she spells her name wrong (ahem . . . KristEn). Thank you for taking on our Magical Gladiator book. For shuffling Ash and Madoc into working order. For pulling out the details that had gotten lost over the aforementioned six years of development and telling us what parts were best. You are a goddess of editing energeia (editeia?).

To the other magical beings at Harper: Caitlin Johnson and Renée Cafiero, who helped us polish up *Set Fire*; Jenna Stempel-Lobell and Alison Donalty, who made this book gorgeous; and Michael D'Angelo and Aubrey Churchward, who got our book to all the right people.

To Cameron from Beacon Book Box not only for being willing to read an early draft of *Set Fire* but for being so, so excited. Your enthusiasm is wild and wonderful and one of the many reasons we adore you. To Katie McGee, for still finding the time even under deadline and release craziness, and Kelly Morton (and all of JosephBeth Booksellers, letsbehonest, every one of you guys has our full hearts), for your early delight in this project.

To Sara's sanity keepers: Kristen Lippert-Martin, Lisa Maxwell, Anne Blankman, Jaye Robin Brown, Olivia Hinebaugh, Danielle Stinson, Shannon Doleski, Shanna, and Angele McQuade; and her loves, Evelyn Skye, Erin Bowman, Rae Loverde, Ashley Poston, Claire Legrand, Natalie Whipple, Janella Angeles, Madeleine Colis, and Akshaya Raman.

And the people Kristen can't write/function without: Mindee Arnett, Katie McGarry, Jen (the muse) Tetzloff, Courtney Forster, and Deanna Fairfield; as well as Jaime and Erin, and Meg and Kass, who always read her books and swoon, the mom friends who keep her sane, and the jazzerfriends who keep her healthy (and okay, also sane). Infinity hugs to you all!

A huge thanks goes to our husbands, Kelson and Jason, for staying encouraging over the course of this book's ups and downs and up agains. To Oliver, for giving Mommy Sara time to write—well, as much as can reasonably be asked of him—and Ren, who inspires Mommy Kristen every day with his limitless enthusiasm. To Sara's parents and sister for their never-ending support. To Kristen's parents, sister-in-law, and parents-in-law for the same. We are so fortunate to have you all in our lives.

From Sara: To Kristen. Saying "thank you" at this point feels disingenuous, because I've gushed over you at great length, and hell, I even dedicated my half of this book to you. But I hope you know that working on this project with you was, and will forever be, one of the highlights of my career. I want another six years of back-and-forth email threads, of nearly incoherent GIF conversations via text (I'm sure there are some more Dwayne Johnson ones we haven't found yet), of knowing that if I got stuck, I could call you, and you'd drop everything to help me find cohesion in chaos. I don't know which god I pleased to have gotten you, but I am the luckiest author, the happiest friend, and my life is richer with you in it.

From Kristen: SAME!! I don't know what I'd do without you, Sara. This project never would have survived, I'm certain of it, without your organization, planning, energy, and Ash-like tenacity. We did it, friend, and I hope you know each time I think of this book, I will remember the magic you taught me, both on the page and off it.

Enough already. Let's go get a cupcake.

Turn the page for a sneak peek of the sequel,
RISE UP FROM THE EMBERS.

ONE

MADOC

MADOC HAD SAVED lives, altered thoughts, and drained the power from gods—but he could not stop the knife swinging toward his gut.

With a grunt, he twisted away, but the steel sliced through the side of his sweat-soaked tunic, a breath away from his skin, and came to a stop beneath his left arm, beside his pounding heart.

"You're not trying," Tor growled, his long, damp hair clinging to his jaw, his tunic stretching across his broad shoulders. He may have matched Madoc in size and build, but that was where the likeness ended. Tor was hardened by years of training; his reflexes were quick as flames. He was a seasoned Kulan gladiator—or at least he had been before his god was murdered.

Now he was an accused traitor, on the run from a vengeful goddess—Madoc's mother—just like the rest of them.

Madoc shoved Tor back and wiped the sweat from his brow with his forearm. They'd been training every day since they'd sailed out of Deimos's war-ravaged capitol, Crixion, two weeks ago. They hoped to find refuge in the Apuit Islands with the goddess Hydra's people, who they'd heard had allied with Florus, the god of plants. But with the gods of fire and earth both dead and Deimos in the grip of Anathrasa, the Mother Goddess, they had no idea how they'd be received. For all they knew, Hydra would think them spies and send her warriors to destroy them.

That was, if Anathrasa didn't hunt them down first.

"This isn't working," he muttered. Though Tor had taught many fighters to use igneia, fire energy wasn't the same as the anathreia Madoc himself possessed. If he was going to be any use to Ash and the others, Madoc needed to learn how to effectively manipulate soul energeia. But whenever he'd used it before, he'd either lost control or nearly killed himself in the process. Even with Tor's lessons, Madoc was no more ready to face Anathrasa now than he had been when they'd fled Deimos.

"Excuses." Tor tucked his blade back into the leather sheath at his belt and wiped his palms on his reed leggings. "I've seen you make a seasoned gladiator cry for his mother. Rip the energeia from a god like a rotten tooth. If you're going to drain the Mother Goddess before she finds a way to claim the other five countries, you'll need to be ready for anything. You're holding back."

Behind him, the ship's rail bobbed against the horizon, churning Madoc's stomach.

He tripped over the hatch cover leading belowdecks as another wave hit the stern. The swells had been bigger the last two days, the air cooler. He could feel it now, needling each bead of sweat on his temple as the sun sank low in the pink sky.

They were getting closer to Hydra's islands.

"If this boat would stop moving, I could concentrate." He staggered to stand, glaring at Tor's steady, wide-legged stance. Maybe he had saved Madoc when Geoxus's palace had fallen, but Madoc was really beginning to hate him.

"Anathrasa doesn't care if you're on the land or sea."

"She'll care if he throws up on her."

Ash lounged on the wooden steps to the upper deck, waving five flame-tipped fingers in front of her face. Since Madoc had returned her igneia—transferred it through the conduit of his body with his soul energy—the fire she created was blue.

Like the dead fire god's.

Madoc had heard Tor whispering with his sister, Taro, and her wife, Spark. They thought Madoc had accidentally given Ash the power he'd taken from Ignitus.

He wasn't sure they were wrong. None of them knew exactly what it meant, but if anyone was strong enough to figure it out, it was Ash.

She was wearing two tunics to fight the cold, but her shins were uncovered, and his gaze had fallen to her bare ankles, crisscrossed by the leather straps of her sandals, when another wave knocked him sideways into the foremast.

She laughed, and he couldn't stop his grin, even as the small crowd that had gathered near the helm above her snickered. Every Kulan on this ship had their sea legs, but Madoc still spent every morning and night with his head over a bucket.

"I'm not going to throw up." *Probably.*

"Focus," Tor ordered. "Anathrasa will be ready. She'll have protection. Aera and Biotus were allies of Geoxus—they'll likely join her now that he is dead. And who knows how many of the god of earth's centurions will rise to her aid once they realize what she can do?"

Madoc shivered. His mother was cunning. She'd survived for centuries by tithing—sucking the souls out of the gladiators Geoxus had offered her. She would not be defenseless now. Those who stood against her would be tithed, and the rest would suffer in silent allegiance for fear that she'd turn on them next.

"You know my intention," Tor continued. "Now stop me."

"Maybe that's the problem," Ash said, snuffing out the blue flames in a closed fist. "You don't really mean to hurt him. When he used anathreia to fight before, there was always a threat to his life." Her dark eyes flicked to his. "Or mine."

Madoc's shoulders drew together as he thought of the Deiman guards dragging Ash out of the preparation chamber at the arena after Anathrasa had taken away her energeia. A new sickness twisted his stomach as he remembered the palace, the tithes—his hollow soul, needing to be filled. His mother had forced him to take Petros's power, even if it meant killing him, to make himself strong. He'd taken Ignitus's power next, then Geoxus's, and it had nearly destroyed him.

If he hadn't been able to give that power to Ash, it would have.

Now a hunger for those same feelings, for the taste of another's energeia, was with him all the time, pressing against his lungs with every breath. But he refused to give in, not when this ship was filled with people who'd risked their lives for him. Not when he knew what tithing had done to Ash. To his sister, Cassia.

If he was going to be strong enough to drain whatever power his mother—the mother of all gods—had left, he needed to find another way to sate this growing need.

"I have no problem making him bleed if that's what it takes," Tor said with a sharp smile.

Madoc winced in Ash's direction. "Has he always been like this?"

"Oh, no." She grinned. "He used to have a training room and full armory at his disposal."

Madoc sighed through his teeth as Tor drew his knife and advanced again, a driven look in his eyes that made Madoc suspect he hadn't been kidding about making him bleed.

He was close enough to strike, and Madoc raised his hands—empty, at Tor's insistence—to defend himself. As they circled on the deck, Madoc reached out with his anathreia, feeling for Tor's emotions, finding the same intense frustration as always.

But it was laced with something else. A thin, pulsing warmth that reminded him, with a jolt of pain, of Ilena.

He blinked back his last image of his adopted mother, holding his face in her hands, telling him they would see each other again, just before she disappeared into the riots outside the temple to find Elias, Danon, and Ava. It was better this way—the farther Madoc was from Deimos, the safer they were—but he worried for them all the same.

Tor's head tilted. "What was that?" When Madoc shook his head, Tor stepped closer, dropping his weapon to his side. "What were you just thinking of?" Warmth spread across the space between them, driving a new spear of hunger into Madoc's soul.

Madoc glanced to Ash, who was now leaning forward, elbows on her knees.

"Home," he said quietly.

He didn't feel comfortable discussing this with Tor—his family was his to protect, even from friends. But if mentioning it helped him control his anathreia, he would do it.

Tor breathed in slowly, his eyes lifting to the horizon. "When Ash was a child, we often traveled for matches and wars. She grew up on ships like this."

Madoc glanced at her, watching him with a confidence he didn't deserve. If she knew how much he wanted to draw that confidence out of her, she wouldn't be so steadfast.

"When she missed Kula, I would tell her that Kula had come with her." Tor stepped closer, resting one large hand on Madoc's shoulder. The warmth was undeniable now, separate from the igneia in his veins, and Madoc held his breath, not trusting himself to swallow the air without a taste of it.

"Home is here." Tor moved his hand to Madoc's chest, where he softly pounded his fist twice. "Not there." He pointed behind them, to the sea. "The things that matter live inside us, and we protect them as we protect any other part of ourselves, with the power we've been given."

Madoc thought of Ilena and Elias. Danon and Ava. Even Cassia. And Ash, because she belonged with them, too. Only now he didn't picture them fighting or running. They weren't being hunted by Anathrasa or tortured in some prison cell as he'd dreamed every night these past two weeks. They were surrounded by a wall higher than those outside the grand arena. One fortified with the hardest, heaviest stones Elias had ever moved.

He locked them safely behind his ribs.

"Igneia is pulled from flames. Geoeia from stone." Tor shook his head in wonder. "You already have a fine source to pull from—your own soul—you're just afraid to do it."

Anathrasa had told him he needed other energeia to feed his power. He'd felt it work when he'd taken energeia from Petros and when he'd warped Jann's mind in the arena. Though he thirsted for it now, he'd never considered taking anathreia from himself.

Whatever soul he'd possessed himself had been broken a long time ago by Petros's hands and Crixion's streets.

"Don't be afraid," Tor said, meeting Madoc's gaze.

When he breathed, he felt the fondness behind Tor's frustration, but he didn't take it. His hunger had changed; it solidified the walls around his fortress. A knot of muscle in his neck relaxed as his anathreia whirled to life inside him for the first time in two long weeks.

Without warning, Tor lunged, knife aimed at Madoc's heart.

Stop.

Tor's hand froze in midair. He looked at it as if baffled, just before the knife dropped from his grip and embedded into the deck with a *thunk*.

"Good." With a grin, Tor spun, reaching out a hand to draw igneia from a lantern posted on the ship's mast. The fire balled in his palm, then sliced across the air beside Madoc's left shoulder. The sleeve of his tunic was charred; the heat seared his skin.

Excitement raced through Madoc's limbs as he rolled aside, then leaped to his feet. The next attack came just as fast, but this time he was ready. Tor wasn't just coming after him, he was coming after Madoc's family, his home. This wasn't about fighting or training. It was about defending what was his.

Madoc raised his empty hands, clutching the cold air as the energeia raced through him, ready for orders. *"Stop."*

The red flames licking Tor's skin suddenly went out. He stumbled back as if hit by an invisible punch, then went straight over the side of the ship.

"Man overboard!" From the helm rushed a flock of sailors, including Taro, Tor's sister. She wore the same glare Madoc had come to recognize from her, though now her eyes sparkled in amusement.

"Can that soul energy of yours give you wings?" she asked. "Because you'll want to be somewhere else when he gets back up here."

Ash giggled, but Madoc only winced.

"Maybe we should leave him down there a few minutes to cool off," he suggested.

"Just delaying the inevitable," Taro said. "It was nice knowing you, Madoc."

He groaned as they laughed. They were joking, of course. Tor wouldn't really kill him.

He hoped.

"Get him up here." Behind them, Spark's voice had dropped. Her worry prickled against Madoc's skin even before he saw it etched into her face. He followed her gaze up to the crow's nest, where a Kulan sailor was shouting to the crew at the helm while he watched the horizon through his spyglass.

"What is it?" Ash tensed beside him, peering into the distance. The sun had dipped below the horizon now, painting the sky an angry scarlet. She snagged the arm of a sailor, a boy no more than fifteen, who was sprinting toward the mast.

"Ships on the port side coming on fast." The sailor's voice cracked. "Too fast for a mortal crew. They've got help."

Madoc's pulse quickened. "What kind of ships?"

Please be Hydra's or Florus's fleet, he willed. Surely the goddess of water had the ability to make her ships cut through the waves at an accelerated clip.

"Black and silver sails." The sailor slipped free of Ash's hold and raced toward the mast to uncoil the lines. "Three of them!"

Madoc turned to Ash, a roar filling his ears. Only one country boasted the black and silver flag: Deimos.

Anathrasa had found them.